Books by The Pathway

The Fairy
The Academy (2)
The Princess And The Orrery (3)

Stand Alone Novels

In The Slip

Praise for The Pathways Tree Series

"The world is Neil Gaiman, jokes are Terry Pratchett, and the politics are George Orwell, all originally made and sewn together by a brilliant wordsmith and storyteller who would please any fans of such authors." Miranda Kane, comedian.

"This is a complex, often dark but still comedic world. It manages to avoid both post-modern tweeness and intellectual abstraction with its earthy characters and F.D. Lee's humour." Andrew Wallace, author.

"If you like Terry Pratchett, or the Artemis Fowl books, you'll like this." Rhonda Baxter, author.

"F D Lee has crafted a wonderful world with a very interesting and wholly loveable protagonist, whose strength of character and self effacing determination to do the right thing made this book, for me, unputdownable." Reader review.

"Lee's imagined world of fairy godmothers, trolls, gnomes, ogres, witches, elves and much more besides living out a troubled existence in an Orwellian dystopia is impressively expansive and detailed." Reader review.

"Lee's witty, satirical storytelling carries the reader with a light touch through unexpectedly dark and twisty territory." Reader review

The Princess And The Orrery

All characters are fictional. Any resemblance to persons living or dead is purely coincidental.

The Princess And The Orrery, The Pathways Tree and all original characters, events and settings © 2018 F. D. Lee (identified as the author of this work). All rights reserved. No part of this book may be reproduced in any form or by any electronic or mechanical means including information storage and retrieval systems without permission in writing from the author, except by a reviewer, who may quote brief passages in a review.

Conditions of Sale

This book is sold subject to the condition that it shall not, by way of trade or otherwise, be lent, resold, hired-out or otherwise re-circulated without the author's prior consent in any form of binding or cover other than that in which it is published and without similar condition including this condition being imposed on the subsequent purchaser.

Cover designed by Jane Dixon-Smith
http://www.jdsmith-design.com

ISBN: 9781790176076

About the Author

Faith is an avid reader, and lives in London and cats. The cats are engaged in a long running battle for the rights to the window sills.

Faith glumly suspects it will all end in tears, and she will be the one buying the kitty treats to make it all better.

Dedication

For my mum, who fights all the monsters.

Sign up for my newsletter at www.fdlee.co.uk and receive information about conventions, special offers, new titles, an invitation to our Facebook group, as well as bonus content for *The Pathways Tree* series!

Author's Note

This book picks up immediately after the events in *The Fairy's Tale* and continues beyond the end of *The Academy*.

THE PRINCESS AND THE ORRERY

The Pathways Tree, Book Three

Dear Stephanie

Be the star in your own theatre!

Faith
xxx

1

Night time.

The strange, blue-skinned creature was crumpled on the floor, clutching its head, back curled, breath coming in short gasps. It reminded Naima, strangely, of a horse her father had once ridden too hard. The horse, however, had not emanated a freezing aura so bitter that she had to wrap her hands in her sleeves.

"That's it? It can't leave?" she asked, her breath clouding.

"Not without my permission."

"Does it... is it in pain?"

"Not precisely." Joseph's gloved hands gripped a golden necklace shaped like a snake, with an opening between the head and the tail so that, when worn, the head would sit just above the collarbone. "From what I understand, they get some enjoyment from the process."

It didn't seem to be enjoying itself. Naima knelt beside it, pulling her jacket closed against the cold. It wasn't what she'd expected. She'd imagined something bigger, stronger. Something marvellous. But it just seemed like a man – a strange man, certainly, but just a man.

"Are you sure it's what you think it is?" she asked.

Joseph tutted, which turned into a cough. He covered his mouth with his forearm, holding the necklace tight. "Quite sure. Of course, if you're having doubts, I can find someone else willing to work with me. Who'd appreciate what I can offer."

Naima wet her lips, regretting it instantly as the cold bit against the moisture. "No, my Lord," she said, not certain of her honesty. "No doubts. I just didn't expect it to react that way. It seems so fragile..."

She reached out to the creature and-

Her body went rigid, muscles she didn't know she possessed cramping as a heavy wave of emotion hit her square in her chest, stealing the air from her lungs and sending her flying backwards, hands at her breasts, clawing desperately at her skin.

Memories, images, smells, senses, feelings all crammed into her mind, a storm of long-forgotten needs, repressed desires, hidden wants. Everything she had ever put aside or grown out of, everything she had dismissed as unnecessary or distracting, rose up from the depths of her. Things she pretended didn't matter, things she'd always believed she was better than, she knew with sudden clarity she desperately needed.

Cold burned her body. Her eyes fluttered and closed. She toppled over, hitting the flagstones next to the creature with a heavy thump.

A voice in her ear – in her mind? In her soul? – soft and reassuring, a dream...

"Everything you want, I can give you. All you need, all you desire. What is it you crave... Respect... Recognition.... To be remembered. Let me help you. Are you not magnificent? Are you not exceptional? Who is this man to make demands of you? Petty he is, with his childish dreams of power, his wicked little mind, his pretence at intellect. Stand on your feet, lift your hands to his face, scratch and claw and bloody him. Take the necklace from him, give it to me, and in return, I will give you what you deserve, what you have always deserved. I will complete you. All you need to do is stand and-"

The voice cut off, and with its end, she found she could think again, that her mind was her own.

Naima opened her eyes and rolled on to her back, dragging deep breaths of chilly air into her lungs. Joseph appeared in her vision, pale eyes watching her with curious, calculated interest.

"What did it say to you? I couldn't hear."

Her head rolled to the side. The creature was prostrate next to her, unconscious. Black liquid oozed from its nose and a heavy bruise was darkening its forehead, turning it from pale cornflower to midnight blue.

Naima turned away, closing her eyes. For the first time in almost forty years, she wanted to cry.

The Princess And The Orrery

Amelia shifted from her dreams into the so-called real world with a jolt. The General Administration's rules for the running of successful Plots state that no scene should begin with someone waking up. But then, Amelia was human and thus not privy to the strict rules governing story management; whereas she was keenly aware that something was wrong.

The orrery was malfunctioning.

She sat up in bed. The click-clack-clack of the cogs and the gentle, lulling whirl of the planets had taken on a desperate edge, filling the observatory with the low scream of metal suffering. She stared, horrified, as the enormous device sped up, the planetary spheres spinning much too fast. The main axle would break, the rotor arms holding the planets would buckle, they would crash into each other, the gears would grind and shatter – two years of work, lost in a moment!

Jumping out of bed, Amelia ran across the observatory, grabbing her toolkit as she flew past it, her feet slipping on the cold stone floor.

Then, as suddenly as it had begun, the malfunction ceased. The spheres slowed down, settling back into their normal speed, rotating in gentle circles around the main column, weaving in and out, over and above each other.

Amelia caught her breath, which hung in clouds of condensation. She shivered. It was late autumn, and the middle of the night; but should it be so cold? Her feet paled as she watched the orrery, counting quietly under her breath, checking each of the rotations.

The orrery towered in front of her, beautiful in brass and iron, glass and crystal, wood and stone. The circular base took up almost half of the vast domed observatory provided to her by her the Sisterhood of Cultivators; when all the planets were attached, it would probably fill the whole room.

Amelia liked living with the Sisters. They knew to leave her alone unless she requested something – and the orrery always needed something new. The larger it grew, the more complex the various components had to be to keep it working. It had taken her the past two years to work out the plans for a structure strong enough to support the planets – not only the four she had already attached, but also the ones she aimed to add in the future – as well as an engine that could power it. A tiny miscalculation in even the smallest cog or the length of a brace, even by the width of a sheet of paper, could ruin the whole thing in moments.

And something had just gone wrong. Luckily, the orrery had righted itself, but Sisters shouldn't be *lucky*. They had to be knowledgeable.

Her counting finished, she darted into the orrery itself, ducking under the planets so she was standing at the base of the device, and checked the engine and the main shaft. All seemed in order. Next, she climbed the narrow ladder attached to the main shaft and, with painstaking precision, began checking each set of gears, rods, and connections. She had built small platforms, encircling the large central column, which allowed her to pause at various intersections to check the mechanics. Each platform was little more than a ledge able to accommodate one person standing carefully but, as she was the only one responsible for the orrery, they were perfectly serviceable.

Two hours later, and she was happy it was working. Once again outside the orrery, she stood back for one last visual check. The four spheres were turning correctly around the central column, each affixed to their own network of cogs and rotor arms which jutted out at different heights and lengths, guiding them on their complex, intricate journeys.

The middle sphere, one of the smaller ones, represented Thaiana, the world Amelia called home. It spun now as it should, diving under and swooping over the others, all turning endlessly on their arcs thanks to a steam engine of her own design, which recycled the wasted steam back into water.

Of the four planets, by far the largest was the darkest sphere, which she had come to think of as the 'black planet'. It had been the first one she completed, and it spun, glacial, on the highest arc, casting a shadow on the other three planets. She didn't know why she had built it first, nor why she had chosen to clad it in dark mahogany. She wasn't interested in aesthetics. It had seemed appropriate, so why not?

Amelia settled at her desk, opening one of her many notebooks. She felt a tingle in her chest, the flutter of a challenge waiting to be beaten. Working on the orrery was like trying to follow a rabbit through long grass, except that the rabbit was changing the landscape as it went. She could see its movements and occasionally glimpse a fluffy white tail. It was frustrating at times, but thrilling, too. A task just for her in a place of numbers and sums and puzzles. Somewhere she could hide where no one would get hurt.

Amelia bent over her notes, the sound of gears gentle and soothing. The malfunction, alarming as it had been, had also brought her something new, another glimpse of the trickster rabbit, another route through the long grass. Why had it sped up? What had caused it? How had the various mechanisms been able to stand it, albeit briefly? What would happen when she was ready to add the next planet?

She chewed on the end of her pencil. The paper waited, ready to be useful. Above her, the stars watched through the giant glass window in the domed, copper-plated roof, eager to see what she would uncover.

Amelia frowned. The possibilities were clear in her mind, but she couldn't settle enough to concentrate on them. She spotted the problem. Barry was still in bed, his head resting on the pillow. She couldn't work without him.

She padded back to the bed and poked Barry in his overstuffed belly. She didn't have to worry that she would annoy him – he never got cross with her, no matter how absorbed she became in her work, nor what strange hours she kept, nor if she didn't want to talk to him for hours or even days on end. He was, above all other things, her best friend.

Barry fixed her with mismatched, button eyes, his permanent smile telling her he didn't mind being woken up. Grabbing his paw, she carried the stuffed bear back to her desk and sat him on the table top by her notebook.

Amelia was twelve years old, the kind of gangly that would one day be tall, with a heavy jaw, olive skin, and a thick mop of brown hair, all inherited from her father. The only thing she'd picked up from her mother – so the family joke went – was her know-it-all attitude. Amelia was also a genius, though she had no idea where that trait had come from, certainly neither of her parents.

And, though she didn't know it, she was less than a year away from destroying the world.

2

A hand rapped the desk, each knock sending Amelia's calculations flying from her mind. She looked up to see a pair of dark brown eyes, much like her own except they were set in a face about thirty-five years older than hers, with warm, rich umber skin and framed by a cloud of neat, shiny black curls.

"You wanted to see me?" Naima asked.

"Finally! I sent that message thirty minutes ago. The orrery malfunctioned last night. It's working again now. But I thought you'd probably want to know. You and-"

"Yes," Naima interrupted, an odd tightness to her expression Amelia hadn't seen before. "Alright. I see."

Amelia shrugged. "I don't mind if we don't tell him. I've got more important things to do. But he said that if anything important happened, I had to report it to him in person."

She waited, drumming her pencil against her notebook, while Naima considered. Why it was such a big deal, she had no idea – she had much better things to do than go traipsing across town. But she wanted Naima to take her seriously, and apparently that meant she had to do pointless things as well as important ones.

Finally, Naima nodded. "You're right. We'd better go." She looked Amelia up and down. "You're still in your nightdress."

"Oh? Right. Yes. I've been working."

Naima went over to the narrow wardrobe by Amelia's equally narrow bed and rummaged through it, finally digging out a shirt with only four ink stains on it. "So, what happened with the orrery?"

"The rotations sped up, the whole thing was moving too fast. I was worried the engine wouldn't hold up, but it didn't last very long before it went back to normal. I checked the orrery. It's all fine. I've been going over my notes since."

"Here we go. Get dressed, little princess," Naima instructed, dropping the shirt and a pair of trousers on the desk. "You don't know what caused it?"

"I'm not a princess," Amelia said in the weary tones of one who'd made the point before. She took the bundle behind her dressing screen. "I need to balance the revolutions, I think."

"That's easy – adjust the ratios to reduce the rotation."

"It's not the gears. It's something else," Amelia replied as she pulled her trousers on. She stuck her head around the screen to look at the orrery, watching the spheres move around the central shaft, the gears turning them at different speeds. It should have been relaxing, like staring at fish in a pond. But it wasn't. There was something wrong...

Amelia's gaze drifted to the black sphere. Maybe she'd miscalculated the weight, and it had pulled too hard on the engine, speeding everything up? But when she'd checked, there hadn't been any sign of that.

"It should work," she said, lacing up her trousers. Dressed and ready to go, she rejoined Naima. "It does work. It just didn't do what it should have done."

"Perhaps you need some help...?"

"No. I'll work it out by myself."

"Ah yes. I forgot what a clever little princess you are. How lucky we are to have you."

"I didn't mean it like that."

"And how did you mean it, then?"

Amelia glared at the floor.

"I just meant it's easier by myself. I understand all my notes," she muttered, not wanting the conversation to continue. Naima, thankfully, seemed to feel the same way.

"Perhaps the orrery's talking to you in a language you don't understand," she said, returning to the point. "Facts can't lie. But *we* can misunderstand."

Amelia considered it. What Naima was suggesting did make sense, in a weird way. Could it be speaking to her in another language? But if that was the case, how could she learn it with no-one to teach her? Language was slippery – another tricksy rabbit darting here, there and everywhere.

"I got told off once," Amelia said. "When I was cold and we had some Prince visiting, I told him to close the window. Mum said I shouldn't have said that. I should have asked him if *he* was

The Princess And The Orrery

cold. But I didn't really care if he was cold, and what if he wasn't? Then the window would have stayed open."

"Politics can be like that."

"What's politics got to do with it?"

A pause. "Nothing. Come on, it's time to go."

Securing Barry under her arm, Amelia allowed herself to be led out of the observatory and through the wide marble hallways of the main building. The Cultivators resided in a purpose-built structure with rooms of different sizes and shapes to accommodate all the explorations in which they were engaged.

The building had had a number of different names over the years, none of which interested Amelia except the last, Castell y Sêr, which meant Castle of the Stars. Starry Castle. She and Barry agreed it was the best name for the place, especially given their set up in the huge, domed observatory with its shiny copper and glass roof.

In fact, Starry Castle looked somewhat like the orrery. There was the rectangular central part of the building, and then the observatory rising up from the roof, like the troublesome black sphere. Around the main building, turrets, towers, conservatories and chambers butted out, each one built onto the primary structure when found to be necessary.

Starry Castle wasn't really a castle, or at least not like the one Amelia had grown up in, which had been white with a massive drawbridge and thin turrets topped with blue, pointy roofs, like upside-down ice-cream cones.

Amelia thought the castle she had grown up in was like ice-cream, decadent and overly sweet. Starry Castle was more purposeful. It was a busy place, with lots of other Sisters – the youngest she'd spotted still at least a dozen years older than her – scurrying around with tasks to do and things to explore. She liked it here.

Naima led Amelia to a side entrance decorated with small statues of proud-looking women who, nearly eighty years earlier, had founded the Sisterhood of Cultivators and formalised the study of the world and its mysteries into the philosophy of elementis. Or, at least, had formalised it in Ehinenden, the Third Kingdom of Thaiana. In fact, the philosophy of elementis had begun much earlier, but that had been in Ota'ari, the First Kingdom, and therefore didn't count – or at least, not as far as the citizens of Ehinenden were concerned.

They made it out of Starry Castle and marched across the gardens, over the square patches of grass, through the gate. A coach was waiting, two large men standing by the door and a third on the driver's seat, holding the horses' reins. The big men held the door open; Naima stepped in first, Amelia following. She sat Barry next to her and looked out the window.

They had maybe thirty minutes' travel through Cerne Bralksteld before they would reach the Imperial Palace. A cold wind washed in from the bay, and the air tasted of salt. Winter was coming, and the nights were drawing in. But Cerne Bralksteld was always slightly darker than it should have been; the city proper sat on the floor of a deep canyon, narrowing at one end to nothing, wide open at the other, onto the sea.

They arrived at the bottom of a steep staircase running up the canyon wall, carved out of the very same rock. Their destination was the huge Palace above them, situated two-thirds of the way up the rock face and extending deep into it.

The people of Cerne Bralksteld had learned how to make the most of their location. The wide bay provided them access to the Shared Sea and all the trade contingent on the same, while the canyon protected them from surprise attacks by neighbouring armies, back when Ehinenden had been prey to internal warfare. The canyon was only a few miles across at its widest point, where it opened out to the sea, but Cerne Bralksteld had found another way to create space.

They built into the cliffs, and the Imperial Palace was the grandest of such constructions. Naima had tried to explain the history of the place to her when she'd first arrived, but had thankfully given up. *Civil* engineering didn't interest Amelia.

Still, she was somewhat grateful that someone found the subject rewarding, as they eschewed the long, steep staircase in favour of the trolley system. Operated via large, steam-powered rotational wheels, one on the ground and one up on the Palace, the two trolleys hung from ropes as thick as oak trees. When one went up, the other went down. They were slow, laborious things, the wind seeping through their windows, ensuring anyone travelling in them got increasingly colder the higher they rose. But still, the trolleys were easier than walking, and as such were reserved only for the use of Palace guests and dignitaries.

Naima and Amelia made the rickety journey to the Palace in silence. Amelia's mind drifted a little, thinking of ways to improve the terminal system so the trolleys didn't swing so much.

They arrived safely, Naima nodding to the guards on the gate, and entered the Palace, home to the man they were meeting:

Joseph, brother to the Baron of the Imperial City of Cerne Bralksteld.

3

Amelia pushed open the heavy door to Joseph's office, dragging Barry behind her, and left Naima waiting outside.

Joseph was sitting at his desk, head bent over one of his little toy men, a paintbrush held between his thumb and forefinger. Amelia could feel his concentration, even from the doorway. Walking quietly, not wanting to disturb something so precise, she approached the table and waited.

While he put the finishing touches to the toy soldier's uniform – little yellow buttons on his blue coat – she allowed herself a moment to enjoy the silence. Joseph was like her, as far as she could tell. She didn't know him very well, certainly, but she recognised in him the same focus she had. Severe, her mother had called him once, citing his reputation and the way he stared at you until you spoke. It didn't bother Amelia, though. She was happy enough to stare back.

The room smelled sharp and sweet. Amelia spotted a round, metal vaporiser standing just behind Joseph. It created a strong smell of rotting onion and menthol, which was supposed to be good for one's recovery. But all it did was remind Amelia of doctors and priests; the type of people you only saw together when something had gone terribly wrong. She tried to breathe through her mouth.

Other than the new addition of the vaporiser, she liked Joseph's office. It was neither too big nor too small, comfortably housing his workstation, his writing desk, the bookshelves – filled with children's storybooks, Amelia had discovered to her disappointment – the globe under the window, and a barometer that stood as tall as a grandfather clock against the far wall.

He even had a miniature orrery, just a little taller than she was, taking up the corner. He'd shown it to her the day she'd first come to Cerne Bralksteld, explaining how the spheres represented all the known planets, including their own world, and how the clockwork

The Princess And The Orrery

and cogs could be used to mimic the way they moved around each other. He'd asked her what she thought of it.

"Clumsy," she'd replied, bending to look between the spheres to the machinery behind them, the pillar of cogs moving with the tick-tick-tick of the simple wind-up engine. The orrery shuddered a little with each revolution, the clockwork running out of turns. "But it has the potential to be elegant."

"Like the worlds it represents?"

She'd straightened and looked at him, not sure if he was making fun of her. But Joseph had just waited for her to reply, his sharp eyes watching her as intently then as they were now focused on the toy soldier's uniform.

"Yes," she'd said. "Potentially."

"I'd like you to realise some of that potential for me," Joseph had replied.

The next day, Amelia's possessions had arrived from home, and she'd moved into Starry Castle.

"Apologies for keeping you waiting," Joseph said now, dipping his paintbrush into the little cup of water next to the toy soldier and carefully wiping the bristles with a cloth. He leaned back in his chair. Wisps of grey smoke from the vaporiser encircled him. He had lost weight since she was last here, the veins on his hands and forearms like blue lines painted on thin parchment.

"How goes the task?" he asked.

Amelia tutted. "There was a problem last night."

Joseph sat forward, disturbing the smoke. "Last night? What time?"

"Probably around three or four. I wasn't really thinking about it."

Someone else might have wondered why Joseph asked about the time and not the problem, but Amelia was too distracted by the cloying scent of medicine. The smoke was nowhere near her, the vaporiser well calibrated to keep it around Joseph, but even so, she felt like her nose and throat were coated in the stuff.

"Interesting," Joseph said. "And what exactly happened?"

"It started running too fast. Only for a moment. I checked everything, and it all appears to be functioning now, but..."

"But you're not sure what made it go wrong?"

Amelia tightened her grip on Barry. "No."

"There's something more," he said. It wasn't a question. "Tell me what it is."

Amelia dropped her gaze, concentrating on her fingers as they dug into Barry's fur. She wished suddenly that Naima was allowed into these meetings.

"The orrery... it isn't doing what I thought it would do. It's not as straightforward as I'd imagined it would be. It's like it's trying to tell me something."

She would have sworn if her mother hadn't taught her not to. Why had she said that? It must have been thinking about Naima – isn't that what she'd said earlier? But when Naima had said it, it had made sense. Now, in this room with this thin, focused man, it sounded like one of the stories in his books.

Joseph stared at her in that way that unsettled so many people, waiting for her to say more. He had a face like a hunting dog: a long nose and sharp cheekbones that pushed his features forward above a small, pursed mouth, and eyes that always seemed to be looking for something to chase.

Maybe Joseph was a bit more like a wolf. Wolves ate tricksy little bunnies up. And people. Ate them all up.

Amelia hugged Barry to her chest. "When I came here, you said you wanted an orrery bigger and better than anyone had ever made before – something complex and remarkable. A mixing of two of the three As, astronomy and arithmetic. You said that I could make people happy-"

"I remember," Joseph interrupted. "And I understood it was progressing well. Until last night, that is, when it reacted to something."

She had expected him to be annoyed, but instead, he sounded thoughtful, questioning even. Like there was some obvious solution, right in front of her, and she wasn't seeing it. Reacted to what? There was nothing new in the observatory, nothing she hadn't requested or made specially.

Amelia didn't know what he wanted to hear. He was sponsoring her place at Starry Castle... If she got it wrong, would he send her home?

The scrape of wood against stone startled her. Joseph had stood and walked to one of the large shelves against the wall. He ran his cadaverous hand over his books, stopping when it landed on a small strongbox, sitting on its own shelf. No, Amelia corrected, not sitting – it was bolted onto the wood.

"Do you believe in magic, Amelia?"

"Of course not," she said, her anxiety momentarily forgotten in the sheer ridiculousness of his question. "I'm not a child."

Joseph glanced at Barry but said nothing. Instead, he fished a key from his pocket, one of many connected to a keyring which was chained to his belt, and opened the strongbox, pulling out another key.

Amelia watched with interest, loosening her grip on Barry.

"Come with me," Joseph instructed.

"Where?"

He didn't answer. Instead, he picked up his cane and exited his office, walking past Naima and down the corridor. She stared at him, and then turned to Amelia.

"Amelia...?"

Amelia met the confusion on Naima's face with her own, no doubt equally baffled expression. She shrugged Barry under her arm and ran after Joseph.

Keeping pace with Joseph was easier than with Naima. The man was in poor health – famously so. But even walking slowly, his cane sinking into the carpet, his breathing was long and thin, like someone trying to mask the fact they'd over-exercised.

They walked through snaking corridors, lit with oil lamps fixed to the walls. No sunlight ever entered the Palace; deep inside the canyon, there were no windows to allow it entry. The stone walls were smooth, sanded and polished to a fine degree. They looked beautiful, but even in the flickering lamplight, Amelia could see the sheen of damp on them. Expensive, thick-woven carpet lined the floors, an attempt to combat the perpetual cold emanating from the rock.

"I'm going to show you something very rare, very special," Joseph told her when they finally reached their destination, which was, apparently, a very heavy looking door, deep in the recesses of the Palace.

Joseph unlocked the door and pushed it open, leaning all of his skinny frame against it, and stepped inside. The room beyond was dark and smelled of old wood.

"Come on," Joseph called.

Amelia hesitated. She didn't like the smell of wood any more than the smell from the vaporiser. But then from inside the room came the click of a tinderbox and the warm flare of an oil lamp, and then a wall lamp lit, and another, and another, chasing away the darkness.

Inside was...

"A toy room?" Amelia asked, stepping through the doorway.

"It's a collection," Joseph said, his tone chilly. It was the closest she'd ever seen him to angry.

"What's the difference?"

"Intelligence."

"Oh."

Amelia looked around. The walls were covered in shelves that ran from floor to ceiling, each holding ranks of little wooden soldiers. Some of them were painted in colours she recognised, some not. There were soldiers from all over Ehinenden, she was certain of that. The ones in red and gold looked like they were from Penqioa, and the ones with the big curved swords had to be Ota'arian. There were hundreds of them. Maybe thousands.

"My father collects trophy heads," she said. "He keeps them on the walls."

"Any idiot can stab a spear into an animal."

"You've met my father?"

She hadn't meant to make a joke, but Joseph tittered, his hand coming up to hide his face. It was a funny gesture; like he was afraid of anyone seeing him smile. Still, she supposed no one was perfect. Even she couldn't help getting overwhelmed with thoughts and feelings, although she was getting better at hiding them away.

The Princess And The Orrery

The toys were interesting, but what really defined the room was the large table in the middle, covered with pretend towns and forests.

At the top of the model country was a city, wedged inside a long, narrowing canyon which opened out onto a wide bay, docks and marinas and jetties brushing against the sea. On the canyon walls near the bay was a structure built half-in and half-out of the rock. The side of the building facing out from the canyon wall was fronted with hundreds of windows in neat, regular lines, each one separated from its neighbour with tall, white columns. Leading up to it were stone steps, but even more fascinating were the little boxes running up the canyon wall on a string pulley system powered by a wind-up clockwork engine. It was not the only building that seemed to grow out of the canyon, but it was by far the largest.

I know what I'm looking at, Amelia realised.

She searched the rest of the model of Cerne Bralksteld and, sure enough, there was Starry Castle, on the canyon floor. She could even make out the lines of metalwork between the panes of glass of her observatory, painstakingly painted onto the model. And there was the library and the various guild buildings, the bank and the hospital, and the tall houses they preferred to build here, all filling the space on the ground as it tapered to a narrow point at the canyon's end.

Moving back to the bay, Amelia saw model boats and the sprawling shipyard that belonged to the O&P shipping company, sitting squat by the docks. Her gaze travelled to a smaller, less ornate building. It was away from the rest of the docks, just beyond where the sea hit the cliffs. A jetty struck out into the water, allowing access to it; otherwise, there was no visible way in.

This building protruded less than the Palace, almost like whoever had made it didn't want it to stand out too much from the cliff face. In the model, it had a wooden gate, but in real life it was iron and stone, thick and heavy, to make sure no one could pass through it without permission. The entrance to the manufactories.

The model was her home, rendered in tiny, intricate detail.

Something was wrong, however. Everything inside the canyon seemed correct, but the land surrounding it, high above the city, was covered in buildings that didn't – couldn't – exist.

Cerne Bralksteld's manufactories were kept underground, inside the canyon walls. As a result, long chimneys snaked through the earth, erupting in steam and smoke-filled stacks, making it impossible to build anything habitable on the plains above the canyon. And yet, there were little models dotted all over them.

"This is Cerne Bralksteld," she said, leaning down to take in more detail. "But it's not accurate?"

"Not yet," Joseph replied. "What else do you recognise?"

Amelia pursed her lips, wondering why they were wasting time on this instead of talking about the orrery, but did as he asked.

She moved down what she now recognised to be the northern side of the table, away from the city. From west moving east, Cerne Bralksteld sprawled out further than in real life, but eventually petered out into empty plains which then turned into farmsteads, little villages, and small towns. Finally, her eyes came to a large, dense forest which began not far in from the coast and stretched across the centre of the map.

On the opposite side of the forest, near where Joseph stood, was another city and castle, this one with white towers and blue, pointed turrets. Something pinched Amelia's stomach, almost like a stitch but far sharper. She told herself the pain wasn't there and focused her attention back onto her side of the table.

Here, the forest thinned to reveal a town much larger than the rest, with a heavy, old-fashioned castle in its centre. A few inches from this town, probably five or six miles in reality, was a smaller, ocean-side town with little docks and simple, stone buildings. She peered closer and saw that someone – Joseph, clearly – had mixed sand in with the paint to achieve a more realistic effect.

"It's Ehinenden." She moved up to the table, back to the largest city, located in the northwest of the bean-shaped landmass. "This is Cerne Bralksteld, there's Skraq, and that's Llanotterly and the docks at Sinne."

"What do you know about Llanotterly?" Joseph asked.

Amelia thought back to her reading. "There was a coronation there, not long ago. The last King had a heart attack, I think. His

The Princess And The Orrery

son's ruler now. It's an old kingdom, but poor. Farms, mostly. Woods. They've got docks at Sinne, but you've got a bigger bay, here."

"Is that all?"

"Roughly sixty thousand people live there, with an average age of forty. General life expectancy is around seventy, though that varies depending on career. The new King's name is John Edward Philip. He's uneducated – his father never sent him abroad to study. Llanotterly has been losing money for a number of years, in part due to the irresponsibility of its past rulers and in part due to the rise of modern machinery, like the steam engines. Cerne Bralksteld has taken away a lot of their trade, thanks to your investment in slavery and, uh, other modernisation techniques."

"Anyone who can read would know that."

"True," Amelia said, annoyed and, beneath it, ever so slightly embarrassed. "I've never really been that interested in geography. Or politics."

"And I'm thankful for it," Joseph replied. Moving around the table to stand next to her, he rested his fingertips on the model of Llanotterly Castle. "Now, tell me what you know about magic."

He was staring at Llanotterly Castle, pressing his fingertips so hard into the battlements they were turning white. This was definitely the strangest conversation she'd ever had. And so, faced with the bewildering sight of Joseph apparently trying to squish his own toy castle, she decided the best thing to do was to answer his demand as sensibly as she could.

"Magic isn't real... but I suppose if it were, it would probably be something we don't understand yet. If we were to travel back in time with one of the tractus engines, for example, and show them to the farmers of the past, they would probably think they were magic. They wouldn't understand how steam can be used to power pistons, how cogs work, that kind of thing."

Joseph looked up. "Exactly. Now that we understand each other, I want to show you something."

Amelia wasn't entirely sure they did understand each other. "You didn't bring me here to show me the map?"

"No, no. Just a happy coincidence. A chance for you to show me what you know of the world. Now, I hope, Amelia, that you are prepared to be open-minded?"

Amelia personally felt open minds were singularly useless – all the information fell out. A tight, strong mind was much better suited to grasping the mysteries of the world. But she'd come this far, and she wanted to know what he was talking about.

"I'm prepared to learn," she said.

"That should work just as well."

Joseph went to the corner of the room, where he unlocked a metal door that had been hidden in the dark. Behind it were shelves made of what looked like iron, holding yellowing scrolls, tools, and yet more strongboxes.

Joseph selected a strongbox and brought it back to the table, straining with the effort. Amelia offered to help, but he grunted a refusal. He placed it on an empty part of the map and unlocked it with the key he'd removed from the very first strongbox, back in his office.

He lifted out a gold snake, curled like a horseshoe, but rounder and bigger. The snake's diamond-shaped head rested about three inches from the dagger tip of its tail. A hinge on the snake's back indicated that the gap could be widened.

It was a necklace, Amelia realised.

The metalwork was exquisite; each of the tiny scales looked individual, and the piece flexed under Joseph's grip, enabling the widening of the gap to fit around a person's neck.

He held the snake out to Amelia. When she touched it, the metal was colder than she expected, given the heat of the room. It tingled against her fingers, reminiscent of the sensation of wool worn too long. The snake wasn't heavy, and there looked to be some tarnish around the hinge.

"Where did you get this?" Amelia asked.

"It was a gift."

"Who from?"

"A friend. Tell me what else you think about it," Joseph said. "I'd like your insight."

"I'm not sure what else I can say without taking it away and studying it. I don't think it's gold. And it isn't plate... copper doesn't shine like that... You should ask Naima. Not that I couldn't tell you more," Amelia quickly amended. "It's just she's more interested in rocks and minerals than I am."

"No. Absolutely not."

"Why not?"

Joseph waved the question away. "It's a secret. I want to give you a piece of it, to use in the orrery. You know what Naima's like, everything has to be written down."

That was true. Amelia certainly found the endless reports and note-taking very annoying. Still, she didn't like the idea of keeping a secret.

"I can get metal from the Sisters-"

"Not like this. Don't you want to make the orrery better?"

"Yes, of course. But it sounds like you think this necklace is magic. I thought you had something real to help me with."

Joseph caught her in his wolf-stare. "And I thought we had just agreed magic is something we don't understand yet. Now, over there you'll find a hot iron – I use it for the models. You know how to work one?"

"Of course, but-"

He handed her the snake. "Think of it as an experiment. I'll wait outside until you're finished. The heat, you see. It upsets me."

Amelia was about to ask why he had a hot iron if he didn't like the heat, but thought better of it. He did look tired, his skin clammy. People were always saying he was sick, weren't they?

She felt a twinge of guilt for arguing with him. What difference did it make, anyway? She might as well humour him. Besides, the quicker all this was done with, the quicker she'd be back in Starry Castle.

"Alright," she said.

"Take a piece from the tail, not the head. Don't damage the hinge," he instructed before closing the heavy door behind him.

It was much harder going than she'd expected. Once the iron, heated in a special oven, was glowing white, it should have cut through the soft metal like butter. Instead, after more than an hour of effort, having to stick the iron back into the oven more than once, Amelia was sweaty, extremely irritated, and had only succeeded in shaving off half an inch from the tail.

F. D. Lee

She dumped the iron in the waiting bucket of water, a cloud of steam rising up, unwelcome against her already sticky skin. She wiped her face with the thick gloves she'd put on and returned to the necklace. The little bit of tail sat separately from the body – and then it twitched.

Amelia didn't gasp, but she did lean closer. The tail twitched again, this time jumping towards the snake proper. She picked it up in her gloved hands, and it stopped moving. It must have been the heat causing the metal to expand and move.

She went to the door and pulled it open with her free hand. Joseph was sitting neatly on a bench, waiting.

"Done?" he said. "It worked?"

"Yes. What now?"

He smiled at her from behind his hand. "Now you're going to melt that down, make a cog or a screw or whatever you like from it, and you're going to use that in the orrery. I hope you're not in a hurry to get anywhere."

4

Preparing oneself to feel pain is rarely a pleasant experience. Will it be as bad as you expect, or are you simply exaggerating the problem? How many times, for example, does the dentist have to reassure the client that the pain of removing a tooth is better than the agony of letting it rot? Some things become bearable simply because we learn to live with them.

And sometimes, even when we know it will hurt, we try again, anyway.

Seven, the last surviving genie, closed his eyes, his hands balled up in fists, shoulders tight. He took a deep breath and pictured a cave in a forest far away, layering the memory piece upon piece until he could almost taste the chill air and smell the soft, mossy ground. He pictured his bed, made by his own hands. It had been unvarnished, barked, and more than a little rustic, but it had also been safe and comfortable and – most importantly – secret, just like the cave.

When the image was crystallised in his mind, he pulled on his magic and *pushed* himself towards the cave, praying that the force would transport him to the safety of his hidden home.

The magic attacked, sharp teeth tearing at his flesh. Layer by layer, scraping and scratching. Fraying, flaying, pulling him apart.

And behind it, as always, the heavy, hazy thrill of pleasure. The clarity of thought, the purity of it, that only the bliss of agony could offer.

All too quickly it passed, the magic leaving his body as swiftly and violently as it had entered. He fell to the floor, spent, spurned, spoiled. For some time he lay there, curled in on himself, his breath ragged. When the torment of the magic, the pleasure and the pain of it, finally waned, he clambered to his feet, wiping black blood from his face with the back of his pale blue hand.

And then he tried again to remove himself from the tower.

Four days were spent like this before Seven finally gave up. In truth, he didn't really know why he tried even once. Joseph had spoken very clearly: 'I wish you unable to travel beyond this room, by any means, without my express permission'. But Seven had been unwilling to accept that his cunning was no match for the simplicity of the wish. So he'd raged against it, poking and pulling it apart for some weakness when he knew, objectively, that there was none.

And so, towards the end of his first week imprisoned, he'd had to accept that there was, aha ha, no escaping the facts. He was trapped in a tower that bulged half-in and half-out of a sheer cliff, without his necklace, at the mercy of yet another person who thought they somehow deserved to get everything they'd ever wanted.

Clearly, Joseph was no fool. The wish was tight, the wording too direct to be twisted – but even if it weren't, the cost of trying to perform any magic without the safety of his necklace was a high one. Once Seven's anger and humiliation eased, he began to think more clearly about his situation.

Even if he had been able to transport himself out of the tower, he'd have arrived back in his cave a broken thing, poisoned by the magic used to make the journey. Without his necklace, he was extraordinarily vulnerable. And how long, exactly, could he survive without it? He was already feeling the effects of its absence: a dull ache behind his eyes, a queasiness in his stomach.

He needed his necklace first, and then he could turn his attention to Joseph.

Seven always got to the root of a person, pulling the truth out of them, devastating them to the point where all they wanted was to be free of him. All the petty things they craved which they'd never admit to were worked loose by Seven, revealing them in a way no person wanted to be revealed. Such people very rarely made a second wish.

Or, in the rare occasions when such strategy failed, Seven was often able to subvert the wish. To get it over with quickly so that the magic had little chance to work its poison on him. Take the infamous 'pickle wish' – Seven had managed to both reveal the man's vanity *and* give him precisely what he'd asked for, though not at all what he'd wanted. Gods, the look on his face when he'd realised what Seven had endowed him with!

The Princess And The Orrery

The memory cheered Seven enormously. Sooner or later greed would get the better of Joseph and he'd be back for his second and third wishes. Then he'd make a mistake, as humans always did, and Seven would have him. For now, it seemed he had no choice but to wait.

At least the tower was well-appointed, with a wide bed, a sofa, a writing desk stocked with paper, chalk and charcoal, and a small, mirrorless room which housed a stone drop-toilet above a pit, and a tap covered in hard limescale that dribbled icy cold water when turned. There was also a little bookshelf filled with nursery stories about fairies and elves, beautiful maidens and handsome men. A joke, Seven supposed, though not a particularly funny one – much like the unlocked door.

During the second week, a young woman came with food and a bucket of warm, soapy water. Seven made good use of all three: washing the sweat and blood from his body, before gorging himself on the food and then, when he felt more like himself again, turning his attention to the woman.

He picked up her hand and examined it. He saw the surprise on her face and shot her a shy smile, carefully crafted. An old trick, boring almost, but useful when it landed.

It took him less than an hour to unravel her, opening her up to experiences she'd always wanted but been too repressed to explore. It was luck, really, that someone so ready to be tempted had been sent to him. Seven had done many terrible things in his life, but there were lines he'd never crossed.

She promised to sneak him in a kitchen knife when she next brought food. When Joseph came, Seven would be ready.

But she didn't arrive the next day, or the next, or the next.

At the beginning of his third week of incarceration, Seven was sent a man in his mid-thirties who looked to be some kind of clerk. He arrived as the young woman before him had, only this time without the bucket – a lesson, Seven was informed, though it seemed the clerk hadn't been told what the lesson was supposed to teach.

He was starving, but Seven realised instantly that this man would not respond well to weakness. So he greeted him warmly, offered him some of his food, and asked about the woman.

"Sent to the manufactories," the clerk said with a sniff. "Don't know why, but it must have been serious."

Seven paused, a grape halfway to his lips. "I have heard tell of these places. Very few survive them?"

"It's the price of progress. Besides, we only send our own down there when they deserve it."

"Is that so? My understanding is you populate these 'manufactories' with slaves. I wonder, my friend, that you can stand such a thing. You are a progressive, are you not? A man of thoughts and ideas, not to be shackled by such barbarous actions."

The clerked preened, pleased with the description – as Seven had suspected he would be.

"I can tell a man of substance," Seven said, pressing home his advantage. "A man destined for great things. Clearly, you are no simple lackey. Your bearing, your intellect, inform me this cannot be."

"Well, yes... actually I work directly for his Lordship, the Baron."

"I am unsurprised to hear it. Indeed, if I may speak truthfully, I am most surprised that you serve. I would have thought you better suited to be master..."

Pulling out the clerk's fantasy was easier than the servant's. Sex, in Seven's experience, was a prize hard won. People were, for reasons he couldn't fathom, much more cautious when it came to consenting to an act that was, really, little more than physical necessity. When it came to their ambitions, however, they were much more willing to be serviced. The clerk left, his mind alight with the promise of power, vowing to return with Seven's necklace.

He never came back, either.

The visits stopped. The door was locked, and a small hatch cut into the wood. The lock was not for Seven, but to stop people coming in should he try to tempt them – which of course he would have done, if it had been a possibility. Food was delivered cautiously, quickly, quietly – and infrequently.

Seven was alone, trapped in the tower with only the steadily increasing pain of his missing necklace for company. It occurred to him after the third month, in a way it hadn't before, that he could very well die here.

5

Management was a thankless task, even before trying to do it well, and Naima found herself in the unenviable position of being both responsible for all the Cultivators at Castell y Sêr and also having to justify their existence to the population. The Cultivators cost money, funding which came from the public purse. And the public, by and large, were losing interest in knowledge for knowledge's sake.

It wasn't that the Cultivators weren't respected. In a general sense, people understood that many of the advancements they enjoyed were a result of the Sisters' work – but equally, the public were also put off by their tendency to make things explode, or change colour, or melt.

Every now and again, Naima's memory would randomly throw up the image of Celia's face just before she turned into a puddle of bubbling, toxic foam.

That incident had done nothing, unsurprisingly, to ingratiate the Cultivators to public. Not only that, but with the rise in steam power and the success of international companies like the Ota'ari & Penquoi Shipping Concern – the famous O&P – and dubious benefit of the manufactories, a lot of people simply didn't appreciate funding what they saw as 'proving the bleeding obvious' or, more damningly, as sexist and elitist due to their strict admissions policy.

Naima had plans, though. The Sisterhood could be what it once was – no, it could be better. With funding, she could open a boys' college; small at first, naturally, but it would be a step towards parity. She even had designs on the manufactories. Technology could revolutionise the work that went on within those cold, stone walls. Minimise deaths. Maybe even remove the need for the slaves completely.

There was so much that could be done, but tradition was a heavy metaphorical rock to reposition, and so far, Naima had barely managed to shift it an inch. And now there was Joseph to

The Princess And The Orrery

contend with, and the repercussions of his 'acquisition' in the tower.

Two such repercussions were currently standing in front of her, having recently filed their preliminary report on their experiences at a Royal Ball held in the small Kingdom of Llanotterly, some thirty miles east.

The report was late, due to the fact the two Sisters had spent three months in hospital, recovering.

Naima spun a curl of hair on her finger as she studied their report. It was easier than having to look at the two younger women standing in front of her desk, one of whom was leaning on a crutch. She'd heard the expression 'holding the tiger by its tail', but had never quite understood its meaning until now. Folding her hands on top of the report, she looked up.

"So, you're claiming that a 'monster' attacked the Ball?" Naima said, pointlessly hoping that somehow the Sisters' report might change on the third telling.

A silent conversation occurred between the two women: an intricate pattern of raised eyebrows, pursed lips, darting eyeballs and, at one point, a slight bobbing of the head.

Naima waited.

"Er. Yes, Sister," the one without the crutch replied at last. She had warm, khaki-brown skin, her hands and forearms covered in thin white scars, like she'd been attacked by a psychopathic pin cushion.

"I can't think of any other way to describe it. I have tried to," the scarred Cultivator continued. "We were in the Ballroom, observing the guests and making some minor anthropological notes, when the glass doors exploded inward and suddenly there was this, this.... huge monster in the room, attacking the guests. Picking people up and throwing them against the walls – I'm certain it killed the King."

"Can you describe this 'monster'?"

"Yes, absolutely." She pulled a thick, well-thumbed notebook from one of her many pockets and opened it at a marked page. The tension in her voice eased as she settled into reading her observations.

F. D. Lee

"It was approximately fifteen-foot-tall and extremely strong, even allowing for its immense size. It was humanoid in appearance, though the creature's head was smaller on its body than I would expect a person's to be, and it had rounded eyes, rather like a frog's, though set like ours in the face. It was also intelligent."

Naima's heart sank. Thank God for her upbringing, which had given her training in putting on a blank face when she needed to. "What makes you think that? The creature's human-like appearance?"

"No, Sister. I'm basing my conclusion on the fact that it could speak. We know because the other... um... monster spoke to it."

Silence, so intense that had anyone bothered to drop a pin, it would have rung out like the Palace bells at noon.

Naima looked down again at the report, not yet officially entered into the records. She needed to nip this in the bud, and the best way to do that was to treat it like any other mistaken experiment.

"This would be the blue man, I suppose?"

"Er, yes," said the scarred Cultivator. "Blue, like I am brown, she is white, and you are black."

"No one is blue, Sisters," Naima said, making sure she sounded like she believed what she was saying. "You must have made a mistake. Understandable, of course, given the circumstance you describe. A giant man is feasible, if allowed the right conditions growing up. Strong, too. And animals might have been trained to attack, explaining the little creatures that hurt you. But a blue man? Have you ever, *ever*, heard of any such race of people?"

The two women shook their heads.

"I'm pleased to see your good sense hasn't left you," Naima said, ignoring the sting of her conscience. Happily, her growing anger made it easier. Facts were facts, and here she was having to make her Sisters believe they had imagined something. Naima drummed her fingers on her desk. The two women waited. Nothing ever happened quickly in Castell y Sêr, especially thinking.

Eventually, she said, "I can understand how the trauma of an attack can rattle a person. The mind plays tricks – the psycharium is full of such people. I think, given your injuries and the stress

The Princess And The Orrery

you've no doubt been under, it would be better if I kept this report and you, ah, reflected on what it is you think happened. The Cultivators are under a lot of external pressure, as you know. We need to maintain our reputation for factual exploration."

The two women shared another look, clearly aware Naima had just cast aspersions on their sanity. But aloud, the scarred one said, "Yes, Sister."

"Good," Naima said. "Off you go."

The two women exited. Naima marched over to her window, overlooking the bay. Her skin itched, her dishonesty as irritating as flea bites. If only she could dig a hole, fill it with herbs, and be rid of the feeling as easily as dealing with such pests.

What could she do? She'd made the agreement now. Joseph wasn't the kind of person to let one off the hook – and that was before he'd got his hands on that *thing* in the tower.

She should have known his offer was too good to be true, the funding and support he promised too generous. That the terms, when first given to her, were too easy. Hell, not just easy – tempting. He'd offered her the chance to reinvigorate the Cultivators, to open up the Sisterhood, to change the world – or to change Cerne Bralksteld, which was near enough the same thing, given the city's influence. To be remembered.

If Naima had been inclined, she would have wished she'd never accepted Joseph's original invitation to discuss the future of Castell y Sêr. Unfortunately, she was now all too aware of the danger of wishes.

※

Next on Naima's list of difficult duties was a trip to the observatory. It had been a month since she'd last paid a personal visit, though she had kept up with Amelia's hastily written updates. What greeted her when she stepped through the heavy observatory door was, however, beyond anything she'd expected.

The orrery had doubled in size since she'd last seen it, and then it had not been small. It now had five planets, all spinning in perfect harmony; a gentle, intoxicating rhythm that lulled the soul.

It had always been relaxing to watch the spheres moving, but now it was something beyond that, as if the device were an old friend reaching out to her, soothing away the stresses and anxieties of the day. There was something just so *correct* about it.

A memory stirred of when she'd been younger, newly arrived at Castell y Sêr, and had first seen the alchemy chambers and the geological catalogues. The moment Naima had realised that she was home, in a way that the barracks, for all its many rooms and distractions, had never been home. The orrery made her feel the same way now as she had then – that she was in a place that made sense, and where sense was made.

"You like it?" Amelia asked, appearing from behind the orrery. She was covered in muck.

"It's... very impressive. You learned how to understand what it was saying, then?"

"Yes, I suppose I must have done," Amelia said, grinning in very smug fashion.

Naima did not appreciate the vagueness. "Have you been keeping records, at least?"

"Most of the time – I keep forgetting. My notebooks are on my desk, if you want to check."

Biting back a sharp reply, Naima moved over to Amelia's desk and thumbed through one of her notebooks. She was relieved to see that there were, in fact, pages of detailed notes and equations, albeit somewhat haphazardly organised. Engineering wasn't Naima's field, but she knew some of the basics.

"You designed a new component?"

"More than one, in fact." Amelia's voice sounded hollow – she was inside the orrery. Naima could catch glimpses of her between the rotating globes. "Speaking of which, can you pass that wossit, no, no, on your right, yes, that one. I need to adjust the speed on this planet. It's not meant to move nearly so slowly."

"I thought going too fast was the problem?"

"I fixed that."

"And how did you decide how fast they're meant to move?" Naima asked, passing the 'wossit' through a gap in the rotation. "You mapped the stars?"

"Yes," came the muffled reply. It was surprisingly dark at the centre of the device, the large black orb at the highest elevation casting a long shadow. "I am in an observatory."

Naima suppressed a smile, despite herself. "Very true. It's not an exact process though, or so I understood."

"It wasn't. I worked it out – I did say you could look at my notebooks."

She debated going back to the desk and really looking through Amelia's notebooks, but not for long. There was something so restful about the orrery. Strange, really. They weren't particularly interesting devices. Certainly not something she would have thought about spending any time on – most people could make one if they had the tools. Garden shed elementis, hardly worthy of a Cultivator's time. And yet, the orrery Amelia was constructing was unlike anything she had seen before.

"It really is a marvel," Naima said. "You should be proud."

There was a *thunk*, and then one of the globes began moving slightly faster on its axis – only by a little, but the change managed to make the whole thing even more satisfying.

"That's good," Naima said over the whirl of cogs and machinery. "Much better." It was like the orrery was even more itself, now. Like watching a fawn grow into a stag; a process so natural, so wonderfully inevitable, it satisfied some deep-rooted expectation she didn't even know she'd had.

Amelia's head popped up from behind the spinning globes. "You'd better stand back."

"Oh? What?"

"Stand back." There was a pause of one rotation, and then Amelia made the jump between the spheres, landing with a tumble on the floor where Naima had been standing. She stood up and wiped herself down. "Was there something you wanted?"

"Mmm – oh, yes, yes." With some regret, Naima followed Amelia to her desk. "I assume you've written to Joseph with your progress?"

Amelia frowned. "He doesn't want to see me?"

"He hasn't asked to."

"Oh. Well. Alright. I'll write something up for him later."

It was Naima's turn to frown. The orrery was spectacular, certainly, but that didn't mean that the girl could ignore her other responsibilities.

"Write it now. You know how we work here, little princess. If you want to be a Sister, you've got to behave like one."

It seemed for a moment that Amelia would refuse, but then she plopped down onto her chair and began scrawling out an update on the first piece of blank paper she came across.

"Now that the difficult work is finished, perhaps you can turn your skills to some of the other projects we're working on," Naima said as she wrote. "There are some interesting discoveries being made in the aqua-"

"Oh, no. I don't think I'll be finished for a long time," Amelia announced, head bent over her begrudging report. "In fact, I'd like you to write to my mum – my parents, that is, and let them know I won't be back until next year at the earliest. I know I was supposed to go home by Winter's Night, but the orrery needs me and Joseph wants it finished, so..."

The implication hung in the air. Politics was not the realm of the Cultivators, but the arrangement that had been brokered between Joseph and Amelia's parents was clear. Two years and the girl went home.

"Don't you miss your family?" she asked.

"No." Scribble scribble.

Naima should have expected that answer. She had a pile of unopened letters in her office from Amelia's mother. At first, the girl had read them and replied, but as the months drifted into years she'd stopped. Eventually, Naima had given up delivering the letters. Instead, she kept them, still sealed, in her office, waiting for the day Amelia might want to read them.

"I expect they miss you," Naima said, trying a different track. "You've been gone such a long time."

"Maybe." Scribble scribble. "I don't know." Scribble scribble. "Probably not." Amelia folded the paper, sealed it with a blob of wax, and handed it over. "Here."

"I'm not your servant, little princess."

"Well, I can't take it. I've got too much to do."

The Princess And The Orrery

The two women glared at each other for a moment, and then Naima took the report. "How much longer do you want to keep working on the orrery, then? Perhaps you can stay until Diwrnod o Olau..."

Amelia spun around in her chair to look at her creation. "That's the candle festival, right, for the end of winter? That won't give me enough time, either. I keep getting new ideas about how to improve it – now I've got the basics pinned down, I'm finally getting somewhere."

"Well... I suppose that's what we want, really," Naima found herself saying. "Improvements. I'll see what his Lordship has to say. It's not as simple as just writing to your parents, you know that?"

Amelia sighed. "Yes, I know. But I want to stay." She sounded suddenly very young and small. "I don't want to go home. Please don't make me."

Naima reached out and patted the girl's shoulder. Behind them, Barry the bear sat on the bed, his glass eyes fixed on the orrery. It would have been difficult in that moment to say which set of eyes was more transfixed.

6

Joseph was sitting in the garden, wrapped under a blanket with a thick scarf around his neck, reading.

Surely it was too cold for such things? The Palace garden was, in fact, a landscaped balcony, jutting out of the canyon wall. They might not get snow in Cerne Bralksteld, but this high up a bitter breeze, unconcerned with sovereignty, travelled straight across the landbridge from the neighbouring country of Voriias.

Nevertheless, Joseph seemed restful, the only indications of his ill-health being the cane resting against his chair and a large jug of thick green liquid he was slowly working his way through.

Naima only vaguely knew what was wrong with him – some wasting sickness he'd had since childhood. It came and went in bouts, often confining him to his bed, doctors from the best hospitals in Cerne Bralksteld hovering around him. They'd yet to find a cure.

Still, he was luckier than most. There was a tradition in Cerne Bralksteld, especially amongst the gentry, of abandoning sickly children to the sea. Anthropology wasn't Naima's particular interest, but from what she understood, it all centred around the fact that so much of the lives of the well-to-do were conducted inside the walls of the canyon.

If a child was born too weak for the cold and dampness of life within the rocks, then a quick end in the waves awaited. Apparently, it had been Joseph's mother, the late Baroness, who had saved him from that fate.

It was Joseph's illness that had first brought Naima to his attention, in fact. The Cultivators' purpose was research, and part of her campaign to re-enfranchise them had centred around the benefit their work might have to areas outside of their traditional remit, such as medicine. But the medical colleges preferred to do things their own way, and with a ready supply of slaves for them to practise on, it had been next to impossible for Naima to convince anyone that the Cultivators might also have something to offer.

The Princess And The Orrery

But Joseph had been surprisingly receptive. At the time, she'd put it down to the desperation of the sick. He had, however, taken a keen interest in all their work, especially engineering, astronomy and history. He'd asked about children's stories, too, and had been disappointed when she'd said they didn't study such things.

She glanced up at the tower, where the creature was kept. In hindsight, the warnings about Joseph's true focus had been there from the beginning – but who would have ever believed such a thing was possible?

"Naima, good afternoon."

She didn't jump, though she had to fight the urge. She'd swear his eyes hadn't left the page.

"Good afternoon, my Lord. Apologies, I thought you were reading."

He closed the book and looked up at her, his eyes narrowed against the bright, early winter sun. "I was."

"Oh. A good book, my Lord?"

He held it for her to read the title – predictably, it was yet another collection of children's stories. This book was very old, the spine fraying at the edges and the picture on the front little more than a pale silhouette. She tried to read the author's name, but it had faded to only a few letters.

Joseph was watching her reaction closely. She handed him Amelia's hastily written report.

If he found it too brief, nothing showed on his face, though he did cover his mouth with his hand at one point. When he was finished, he folded the paper up and tucked it in his pocket. Naima would have left then, if she could. Unfortunately, there was more to be discussed. She just wasn't sure how to approach it.

"She's made a lot of progress, my Lord," Naima offered.

"She has."

"And you're pleased?"

"Certainly."

"Ah... good. She's working very hard. You, ah, never did explain why you wanted her to build it. Nor why you want that thing in the Palace," she added, hoping he might pick up the conversation.

F. D. Lee

Joseph sat quietly, watching her with eyes that didn't seem to blink. She tried, unsuccessfully, not to think about how creepy he was.

It's the way he looks at people, Naima thought as she tried to maintain eye contact. He was always studying you, scanning your features for clues, waiting to see what you would do or say. It wasn't just that his staring was rude… it tripped over into something else. She could imagine the same intensity in a child faced with a stranger, trying to work them out. While she might find a toddler's scrutiny mildly annoying, in an adult it was downright disturbing.

Her father had had an infantry man executed once. She'd asked him what the criminal had done, but he'd refused to explain. She knew now, of course. War made people do terrible things, certainly, but there were some who needed little convincing. And, once the battle was done, they found they had developed a taste for bloodshed.

That man had liked watching people, too.

Naima held on to the silence for as long as she could bear, but Joseph was always going to win any conversational tug-o-war.

"Well. I'm pleased that you're pleased, my Lord," she said, giving up. "However, there may be an issue."

"Surely not?"

"She wishes to keep working on it. To extend her stay."

"Is that a problem?"

Naima found herself falling into the pose she used to adopt when she was receiving some accolade or another as a child: a stance called 'at ease', though it rarely was.

"What about her family, my Lord?"

"What about them?"

"I understood the girl was only to remain with us for two years."

"Do you need more funding? You know, I can always speak with my brother about your finances."

Naima paused. "No, my Lord. Thank you. The Palace is very generous."

"Well, then," he said, picking up his book, "I see no problem with her extending her visit, do you?"

The Princess And The Orrery

"...No, my Lord."

It would have been a relief to send Amelia home for a few months. The letters from her mother were growing increasingly frequent, and as the pile rose, unopened, in her office so did Naima's guilt at keeping Amelia. Not that the girl wasn't bright. She'd make a good Cultivator one day – but she was too young and too focused, obsessed in fact, on the orrery. It wasn't healthy.

And that was without the nagging unease that Joseph's interest in her work elicited. The man in question had returned to reading his book as if she wasn't there.

Naima coughed. "Will you inform her parents?"

"If you need my help, I'm happy to give it," he replied, closing the book in a way she thought was rather pointed. "Is that all? Or do you have any other issues you need me for?"

"Actually... yes, my Lord. One more thing, if she's going to stay. The orrery takes up a lot of her time. Too much." She caught the accusation in her tone and swallowed it. "She's missing classes. Her biology, geology, anthropology," she glanced at his book. "Folklore... any subject that isn't related to engineering or astronomy is suffering."

"I thought the Cultivators encouraged specialisation?"

"Yes, my Lord. But only when one has a solid foundation in all the major subjects."

"And you consider folklore to be a major subject? Your expression just now didn't suggest that. Even knowing what you know."

"I don't believe we should privilege any one type of knowledge over another, my Lord."

"A little bit of knowledge is a dangerous thing, though, isn't that what they say?" Joseph replied. "Perhaps it would be better to have her focused on one task."

That wasn't the right meaning of the quote, but Naima didn't correct him. Instead, she said, "A good foundation in all the subjects is beneficial, my Lord. It helps us to see things from different points of view, to solve problems."

"All the more reason for her to stay, then," Joseph parried. "Let her catch up."

Naima gave up. "Yes, my Lord."

"While you're here, Naima, I have a question for you. I've been thinking about our guest, the one in the tower," he clarified unnecessarily. "Tell me, have you ever thought about absolutes?"

"The philosophy of elementis teaches us that there are truths to be found, my Lord," Naima said, falling back on the blessed structure of the Cultivators rather than acknowledge the sickly heat in her stomach at the mention of the blue-skinned creature. "But I can't say whether they are absolute."

"But some things are fundamentally true, are they not? Pain is always painful. Happiness is always happy."

"...I suppose so, my Lord. But people experience them differently."

He tapped his book against his chin. "Ah yes. True. Still, it's something to think on. Perhaps, when I'm in a position to help you open your boys' college, you might permit me to guest lecture on the subject?"

"Of course, my Lord. It would be an honour."

"Excellent, Naima. Thank you."

And that was that. Joseph opened his book again and started reading. For a moment she didn't know what she was supposed to do, a decidedly unpleasant – and increasingly more frequent – feeling.

Her brain, thankfully, came back to her. Naima bowed and left him in the garden, reading his book of children's stories as the cold night drew in over the bay, pulling the winter behind it.

An hour or so later, Joseph closed his book. He'd read it many times over, and plenty more like it. Naturally, the stories differed. Time changed them, as did the personal interests of the author.

A lot of them appeared to be based on oral histories and folk tales, adapted slightly for whatever the current fashion was when they'd been written. But there was a seam of truth to be mined, if you read carefully enough. And everything he'd read had been corroborated, one way or another. He wasn't just relying on the literature, as the Cultivators would say.

The Princess And The Orrery

Words were important, that much was obvious. He'd worked that out as a child, stuck in his room with only his stories for company. Almost every genie tale had someone being caught out by the words they used.

He'd been careful so far, and so far, he was winning. It had been interesting, nevertheless, to see how the genie had tried to break free. To watch its famed manipulation in action as it attempted to convince his people to turn on him. If anything, Joseph had been rather disappointed: the genie's tactics had been obvious, dull – clumsy, even, especially where Naima was concerned.

Though, to give credit where it was due, he could allow for the fact the genie hadn't been at its best when it had tried to get Naima to kill him, and both the scullery maid and the clerk had been absolutely determined to carry out the genie's instructions. If Joseph hadn't been waiting safely outside the door with some Palace guards to capture them and dump them in the manufactories, they might even have succeeded.

Of course, he'd also taken risks; every hero had to face trials, after all. Having Amelia break the necklace had been his most recent gamble, but he'd made sure he was safely behind a heavy door when she'd done it. And from the report tucked in his pocket, it seemed like his plan had worked perfectly. *Was* working perfectly. In truth, he hadn't anticipated the orrery reacting to the genie's necklace so quickly – it was so tempting to try to rush things along, but he knew he had to hold his nerve.

Temptation was the sure-fire way to lose the upper hand when dealing with a genie. Naturally, with two wishes left, he had thought about skipping ahead. Dumping Amelia, wishing the orrery complete, and using his final wish to fulfil his destiny. But Joseph was smarter than that. There was too much space in a wish like that for the genie to find cracks, to break it open.

The other constant in all the stories were the limitations. Three wishes, no more, and the genie and its lamp – or, as he'd learnt, necklace – had to be together. It seemed a design flaw, but then design flaws were an inherent aspect of the genie's condition. The magic clearly hurt it, for all the rumours that it also brought pleasure. The servants Joseph sent infrequently to drop food off to the genie, with strict instructions not to speak, enter the room or dally, told tales of sickness and the stench of blood.

The genie, it seemed, suffered an illness, just like him. But that was the trouble when things were left up to nature, Joseph thought, reaching for his disgusting green medicine: so much was poorly put together.

But not for much longer: just until he worked out the perfect wording for his second wish. And, if it was as strong as he suspected it would be, he'd never need his third one. Soon, he'd have everything that he could ever wish for, and he'd *still have the genie*. That was the beauty of his plan, and why he could stand to wait.

He was so close! When it all worked out, as it surely would, he'd be a hero, a saviour: the man who made Cerne Bralksteld the greatest city in all of the Third Kingdom, hell, in all Five Kingdoms of Thaiana. And unlike all those idiots in the stories, he wouldn't be caught out by the genie's tricks. His time was coming.

There is a saying that even a broken clock can tell the time twice a day. It's true, of course. And yes, the time may well be correct for those brief hours, but it's wrong the other twenty-two. Broken clocks can fool you into thinking they aren't, if you don't pay attention to them.

And no one, really, paid Joseph any attention at all.

7

Seven lay on his bed, cornflower blue fingers pressed to his temples as if the pressure would ease the pain. It didn't.

Six months had passed without his necklace, and his head was in constant torment. Food was shoved irregularly through the hatch in his door, and what was given to him was meagre fare: hard bread, apples, bowls of gruel. If Seven had been human, he probably would have starved. The door remained locked, and those charged with bringing him his meals never tarried.

Or so it had been, until today.

A knock at the door jolted him out of his bitterness with a start. Even moving gently, it felt like there was a cannonball in his skull when he lifted himself from the bed. His arms and legs were no better, heavy as lead and yet, perversely, weak as straw.

Shuffling over to the tap, pausing only to let the cannonball settle after the exertion of movement, he splashed water on his face. Next, he tightened the cord of his dirty linen trousers so they sat snug on his narrow hips and rearranged his tunic to display a triangle of smooth, cornflower blue skin. At least on the outside, his body showed only minimal signs of affliction; he was thinner, his hair greasy, bruises appearing and then fading all over his body without his having touched anything. But he was still tall, muscular, handsome.

Beauty was natural to the genies in the way sharp teeth were natural to a shark, and for the same reason. Still, what he wouldn't give for five minutes with a mirror, a proper tap with hot running water, some clean clothes, and his kohl eye-liner and jewellery – his necklace top of the list. But he made the best of himself, given his situation.

Seven leaned against the desk, forcing back the ache in his head. "Come in," he called, his voice rich and indulgent as honey.

A man stepped into the room, holding a tray of food. Despite the low, desperate rumble from his stomach, Seven didn't allow his gaze to fall on the tray. Instead, he put all his energy into a dazzling smile for the man carrying it. He was middle-aged, plain and pale, the skin under his eyes almost translucent. At his wrists, veins strained against thin arms as he gripped the tray. A slave, Seven surmised, released from the underground manufactories and charged with feeding the prisoner. What was Joseph playing at…?

"Welcome," he said, brushing his dark blue curls behind his ear, tilting his head just so. He was desirable, he was kind, he was interested. "It is a pleasure to make your acquaintance, my friend. What delights have you brought for me?"

The slave stared at Seven, then at the food, as if the pile of hot, fresh bread and sweet fruit could help him.

"Tell me, sir, what is your name? You surely know mine, do you not? Most of you seemed to."

Again, the slave said nothing, which was unexpected. Usually, Seven couldn't stop the humans talking to him. He let a quick smile flutter across his lips, suggesting a comforting vulnerability.

"I suppose I must look very strange to you. The blue-skinned creature in the tower – what a sight to behold! And yet, here I am. Not so monstrous, I hope? Indeed, I would think you have seen worse. You have nothing to fear from me, friend. Watch, and I shall prove it to you."

Seven pushed himself off the table and sauntered towards the door, lithe as he was able. Walking took concentration, but he didn't want to lose his allure by showing weakness, showing pain. Not that displaying pain was without its uses, but it had to be the right kind of pain. Physical distress was not the route to this man, Seven sensed. He reached the open doorway without upsetting the cannonball too drastically, and pressed his hand up to the space.

It was as if an invisible barrier splayed his fingers. The slave gaped. Another quick, shy smile from Seven, and then he pressed himself against the door at an angle impossible to maintain without support, pushing his head against the invisible barrier, flattening his dark blue curls as if against a window. When he felt his point was made, Seven pulled back. Nausea rolled in his stomach with the action.

"Now, my friend, you try. But I would advise you not to lean so, lest you hurt yourself. A hand should suffice."

The Princess And The Orrery

The slave, wary, scuttled up to the door. He shifted his grip on the tray to one hand, and pressed his other into the open space. It passed through into the corridor without any trouble.

"There, you see. You may leave here whenever you wish, I cannot follow you. If you prefer, you could even feed me from the corridor." Seven shot the slave a mournful look, a seemingly effortless expression that felt like sand grinding in the soft tissue of his face. "Though I hope you will not?"

The slave tried the door again, this time with his foot. It was the same. He turned questioning eyes to Seven.

"You were warned that I am dangerous," Seven said. He let his voice drop, softening his tone even further. "I wonder why... Do you think they care about you?"

Seven touched the man's chin, very lightly.

"Open your mouth."

The slave obeyed. Instead of a tongue, Seven saw a twitching stump of raw muscle, inexpertly healed. He let his head drop sadly– the cannonball thudding into the bone behind his eyes – sympathetic, but not patronising.

"Ah, no," Seven sighed. "I think they do not care for you. You may close your mouth. Was this inflicted upon you for my benefit?"

The man nodded. The tray rattled in his hands.

"For this, I am truly sorry."

Gently, Seven took the tray from the slave. The man's fingers twitched towards his, and when he crossed to his desk, the slave followed. Seven put the tray on the desk and turned back to him.

Any sensible creature would have taken the chance to run, would have realised something was very amiss with this prisoner and his prison. But for the slave it was already too late. Seven could feel it, churning in his stomach like a rotten meal: the way the slave's mind spun with want, with hope, with relief. An old, broken little mouse, longing for the claws of the cat, if only for the attention.

Why Joseph would send him such a person was anybody's guess. Probably another little test of his abilities after six months without his necklace, on someone Joseph assumed to be worthless. Oh, but this slave wasn't worthless, not to Seven. It would hurt, but if he could convince the slave to help him, what did more pain matter?

"Such cruelty is abhorrent, the actions of a base man," he said to the slave. "But I speak only of that which you already know. The world is full of such people, sadly. Those who see individuals like you – like us – as little more than pieces on a board, to be moved around or discarded as they see fit. Is this not the story of your life?"

Hesitation from the slave, then a quick nod.

Putting his arm around the man's shoulders, Seven led him to the sofa, guiding him onto the plump cushions. Seven slid to the floor, settling – blessedly still – at the slave's feet. The skin showing between the man's trouser cuff and his cheap shoes was paler even than his face and arms. His ankles were all bone and tendon.

"What a world these people seek to create," Seven said, shaking his head sadly, blinking away the pain, hoping it would pass for an overabundance of emotion.

"Slavers and thieves. I dare not imagine what they have stolen from you, and yet I cannot help but think on it, on your suffering. They take your tongue from your head and send you, all alone, to feed the monster. Why do you think they do such a thing? They send no one to collect my waste, nor to deliver me my water. Why, then, send someone to feed me? Attend. It is because they forgot that you are a person, or they never bothered to care. Which do you think is the truth? I suspect the latter, and so should you, if your good sense they have not also amputated. Just nod."

The slave nodded, his head down, staring at his knees.

"Poor thing. Do you know why they chose you, specifically, for this task?"

Shake, no.

"I am glad, though, that they did. I have been so..." Swallow. Hesitate. "So very lonely. For all the pain inflicted upon me, it is the abandonment that crushes. I have never before felt so helpless, so weak, so casually misused."

The man looked at him from beneath his lashes, his eyes shining. Seven rose up in one fluid movement, so he was kneeling between the man's legs. Giddiness swayed him.

"Do you know what it is to be so very alone? To abandon even yourself?"

The slave blinked, tears rolling down the sharp planes of his face. He nodded.

"I knew that you would."

Seven brushed away the man's tears. The slave was with him now, but Seven's precarious balance on his health was shifting with the human's increased focus on his need. Guide or push? With his necklace, it was an art. Now, it would have to be what it was.

"My friend, I can help you... and you can help me. This is my summation: they took your tongue from you because they assumed, mistakenly, that if you could not speak to me I would not know you. But I know you as intimately as I have ever known a person. I know what you strive for."

Seven caught the slave's chin in his fingers, forcing the man to fix his gaze on Seven's featureless eyes, peacock blue from lid to lid, devoid of pupil or iris. A genie's eyes: promising everything, revealing nothing.

"My eyes seem strange to you, do they not? Unlike any you have encountered before. What can I see, when there is nothing there to see with, you wonder? This answer is this: I see everything. I see your pain. I see your frustration. I see..."

Bracing himself, Seven skimmed the surface of his magic.

The pain came, worse even than the constant, pounding nausea caused by the absence of his necklace. For all that Seven barely touched the power inside him, stinging whips of agony crackled along his muscles, filling his veins with a frozen purity that was both indescribable torment and, chasing behind it, the sweetest, purest pleasure he'd ever known.

"I see your home," Seven whispered. "Far from here. A long pathway, with stones that press through the soles of your shoes as you run along it. A tree with fat, sweet fruit hanging from its branches. There were books in your room, and a friend you used to play with as a child. Ah, yes, and sometimes as an adult, too. I see... I see the raiders, and fire, and the dark belly of a boat... I... Darkness and heat... the steam burns you..."

F. D. Lee

Seven pulled back from his magic, though it remained hot and sharp on his skin, like the memory of nails scratching. "Would you not wish to be back in your garden, listening to the birds sing? I, too, have a home I would return to. Yes, my friend, we can aid each other. Let it be so. When you leave here, do not return to your post. Go instead to–"

He stopped, his words shrivelling in the sudden dry heat of his mouth. His stomach knotted, the skin on the back of his neck tingling.

Seven's head snapped to the door.

Joseph stepped into the room. There was something in his hands, bound in heavy material, only a tiny flash of gold visible, which Joseph pressed the edge of his thumb to. Seven didn't need to see it to know what it was: his necklace. Joseph held it close to his mouth, whispering to it.

The temperature dropped; the breath on the humans' lips began to steam. Joseph quickly removed his thumb, covering the shard of Seven's necklace in the material.

The wish gripped Seven like bindweed coiling around a plant, its intentions clear. Too late, he realised the slave's true purpose – a distraction, a test, a feint. He screamed as the wish tightened its hold, securing itself to the power inside him.

Panic made his heart pound, his skin sting, his stomach clench. He was only faintly aware of the hard floor beneath his knees, of the keening wail from his throat, the weight in his limbs and the agony in his head. The wish was too much, too strong – he needed his necklace. Even so close, it was too far away.

And yet, for all that his body was descending into seizure and panic, his mind was soaring into raptures. The heavy, hazy thrill of pleasure danced along his screaming nerves. The clarity of thought, the purity of it, that only the bliss of agony can offer.

Music surrounded him, music only he could hear: the heartbeat of the universe, the melody that held the worlds in place. Stars filled his once empty eyes, spinning and turning like the end of the universe, the end of time, the end of life.

Seven crashed to the floor, pain and pleasure dancing reels across every nerve ending in his body, the wish rooting itself in the

The Princess And The Orrery

magic inside him, a reservoir beneath the earth of his consciousness.

Joseph's second wish was made, and Seven was bound to it.

The last thing Seven saw before unconsciousness claimed him was the slave dropping, prostate, at Joseph's feet.

Ignoring the slave, Joseph walked up to the prone figure of the genie and prodded him with a slipper-clad toe, still cradling the wrapped necklace. The genie shuddered, but otherwise gave no response.

Joseph's mouth twitched, the nearest he would come to a smile while unable to hide behind his hand. The wish had worked, he could feel it! All those months spent delaying, denying himself – each and every day, hour and minute, validated in this moment. The second trial was complete – he'd bested the genie! He'd done what so many other heroes had failed to do.

There was just one last test to overcome, and he needed the orrery for that. A little more patience was required, that was all. All in all, Joseph was happy.

Very happy indeed.

8

Spring never exactly sprang in the fae city of Ænathlin. It slid into existence. Or, more accurately given the city's overcrowded streets and poor sanitation, *oozed*.

There was nothing like waking up to the heady scent of emptied chamber pots and rising heat. Still, winter was waning, change was in the air. The seasons shifted slowly, but change always came, eventually.

In the sticky-floored pubs by the wall, groups of fae huddled over watered-down beer and vinegar-sharp wine, talking in whispers:

"It's been a month and they still ain't reopened the Academy. I heard they're not gonna train anyone anymore, that they don't have recruits. I heard the GenAm don't know what it's doing."

In the markets, amidst the shouts of hawkers and the street performers, *sotto voce*, the conversation spread:

"My friend's cousin's friend knows someone who was studying there. They said there was an accident. The building collapsed and people died. They said the GenAm is failing."

In the dragon's dens, hidden behind the thick, pungent smoke from the fenlandriz pipes and the soft murmurs of the storysells, the rumours burned:

"They said the GenAm lost control of the Headmistress, that she was an Anti. If the GenAm can't control the Academy, how can they control the city? How can they keep us safe?"

In warm, dark rooms in the city centre townhouses, where wealthy families lived distant, disconnected lives from the poor and the downtrodden, discussions were held:

"The city's on a knife-edge. The Mirrors have only just begun working reliably. Trade is unpredictable. The peace is fragile. Perhaps now it's possible to, ahh, encourage the GenAm to see the error of its ways."

And in the dull, beige office belonging to the imp Julia, the Head of the Redaction Department, those rumours – and the names of the people spreading them – reached her in the form of reports from her network of informers.

Julia folded one such report, pressing the paper into a sharp edge, and then another and another.

If only she had the Beast. She could have sent it out onto the streets and all those nasty little rumours would have shrivelled and died in the throats of the people spreading them. Redaction worked well enough, but it had to be used effectively. Dead-head too many citizens in quick succession and you risked a revolt. The Beast, on the other hand, would have been a visible yet distant show of power. A reminder that The Teller Was Watching Them – with three pairs of eyes inside a body that could find you wherever you tried to hide, no less – but not an overt attack.

She added another fold to the report.

But instead she was stuck with Mistasinon. A weak, snivelling waste of space when she'd been promised a monster. And even so, despite the insult and the disappointment of it all, she'd found him a position in the Plot Department when he'd refused her offer of a white suit. She'd supported his plan for the genie, to the point of holding off Redacting that bloody cabbage fairy because she'd thought it would send him over the edge.

And how had he repaid her? By stealing the GenAm's best assets, the Redacted protagonists, and allowing their creator to disappear, no doubt dead somewhere in the snow.

It was very disappointing; clearly, the result of the pernicious influence of the cabbage fairy, Buttercup 'Bea' Snowblossom. The Mistasinon of a year ago might have tried to bring the genie in willingly, but he would have used force if he had to. And he certainly wouldn't have got all misty-eyed a handful of Redacted characters when Ænathlin's wellbeing hung in the balance.

Julia ran her thumb an edge of the folded report, sharpening the crease. Without looking up, she said, "He hasn't been to see the cabbage fairy since returning to the city?"

"no my lady he has been working in the plot department"

"That's good. I want to know if he does."

"yes my lady"

"We have to be careful. Mistasinon is a bridge to the old regime, one that will prove useful to me when the time comes,"

F. D. Lee

Julia said to the goblin. Or, more likely, to herself. Redacted fae weren't exactly capable of involved conversation, but they were useful, nevertheless. The dead-heads did as they were told and were loyal, both traits which Julia valued very much.

"yes my lady you have said many times that the beast is tied to the general administration he believes that The Teller Cares About Us"

"And so the Teller does, even now. The only difference is that it's down to me to interpret that care. Mistasinon is a simple thing. Confused, yes. But not complicated. He just needs to be pointed in the right direction and his training will take over."

"would you like me to move him my lady"

Julia chuckled, her eyes fixed on the paper as she continued to fold it, edge over edge, seam against seam. "No, I wasn't speaking literally. I know how to finish the game, but I have to set up the board first. Put him in his place. Just bring me a list of suitable informers."

"yes my lady"

The dead-headed goblin left. Julia put the finishing touches to her paper sculpture and sat it on her desk to admire it: a tiny, neat little dog with three heads. She pushed its tail, and the heads bobbed up and down.

A smile settled on the imp's green face.

Step by step, fold by fold. You could control anything, if you knew the right movements.

"Mortal gods, what have you done to yourself?" Ivor exclaimed, dropping his dice in shock.

Bea patted her dark green hair, which now brushed against her jaw in a messy bob. "Do you like it?"

Ivor leaned on his stool, grabbing his bony knees for balance, and sucked on his teeth. It always surprised Bea that he'd never accidentally swallowed one. But then, a lot about Ivor surprised her. For one, it was a genuine mystery how the gnome managed to survive, given his lax attitude to personal hygiene, nutrition, and exercise. She was sure she'd never seen him leave the little lobby of her building, and she'd certainly never witnessed him eating anything that didn't come wrapped in greasy paper. Maybe it was all the sticky, sour, Ænathlin-made alcohol he drank that held him together? Speaking of which...

"I got you something, too, to say thank you for keeping my room while I was at the Academy," she said, pulling a bottle from her bag.

Ivor was still staring at her.

Bea held the bottle out.

Ivor continued eyeing her.

She shook it, hoping to entice him.

The gnome took the bottle, pulling the cork out with his spindly fingers, his gaze still fixed on her, or, rather, her hair. He took a swig. There was a pause, a grimace, and another swig. Finally, he blinked.

"Looks alright," he allowed. "Ain't you gonna make it grey again?"

"No."

"You'll get stick for it."

"Probably," Bea said, pulling up a stool on the other side of the desk. She picked up the bottle and studied her reflection, distorted in the glass. It wasn't exactly flattering – her chubby face was stretched around the curve of the bottle like someone had grabbed both her cheeks and pulled, but she wasn't interested in that. She fluffed her newly cut, naturally green hair, and grinned at herself.

"I'm a garden fairy," she said to both her reflection and Ivor. "The least I can do is look like one again."

She glanced up at him and, with something of a flourish, took a swig from the bottle.

Ivor grinned. It occurred to Bea that she might have just lost a game the gnome had been playing without her consent. She held her composure for as long as she could, and then let out a spluttering wheeze.

"Mortal gods, what *is* this stuff?"

"Heh. Lemme guess, you traded for this after your decision to go full cabbage fairy?"

Realisation dawned.

"Bloody hells," Bea muttered, handing the bottle back.

"Told you. You'll be lucky if bad trade's the only thing that new hair-do gets you."

"Well, never mind that." She couldn't help touching her hair again. "I like it."

Ivor waited a moment, eyebrows raised. Then he said, "That's it? No twenty-minute lecture on why the whole world is wrong to treat fairies so bad, and how you cabbage fairies have it worse than anyone, and how you're gonna change it all? No angry desk thumping and swearing and shouting?"

"Nope."

His face was a picture of disappointment. "Huh. Suit yourself. I'd think you'd gone soft, but I s'pose not. Not with that hair on display. You wanna hear a story?"

"Go on, then."

"You'll like this one. Go check the doors."

Bea did as she was told, making sure no one was hovering around either the main entrance or the door leading up to the bedsits. You could never be too careful. The Redaction Department had informers everywhere.

"All clear. Is this an illegal one?"

"Not illegal, just not exactly endorsed by the GenAm, neither."

It was Bea's turn to raise an eyebrow. "Interesting."

"Wait 'til you hear it. It's about the Teller and the Beast-"

Bea jumped up as if the old woollen cushion had caught fire.

"I'm sorry, Ivor. I just remembered I've got... I left... I need to do something. Sorry! Maybe later? Sorry!"

She shot him an apologetic look as she hastily closed the stairwell door on his startled expression. She stood at the bottom of the narrow staircase, trying to calm her breathing, which was much easier than calming her mind. It was like she'd had no control over herself, her body and mouth deciding she needed to get away as fast as possible and not bothering to consult her brain.

Though, to be fair, it wouldn't be the first time her brain had been left out of important meetings. Sighing, she began the climb to the fourth floor.

Is that the plan, then? she asked herself. *You're just going to run away every time someone mentions the Beast?*

The Princess And The Orrery

For a brief moment she entertained the thought. How hard would it be to make a judicious exit whenever conversation turned to the Beast? Chances were, people would just assume she was frightened – that was the whole point of the GenAm employing a three-headed, dog-like monster, after all. Keep the city afraid, keep people in line. Catch the dissenters, the Anti-Narrativists. Drag them to the Redaction Department in the middle of the night. A brief interrogation, then onto the Redaction Block in the main square and a cold, white Eraser to the forehead.

And then... nothing.

Bea flung herself through her front door, slamming it behind her. She slid down the old, chipped wood and landed in a soft pile on the floor.

The Beast. The monster that came in the night and stole people away.

And she'd saved its life.

Well, alright, not exactly. She'd saved the life of the man the Beast had been turned into. Mistasinon. Nice, kind, sort-of handsome Mistasinon, with his summer rain smile and big brown eyes, who still thought the GenAm was amazing and that The Teller really did Care About Them, despite everything they'd done to the city. And to him.

While Bea didn't regret her decision to save his life, she wasn't entirely convinced she knew what to make of it. Or him. He wasn't the Beast, not anymore. She was certain of that, or she wouldn't have saved him. But at the same time, he *had* been, once. Everything that creature had done, Mistasinon had done. He'd admitted it himself.

See? That was the problem. Everything was confusing when it came to him.

And she hadn't seen him in a month. Bea had been keeping herself busy with Joan and Fairies United, with no word from any of her Academy co-conspirators. They'd all decided, Mistasinon, Chokey, Hemmings and herself, that they should keep their distance from each other until the dust had settled. Sensible, certainly, but the reality was turning out to be much harder – and the interval much longer – than she'd expected. And there was no sign of the mess caused by the Academy's closure clearing up anytime soon.

Bea did the only thing she could think of in the circumstances; the only thing that made sense: she let rip a torrent of loud, extremely rude words. It did make her feel marginally better, but after the echoes died away, she was still alone, still confused, and still embarrassed to have run away from Ivor, of all people.

She wished she'd kept the bottle of cheap, stinging alcohol for herself.

9

Mistasinon wondered what it was he was expected to achieve, and whether he was being punished for something.

The fact he could think of plenty of things he'd done that merited punishment did nothing to ease his anxiety. A few weeks ago, he might have thought his current psychological dilemma was the result of having three heads, each with very distinct motivations. But since he now only had one, he was instead harbouring the bitter suspicion that such conflict was a matter of fact in his new life.

After all, when you were born a three-headed dog-like creature and were then transformed into something man-shaped, it was, he felt, not entirely unsurprising that along with the arms and legs and the singular head, one also found they had acquired an identity crisis. He was also unsure whether he was a cynic. Having never been just himself before, he wasn't sure whether having cynical thoughts meant that you were inherently cynical, or simply that you were realistic.

The fact that this was almost certainly the response a cynic would give was not lost on him. He'd spent hours the night before, lying in bed staring at the ceiling, trying to work it out. Eventually, he'd begun to wonder if he was not only cynical but also neurotic.

Stifling a yawn, he turned to the brown-suited gnome sitting next to him at the desk.

"How many more are there?"

"Twenty, my Lord."

"Twenty?"

"Yes, my Lord. In today's batch."

"Mortal gods... Why did we allow so many to enrol?"

The brown suit gifted Mistasinon with what he felt was a tacitly blank expression.

"I couldn't say, my Lord," she replied. "That's Plot Department business."

Of course it was. Everything was the Plot Department's responsibility since the Academy shut down, which meant it was all his responsibility.

"Fine. Yes. Thank you. Can you ask the next ones in, please?"

Picking up her clipboard, the gnome stood, pointedly replaced her chair under the table, and chuntered off through the double doors at the end of the room. Judging from the way the morning had gone, Mistasinon had a few minutes to himself before the next family were brought in to be formally apologised to. He buried his head in his arms, closed his eyes, and tried to relax without – and this was the tricky part – falling asleep.

He might as well have not bothered. He'd barely shut his eyes before his consciousness was hit with the sharp, acidic yellow-red scent of righteous anger.

While not entirely sure exactly what he was, Mistasinon knew what he *wasn't*. He might look similar to an elf, barring their pointed ears and pale skin, but an elf he was not. Nor was he a human, despite his height and tawny brown complexion – at least as far as his experience of them suggested. Mistasinon was yet to meet a human who had his sense of smell, speed, and strength, even if these skills were somewhat erratic.

The door banged open. A red-faced female dwarf marched towards him, holding a large, rather shabby handbag like a shield. Or, Mistasinon corrected, a battering ram. The yellow-red of her fury was overwhelming. The brown-suited gnome was noticeably absent.

Standing up, Mistasinon reached into his top pocket for his handkerchief and discreetly rubbed his nose with it, transferring a minuscule amount of diluted peppermint oil to the skin below his nostrils. It wasn't a perfect solution to the problems with his nose, but what else could he do? So far, as long as he was quick, it worked as a kind of blanket that blocked out everything else.

"Hello, thank you for coming today," he began, tucking the handkerchief back into his pocket. "My name is Mistasinon, and on behalf of the Plot Department I would like to-"

"I want to know exactly what you people think you're playing at," the dwarf announced, coming to a stop in front of his desk with the terrifying finality of an avalanche. "How dare you push my children to the bottom of the list?"

"The bottom of-"

"Don't you know who I am?"

He glanced desperately at the list of names on the desk. "Aren't you Mistress Chesterton-Finkbeetle?"

The dwarf pulled herself up to her full height and glared down her nose at him. Such was her resolve, Mistasinon found himself cowed, despite being at least two feet taller.

"Who's your supervisor? I will speak to the person in charge, by the mortal gods."

"I'm the Plotter in charge, Mistress, that's why-"

"Exactly what kind of a Department are you running? I sent my darlings to the Academy to receive an education – to become suits and to work for the General Administration. Instead, I find them back home early because the building collapsed!"

"It was just one room-"

"And that's how you manage things, is it? What do you intend to do now? I demand answers, my Lord, and I will not leave until I have them. Satisfactory answers, may I add – Dea'dora and Hemmings might have been killed."

The penny dropped.

This was Chokey and Hemmings' mother.

When Mistasinon had first met Chokey at the Academy, the young dwarf had warned him in no uncertain terms that he would not want to have to deal with a complaint from her 'Mama'. It turned out she was right.

Sitting down, Mistasinon said, "Mistress Ogrechoker? Please, take a seat."

The dwarf pursed her lips but deigned to do as asked.

"Firstly, please let me apologise for keeping you waiting. We've been working through all the parents alphabetically and-"

"Working through? *Working through*? What do you think this is, my Lord – a stock take?"

Mistasinon took a deep breath, forgetting the peppermint oil. For a moment he was lost in an ocean of stinging whiteness. When he came to, Mistress Ogrechoker was still in full steam.

F. D. Lee

"...simply not good enough. We traded for their places at your wretched Academy, and then my two darlings turn up halfway through their training full of stories of missing Headmistresses and witchlein burning to death. In addition to this huge negligence, you haven't even fulfilled the contract. Dea'dora was never placed and Hemmings hasn't begun training. Too much time has passed in which absolutely nothing has happened! How do you account for that?"

Mistress Ogrechoker sat straight-backed, her handbag square on her lap. Mistasinon stared at her, waiting to see if she had finished. Then, cautiously, he began to speak.

"Mistress... On behalf of the Plot Department, we are of course very sorry for the occurrences at the Academy..." He glanced down at his script. "The General Administration takes the safety of its recruits very seriously, and an investigation is currently underway. I can assure you, the full weight of all four Departments, and indeed the Teller, *whocaresaboutus*, himself, is being brought to bear in the resolution of these matters. Strength and stability are the watchwords of the General Administration, especially at this difficult time. We thank you for your continued support, and I would like to personally offer you my assurances, as the senior Plotter in charge of the investigation, that your children's training will be continued at the earliest possible moment with, of course, no impediment to their future careers with the General Administration."

Silence descended.

Mistress Ogrechoker held Mistasinon's gaze.

A long time ago, Mistasinon had overheard a general speaking about a siege he had maintained for ten years, holding the beleaguered city captive within its own walls. *This isn't the same*, he found himself thinking. *This is a courtesy meeting in the Plot Department. I could get up. I can ask her to leave. I'm in charge.*

And yet he found himself rigid, unable to look away.

Tortuously slowly, Mistress Ogrechoker lifted her hands to the two sturdy metal clips holding her bag closed, and unlocked each one.

Click. Click.

Mistasinon swallowed, his neck suddenly aching. Unhelpfully, he remembered the final part of the general's story, the bit where he explained how he'd finally managed to break the siege by hiding his troops in a seemingly innocent container.

"Mistress Ogrechoker," he said, his voice hoarse, "I'm afraid there are more parents I need to see..."

Ignoring him, the dwarf opened the bag.

Mortal gods, was he holding his breath?

She removed a sheaf of papers at least two inches thick and placed them on the table.

"This is what I expect for my darlings," she stated, bringing her hands back to her bag but not, he noticed, closing it.

Brilliant white flashed across his vision, reminding Mistasinon that he couldn't breathe deeply. He longed to wipe his nose, realising that he had misjudged the impulse to protect himself from her anger. Always making mistakes...

He pulled the papers towards him and, with more effort than he cared to admit, broke eye-contact with the dwarf to glance down at the documents. A glance quickly turned into a detailed perusal.

Mistress Ogrechoker waited while he read through the first page, and then the second, and then the third...

Ten minutes passed before he spoke again. He was roughly a quarter of the way through the paperwork.

"This is... I mean... You can't..."

"I can and I will."

"This is blackmail!"

Mistress Ogrechoker shook her head.

"This is business, my Lord. I am a business dwarf. The General Administration took supplies from me in return for the education and employment of my babies. The General Administration continues to take supplies from me. And in the meantime, you put my children – my darlings – in mortal danger. You secreted them off in some mortal gods-forsaken backwater even the characters wouldn't bother with, and then you summarily failed to either educate or employ them. A deal was struck. I trust you, as a 'senior' representative of the Plot Department, understand the importance of a bargain made?"

"Of course I do! But you're threatening to close half the market! It's spring – the space between worlds is thinning – you can't seriously be suggesting such a thing during one of our best Mirror times?"

"It would certainly pain me to do so, but for my children? I would close the markets and more."

"I don't even believe such a thing is possible!"

Mistress Ogrechoker reached back into her bag and removed another thick ream of paper, placed it on the table and spread it out, fanning the sheets with the quiet satisfaction of a poker player who'd found their mark.

Title deeds.

Manifests.

Business contracts.

She had to own half the city. Eyes watering, Mistasinon sank back in his chair.

"Chokey and Hemmings... What do they want?" he asked.

"They want what I want, my Lord, as all good children do. And I want to see my darlings in suits. To see them respected, like I respect you."

"Respect? This is hardly respectful – you're holding the entire city to ransom!"

"If I didn't respect you, I wouldn't be here now, advising you. Even though you didn't prioritise seeing me," she added with a sniff. "Even though you put my darlings in mortal danger."

Mistasinon opened his mouth to argue, but there was no point. Even if he did have the means to counter her threat, he didn't have the wherewithal. Besides, something had to be done about the recruits. Mistress Ogrechoker was right: fees had been paid, bargains made. The Academy shutting its doors was a huge, public failing of the General Administration. Worse, it suggested that the General Administration *could* fail.

As each day passed and the Academy remained closed, more and more fae gathered in the square outside the GenAm buildings. They weren't protesting – no one would be that stupid. Even so, the Redaction Department was maintaining a minimal yet conspicuous presence, with three white suits keeping watch from the Redaction Block. They didn't mingle with the crowds. They

The Princess And The Orrery

just stood there, day and night, to remind those present that trouble would not be tolerated.

But still fae continued to arrive in the square. And Mistasinon knew what they were waiting for. They were waiting for an explanation. For reassurance.

Maybe Mistress Ogrechoker's plan wasn't so far-fetched: apprenticeships, pairing the recruits up with working Fiction Management Executives. The FMEs wouldn't like dragging around a trainee on their Plots, but it resolved the issue with the recruits and showed that the GenAm was still in charge, still making decisions. The absolute worst thing that could happen, Mistasinon was certain, was for the city to fall into instability. Rightly or wrongly, the GenAm needed to maintain control. To protect the Mirrors. For the good of the city. To avoid a civil war.

Standing, he offered Mistress Ogrechoker his hand. "Very well, Mistress. I'll see what can be arranged."

The locks on the bag were snapped shut.

"That's all I ask," Mistress Ogrechoker said, giving Mistasinon's hand such a firm shake he had to bite the inside of his lip.

Mistress Ogrechoker departed, leaving her paperwork on the desk. Mistasinon pulled a fresh handkerchief from his pocket and wiped the peppermint oil from his upper lip.

He picked up the paperwork, shoved it into his battered satchel, and called for the brown-suited gnome to bring him the names of the most experienced FMEs.

The list of people he had to speak to was about to double in size.

10

One such FME was Melly, though she wasn't currently worried about a Plot. Instead, she was wondering how many times she could perform the same task with the same results before she went insane.

'Once more' seemed to resolve the first part of her question. She was worried the second part had been answered a month ago, when she'd made the bargain that now had her endlessly trying to connect her illicit Mirror to the Imperial City of Cerne Bralksteld. She took a long drag on her cigarette and checked her list. It wasn't impressive, but it provided a nice illusion of control.

1. *Check Mirror for cracks or hairline fractures*
2. *Keep calm, think about the genie*
3. *Connect the Mirror*
4. *Get the genie, bring him back to Ænathlin*
5. *Hand him over to the GenAm*
6. ...

The end of her cigarette burned red. She couldn't bring herself to write item 6. It would come when it came, and that was that.

Or, at least, it would if she could get her Mirror working.

Cigarette ash fell on her black skirt. She stood, brushed herself down, and decided on one more try.

She went to her Mirror, which she'd brought down from her upstairs landing to lean against the kitchen wall. There wasn't space for it in the living room, thanks to cabinets housing her china collection and the pipes which crisscrossed the walls.

Would she be able to take her collection with her when she left? Probably. Perhaps she could even grow it. After all, she'd be moving from a two-up, two-down cottage nestled in the Sheltering Forest to a castle. Plenty of room for more china shepherdesses and little glass animals. And she was sure she could find another

The Princess And The Orrery

human to set up her iron pipes so she wouldn't need a fire when winter rolled around again. Hells, she wouldn't even need to trick them into it. No doubt it would all be arranged for her by the King.

If she could get her Mirror working.

Stubbing out her cigarette, she returned to the task. She held a picture of the genie in her mind, focusing on his blue-skinned handsomeness, his arrogance and charm. She'd only met him twice, but genies were designed to impress. Specifically, to impress upon you all the things you wanted and thought you needed, and then to twist those hopes and dreams up and distort them for their own amusement.

Wish on a star, by all means; but never wish on a lamp.

That was the problem with the younger fae, like Bea and Joan, who'd only ever lived under the GenAm's strict governance. They didn't know what it had been like before the Teller and the Plots. They assumed that the irregularity of the Mirrors and the resulting curtailment of their liberties was the same as the madness that went before. They didn't understand the cruelty of the fae when all they had to worry about was who could tell the most memorable story.

History reminds, but it rarely insists.

The image of the genie clear in her mind, Melly placed her hands on the Mirror to make the connection to him. It should have been easy enough – she even knew which city he was in, thanks to Ana. But instead of blackness bubbling over the Mirror's surface, showing that the connection to the human's world was being made, all she saw was her own, frowning, face.

Something was blocking her. She brought to mind the castle at Llanotterly, pressing her hands again to the glass. This time the surface rippled black, inky milk-like bubbles roiling around the edges before converging in the centre and then, a minute or so later, pulling away to reveal Llanotterly Castle's battlements. The drawbridge was down, as King John preferred it, though two guards were stationed either side of the entrance, as Ana, his Royal Adviser, insisted. There was no sound – the Mirrors could only show and transport – but that didn't matter. All she wanted to do was confirm that the thing was working. Melly waved the scene away.

F. D. Lee

It had to be the genie. He must be doing something with his magic to stop the Mirror connecting to Cerne Bralksteld. Melly picked up her mug of tea, now cold, and took a sip.

There was a knock at the door. Melly jumped, nearly spilling her tea. She threw a sheet over the Mirror and then, brushing her red hair back off her face and readjusting her antlered crown, went to open it.

"Message, Mistress," said the tompte, hovering at face height, wings buzzing in a blur, his little arms weighed down with a letter.

"Oh. Yes, thank you." She took the letter. It was probably another message from Bea.

"You're a long way out," he said, rubbing some life back into his arms. "Ain't you worried about the orcs and gnarls?"

"Not really," Melly replied, fishing into her sleeves a tip him. All she had was tobacco leaves and a thimble. She passed the latter to the tompte, who looked at it nonplussed. "Sorry," she said, shutting the door on him.

Pretending she didn't hear what he called her through the door, Melly turned the letter over to open the seal. Only instead of the lump of cheap wax she expected, she found herself looking at two ornate letters pressed into the red seal: **G.A.**

The General Administration.

Melly considered calling the tompte back and asking him to return the letter to its sender, pretending he hadn't been able to find her. Stupid. The GenAm knew exactly where she lived.

That was another mistake the younger fae made – thinking that the GenAm didn't give them choices. Of course it did. There was always a choice, Melly knew. Knew it better than most. Every day, the GenAm offered its citizenry a choice: rebel or conform. They just didn't care to make it.

For all the whispered complaints after one too many drinks about the white suits and the rules governing the Plots, no one ever actually did anything to stop it all – well, except for Bea.

Bea was the kind of person who'd would walk into a lion's den and protest the smell of cat's pee. Even the Anti-Narrativists did little more than complain and occasionally try to upset the Plots, and they were an organisation set up to cause trouble for the GenAm. Yet, in under a year, Bea had managed to uncover not one

The Princess And The Orrery

but two GenAm conspiracies *and* drag Melly into both of them. It was a miracle the Beast hadn't caught up with them already.

Like many of the fae, Melly had heard the rumour that the Beast had been sent out to capture a threat even larger than the Anties. Unlike many of the fae, however, Melly was certain she knew what that thing was: the genie. What she didn't know was why the Beast had failed, nor why the GenAm had panicked and sent an ogre to try to bring the genie in.

She turned the letter over. Open it or ignore it? That was another choice, wasn't it?

She opened the letter and read it. And then she read it again.

It was from that Plotter Bea and Joan seemed so keen on, the skinny one with the tan skin, long face and thick eyebrows above sad, brown eyes, whose tribe Melly couldn't place. Mistasinon. She was to take on a student, it seemed, and he wanted to introduce her to them personally.

He wasn't Melly's Plotter. She just picked up the jobs she wanted when she needed more GenAm ration tokens to trade with. She'd spent hundreds of years cultivating the GenAm's trust into a general disinterest in her, and now, when she needed them to leave her alone, she was getting personal requests on official stationery.

She could wring Joan's neck! She knew it had been a mistake involving Mistasinon in that business with the Redacted characters. Now she was on his ledger. Was it Narrative Convention, or just bad luck?

Melly reached for her onyx cigarette case before realising she'd left it in the kitchen. Muttering the kinds of swearwords even Bea would be surprised she knew, she stalked back through to the kitchen, grabbed a cigarette and lit it, drawing deeply. She felt a wave of queasiness from the sudden inhalation, coughed and spluttered, and then took a more measured drag.

It couldn't be that bad, she told herself. Mistasinon was just as involved in that business at the Academy as she was. More so, from what she'd pieced together. Melly might have used her Mirror to smuggle the Redacted women out of the Academy to Ana in Llanotterly, but it had been Mistasinon and Bea who had done the actual rescuing.

F. D. Lee

'Stolen' them, she supposed the GenAm would say. Not that wording mattered; the Redaction Department wouldn't be interested in semantics. Nevertheless, there was nothing Mistasinon could do to her that he wouldn't also be doing to himself. Strange as he was, Melly doubted he wanted to be dead-headed any more than she did.

Still, it meant she was out of time. Mirror or no Mirror, she had to get the genie and bring him back to Ænathlin. Then she would turn him over to the GenAm so they could use his wish magic to maintain the Mirrors. She would save her friends and her city, even though she knew it meant condemning the last surviving genie to a slow and gruesome death. And then she would leave the Land and never return.

Because there was always a choice, even if you wished there wasn't.

Melly was not the only one faced with a difficult decision. Back in Ænathlin, Hemmings was trying to decide the best way to commit matricide. It was a genuinely interesting moral puzzle.

On the one hand, murder was clearly wrong. While it was true that death was the natural goal to which all living creatures must aspire – for, Hemmings mused, without death how could one ever truly make meaning of their life? – it was nevertheless a supreme arrogance to take that journey away from another.

Indeed, murder was the *crime absolute*. The ultimate theft, stealing not only from the person murdered but, by taking away the possibility of their future, also robbing the world. Life is a state of constant dying, an addiction picked up from birth, but that constancy was important. It was a process that had to be extended to its conclusion, naturally and without interference.

On the other hand, he was absolutely mortified, and it was all his mother's fault.

"Oh, darling, do stop sulking," Chokey sighed. She was sitting on one of the sofas in the upstairs lounge of their townhouse, fiddling with her braids. "It's so terribly boring to watch you pacing around the room."

"I'm not sulking," Hemmings said, turning on his heel to begin a new circuit. "I'm thinking."

"You are sulking. I can tell by the pout."

"I am engaged in unravelling a complex and unique moral quandary, exactly the type of thing that thoughtsmithing was designed for."

"Of course you'd say that, darling. I rather think you make the rules of thoughtsmithing up as you go along," she said, displaying a lot more insight than either she or Hemmings realised. "I suppose this is to do with Mama visiting the GenAm?"

"Well, honestly, aren't you in the least bit cross with her?"

Chokey awarded him with the kind of long, hard stare only a sister could bestow. Then she clambered to her booted feet and stood on the sofa, so she was roughly as tall as him. Chokey, like their mother, father and infant sister, was a dwarf. Hemmings, on the other hand, was an elf, adopted into the family as a baby. He was also, he realised, in for a telling off.

"Come here," Chokey said.

"I know that look. You're going to hit me."

Chokey folded her arm behind her back. "No, I'm not. See? Now come here, don't be a bore."

With extreme reluctance, Hemmings crossed the lounge to stand in front of his sister.

"Listen to me, darling," she said, hands still behind her back. "I know you're terribly clever and all that, and I'm just your silly sister, blah blah blah, but I really don't see why you're making such a fuss. You want to join the GenAm, isn't that right?"

"I suppose so."

"Of course you do. And if Mama hadn't dashed off and sorted it all out, do you think you'd be about to begin your apprenticeship?"

"No."

"Well, then. At least you've got something to go to. Even Mama can't make them re-open the Academy and assign me a role. And you're going to be a villain! That's one of the best ones."

Hemmings squirmed. She was right – at least he had a role to go to. Of course, that didn't make his mother's interference any better, but it did mitigate it somewhat. Was there a case for intentions, if well-meaning, over-riding actions? And if so, by what amount?

One could hardly say that Redaction was justified, even if it did mean troublesome elements were denied their ability to cause havoc. Redaction was like murder, the cessation of a person's potential, their future. Redaction, in fact, was worse than murder.

At least when someone died, they were laid to rest, their body burned and one of their bones filed and carved into the family symbol and placed in the Hall of Faces for mourners to visit. Redaction just emptied a person, leaving their body a walking, talking shell to be ordered about. There had to be limitations. Otherwise, anything could be made to sound as if it were-

"Ow!" he squealed, his train of thought shunted into a barrier of sudden pain. He rubbed his cheek, the one that wasn't covered in fine, tiny scars, and scowled at his sister. "You said you wouldn't hit me."

"And I didn't," she grinned, her arms now hanging incriminatingly at her sides. "That was a pinch." Grabbing him, she pulled them both down onto the sofa. "You were disappearing off down one of your thought holes and you know I hate it when you do that. Oh no, darling, please, don't try to explain it," she said as he opened his mouth to lecture. "You know I'm really very proud of you and all that, but let's not. Now then, do you know who your mentor will be?"

"No," Hemmings said miserably. "I'll find out tomorrow. I've got to go to the GenAm."

Chokey offered him a bright grin. "Cheer up, darling. At least you might see a friendly face there."

"A friendly face...?"

"Mistasinon, you goose. He's the one Mama spoke to, after all. Doesn't it just feel like an age since we saw everyone? Honestly, after all the excitement and adventures, everything else has been *frite-fully* boring, don't you think? I should almost wish we were back at the Academy. We made a wonderful team, didn't we? Saving all those women, uncovering a mystery! You know, I really do think it's been too long since we all got together. I saw a poster the other day for a Fairies United thingy, tomorrow, in the square by the Grand. Buttercup's bound to be there. I'm going to go.

The Princess And The Orrery

There, it's decided – I'll pop along after seeing you off. I say, speaking of fairies' rights, did you hear about Althaus? You'll never guess what Tiff told me..."

Hemmings let his sister prattle on, for once too depressed to say anything clever.

F. D. Lee

11

The seasons in Ænathlin might be slow, but certain points in the calendar were still marked: the long day, in the middle of summer, and its counterweight at the other end of the year, the long night.

And, most importantly, the balance between the extremes. The turning points that were neither *this* nor *that,* but were something between the two, when the air tingles and the world changes. Calan Mai, Beltane, La Fête du Muguet, Kevadpüha, Hexennacht, Samhain... the name hardly matters. It's the time that's important, the moment when the darkness begins to ebb and the light to flow, and vice-versa. When the worlds are in flux, open and malleable...

In Melly's absence, her Mirror wobbled, as if a tremor had run through the cottage floor.

Black, viscous bubbles formed at the edges of the glass, popping and spreading inwards until the whole surface was dark. A sharp crack appeared, spiderwebbing around the edge of the Mirror, framing it with ominous promise. Still the black surface bubbled, a high, screeching hiss filling the cottage.

The Mirror cleared, showing the fractured image of a blue figure: male, beautiful as the stars, lying on a bed in a dirty white tunic, staring at nothing. His mouth was a thin line of concentration, his chest rising and falling in uneven, stuttering motions, the tendons in his neck taut as the ropes that held the O&P steamers in dock.

The image flickered as the connection wavered, a tether loose of its mooring. The orrery appeared, now with six planets weaving and dancing around each other. Something like lightning crackled across the surface of the black sphere, gone in the blink of an eye.

The Mirror went dark.

The wail of tortured glass rose higher still.

The blackness rolled back, revealing something foul and dreadful. Something old, narrow-minded and cruel. Something *hungry*.

The Princess And The Orrery

It turned a yellow, bulbous eye towards the Mirror, searching for a way through. The edges of the Mirror bubbled blackness, almost as if it were fighting the connection.

From somewhere – from everywhere? – came a distant drumming, like an army approaching from over a hill, not yet in sight but very much inevitable.

Then, just as suddenly as it had appeared, the creature vanished.

Amelia looked up in horror as the orrery ground to a halt, all the spheres, including the newly installed sixth planet, slowing into stillness. The last one to cease its revolution was the largest, the black orb at the top of the device, its momentum pulling at the clockwork and gears until, finally, it too ground to a halt.

Not again, not again, not again...

Racing across the observatory, Amelia jumped between the stationary planets to the centre of the orrery, her heart pounding, her brain spinning a mile a minute, and began frantically unscrewing the cover of the engine – and then she paused.

Closed her eyes.

Took a deep breath.

Nothing bad was going to happen. She was in control. It was safe.

But she did need to think. To be calm and methodical. Rushing things, getting over excited, was how mistakes were made. She hummed a few bars of a tune, concentrating on the notes and the rhythm. Let it ease the sparking, jumping currents of panic taking hold of her brain. She didn't know where the tune had come from. It wasn't one of the ones her mother was always singing. It had just been in her head the last few months... maybe she had invented it?

Either way, it worked. She felt her breathing even and her mind slow to a speed she could think at.

She opened her eyes and undid the engine cover. Everything appeared to be in order, except for the fact the orrery was unmoving. She uncoupled the spinning barrel, releasing the engine from the orrery. The moment it was free, the detent escapement mechanism – a disc with long sharp teeth which turned the initial cogs – began spinning again.

The engine was working, which was a relief. Amelia turned her gaze upwards, to the inner workings of the giant structure.

It was like looking up at the canopy of a dense jungle, trees merging and blending as their branches reached out to each other, vines roping across the gaps in a tangle. Except that instead of wood and leaves and the sickening smell of the forest, what she saw were tall metal columns connected with delicate, clever networks of cogs, rotors, more escapement mechanisms – detent, cross-beat, even some verge escapements, the earliest devices used in clockwork machinery, which she'd adapted to control the vertical movements of the planets.

But there was no reassuring click-clack-clack of her mechanisms working, only the gentle *kerchunk* of the steam engine as it chugged away, endlessly recycling its own water.

She was going to have to go through each mechanism individually to find the one that was broken. She might even have to dismantle the whole thing.

Amelia's hand came to her mouth, muting her howl of frustration before it had a chance to escape. She pushed it deep down inside her where the bad things went and climbed the ladder inside the orrery to begin checking each element for the fault. As long as she could explain what had happened, they'd have to let her stay to fix it.

In fact, it only took her thirty minutes to find the culprit: the little golden cog she'd made from Joseph's snake necklace. Her excitement at having found the problem didn't last long, however.

Sitting on one of the narrow platforms that encircled the central column, she studied the cog. It was submerged in a sticky, thick, clear substance. She reached into the pasty mess to fish the cog out but pulled her hand back sharply before making contact – the cog was freezing; so cold it pinched her fingers just holding them near it.

She rolled up her trouser legs and pulled off her socks, slipping them over her hands, and tried again to disconnect it. The strange gunk made it hard to pull free, but she was able to get it. She held it in her palm and began wiping off the goo. It hurt despite her

The Princess And The Orrery

makeshift gloves, the cold making her nimble fingers stiff. Still, after a few stops to warm her hands in her armpits, she managed to remove the worst of it.

Carefully, she reattached the freezing cog, climbed back down to the engine, reconnected it, and waited as the chain-reaction of the clockwork fired up. Above her, the mechanisms began to move again, slowly, a cascade of whirring and clacking. She watched as the chain climbed higher, reaching the section where she had inserted the snake-necklace cog, near the black sphere.

The reaction reached the intersection with the cog. On the outside of the orrery, the planets had begun spinning again. The black planet shuddered and moved, and then turned, and then spun-

Then the whole thing ground to a halt again.

Amelia climbed back up to the faulty cog. It was once again covered in the thick, translucent substance, gumming up the workings.

A groan from below. Amelia's head snapped down. The engine was struggling to keep the orrery moving against its will. Half climbing, half falling, she raced back to the bottom of the device and uncoupled the engine. The groaning ceased, just the like orrery.

Right then, something else. She went to the large storage unit where she kept her parts, selected a new cog of the same measurements, and replaced the freezing cog. Turned the engine on. Once again, the orrery began to move, each planet slowly shifting, until the chain reaction reached the new cog.

There was a *zing,* and the new cog came flying out of the device, smashing against the observatory wall. The same thing happened with the next ten cogs Amelia tried. It was like the orrery was rejecting them, as if now it had experienced the snake-necklace cog, no other would do. Which was ridiculous. The orrery wasn't alive, it couldn't *decide* which pieces it wanted.

And yet...

Amelia couldn't fix it. She didn't know what was wrong. The orrery seemed to only want the new cog, but it was creating this mysterious slime, gumming up the machine.

F. D. Lee

The howl she'd held back earlier broke free from its cage, rampaging up her throat, crashing against her teeth, and this time she didn't try to stop it escaping.

12

Years ago, when Melly had first accepted the Teller's offer and joined the General Administration, she had comforted herself with the fact that she would at least be working alone.

It had been her only sticking point, once she'd read the writing on the wall. Or, more accurately, the GenAm slogans on the posters, banners and signs that had sprung up overnight across the whole of Æenathlin. Either way, she had held her ground and the Teller, perhaps recognising that it would make the transition easier to have her on side, had agreed.

She would publicly support his usurpation, and then she would be allowed to fade into the background, lost in the system he was creating. As long as she kept quiet and stayed out of the GenAm's way, she would never again be responsible for anyone else, beholden to anyone else, reliant on anyone else.

Nor, and this was the point she kept returning to, would she ever have to take part in any kind of committee. In her experience, if you wanted something done, the very worst thing you could do was involve other people.

Ana, the King's Royal Adviser, saw things differently. The term 'collective decision-making' was new to Melly, but she had quickly decided it was synonymous with 'speaking in endless circles'.

She lit another cigarette while the humans continued their argument.

"Damn and blast it all," John said, rolling his wheeled-chair away from the map taking up almost the whole table in his study. "Remind me again why we can't use the pirates?"

Ana pinched the bridge of her nose. "Because if something goes wrong, we'll expose the network we've spent months building up. We wouldn't be able to rescue any more slaves."

"So the whole thing's a rum job? We can't get Melly into the Imperial Palace." John poured himself a snifter of fortified wine. Melly bit back the instinct to tell him not to drink too much.

Human bodies were so frail, and John had already suffered a near-fatal injury. But he was also a King, and Melly understood that Kings could not be – what was the word he used? – ah, yes: mollycoddled.

"And we're set on the fact that he's in the Palace?" John asked.

"Yes, yes. Everything we've heard supports that," Ana replied. "You've read the reports from the rescued slaves, the defectors. It has to be him."

"Damn and blast," John said again, draining his glass. "Well, then. Plan B. We send an official retinue. Pomp and ceremony. Whizz her in under the cover of intranational relations, what?"

"No," Ana replied, glaring at the map. "Firstly, we can't be associated with this. We're already on frosty terms with pretty much every other power in Ehinenden after Seven kidnapped that bloody Countess."

"So why not try to track her down? Countess thingamajig? Ghislain?"

"Because she hasn't been seen since the Ball, either. And the Count's keeping his lips firmly sealed – probably embarrassed about being cuckolded. Look, if we're caught, none of the other local rulers will help us, and we can't stand up to the Baron on our own. Which leads me to the second reason why that's a stupid idea. We don't have the money for even a small official visit."

Ana finally lifted her gaze from the map. Her mossy green eyes landed on the empty glass next to John, and she shot him a sharp look.

Melly was rather impressed: Ana's glare was almost as good as an elf's. Quite the feat for any human. Elven power was tied up in their beauty. They mesmerised. Not to the extent that the genies had managed it, she knew, but well enough to make most humans feel small and inconsequential. Ana, however, managed the same effect without a fraction of the beauty. It had to be something to do with her nose. Even Melly preferred not to be caught on the sharp end of a pointed stare from Ana.

Ana marched over to where John was sitting in his wheeled chair, snatched up a glass and poured herself a drink. The King leaned over and rubbed her arm. "Buck up, there's a good gel. We'll work something out."

The Princess And The Orrery

"It's a bloody mess," Ana snapped. She turned to Melly. "You're certain you can't use your magic mirror?"

"Certain," Melly said. She took a long pull on her cigarette. "There might be another problem, too."

"Course there is," Ana sighed. "Go on, then. Let's hear it."

"I've been summoned to the GenAm tomorrow. I've got to take on an apprentice. They'll be with me for the next few months, learning how to be a villain."

The two humans fell silent. Melly had expected more of a reaction, especially from Ana. Instead, the news seemed to knock all the air out of them. Somehow, that was worse.

"We might have to delay our plan. Just for a little while. There are too many..." Melly struggled for a moment. "...too many sub-plots. Too many threads."

John's face fell. "I s'pose you're right. Silly really, but I was rather looking forward to seeing Seven again. Wanted to look the fella in the eye, ask him what the bloody hell he was playing at. I did think of him as a chum, once."

Ana caught Melly's eye and gave her a warning look. To John, she said, "I know."

Their spirits abandoned them not long after. John and Ana carried on suggesting and dismissing ways to get into the Imperial Palace once Melly had finished her mentorship duties, but everything came back to the lack of funding and support for Llanotterly. The whole plan had been reliant on Melly using her Mirror to get in and out, quick and tidy. Eventually, John was called to his other duties and, bidding Melly a fond farewell, he wheeled off, head low.

"He thinks we're bringing the genie here," Melly said. "You haven't told him."

"He wouldn't understand."

"He wouldn't agree, you mean."

Ana put her hands on her narrow hips. "And you've told all your friends, have you? Bea? She and Seven got on very well, from what I remember."

"It wasn't a criticism," Melly said. She walked over to the map. It was strange to see the human world laid out flat. Geography wasn't really a subject the fae spent any time on. Human lives were conducted in cottages, castles, towers, caves; places where the Plots were set. And in the Land, the only places that mattered were Ænathlin and the Sheltering Forest that surrounded it. The rest of their world was sand and dust, the result of the Rhyme War, many hundreds of years ago. Of Yarnis and her mad attempt to seize control of the Mirrors.

"It sounded like a criticism," Ana said, coming to stand next to her. "This was your idea, remember. Your bargain. You get the genie, and we get you." She pressed a thin finger to the map, above the drawing of Cerne Bralksteld. "And then we stop the slave trade."

"I remember."

Ana sighed. "Perhaps something will present itself in the meantime." A pause. "Melly?"

"Yes?"

"Look. I just wanted to say. For all this. Keeping your word." Ana reached out and squeezed her arm. "You know. Thanks."

"Yes. I know," Melly said. She didn't add that when she brought the genie to the GenAm, she'd need Ana as much as Ana would need her. She didn't need to. Ana knew well enough what they were doing. If everything went to plan, all they would have was each other.

Ana offered her a thin smile. "Right then. I suppose we should keep working? You can stay for a couple more hours?"

For a moment, Melly considered refusing. She was an elf and a witch, not some lackey to be bossed around by a character. But Ana wasn't just some character, not anymore. And it had been a question, not an order.

Everything made her tense at the moment. Every word seemed like a threat. The sooner this was done, the better.

"Actually, I can stay here tonight. We can work through 'til morning. Then I'll head back to the Grand-"

"What about the checkpoints at the Grand Reflection Station? They don't know you're here, do they?" Ana asked, frowning. "We don't need that kind of trouble, not on top of everything else. And I don't want anything happening to you."

Melly laid her hand on Ana's shoulder, brushing her thumb across her collar bone. Ana was right to see the fae as a threat. If she were completely honest, Melly thought Ana should be more concerned with her kind than she was with the Baron. But, hopefully, their plan would come off and Ana and John would never have to fear the new moon, or the sweet, luring song of the adhene, or the mischief of the imps...

Or the laughter of the elves, on the hunt.

"It's risky, but I've still got my permit from healing John. Besides, I won't have time to get into Ænathlin from my cottage if I stay here. You *do* want me to stay…?"

Ana rolled her eyes as if the answer were obvious. Then she poured them both a drink, ordered some vegetable stew, and they set to work.

13

"Amelia, open the door. Amelia. Come on."

Naima leaned against the door, her patience burning low. How the hell had the girl managed to lock the door from the inside, anyway? Naima would swear she hadn't noticed anything unusual the last time she was in the observatory.

But then, the orrery had taken up so much of her attention. Naima had no choice but to admit that Amelia could have installed a double-bar lock across the door and she probably wouldn't have noticed.

"Do you know what happened?" she said, turning to the Cultivator who'd to alert her to the situation when the porters had tried and failed to bring Amelia her lunch.

"No, Sister. We were informed the door was locked, and I was sent straight to you."

"Blast it. Alright. How long has she been in there?"

The woman consulted her notebook. "Ninety minutes, maybe two hours."

"Not long, then." She turned back to the door. "Amelia, I am instructing you to open this door."

Amelia's voice came through the wood. "I want to speak to Joseph."

Naima's stomach filled with needles. She paused, let the feeling subside, and then asked, "Why? I'm sure I can help you."

"No. It has to be Joseph."

"We really don't want to make him go to all the bother of coming here, do we?"

Silence.

"Let me know what's wrong. I'll get our best Sisters to help."

Silence.

Naima tugged at her curls, a habit she'd picked up as a child when she was anxious. She didn't want Joseph here. He didn't belong here. Not because he was a man – though, God knew, that would be reason enough for many of the senior Cultivators. Ever since their discussion on the balcony some six months ago, she'd done her best to avoid the man. She'd even stopped delivering Amelia's reports herself, instead trusting them to her most reliable porter, in three envelopes, twice sealed with thick wax.

Joseph hadn't commented on the new method of communication. She'd heard a rumour he'd been confined to his bed again over the winter. She had no idea if it was true. She hadn't wanted to taste his name on her tongue to ask.

Naima had given up trying to decide which scared her most: the thing in the tower or Joseph. The memory of her first and only meeting with the genie still tormented her, often reappearing when she least expected it. The feeling of being completely opened-up, all her hidden wants and secret desires laid bare in front of her, the absolute and sudden certainty that she was selfish, and that the things she wanted, laudable as they were, she wanted only for her own ego, her own advancement. That she was not, and perhaps never had been, the person she'd thought she was.

And then, there was the way Joseph had just eyed her curiously, wanting to know what the genie had uncovered. His quiet, polite interest and the stillness in his eyes as he regarded her pain, her embarrassment. There were two monsters in Cerne Bralksteld, Naima now knew. Three, if she counted herself and the results her choices had brought…

She rested her head against the locked door. Had anyone, ever, been as stupid as her?

The other Cultivator coughed. "Sister... perhaps if you try another method?"

"What do you suggest?"

"Well, my sister has children, and I've often observed that sweeties work well as an incentive. I've got some boiled mints," she said, reaching into her pocket and pulling out a little paper bag.

"Do you think that will work?"

"It can't do any harm, can it? Little girls like sweets."

Naima wasn't at all convinced, but she was willing to try anything. "Amelia," she said. "If you open this door, I've got a treat for you. Some lovely sweeties – boiled mints! Doesn't that sound good?"

There was a noise from the other side of the door, like someone moving around. The younger Cultivator grinned at her in triumph.

The door thudded as if something had been thrown at it.

"I'm not a child!" Amelia shouted through the wood. "I want to speak to Joseph! He's the only one who can fix it!"

Rubbing her head, Naima turned to the other woman. "What's your name, Sister?"

"Kamala," she replied. She looked like she would have happily given a false name if she'd had the wherewithal to think of one.

"Well, Kamala, I would like to put forward the suggestion that your sister has absolutely no idea what she's talking about, and neither do you."

"Yes, Sister."

"Clearly boiled mints are sweeties aimed at a younger audience."

"Yes, Sister."

"I don't suppose you have any more... mature... sweets about your person? Some..." Naima struggled a bit, but she rallied. "Some liquorice, perhaps? Or that pink, sugary stuff that comes out of Ota'ari?"

"Ataji Delight?"

"Yes, that's the stuff. I'm sure I heard that a child would give up their whole family for a piece."

"I think that's only boys, Sister."

"Really?"

"Yes, Sister. I'm not sure why."

"Well, it's got to be worth a try. Do you have any?"

"Boys or Ataji Delight?"

"Ataji Delight, of course!"

"No, Sister. Just boiled mints, Sister."

Naima glared at Kamala. And then she noticed the fine scars on the woman's hands, clutching the bag of sweets. "You were at that Ball last year? With the attack?"

"Yes, Sister."

"Why are you – I thought you were studying anthropology?"

Kamala shook her head. "Well, I was. But after the, ah, feedback on my report, I thought perhaps I would be a better astronomer than an anthropologist, so I moved over here." She looked at the door. "I think perhaps I underestimated the complexities of the field, though."

Naima swallowed the bitter taste of guilt on her tongue. "Yes. Well. This situation is rather unique. Don't let it put you off your studies."

"Thank you, Sister, I'll bear that in mind. What do you think we should do? She can't stay in there forever. Maybe if we just leave her, she'll come out on her own."

Just then, a letter appeared under the door, sealed with Amelia's family crest. It came as no surprise to see Joseph's name written on the envelope.

"I have to speak to Joseph," Amelia said through the door, her voice low, determined. "Give him this letter and he'll understand why."

Naima stared at the letter, feeling all at once extremely tired and alone. Then she picked it up and left Kamala with instructions to watch the door until she returned.

The Imperial City of Cerne Bralksteld was a place of contrasts. The city itself, the buildings and the streets, the theatres and the markets, the banks and the shipping yards, the pubs and the prison, all rubbed against each other, snug and safe, protected by the cliffs on either side and the ocean in front.

For a time, it had been enough. The land was verdant, the soil enriched with minerals. The city grew. Docks and jetties were built, and with access to the sea and thus the other Kingdoms of Thaiana, trade flourished.

It wasn't long, however, before the fledgling city's rulers realised the downside of their location. Protected they may have been, but they were limited, too. The valley was finite. Space, first and foremost, became the issue.

So, they began to build into the rock. The Imperial Palace, half external and half internal, was the first structure, though others quickly followed. With each passing generation, the expertise to build better, stronger, deeper, increased. The secrets of steam power travelled across the Shared Sea from Ota'ari and landed in Cerne Bralksteld. And all those clever Bralksteldian minds knew how to best utilise what was seen, at the time, as nothing more than a way to make toys or simple devices.

Steam power may have been discovered in that distant land, but it was industrialised in Cerne Bralksteld.

The manufactories came. Buried deep inside the earth, accessed via a long and hellish tunnel from the sea, they were the life and death of many hundreds of slaves. And yet, in the city, you would never know the pain and degradation suffered by the enslaved. Cerne Bralksteld proper was a beacon of modern civility. The riches gained from the manufactories ensured the streets were clean and schools and hospitals were plentiful.

Soon, the great and the good were travelling from all over Thaiana to the city. Probably they knew something of the plight of the slaves, in a distant and disapproving kind of way. But the promise of the life Cerne Bralksteld offered overcame any lasting moral objections, especially to those coming from Voriias or Penquio. Even the poorest areas of Cerne Bralksteld enjoyed a level of development far outstripping many of the wealthiest of Ehinenden's other towns, fiefdoms and – to the civilised minds of the Bralksteldians – *minor* kingdoms.

The truth was, the people of Cerne Bralksteld were happy, and this happiness and the resulting productivity were made possible because of the manufactories and the rise of international trade, and the large bay that allowed the O&P to take full advantage of this.

Joseph knew all this, and the careful precision required to maintain it.

It worked, but only in so much as it was unthreatened. If anyone – or anything – ever tried to take the city, Joseph suspected they would find themselves with a ready rebel army, sitting inside the very stone walls which for so many years had protected them. The slaves posed a threat, even weak and half-starved, their skin burned from the steam engines and the boiling heat that could only escape via narrow chimneys worming their way through the earth.

He tried again to explain this to his brother, the Baron.

The Princess And The Orrery

"Won't happen," the Baron said around a mouthful of chicken. "You're paranoid."

"We need to think about alternatives. Enforced slavery is not sustainable-"

Another mouthful of chicken. "It worked well enough for Father."

Joseph did not shudder or frown. His mouth remained relaxed, his expression blank. He ignored the line of grease dripping from the Baron's lips and running over his pink, spotty chin.

"That was a different time. When our father began this endeavour, the rest of the world was two steps behind us. No one looked much beyond the borders of their own lands, let alone to the advancements being made overseas. Now, alas, the world is more becoming aware."

The Baron set his knife and fork down. "So what? Let them be aware. We've nothing to hide. Hell, it's our investment in steam power that has pushed the entire Third Kingdom forward. Even those savages in Skraq are using tractus engines for their harvests. Heh. Imagine what they'd make of our textile plants."

'Our' work. Joseph wondered what might happen if he were to pick up that fork and jam it in his brother's eye. He tightened his grip on his cane.

"As you say, brother."

"You don't fool me, Joe." The Baron picked up his cutlery and resumed his meal. Bits of meat, pale and glistening, were shredded, moved to his mouth and masticated upon loudly. His eyes, however, stayed locked on Joseph's.

"Everyone else might pity you. Skinny boy, always so sickly. But I watched you grow up. Hiding behind Mother's skirts. Playing with your little toys. Nose always in a kiddie's book." Shred, lift, chew, speak. Shred, lift, chew, speak. "A man shouldn't be so wet, Father used to say."

"Can I at least have some more funding for the Cultivators? And the hospital needs more space."

"They won't find a cure," the Baron said. "There's only one cure, and it's too late for that."

"I'm not looking for a cure. We need something positive to offer the subjugated population-"

"The Savages."

"Yes... The Savages... to offer them something to admire. To want to be part of. Healthcare. Education. Arts. Technology. *Advancement*. People behave so much better when you make them happy."

The Baron laughed. He didn't cover his mouth. "Happy ever after, eh? Just like in your storybooks. Oh, very well, if it means getting me some peace." He waved his hand, and a clerk appeared at his side. "Send word to the Treasury to give my brother a further thousand coins."

The clerk scribbled a note, then slipped back to the edge of the dining hall. Joseph bowed, was dismissed, and took his leave. He made his way through the Palace corridors, the flickering light from the oil lamps in the walls turning his pallid skin an unnatural orange.

Savages! Was the Baron really so stupid? These were their own people – Ehinen people – they were advancing on. Not raider ships, leaving the docks in the night and returning weeks later with hulls full of foreigners no one would care about. The only reason they'd gotten away with it so far was because they'd only focused on smaller townships and villages.

Even so, there were rumblings from their neighbours. At the moment, such complaints were limited to weakly-worded diplomatic overtures, but dissent was growing. In Llanotterly, their milksop new King had only just managed to quell some kind of rabble uprising to cut off Cerne Bralksteld's supply of wood. Moreover, the tithes Cerne Bralksteld demanded from the smaller Kingdoms, including Llanotterly, were increasingly delayed and – worse – often short.

Cerne Bralksteld didn't need the money, of course. It was the principle. The old Baron had set up the tributary system as a promise of goodwill to their neighbours. Keep us happy, and we won't find cause to make you unhappy.

But his brother didn't care about that. He thought they were too big to fail. And with each success, his brother grew bolder and, clearly, more arrogant. For the briefest moment, Joseph considered using his secret weapon. How quickly he could be rid of all his problems, his brother first and foremost.

The Princess And The Orrery

But no. With great power came greater difficulties, and he knew the dangers of reckless wishes. Besides, Joseph had a plan. And after so many years of painstaking preparations, it would be beyond foolishness to give in to whim, now. So, instead of heading to the tower, he went to his office. The money his brother had given him would need to be carefully allocated to keep everyone happy but still needy.

When he arrived at his office, Naima was waiting for him, a letter in her hand.

14

"Something's happened," Naima said, handing over the letter.

Joseph broke the seal and read it. When he'd finished, he folded it up and slipped it into his pocket. So, the orrery had broken – or, it seemed, the genie's necklace was breaking it. He hadn't accounted for that.

His research had told him that genies and their conduit – lamps, necklaces, rings, whatever – needed to be together, but he had understood that it was for the genie's sake. He'd certainly seen the effects of his wishes on his 'guest', but he'd put that down to the fact that, currently, the genie was both without his necklace and burdened with the inability to fulfil the second wish. It hadn't occurred to him that the metal itself might also suffer from the separation.

He felt his left eye twitch, an early sign of a flare-up, and covered it by bringing his fingers up to both eyes and massaging the lids.

"My Lord?"

He pulled his hand away. "How long has she been locked in the observatory?"

"The whole day."

"Just one day, though?"

Naima stood in her soldier's stance. It wasn't half bad, Joseph acknowledged. Not as good as his models, but then they were made of wood, which gave them the edge when it came to rigidity.

"Yes, but we can't get her out, and you know how stubborn she can be," Naima said, apparently feeling the need to fill the silence. People always did, he'd found. Strange, really. Most of his life had been conducted in silence, just him and his books, his ideas. He had no idea why other people found it so uncomfortable.

Naima continued, "I wouldn't put it past her to starve herself to death just to win an argument. Perhaps we should send for her parents, my Lord? She's been here longer than originally agreed.

Perhaps it's time to send her home? You have your... the thing in the tower..."

Her anxiety over the genie was irritating – no, worse: insulting. Why couldn't she accept that he knew what he was doing – this was his destiny, for God's sake. Of course he had it under control.

"Does Amelia want to go home?" he asked mildly. His brother had taught him well how to hide his feelings.

Naima fell silent. Did she know she jutted her chin up when she was thinking? So many people looked down when they were uncertain. Perhaps she might model for him, if he offered her some more money for the Cultivators? She'd be a wonderful model.

Joseph had given up buying pre-built figures years ago. He had the time to make them, after all, and besides the figure-makers didn't seem to want to build many women, and the ones they did were frankly preposterous. He'd had to strengthen their bases just to stop them toppling over. And the armour! Good God, the armour. If they were real soldiers, they'd die of exposure before ever seeing a battlefield.

If Naima did model, he'd paint the first figure after her. Ebony skin and thick, curly hair. Gold armour. A sword, the point facing the sky – no lackadaisical demure pose. Then he'd make a whole army of women, pink, brown and black, auburn, brunette, blonde, to join the ranks of multi-hued male soldiers he already had. Something representative of the city he was building.

No more old, fat men with old, fat thoughts.

"Well?" he asked.

Naima's expression flickered, some feeling apparently strong enough to break through her guard. "It isn't right to keep her here."

"So many things happen that aren't right. I thought we had agreed to put a stop to some of them?"

Silence.

And then Naima replied. "Yes, my Lord."

He tilted his head, trying to catch her entire expression and commit it to memory. She really was marvellous. He was very glad he'd chosen her.

"Come now," he said. "There's no need to look so worried. Everything will end happily, I promise. Now, let's visit our guest.

I'm sure it will have something to say on the matter – it usually does."

Naima stopped outside the door. "My Lord, perhaps I should wait outside?"

"Whatever for?"

Whatever for, indeed? "If I'm present, you might have to limit your conversation. I'm no politician, my Lord. There are things I probably shouldn't hear."

Joseph pushed the door open and then stepped back, arm extended. "Nonsense. After you."

Taking a deep breath, Naima steeled herself and stepped into the room where the creature was kept.

Nothing happened.

She turned and looked at Joseph, questioning him with her eyes. He responded by lifting his hand to his mouth, covering his smile.

"See? Nothing to worry about," he said cheerfully. "Let's see how it's doing, then."

The creature lay on the bed. How had such a thing addled her so? Look at it – wrapped in dirty clothes, hair slick with grease, a strange black substance dried and flaking at the corners of its mouth and around its nostrils. And the smell – God, it smelled awful. Stale sweat and bad digestion. Even the strange blue of its skin and hair did nothing now to intrigue her.

Or so she told herself, shoving her hands in her pockets to stop them reaching to touch it. Even unconscious and mired in filth, the genie still seemed to exert some power over her. It was like her brain and her body were working to different masters.

"Is it...?"

Joseph didn't bother to look at her. "Unconscious? No. Just making a fuss." He jabbed the genie with the head of his cane. "Wake up. I want to see what you can do."

Its eyes fluttered, a long breath escaping through its cracked lips. Its body jerked, almost like someone was pulling it, but then it collapsed back onto the bed, a low whine hissing through its teeth.

The Princess And The Orrery

Joseph clicked his fingers. "Pass me some water."

Naima went and filled a small wooden cup from the weak tap in the bathroom. She stepped toward the bed and stilled, her heart thumping.

It was colder, nearer the creature.

She found herself thinking about the geology department, and how excited she'd been when she'd first joined the Cultivators. It had been too long since she'd done any real work. If only she could return to her real passion-

A scream, shaking her from her thoughts. The creature curled up on the bed, clutching its head, face hidden behind its arms.

"It tried to get into your head?" Joseph said, taking the cup.

Naima nodded. When she spoke, thin clouds of steam formed in the air.

"Yes... but it wasn't like before. It was gentle, soft. Like waking up hungry, but knowing there's food."

Joseph tipped the water over the genie. The creature shuddered, coughing a thick black substance onto its pillow.

"Tell me, why did you try to upset Naima?"

The drenching seemed to help the creature, or at least it found its voice.

"You know the answer." Even rasping, it had a wonderful voice. Soothing and soft; breakfast on the patio, in the sun, warm sweet tea with bread and jam.

"I want to hear you say it," Joseph said.

The genie glanced at her with its strange, featureless eyes.

"To prove to her that you are my master," it said. "To show her I cannot tempt her or anyone else without your wanting it to be so."

"Splendid," Joseph said. "Now, tell her. Does this mean that you are safe?"

"Yes."

The genie shuddered and twisted. It was like seeing someone being burned, invisible pokers making him jump and flex as he tried to avoid them. Yet Joseph was just watching him, his face blank.

Naima tried to imagine what her face must look like, watching the creature writhe, pain evident in every movement. She hoped she looked as horrified as she felt.

"My Lord, what's happening?"

"It's alright," he said, still watching the genie. "Albelphizar, you know the nature of my second wish. I want an honest answer to my question."

Naima blinked. Joseph had made another wish?

"Yes ...and no," the genie wheezed. "If you died, I would be free. If I had my necklace, I could, perhaps, overcome it. But this is a distant and unlikely prospect, made more unlikely with the passage of time. I am beholden to the wish and without my necklace, the weight of it crushes me."

"Excellent. See? Isn't it better to just accept your position?"

The genie's body fell slack. "Yes."

"I want to ask you some questions," Joseph said. "I'm working on a device, and I had hoped your necklace might help. It appears not. Why is that?"

He had to be talking about the orrery, Naima realised. But what had the genie's snake necklace to do with it? And there was, of course, the question that had been driving her to distraction ever since that first night in the tower: if Joseph had a genie, why did he need Amelia or the orrery? Couldn't he just wish for whatever he wanted? The thought of what he might be saving his wishes for terrified her, and now he had made another one and she didn't know what it was.

"When you broke the necklace, you weakened it," the genie answered. "Just as you weaken me, keeping me from it."

"So, if you were reunited with the broken piece, it would work again?"

The genie paused. "Possibly. I know not what you intend for it, or for me."

Joseph ignored the comment, turning instead to Naima.

"You can see, I hope, that the genie is fully compliant? That he poses no danger?"

"I... it appears to be the case, my Lord."

Joseph nodded. "Then you will have no objections to my solution. Right then," he said, turning back to the creature. "On your feet. We need to get you presentable. I have a new task for you."

F. D. Lee

15

The orrery stood still as a mountain. Amelia hugged Barry, refusing to cry.

Naima and Joseph would send her home if she couldn't get it working. It was awful. She had replaced the snake-necklace cog, if only to feel like she'd done something. It still wasn't working, the clear, gummy paste thick in its teeth, bleeding onto the normal cogs surrounding it.

But she wasn't going to cry. She hadn't cried in years. Not since... Anyway, she wasn't going to start crying again. If she started, she didn't think she'd ever stop.

She buried her face in Barry's fur, just so she didn't have to look at the orrery. For the briefest moment, she wished her mother was with her. Her long, pale arms around her, black hair tickling Amelia's nose instead of Barry's brown wool.

A knock at the door.

"Amelia Sophia Bethany Ghislain," came Joseph's voice. "Open this door. I have a gift for you."

Relief washed over her – he'd read her letter! He must be here with more of that strange, icy-cold metal.

Amelia gave Barry a big squeeze and dashed across the observatory, ignoring the orrery as she passed it. She fiddled with the complex locking mechanism she'd devised and, finally, pulled open the door.

Joseph stood outside, Naima to one side of him, a stranger on the other. Amelia's happiness evaporated.

"What – I thought you'd bring – who's that?"

"Manners, Amelia," Joseph said. "This is my good friend, Albelphizar."

Amelia glared at this 'good friend'. He was leaning against the door frame like he was drunk. Despite his lop-sidedness, she could tell he was quite tall, with a wide jaw and a long, rounded nose. Not too long, she noted. Just long enough to offset his high cheekbones. He had thick, curly hair that looked a little damp, and

The Princess And The Orrery

he was wearing make-up, his odd eyes lined black. He was also blue, which was unusual but not particularly interesting – certainly not interesting enough to make up for Joseph bringing him to her instead of the piece of metal she'd been expecting. How could she get the orrery working without it? Hadn't Joseph understood her letter?

"Amelia, say hello," Joseph said, a note of displeasure in his voice.

"Hello. Are you from Ota'ari?" she grudgingly asked. "I can't remember if I'm supposed to bow or curtsy if you are."

The stranger seemed taken aback. He blinked slowly. Definitely drunk. "You think me...? Why do you think that?"

Amelia shifted her grip on Barry. "You're wearing the same type of clothes they wear over there. And you've got the nose."

"There is nothing else that strikes you... foreign... about my appearance?"

"Well, yes. Obviously. You're blue. You've got funny eyes, too. And probably a rotten liver." She turned to Joseph. "The orrery's broken. I can't make it work. I explained in my letter..."

"You did, quite adequately," Joseph said. "Let us in, and we can see if we can help."

Amelia stood aside, unsure what was going on. But at least they weren't sending her home. Yet.

Joseph entered, the blue man stumbling along behind him. Naima hung in the doorway a moment and then stepped through. She took herself to Amelia's desk and perched there, not saying hello or calling her 'little princess' or even telling her off for locking herself in her room.

The drunken stranger stared at the orrery.

"You are building an *es'hajit*?" he asked, his tone growing increasingly frantic. "With my necklace within it? You must not use such a thing, not now, not when I am present. It is-"

He came to a sudden halt, swaying woozily. He gripped his stomach, sweat breaking out across his forehead.

"You cannot, you must not. Destroy it, melt it, bury it. But do not have it here. It is-"

Joseph held his hand up. "Enough. This outburst is extremely disappointing – I expect you to behave properly, as we discussed."

F. D. Lee

Something passed between the blue man and Joseph. It seemed to upset the blue man, from the way he stiffened. His mouth twisted, his face scrunching up like old tissue. Then, his voice thin, he said, "Apologies, apologies, my Lord, I did not mean to offend – I will do as you wish. I did not mean to upset. Please."

Joseph lowered his hand and leaned on his cane. "Very well. Tell us what you know about this device. Rationally, I will add. There will be no more hysterics."

The blue man moved closer to the orrery, stumbling once but recovering his balance to reach out and press his fingers against one of the spheres.

"This is your planet, Thaiana," he said, correctly. "And here, this one is the home of someone I know – they call it the Land." He stepped back and looked up at the remaining planets. "That one I know not, but the one above it I heard tell of, long ago. You have it misaligned. Where is... oh, yes. There it is." He was looking at the second highest sphere, which Amelia had painted dark purple. "I always imagined it to be red."

"I didn't imagine anything," Amelia said, her annoyance at volcanic levels. "It's all based on observation. The *or-reh-ry* is an astronomy device, for mapping the stars and planets. They were invented about fifty years ago, by a man called-"

"Pfft. You merely rediscovered them," the blue man muttered. "*Es'hajit* were old before my kind ever walked upon this wretched land."

"Enough," Joseph snapped. "Help her find the answer to her problem. Use your gift."

The blue man wobbled, hands moving from his stomach out to his sides, steadying himself. It was like he was trying to resist something pushing against him. If Amelia hadn't known better, she would have gone up to him just to check there was nothing there. But she did know better, so she folded her arms and glared at him instead.

"Problems are just... like tangles of... wool," the blue man managed, his words interrupted by deep, quick breaths. "Truths hide within... Lies.... But a sharp mind can untangle the knots." He bared his teeth, a high noise escaping him, like the whine of an animal. "A mind like yours could so easily... find the answer...You look for improvements..."

As if from nowhere, Amelia found herself thinking about her home, growing up with her family. About her workroom, and the hours she'd spent in there, tinkering with things. Happy memories of being clever and busy. She could always solve any problem, no matter how difficult. Surely she could find the answer to the orrery...?

And then, suddenly, she was running through the forest... the sound of things chasing her... the realisation she'd made a terrible, terrible mistake – Amelia slammed the door on the memories, shutting them off.

The blue man sunk to his knees, hands wrapped tight around his body. "A clever little rabbit... Trees and darkness... Wolves... I... I cannot..."

"Very well," Joseph sighed. "You can help Amelia the traditional way."

"Help me?" Amelia snapped, the taste of her unwelcome memories still rancid in her mouth. "I don't need his help! He wants to melt it down!"

Joseph waved her words away. "Albelphizar can-"

"Seven. My name... Please..." the blue man mumbled from the floor.

Joseph shot him a look.

"Please... my Lord."

"Yes, fine. 'Seven' is a very quick study, an expert in things we are not. I promise, he can help you."

Amelia gaped at him. "You can't be serious? He doesn't even know what it's properly called!"

"I am perfectly serious," Joseph said.

"Look at him!" Amelia shouted at Joseph and Naima, not sure who she needed to convince. "He can barely stand up! What if something happens to him? What if he does something to my orrery?"

"He'll be right again, soon enough," Joseph stated. "And he certainly won't damage the orrery. There's nothing to worry about, is there, Seven?"

The blue man managed to pull himself up, so he was sitting on bent legs. He wiped his hand across his mouth. "No, my Lord."

"I – well – surely…" Amelia couldn't find the words. Clearly Joseph and Naima had both gone mad, bringing this drunken, no-doubt saboteur into her observatory when all she really needed was another piece of the secret metal.

Joseph placed his hand on her shoulder and squeezed. "You can think of him as your assistant if you like. I want it working, Amelia. I want it perfect. Can you manage that?"

Startled, Amelia could only nod. He'd never laid a hand on her before, and now her shoulder was a sharp site of pain.

"Good girl. And I want you to help her, Seven, to finish the orrery. Your focus on this and only this is what will please me. I give you permission to use this room as you see fit, but you are to go nowhere else. These instructions give you enough freedom, I believe?"

"Yes, my Lord."

"But not too much?"

"No, my Lord."

Joseph released Amelia's shoulder and stood back to take in the orrery. "Excellent. Get it working again, and then report to me – and remember, my happiness depends on this device. By either action or omission, you are to allow nothing to stop its completion, whatever name you choose to give it. Naima, come along."

Naima pushed herself off the desk, scuttling past the rude, oddly named blue man, her head turned away from him. She stopped when she reached Amelia.

"Listen to me. If you need anything, or if anything... feels amiss... you send for me. I'll keep up my visits."

Amelia wasn't sure exactly why Naima bothered with the last bit – why would she stop her visits, anyway? But there was something her voice that made her anxious. Amelia nodded.

The older Sister looked like she wanted to say something else, but Joseph was waiting by the door, watching them impatiently. Naima joined him, her eyes on Amelia as the heavy wooden door swung closed.

"Remember," Naima said at the last moment, "I'm here if you need me."

The Princess And The Orrery

"Seven's a stupid name," Amelia said, once the door had closed and she'd heard Joseph's and Naima's footsteps receding.

"It is the name I chose for myself," the blue man replied. He was still sitting on the floor but had – against all her expectations – managed to pull himself together. Well, then. At least she didn't have to worry about him dying on her. She simply had to put up with him getting in her way.

Amelia glared at him and then turned on her heel, returning to her notebooks. She was just sinking into the right space in her mind when a rattle pulled her back into the room.

He was climbing the orrery! Awkwardly, admittedly, his movements laboured – oh, God, that was even worse, wasn't it?

"Hey! What – get down from there! You're going to break it!"

"I will not."

"Yes you will – your leg just slipped! Get off it right now! It's mine!" No, wait. What would her mother have said, if she were here? "You'll fall and break your neck!"

"Unfortunately, no." Seven pulled himself up from the lower planet he was standing on to one of the middle planets, arms shaking. "Moreover, I hardly think you would spend any great deal of time wearing the black, should I perish."

"No, I wouldn't. Death doesn't bother me. But you'll break it."

He came to rest on the globe, his chest heaving. "That is a lie, my Lady."

"No, it's not. Only I know how it works."

"If we are to work together, you should at least aim for honesty. Perhaps, with practice, you might at some point hit your mark."

Seven shifted so he was lying across the globe, his head hidden in the shadows at the centre of the orrery. Amelia was going to explode! What was he doing?

The orrery groaned.

"Stop it! Stop it right now! You're breaking it!"

She ran forward and jumped up and down, trying to reach the hem of his loose trousers. She'd pull him down and, and, and *damn* the consequences! He was breaking it! He was-

A shudder, and the planets began to move again. Seven slid from the sphere as it dipped, landing in a pile at her feet. If he wasn't blue, she might have said he looked green.

"There... it is restored."

Amelia was dumbstruck. "But..."

"As I said, it was misaligned. Now, my Lady, I beg your forgiveness, but I feel I must rest."

He flopped down on the floor – the floor! – and lay on his back. He was breathing very heavily. Probably a smoker as well as a drunk. But she was stuck with him, it seemed. And the orrery was moving again...

Amelia thought back to her conversation with Joseph, about things that weren't understood seeming like magic. She didn't put much stock in his opinion, but Naima had also said that it was possible to misunderstand facts, if they spoke to you in a different language.

If she was going to be taken seriously, didn't she need to understand everything? And the more you knew, the less likely you were to make mistakes. That was why she'd wanted to come here in the first place. Why she admired Naima so much – the woman who, at thirty, had spotted one of the most serious mistakes the Cultivators had ever made and fixed it. Had saved lives.

Amelia came to stand next to Seven.

"So why are you blue? And your eyes are odd. How do you see anything?"

He brought his arm over his face, and grunted. "I have no idea how my eyes function, simply that they do. And my skin is blue for the same reason you are tan. Family. Blood. Inheritance."

"Not always. My Mum's pale, so was... I got my colouring from my Dad. Don't people find it odd, you being blue?"

"Most do not see it."

Amelia felt a tingle of pride. "Really? Why not?"

The man removed his arm from his face, fixing her with a peevish look. "Does it matter?"

"I don't know. That's why I'm asking."

"Very well. In the past, people did not see because I ensured that was the case. However, recently I have been – as you might note – unwell. Thus, I am revealed. I do not care for it. Is that enough?"

"Sorry – I've just never seen a blue person before. So, where are you from? Not Ota'ari?"

"Ota'ari is the land I was born in. Are these endless questions to be the norm?"

"Naima says that all good Cultivators seek answers to their questions."

"What a delight. I should like to spend some time alone with her. What questions she might ask me…"

"I think she'd want to know why you're blue and why your eyes are weird."

Seven lifted himself onto his elbows. "You are a very singular child."

"I'm not a child."

He tilted his head, like he was really looking at her. How did he manage that? His eyes were... nothing. Just blank, blue ovals, a slightly darker shade than his skin. And yet, she knew he was studying her in the same way she knew when she'd found the right answer to a problem.

"No," he said, finally blinking. "You are indeed no child. I am sorry."

"That's fine," she said, shrugging. "Everyone calls me one, even though I tell them not to. What did you do to the orrery – I know it wasn't misaligned. I checked and rechecked all my notes. It was the first thing I did."

"Does it matter if it functions? And now, if you please, I must rest." And with that, he rolled over, his back to her, and fell asleep, right there on the floor.

Amelia considered kicking him awake but decided against it. Instead, she clambered up the ladder inside the orrery until she reached the snake-necklace cog. Frowning, she held her hand just above it – still cold, but no longer painful to have near her skin. More than that, the strange oil seemed to have diluted. The cog was still sticky, but the teeth were no longer gumming up the rest of the mechanism.

She *knew* it hadn't been the alignment.

Amelia shimmied back down the orrery and jumped out. She stood for a while, staring at the sleeping figure on the floor. And then she went to her wardrobe, grabbed a spare blanket, and laid it over him.

16

Old, heavy minds moved with unstoppable, glacial energy. Deep thoughts, so old that even many thousands of years ago they would have been arcane, filtered through layers of instinct and formal, precise logic, arriving at a memory.

Warmth.

Food.

Ours.

For so long, the way had been narrowed, impossible for them to traverse. But now it was opening. The creatures turned their attention to the thing that had revealed the pathway, the gate. Not wide enough for them, yet. But slowly, surely, the gate was swinging open, and the pathway beyond becoming ever more tantalizingly visible.

Soon.

17

Naima, in fact, had many objections to Joseph's suggestion. Which was why she found herself following him back to his carriage.

He paused by the door. "Do you intend to accompany me all the way back to the Palace?"

This was it. Naima took a deep breath, ignoring the voice in the back of her mind that was recounting every horrible, vile fact she'd heard about the manufactories. "No, my Lord. But I hoped… perhaps we might talk some more. In private."

"What about? Do you need more money?"

"No, my Lord. Thank you."

She waited, hoping he would invite her into the carriage. After a few moments, however, it became clear he had no such intention.

"I don't think you should have that, that *thing* working with Amelia," she said, lowering her voice. "What if it does something to her?"

Joseph's expression didn't flicker. She wondered what he'd been like as a child, staring out at the world with those sharp, cold eyes in that still face. Everyone knew he'd spent most of his youth unwell, confined to his room while doctors, at his mother's insistence, tried to find a cure. But there were rumours, too, about the reason his father had refused to even be in the same room with him, even when he'd been near death.

At first, Naima had ignored them, putting it down to the barbaric superstition the wealthy clung to in Cerne Bralksteld of killing sickly children as babies. Perhaps, she thought now, she should have paid a bit more attention to the warnings. But like so much of her adopted home, it was something she'd never reconciled herself with, like the use of slaves. And, again like so many things that happened here, there was nothing she could do about it, not currently. She might be a figurehead for the Cultivators, but no one outside the walls of Castell y Sêr – and very few within – took her suggestions for change seriously. No one until Joseph…

The Princess And The Orrery

"Very well. Come in," Joseph said.

He stepped up into the carriage and took a seat on the bench, his breathing laboured. Naima followed him. Joseph waved her onto the opposite bench and then fiddled with a miniature vaporiser hanging from the ceiling. After a moment, thin threads of cloying smoke began to fill the small space.

"For my lungs," Joseph said. "Now then. I don't understand your concern. You saw that the genie can't do anything without my command."

"Yes, my Lord. But can you trust it? She's only a girl."

"I'm surprised to hear such dismissiveness from you, Naima," Joseph said mildly. "Amelia is, by your own admission, exceptionally bright. It was you who suggested she might become a Cultivator, after all."

"Yes," Naima said, trying not to let her voice dip into frustration or, worse, anger. "But I also said when she was of an age. She's too young to be here. She shouldn't even still be here – the deal set with her parents was for two years, while she worked on your device."

"And she remains working on the orrery. I thought we resolved this matter last winter. I have informed her mother. I fail to see the issue."

"The genie is the issue, my Lord!"

Naima's breath caught in her throat. She had shouted at him. She had shouted at the Baron's brother, her benefactor, the man who could close Castell y Sêr and throw her and all the other Sisters into the dark, steaming manufactories, never to be seen again. She wouldn't be the Sister responsible for opening a boys' college or refining the manufacturing processes to reduce – or remove – the need for slavery. She'd be the Sister that caused the death of the Cultivators.

Joseph leaned back. Naima gripped her knees, but held his gaze. If she was going to be punished, she would face it as a professional and take sole responsibility. As her father would have expected. He would be so disappointed if he could see what she'd become...

The vapouriser continued to release its heavy, pungent smoke, winding and circling around Joseph's head.

"Naima, I admire you. Respect you. I want the Cultivators to succeed. I thought you were of the same mind?"

Of all the things in the world that Naima wanted – all the dark, secret desires the genie had pulled out of her that night – being of the same mind as Joseph was not one of them.

But aloud, she said, "Yes, my Lord. Of course. But the genie could hurt her. Twist her mind. It's not... It's not right to subject her to it. She's a child."

"There you go again, dismissing her. And what is a child, anyway? Something we created. We have 'children' younger than her in the manufactories. They are some of our best workers, in fact."

"I don't think – the manufactories aren't relevant, my Lord. Amelia is the daughter of-"

"I know who her parents are. I wasn't suggesting she work there, merely making a point. You seem quite agitated, Naima. Are you well?"

"Yes, my Lord. Thank you. But I, I feel my concerns are valid. The genie is dangerous." A thought struck her. "You know it yourself, my Lord. Discovered that fact – you were sensible enough to lock it away."

His hand fluttered to his mouth. "Indeed. And me, a man, as well. Just think what all those young men will add to your endeavours when you are able to admit them. Think of all the people we could remove from the manufactories and train – the skills we can add to our city, to the whole of Ehinenden, when I have the power to help you make the changes you so rightly desire. When the Cultivators are properly funded. All I need to achieve this is the orrery."

She'd walked into that. "But you have the genie, my Lord. Why not... why not just wish for what you want?"

"Let me tell you something, my friend," Joseph said, threading his fingers together and leaning forward, disturbing the smoke. "Many, many years ago, when I first read about the genies, they fascinated me. I devoured everything I could find on them. The more knowledge I gathered, the more convinced I was that they had to be real. My family thought I was mad, even my mother, at the end. But there were too many coincidences, too many similarities, in all the stories from all the Five Kingdoms, across hundreds, thousands, of years. And at first, I had in mind I would wish for my health. But I realised the folly of that, soon enough. Such a selfish wish. And besides, had I not been as I am," he gestured vaguely over his person, "I would not have been granted the luxury of time and peace to do my research. I would have been forced into the same, ha, training for leadership my brother endured at the hands of our father.

"So, alone and ignored – quarantined, even, at times – I continued my search for the truth of the genies. I would say that, of all the people who have ever lived, I am the sole expert on them. I know what their power is, how it works, and how they use it. How it uses them. The genie, Naima, is mine. There is nothing he can do without my say-so, even when I am not there. When the orrery is built, everything will come together. You'll see. It will be my legacy. But in order to achieve it, I need the orrery. And for the orrery to work, it needs the genie. Do you see, then, the situation as it stands? I hope so, because I want you to be happy, Naima. It means a lot to me – a happy ever after, just like in the stories, for all my favourite people. I should hate to think that you didn't want to be happy."

Naima's knuckles pressed against her skin as her fingers bit into her knees.

"My Lord, I'm only worried for Amelia's safety."

"Then you have nothing to worry about," Joseph said. "She is quite safe. The genie can only help her, my wish has seen to that. Of course, if you would rather excuse yourself from this enterprise, I'm sure I can find somewhere else for your talents..."

"No, my Lord. No, thank you."

Joseph brushed his hands together as if he were cleaning crumbs from his fingers. "Excellent. Then I suggest you return to your work and leave Amelia to hers. And me to mine, of course. I'm sure you have a lot to be getting on with – it won't be long now, after all, until you can have your boys' college and your scholarships, all the things you told me you would do, if you only had the means, the support."

He picked up his cane and used it to push open the carriage door. Naima stood, her mind spinning. She was arguably one of the most intelligent Sisters in Castell y Sêr, and yet for all her intellect, this was a situation she had no means of grasping. Give her a pile of dirt and she could have sifted it and separated it and categorised it in moments, recognising all the different textures and minerals and the story they told of their history, and the history of their home. She could tell the difference in the shades of green between *torbernite* and *olivine* by sight, both of which were beautiful but only one of which caused blood lung.

But Joseph was not a rock, and his plans were not as simple to understand. Every move she made he countered, and then he moved again while she was still grasping for the right words. There had to be something she could do, something she could say. But nothing came to mind, and now he was ushering her out.

"Oh, Naima, I heard your conversation with Amelia," Joseph said as she climbed out of the carriage. "I think it might best if you leave her alone, just for a while. The genie clearly upsets you, and you wouldn't want to pass that anxiety onto the girl, would you? I would hate to hear that you – or she, of course – were under any, ah, unnecessary stress. And, of course, the genie is under instruction to see the orrery completed by *any means* necessary. It would be a shame if he were placed in a position where he had to take… corrective… action, don't you think?"

"I... yes, my Lord. I understand."

"Good. I'll contact you when it's time for you to involve yourself again."

With that, Joseph closed the door, leaving Naima standing in the street outside Castell y Sêr. The driver shook the reins, and the carriage drove off.

"Shit," Naima said.

There didn't seem to be anything more to say.

18

Someone was poking him. Seven forced his eyes open. In truth, it was not the first time he had been roused by something jabbing into his person. Historically, however, such rude awakenings had promised something more exciting than an impatient face and a heavy pile of books dumped on his stomach.

"Come on, wake up. You've been asleep for hours."

Seven heaved himself onto his elbows, scattering books. "I thought you did not want my aid?"

"You're not aiding me. I'm your boss."

"Ah, so? In which case, I think it only right that you should take better care of me – the floor is hardly a suitable bed."

"Well then, you shouldn't fall asleep on the floor, should you? You're too heavy to move. Eat something and then we can get started. There's some porridge, hot mushrooms, bread, and fruit," Amelia said. "They'll bring you anything you want if you don't like that."

"In that case, I should much prefer a large bottle of strong spirit."

Amelia nodded in a way that suggested she had expected as much. "You can't work if you're drunk."

"Peh. You underestimate me."

"I think my estimation of you is accurate." She wrinkled her nose. "This is an alcohol-free observatory."

Seven was in no mood for conversation. The floor had not been a kind bed, his head ached and his tongue had been replaced in the night by something malignant and furry. The fact that he had been so rudely awoken only added to his growing litany of misfortunes.

"My task is to aid you in building the orrery, is it not? As long as I fulfil my obligation, my sobriety makes no difference."

The girl folded her arms and gave him a stern look. "I won't work with a drunk."

Joseph's wish gripped him in warning, like the hands of a thug on the shoulders of a debtor trying to weasel their way out of paying: a promise that should he continue down this path, pain would be at the end of it.

"Fine. Sobriety, then," he relented. "But I want some paper and drawing materials – and a bed."

"Fine. Now eat. *I* want to get started."

Seven, begrudgingly, opted for the porridge and was surprised to find it was amazing. Warm and comforting, reminding him that he hadn't eaten well in months. He forced himself to take little mouthfuls, for all his stomach's growling insistence to be filled quickly. Too much food and he would be sick. It was bad enough to have humiliated himself the night before, collapsing on the floor.

Amelia started picking up the books he had scattered. He watched her as he ate.

She was slightly out of proportion, her arms and legs a little too long for her body. No doubt in a few years she would be strikingly tall, but what did that mean except more expensive trousers? She had a square jaw, fierce brown eyes and warm olive skin. The Ehinen people, generally, were darker towards the south-east of Marlais and in Sausendorf, and paler here, in the west, though the population had moved so much over the past hundred years, Seven was loathe to put much faith in skin tone to tell him anything about her.

Hells, in a city like Cerne Bralksteld she could be from any one of the Five Kingdoms, let alone Ehinenden. Still, he thought she was probably Ehinen. She spoke with the clipped, neutral tone that implied money, but there was the faintest trace of an accent – Marlaisan maybe? But again, that wasn't much to go on. She might have just as easily had a Marlaisan tutor.

More telling was the way she moved around the observatory with the easy confidence of someone in their own space. Strange, for one so young to be so at home here, when everyone else he had spotted was so much older. He had also noticed that she'd locked herself *inside* the observatory. What kind of person locks themselves in their room? She hadn't seemed particularly fearful of Joseph, more fool her.

So, the kind of person who fears being released, then...?

"How long have you been stationed here?"

The Princess And The Orrery

"Two and half years," she answered. "Me and Barry."

"Barry?"

"My bear." Amelia nodded towards the bed, where an old stuffed bear sat on the covers. "He was my brother's, actually."

She hadn't meant to say as much, Seven could tell by her expression and the tingle against his skin. Humans. Always thinking about what they wanted, even when they did not intend to. Nevertheless, it hinted at some deeper need buried inside her; something he'd glimpsed when he'd tried to sense her desires. If he could discover what she wanted, what she needed, he could use it. Without being able to access to his magic, though, he would have to employ other skills. Trust was the first thing to fashion.

"It is a fine creature," Seven said, taking another spoonful of porridge.

Amelia eyed him. "You're not going to say it's a child's toy?"

"People never give up their toys, my Lady – they simply move from one type to another. Those who claim otherwise are lying."

"Mmm. You said you were from Ota'ari? They discovered clockwork there," Amelia said, deceptively casual – a trick Seven knew well, and was better at. "Do you know anything about, I don't know, a special metal they might have there?"

She was asking after his necklace. Did she know what it was that she had hidden within the *es'hajit*? Doubtful. The secret truth of the devices had been buried – though clearly not well enough. Joseph had to know what it was he had commissioned, though Seven doubted he understood the full scope of the device.

Just enough to get me killed, Seven thought. Well, if the wish didn't get him first. He'd need to be careful, that much was a given. But at least his brief climb into the device had confirmed a piece of his necklace was present. Even if he hadn't seen it, his recovery from the trauma of the previous day was evidence enough that his necklace, or a part of it, was here.

This was not, entirely, a good thing. As much as the small piece of his necklace offered him some restoration, some protection, he would be having an equally strengthening effect on the connection the fragment was forming with the *es'hajit*, the 'orrery'.

Seven glanced at the black planet, careful not to let his head move so the girl wouldn't know; one of the many benefits of having eyes that humans found so hard to read. If Joseph truly did know what an *es'hajit* was – if he, unlike this girl, had not mistaken it – Seven needed to get away from here as quickly as possible. But the wish bound him to this place. What good was an escape if he died as a result of it?

He needed to think. To work out the boundaries of Joseph's wish and to find the pathway through it. If only he could get his hands on his necklace, whatever remained of it. The piece inside the *es'hajit* was too small to be of any real use. But if he had his necklace? Then he might, perhaps, survive Joseph's wish long enough to get as far away from the *es'hajit* as possible.

Who knew? Maybe he'd survive long enough to deal with the man himself. And, *oh*, he wanted to deal with Joseph. And The Woman who had brought him here.

He couldn't bring himself to say her name, even in his head. The very thought of her made his stomach knot, his throat burn, his eyes sting. This had to be what hate felt like. And was he not entitled to his hatred? The Woman had betrayed him, thoroughly and completely. She had taken his love – the love of a genie, a creature so far above anything she had any right to – and defiled it, using it to bring him to Joseph.

"Well?" Amelia said, glaring at him impatiently. "Do you know anything about a, ah, special metal or not?"

"Apologies. My mind wandered. I am afraid my talents do not stretch to smithing," Seven said, deliberately vague.

"Fat lot of good you'll be, then."

"Why do you want to know?"

She pursed her lips, clearly trying to decide how much to tell him. Seven, had he been able to use his magic, would have had no trouble eliciting her need to show off; her very being was woven with the desire to be taken seriously, to be recognised. All he would have needed to do was pull a little at the thread, and she would have unravelled. But, alas, he could only hope she would do the work herself.

She didn't. "It doesn't matter. Do you know anything about engineering, at least?"

"It is the mastery of clockwork and steam. Of mathematics."

"And astronomy?"

"Mastery of the stars."

"Mmm. You might be some help, then. Since you're so good at alignments, you can make a start on the sums for the seventh planet. You'll need to go over the notes I made for the first ones, but I can get you any other books you need from the library. While you're doing that I'll look into the machinery and-"

"I cannot help you in this," Seven said.

"But you just said-"

"My Lady, I said only that I know what these things are. I have not the mastery of them. I have never needed the skills they require."

"But how did you fix – how did you know about the misaligned planet?"

Seven put down his bowl.

"I have travelled, my Lady, and in my travels have met many strange and brilliant people, seen many strange and brilliant things. I may not understand completely the nature of all my observations, but I recall them clear enough. I have knowledge in these areas, I assure you, I simply lack the means of dissecting it. However, this is surely where your own strengths lie? I cannot resolve your problems with this device but, perhaps, I can provide you with information which you might put to use?"

Amelia considered his words. He waited, trying to ignore the tight knot of apprehension in his chest. If only he had the strength to use his magic against her. If only she were older and more inclined to be dazzled by him. If only he had never come out of hiding, never tried to find The Woman, whom he had loved and who he thought had loved him...

If only, if only, if only. What a weak, whelpish thing he had become. And yet he waited, hardly breathing, to see if Amelia would accept him.

"Naima says that knowledge is the first step to understanding," Amelia said at last. "She says a lot of people think knowing things is the end result, but it isn't. Anyone can read a book, she says, but very few people can actually think about it, understand it, build on it. She calls it 'quotation masking innovation'. But if you can quote to me, I suppose I can innovate from you. Deal?"

Seven smiled at her, for the first time in months feeling like his old self again.

"Deal," he said.

19

Melly was not given to vanity, unlike many of her tribe. In the past? Well, perhaps. But not for a long time. Still, there were limits. She took the brush to her hair again, trying to deal with the mess Ana's bed had made of it.

The brush was too soft. Elven hair was thick as wool. Not like the char-

Melly caught herself. Not like the *humans'* hair, which was ridiculously fine. Fine and easily broken, just like them. She pulled the brush again through her long red mane, following it with her fingers, letting it tug at her scalp.

"Oh, for God's sake, let me," Ana said from the bed.

"I didn't realise you were awake."

"Awake enough to realise you're going to scalp yourself if you carry on like that."

Ana padded over to stand behind Melly at her dressing table, her tall mirror covered at Melly's insistence. She picked up the brush and began working. Under her ministrations, Melly's hair slowly returned to its usual lustre.

"So, do you regret last night?" Ana asked, breaking the silence. There was no accusation in her voice. It was just a question.

Melly turned and met her gaze "No, not at all."

"That's good."

"Do you?"

A smile ghosted across Ana's face. "I never do anything I don't want to. You remember the Ball – the one last year, that started all this? You made me laugh. When Seven was being... being his usual self, I suppose. Anyway, you made me laugh at him. I've liked you ever since, even when you were causing me no end of bloody trouble."

"Elven magic."

Ana tugged Melly's hair. "Sure." A pause. "But I thought your lot weren't allowed to have sex with the 'characters'?"

"Relationships. And no, we're not. It confuses the Plots. In the past, it caused problems."

"For you?"

"Oh, yes. Absolutely. Some of the things we did – you'd think I was describing a dream. Or a nightmare, from your point of view. My husband and I had a tremendous row once over a human woman. It caused all manner of problems."

Ana stopped brushing. "Your husband?"

Melly turned to face Ana, who was ever so slightly taller than her. Most humans were. Still, it was strange that she'd never noticed before.

"Yes. Do you… is that a problem?"

Ana snorted. "That you've been with a man? Hardly. But if you're married? That's different."

"He's dead. Or Redacted. Gone, anyway. For a long time."

She watched Ana's face as she digested this new piece of information. It was strange to talk about her husband, even in such vague terms. She hadn't allowed herself to think about him for years, and then, in the space of a few weeks, she'd confessed to Joan and now to Ana. Getting soft. Getting attached.

But then, if she was going to give up her life, what better reason was there than attachment to those around her? Love. Yes. She loved Joan and Bea. That had crept up on her, hadn't it? Chipped away at her over the last six years. And she loved Ana and John, too. Four people. Not exactly the extensive court she'd once had responsibility for, but they were her people, all the same.

"Do you miss him?" Ana asked.

"Sometimes. It doesn't hurt like it used to. You'd have liked him."

"Oh?"

"He was almost as bloody-minded as you. Honourable, too, at the end."

"You've got good taste, then," Ana said, deadpan as ever. "So. Back to fairyland?"

"Back to fairyland." Melly lifted herself up onto her toes and kissed Ana. She'd meant it to be a little goodbye kiss, but Ana had different ideas. Her hand found its way into Melly's hair, her fingers threading through the newly-untangled locks, her mouth hot and hard and demanding. When the kiss finally ended, Melly was not entirely unsurprised to see that Ana's lips were redder than usual. The mortal gods knew what she must look like. She didn't care.

"You've ruined your hair," Ana commented, sauntering back over to the bed with a sly grin. She dropped down on the mattress, heavy as a sack of potatoes for such a skinny woman, arms at her sides.

Melly shot her a smile and turned back to mirror, smoothed her hair, and then uncovered the glass, placing her hands on the cool surface. She concentrated on the Grand Reflection Station and, after a short delay, the mirror flickered and the station appeared. It was, as usual, manically busy, hundreds of fae bustling about, brown suits marching around trying to maintain some kind of order. The Mirrors were working and the GenAm was running as many stories as possible to take advantage of the fact.

Melly supposed it had to be the residual belief still coming in from the stories with the Redacted protagonists – the mess that had closed the Academy. It would begin to wane soon, and then the Mirrors would start breaking again.

A vile image of Ana, glassy-eyed and smiling faintly, obediently, slid into her mind.

Melly had only seen Bea briefly since the events at the Academy, but she'd said that she'd burned down the woodshed that had housed all the Redaction drink the GenAm had been using on the humans. Melly had asked her if that meant it was over, and Bea had looked away, a shadow passing across her face, and simply said that she hoped so.

Hope wasn't good enough. They needed the genie.

"I'll never get used to that," Ana said, watching the scene in her mirror. "It looks a bloody shambles, too."

"To be honest, I've never really liked it. I'd rather go home and walk."

"So do that."

"I can't. I'm expected at the GenAm. Trust me, I've a better chance of explaining my way through a checkpoint than explaining why I refused an official summons."

F. D. Lee

Ana looked singularly unconvinced. Indeed, 'mutinous' was probably the best way to describe the expression that had settled on her face. "You and Bea both spent a very long time explaining to me what this GenAm is like if you break the rules. I was at the Ball, don't forget. I saw what they did. That *thing* they sent to attack us."

"And that's exactly why I've got to go back. We discussed all this."

Fury caused narrow, hard lines around Ana's mouth. But she gave a curt nod. She was, Melly knew, first and foremost a realist. A thinker. Passionate, too. But she knew when and how to direct that passion. It was one of the things Melly had first liked about her.

"You're right," Ana said. "Go. But you are to return here as soon as you can. This is my bargain. Do you accept?"

It was a remarkable pincer attack. "Clever girl," Melly smiled. "I accept the bargain."

With that, she stubbed her cigarette out on the inside of her tin, squirrelled it away, and disappeared through Ana's mirror...

...appearing a moment later through a Mirror in the Grand. It was still busy. Melly pushed her way through the crowd, her confidence and her witch's uniform silencing any disgruntled complaints from the fae stuck queuing to get out.

She reached the checkpoint and was immediately accosted by a brown-suited gnome from the Contents Department.

"Where have you been?"

"Ehinenden."

"The Indexers are over there, take your Book to them."

"I don't have a Book. The Plot Department sent me on a task." Melly handed over the slip she'd been given many months before. When John had first had his accident, the Plot Department had allowed Melly special access to Thaiana to heal him. It was all, naturally, very hush-hush. The GenAm had not officially accepted responsibility for – or even acknowledged – John's broken spine and their part in it. But they had allowed Melly, as an elf and a witness, to apply her healing talents to him.

The Princess And The Orrery

But her permission slip was out of date. Luckily, the brown suit, eying the queue behind her, had too much to worry about and seeing the official stamp at the top of the paper, waved her through.

Outside the Grand, it was even busier. In addition to the usual thronging crowd, there was a large rabble of jeering fae, all shouting slurs and threats at a contingent of... fairies?

Melly, standing on the steps of the Grand, read one of the banners they were waving: *Fairy Rights Are Fae Rights.*

It was a Fairies United protest. It seemed to be mostly made up of house fairies, but she spotted a few splashes of colour, which meant there were also flower fairies in the mix. And then she saw two figures she recognised. One was shorter than the other, one fatter: Joan, with her yellow haystack hair and Bea, who had apparently cut off her long grey hair, leaving only her natural green hanging around her jaw. They were holding signs and chatting happily to each other.

Melly didn't want to be seen. Didn't want to have to make up some story about where she'd been or, indeed, why she'd been too busy to see since the events at the Academy. She couldn't tell Bea or Joan her plan – they wouldn't understand, Bea least of all. They'd try to talk her out of it. Try to save the genie's life. Good intentions, she knew. Good intentions from good people – the best. All the more reason not to taint them with the horror of real choice, real responsibility.

Something flew through the air, hurled from the jeering crowd at the group of fairies.

Melly darted forward, her hands tingling as she activated her elven gift of healing, and then she saw what had been thrown.

An egg. Just an egg. Sickly yellow goop spread across the cobbles at Bea and Joan's feet. Bea looked up, shouted something Melly couldn't hear. Joan burst out laughing, and Bea shot a very rude hand gesture in the direction the egg had come from.

Melly turned and walked quickly away, letting the space where she'd been standing fill with strangers.

20

Hemmings felt he bore things very well, generally. It was, he considered, part of his nature to rise above those misfortunes that would defeat simpler minds.

When the other elves had bullied him for being a dwarf, and the dwarfs had bullied him for being an elf, he'd risen above it. When Chokey's idiot friends had sent her crawling into his bed to lie next to him, determinedly not crying, he had pushed aside his anger to be what his sister needed him to be. When he'd found out what the GenAm had done to those characters, Redacting them for the sake of easy stories – when, surely, the point of stories was to explore the horror and the beauty of the world and make sense of them both, not to bastardise and simplify it all? – he had overcome his fear and helped rescue them.

And so, he told himself, he would rise above this.

"My baby boy, look at you," Mistress Ogrechoker said. "So handsome! So grown up! Though I do wish you and your sister hadn't put all that red dye in your hair. You look like you belong at the wall." She reached up and fiddled again with his cravat. "At least we managed to get the worst of it cut off. You're so handsome, my boy, you don't need to hide away the way you do. I remember the day I found you, all swaddled up and crying – the lungs you had – and I knew you were meant for greatness. Dea'dora, darling, don't you remember?"

"Not really, Mama, I was only a bit older myself." Chokey shot her brother a look he had learnt to dread. "But I do so adore hearing the story! Do tell us again, won't you?"

"Oh, my little baby boy, my darling! Nobody thought we should have you. An elf, they said; cruel tribe, cruel and selfish. But I knew the moment I saw you how special you were. To have survived what torments I shall never know, abandoned in a handbag, your dear little face all covered in scars, oh, oh, oh," Mistress Ogrechoker pulled out her handkerchief and loudly blew her nose. "And now here you are, about to become an official

Fiction Management Executive! A villain! And just when the GenAm need people like you, too. The Ogrechoker name has never been so well placed. Oh, my sweet little boy," she finished with a sob, wrapping her thick arms around his middle, her head resting against his tummy.

Hemmings tentatively put his arms around his mother's shoulders and glared at his sister over the top of her head. "There, there. I'll do my best."

Mistress Ogrechoker gave him a squeeze, narrowly avoiding breaking his ribs. "I know you will, Hemmings, my darling." She held out her arm for Chokey, who dived into the hug. "And you, my eldest girl. I shall find a place for you as well, never fear. Nothing holds the Ogrechokers back, you remember that, my babies."

Ignoring the stares from the other recruits being dropped off at the GenAm, Hemmings dropped a kiss on his mother's head. "Thank you," he mumbled.

His mother and Chokey wished him luck and waved him goodbye from their carriage, Chokey demanding that he keep up his journals and his mother giving her a sharp clip around the ear for encouraging him in his nonsense, and then they were gone.

Hemmings readjusted his cravat, straightened his waistcoat, fiddled with his newly much shorter hair, trying to cover the scars that ran down one side of his face. He checked his pocket watch. Brushed the toe of his newly polished shoe against the back of his leg. Checked his pocket watch again.

It was time.

He walked around the main entrance to the GenAm, past the towering bronze doors that fronted the Redaction Department and, high above, the Teller's spire, to the more subdued entrance of the Plot Department. Following the instructions sent to his mother, he navigated a maze of seemingly identical beige corridors, only needing to ask for help a half dozen times, until he found himself in... surely the wrong place?

The corridor was, even by the benchmark of those he had travelled, drab and dull. The carpet was the kind of brown that must have been chosen only for its capacity to absorb stains into its hideousness. He double-checked his instructions, then realised this was pointless as he had no idea which way he had come, and instead started trying doors. The first was locked, the second some kind of broom closet.

The third door stuck against something, which turned out to be a chair.

"Hemmings? Well met. Sorry about the, well, the office, I suppose," Mistasinon said, his voice slipping through the gap. "Hold on a second."

A few busy moments passed before the door opened wide enough for him to wiggle through. Inside, the room was extraordinarily full. The wide desk might have just about fitted, if it weren't also for the cabinets and shelves full of Books, papers, rolled up scrolls and the mortal gods knew what else. Hemmings was prepared to admit that his life so far had given him advantages others lacked, but he'd not realised, until this moment, quite how much he took *space* for granted.

Wedged into all the chaos was Mistasinon and Melly, Bea's friend. She was smoking. As if the room wasn't cramped enough, even the air had to struggle for space, shifting to make room for the blue, sickly sweet smoke.

Mistasinon shot him an apologetic smile. "Please, take a seat. You know Melly, of course?"

"Yes. It's good to see you again."

Melly offered him a curt nod. "And you. I trust your sister is well?"

"Yes, thank you."

Surely they couldn't fit anything else into Mistasinon's tiny office, and yet, somehow, an awkward tension managed to squeeze itself in as well. Hemmings sensed he had walked in on an argument.

Mistasinon seemed momentarily at a loss. And then, rubbing his neck in that odd way he had, said, "Well, I suppose there's no point pretending we don't all know what we know. Melly and I were just, um, discussing your working together, Hemmings. I think the two of you are much safer together – you'd have both been placed with someone, whether you liked it or not, so better someone you don't have to lie to."

Melly drew on her cigarette, but said nothing.

"I'm very pleased to be here," Hemmings said, sensing the explanation hadn't been for him. "I know this wasn't your idea. I'll do my best not to let you down. Our best is all we can ever do, naturally, but it is very much my intention to aim for it."

"Ah? Yes, good," Mistasinon said. "Thank you."

Melly dropped her cigarette into a half-full cup on Mistasinon's desk. It sizzled and died. "I expect you have something to be getting on with, as do we." She stood up, offering a shallow bow to Mistasinon. "If that's all, my Lord?"

The Plotter stood too, bowing more politely. "Of course. Um. Actually, I wonder if I might speak with Hemmings a moment. Privately."

"Very well," Melly said. "I'll wait at the end of the hallway."

She squeezed past Hemmings, pulling the door closed behind her.

Mistasinon leaned across the desk and whispered, "I was wondering... that is... if maybe you'd seen, uh, seen Bea at all?"

"You said we shouldn't," he whispered back.

"Ah. Yes. I just thought perhaps – you know Bea. She never listens to anyone."

A weight formed in Hemmings' stomach. He tried to pretend it wasn't there. "I'm sure she'd like to see you."

"Really?"

The weight got heavier. "Of course. She's quite fond of you, I think."

"It's a bit... complicated between us. I wasn't sure if I should..." Mistasinon's voice, already hushed, trailed into nothing.

Hemmings thought for a moment. "All life is complicated, Mistasinon," he whispered. "Bea knows that, I think. We can never be sure of what we do. Only that we act with the best of intentions, and seek to avoid harm."

Mistasinon offered him a smile. He pulled back, raising his voice to a normal level. "Thank you. I do wish I was as good at thinking as you. Perhaps, when you're back from training, you wouldn't mind... I mean, maybe you could teach me how to do some thoughtsmithing."

"Really?"

"You did offer, once. Would you?"

Hemmings went to brush his hair forward, covering his scars, and then remembered his emergency haircut. His hand found its way into his pocket, where it could fiddle with his pocket watch instead. "Of course – it would be my pleasure," he mumbled. "Do you know what you want to think about?"

"Morality. Choices."

Hemmings perked up. "Oh, that's no problem at all. I've piles of journals on those subjects. It's... well, I mean, it's mostly my own work, you understand. The Teller, *whocaresaboutus*, doesn't allow the Contents Department to lend out any books on thinking."

"Not at all. I'd rather learn from you than from a stranger."

"Thank you."

"Really, I should be thanking you, but after the visit from your mother, maybe this could make us even?"

"I really am terribly sorry about-"

Mistasinon held his hands up. "No, no. I was teasing. I'm sorry. Anyway, I shouldn't keep you any longer."

Hemmings stood up. "Um. Chokey mentioned there's a Fairies United rally today. She thought Bea might be there. I, uh, I think she was thinking of going..."

"Oh? Well. Yes. Maybe I'll stop by, when my work's finished."

Hemmings nodded and slipped out of Mistasinon's tiny office. Melly was waiting for him at the end of the hallway, her cigarette burned down to a stub. From her expression, it seemed her patience was at much the same level.

As Hemmings trotted down the hallway to join her, he tried not to think about how much he'd rather be with Chokey or, better still, teaching Mistasinon thoughtsmithing.

Life was, indeed, complicated.

21

"That's someone hanging on by their fingernails if ever there was one," Melly said, apparently without irony, as she lit a new cigarette from the butt of her last one.

They were making their way to the Grand Reflection Station, travel documents freshly secured.

"Mistasinon? Considering what he's been through, it's hardly surprising," Hemmings said as he tried to keep up with her. "One can only imagine what it was like."

"What what was like?"

"Being Redacted."

The witch came to such a sudden halt, Hemmings overshot her by a few paces and had to turn back.

"Excuse me?"

Hemmings lowered his voice, conscious they were standing in the middle of the street. "At the Academy, when Bea found him. He'd been captured by West, the woman responsible for all that unpleasantness. He was dying. Bea told us the only to save him was to give him some of the Redaction drink. I was shocked at first, as well," he said, completely misinterpreting the look on Melly's face. "Redaction is an unforgivable act. But when she explained, it all made sense. Things often do, if they're explained properly."

The witch grabbed him by the arm, almost as hard as his sister's grip, and dragged him into an alleyway. Honestly, Hemmings thought, it really was a stroke of genius that Ænathlin was so intricately designed. It was almost as if the city had been created expressly for the purpose of secret conversations in shadowy corners.

"And exactly how did he survive the Redaction?" Melly asked, her emerald eyes narrow. Probably against all that ghastly smoke. "There's never been a member of the fae able to overcome it."

F. D. Lee

"I surmised it was because it wasn't really a Redaction. The drink West concocted was a weakened version. Didn't Bea explain all this?"

"She told me about the Redaction drink and the woman, West. She failed to mention she'd used it on someone."

"Oh. Well." Hemmings felt unaccountably embarrassed, especially considering all he'd done was educate. Normally, when he explained things, he felt ignored or ridiculed or simply isolated. Rarely embarrassed. "She did have a good reason."

Melly threw her latest cigarette on the cobbles, stamping it under her heel. "Right. Yes. I see."

"Wisdom is often attained when one is prepared to open one's eyes."

But the witch wasn't listening. "I told her not to get involved with the GenAm, or with the genie, or the Plotter, or the Academy, and she didn't listen to a word I said. That bloody fairy! She's determined to get herself Redacted!"

"I'm sorry? The genie?"

Melly seemed to remember he was there. "What genie?"

"The one you just said Bea shouldn't have become involved with. I distinctly heard you."

For a moment, the two elves stared at each other.

"Blast it. Alright. Come with me, Mister Thinker Elf," Melly said, stalking out of the alleyway like it had personally offended her. "I'll explain when we're in Thaiana."

Hemmings tried again to wring the water out of his coattails.

Melly had brought them through a Mirror in the Grand Reflection Station to a river in a forest, using the image cast back in the water. As a result, both elves were now standing on the riverbank in sopping wet, black attire.

Mind you, Melly seemed to be drying off much faster than him. She wore a simple, long black dress, the traditional witch's costume. Hemmings, on the other hand, had to deal with the fact his silk shirt was sticking to him, his waistcoat was drying rigid, his trousers were so heavy they were slipping down his hips, his lovely new shoes with the silver buckles had apparently turned into buckets, and his frock coat was, frankly, frocked. The braiding would never be the same again, that was certain.

It was remarkable, really, how two such similar personages could be so very different.

Melly, like Hemmings and indeed all elves, had an innate grace and beauty, but she seemed to have a bloody-minded determination to minimise it. Her dress was plain and, Hemmings couldn't help but notice, rather tired. Not grossly so, but just in the way things get when they're used and reused. Even the elves by the wall made an effort, cobbling together something presentable from bits of scrap. She wasn't wearing any jewellery; the pearl and antler crown he remembered so admiring when they'd first met was gone. And the smoke from her foul little cigarettes! She might just as well have renounced her tribe and claimed she was a bonfire.

Beauty, elegance, grace. These were the things that defined the elves. It was what had made the tribe so successful with the stories, before the Teller had sanitised the Plots. It was a history that many elves still clung to. For some reason, the characters tended to overlook cruelty when it was wrapped up in a pretty form, and the elves had, once upon a time, taken full advantage of that fact. Nasty stories always garnered belief. Their tribal talent for healing had also helped them in this regard, though not in any way a true healer would want to be associated with. You could have a lot of fun with a creature when you knew that broken bones could be easily remedied.

The trouble with imagination was that it was available to everyone.

At least Hemmings and Melly didn't support that kind of behaviour. Or so he'd thought. From the way she was smiling as he tried to dry himself off, Hemmings wasn't entirely sure Melly had given up *all* elvish cruelty.

"I thought we were going to a castle?"

Melly managed, with some degree of success, to straighten her face. "We are, but you want to know about the genies. It's better to get it out of the way here, where we won't be disturbed. Come on."

Hemmings squelched after her. "Our governess told us about the genies when we were little. She said they weren't very good storytellers. There's no need to believe in something if you can just wish for it."

"And if that's what the genies had done, she'd be right," Melly said, pulling her cigarette case from her sleeve. Miraculously, the contents were dry. She struck a match against the inside of her case, lit up, coughed a bit, and continued. "The genies didn't use wishes to give people what they wanted. Listen, you think the King and Queen of the fairies were bad? That the stories they told were irresponsible, selfish, cruel? What about Rumpelstiltskin – he tricked the characters, enslaved them, killed them. Locked young maidens away, all of that. And then, before him, there were the stories that focused on the young ones. Did you know the fae used to eat children? No, I thought not. The Teller's done a good job of protecting us from our past."

She took an angry drag on her cigarette. "No one understands what it was like, before the Teller. Short memories only ever seem to go as far back as the 'good old days'. Anyway. The genies didn't grant wishes, not in the way your governess meant. All our wickedness is because of the genies – they taught us what was possible. It was a game to them, and by the mortal gods, they were good at it. Some poor soul would wish for the boy or girl of their dreams to fall madly in love with them, and that's exactly what they'd get."

"All the Teller's Plots are about falling in love and Happy Ever After."

Melly snorted. "They're not the same – that's the point. Have you ever had someone *madly* in love with you?"

"No."

"Be grateful for it, because that's exactly what the genies would deliver. If the wisher was lucky, the worst it would get was having to change their name, leave their friends and family behind and start a new life, far away. If they weren't lucky... Love can be a very aggressive emotion. They might not have any friends and family left to leave."

Hemmings shuddered.

The Princess And The Orrery

"Now imagine if your sister died," Melly said. "Wouldn't you wish to have her back?"

"Of course I would – oh. Oh, no."

"Exactly. The genies manipulated everything, twisting people's desires and needs into something that would amuse them. They lived for it. The more subtle the trick, the better. The belief they generated was masterful. The characters would always, *always*, make the wish because of the promise it offered and then, when it was granted, they put all their energy into believing they could undo it. The genies had them coming and going."

"Belief untempered by thought, poisoned with the promise of hope."

Melly gave him an appraising look. "Exactly."

"Thinking is its own reward if one makes the effort," Hemmings said. "But if it's as you say, where are the genies now? With that kind of power, one would have thought they'd be in control of the whole of the Land. The Mirrors must have thrived under them."

"They weren't interested in us or the Mirrors. They just wanted the game. Their power works on us, to be sure, but it works so much better on the humans."

"So they're here? In Thaiana? Is that how Bea got involved with one?"

Melly took another drag on her cigarette. For a moment, the only sound was the crackle of the paper burning and the crunch of the forest floor under their feet, muted slightly where Hemmings' sodden shoes fell. The witch seemed to be struggling under some internal weight, eyes fixed on something only she could see.

And then she let out a sigh, returning from wherever she'd disappeared to in her mind.

"No, they're not here, not anymore. The Teller found a way to use their power to help charge the Mirrors, to subsidise the belief from his Plots. To fix the ones that broke. It was what, ultimately, allowed him to steal the Chapter from the King and Queen. That and his Beast," she added, scowling. "When the Mirrors started breaking again, I assumed the genies were all dead. It was the only thing that made sense. But last year, when Bea was working on a Plot, she met one. A real, living genie. He was involved in her story and Bea being Bea, she didn't report him to the GenAm like she should have done. Like any sensible person would have done! And now, here we are! Everything that's happened since – the Mirrors breaking, the Redacted women, the attack on Llanotterly Castle – all because Bea felt some kind of sympathy for that thing."

Hemmings pulled up, his back stiffening. "One should always act with kindness. It's our duty."

"Oh, really? If the GenAm had that genie, the Redacted protagonists you were so worried about wouldn't have happened. There wouldn't have been any need for them. I had to deal with a human woman who'd been maimed and tortured, murdered, all because the GenAm needs a way to fix the Mirrors without the genies' wishes. Is any of that kindness? To put all those people at risk because of one genie's sob story about falling in love? What does all your clever thinking have to say about that?

"The only thing anyone should be thinking about is that the Mirrors are breaking," Melly continued. "And desperate decisions are being made as a result. Without the General Administration and the Teller keeping control, what do you think will happen?"

She caught herself. Glanced around. Lowered her voice. "Hells, I don't want to see the old stories coming back, the blood and bone. The Anties, whoever they are, think that we only need to go back to the way things were and everything will be right as rain again. It's never that simple. This isn't a story. Once upon a time when the Land was good and just? It never was, that's the truth. And some Prince isn't going to turn up in the last few pages to save us. We have to find a way to save ourselves."

Hemmings was, unaccountably, at a loss. He knew he didn't agree with her, but he couldn't disagree, either. None of his thoughtsmithing could help him find an answer.

"I know this is hard," Melly said. "I didn't want you involved. I tried to get that Plotter to change his mind, but he wouldn't listen. There's no time to wait. You understand?"

"Yes and no. We must all help the tree to grow."

She frowned but, disappointingly, didn't ask him what he meant. "We're going to meet Ana and King John – they're humans. I've struck a deal with them, the details aren't important right now. But I'm going to fix it all – if we can just work out a way into that bloody city."

"What city? Fix 'what' all? You mean the Mirrors? How?"

"I'm going to get the genie and then I'm going to give him to the GenAm. And since I've been lumbered with you, you're going to help me."

22

Thus, on the same day Seven began work on the orrery, Hemmings and Melly arrived at Llanotterly Castle. Brief introductions were made, and Melly explained the situation regarding her new apprentice to John and Ana.

Ana had taken it as well as could be expected; John, in fact, rather got the impression she'd known about it beforehand and was putting on a bit of a show on his behalf. As if he hadn't noticed the way she and Melly managed their meetings so they would always finish the day working alone.

It was, he thought, rather endearing to see two such arrogant, stern women trying to skulk about each other for months on end, neither one wanting to be the first to show the white flag. But the flag had clearly been waved at some point in the recent past, if their little glances and stolen touches were any clue.

It was the only bit of jolly news he could lay his hands on, that was for damned sure. Perhaps when all this madness was finally capped, he might spend some time looking for a little bit of the ol' puppy-eyes himself. If this madness ever did get capped.

King John wheeled himself away from his window. Had he ever had so much to worry about? Well, yes, he had. Getting his spine cracked near as damn it in two by an ogre had certainly been a jolly rum job, and the blessed wheeled chair had taken some getting used to, that was a fact. But still, there was no denying it. They were in a bind.

There was so much to take in. When he'd been a lad, things had been straightforward. None of this elves and witches nonsense, leastways not beyond the nursery walls – and rarely within it, truth be told. His aunt hadn't approved. Ye God. Now there had been a real monster, no two ways about it. Aunty Constance, a woman who had lived up to her name when it came to regular discipline and a severe distrust of anything even remotely enjoyable.

John couldn't help wondering if his father hadn't had the right idea, eating himself into an early grave just to escape her. Damn shame really that the old bat had died before him, leaving King Edward with the freedom he'd always craved and a heart condition that would see him off not two years later, leaving John at twenty-seven years old the sole ruler of a Kingdom that was about as down on its luck as it was possible to be.

Or so he'd thought. He'd tempted fate with that one, really. Now not only did they owe a King's ransom – ha, ha – to the Baron in back taxes, but they were also involved in clandestine people-smuggling from the very same Baron's slave pits *and* were working with an elf – correction, two elves! – to get back a genie in order to stop that Baron taking even more slaves.

Hell's teeth. He'd only ever wanted to run Llanotterly well. Maybe earn a bit of respect, make up for the fact he was about two decades too young to wear the crown and had missed out on his education.

"I thought I'd find you in here."

John spun around. Ana was standing at his door. She hadn't bothered to knock. She wasn't a knocking kind of gel. John wasn't entirely sure how he'd ended up with Ana as his Adviser after Seven had disappeared. He'd been holed up in bed after the attack, doing the ol' recoup with Melly's magical assistance, and somehow she'd just started doing the job. Not that he minded; Ana had proven herself a true and trusted friend.

"Only place I can find any peace. I thought elves were supposed to be gentle, relaxing things, more fool me. Well, come in then, madam. No good haunting the door frame, what?"

Ana stepped into the room. John's private quarters were rather homely, he liked to think. He didn't go in for all the pomp of his predecessors. He collected antiques, bits and pieces brought into Llanotterly's modest docks in the fishing village of Sinne or carried through by traders. And plenty of books. Books were the answer, John felt. He just wished he knew what the bloody question was.

The room itself was small, at least in comparison to the others in the castle. Seven's quarters – well, Ana's now – were at least twice the size. Large enough for a giant bed, desks, two wardrobes and still enough floor space for a pretty reasonable shindig, plus a privy in an adjoining room.

F. D. Lee

John had opted to stay in his childhood bedroom after his coronation. Even when he'd been put in the wheeled chair, he'd refused to move to a more accessible room. Ana had smoothed out all the creases though, getting the steamer chair lifts working on the main staircases, planing down the floors on his most common routes through the castle, knocking through a wall so he, too, now had a private bathroom with various bits and pieces to help him use it in peace.

Didn't make her hen-pecking any more bearable, but he had to admit she was a good sport, all in all.

"They're neither of them what I would have imagined an elf to be like," Ana conceded. "What do you think about the new one?"

"He's a bit of a popsie. Got the air of someone who's yet to get a good kick in the arse from life, frankly."

"Melly says we're stuck with him."

John laughed. "You catch the look on his face when she said that?"

Ana grinned. "I did, yes. God, this is getting more complicated by the day. We need them out of the castle, John. We need to get moving."

"You don't have to tell me that. It's only been a day of her glaring and him reciting all that codswallop – I could go a lifetime without ever seeing another pointy ear. But if they can help us get S., Seven I mean, back, I'll take them."

Ana took a seat at his reading desk. She seemed pensive, even by her normal standards. "What is it about Seven that makes you want him back?"

"Same thing as you. He can help us get out from under that blaggard, the Baron. Sort out all this mess."

"No. That's why we need him. Why do you *want* him back?"

"He's my friend," John said simply.

"No he's not. He used you, used all of us, to kidnap the Marlaisan Countess."

John drummed his fingers on the arm of his wheeled chair. Ana had a bee in her bonnet about Seven. He'd figured this conversation would happen at some point. Might as well be now.

That was the thing about John. He was young and handsome, in a chinny sort of way, and spoke like someone who'd never seen

The Princess And The Orrery

the outside of an ermine cloak. Everyone knew the crown hadn't had the money to educate him. At best, people felt sorry for him. In over his head. Funny ideas about modernisation. Took in some strange foreigner to be his Adviser, and look how that ended up. A year ago, even John had believed it all. Now, he had a different point of view.

"Listen to me," he said. "I don't hold with all that, not one bit. S. was an odd-bod, I'll give you that. But he cared about Llanotterly. He wanted to help us. I've heard what Melly has to say about genies and mind control, and it doesn't add up. If he'd wanted, he could have had me wish for all kinds of nonsense. He never did, you hear? Not once. I've spent a long time thinking on that." John rapped his knuckles against his chair. "Had a long time to think. I can't recall one single instance where he led me into wishing for something, not one. Truth be told, I think he tried to avoid it all. Always in that damnable puggaree, covering himself up. Used to drive me up the wall, I don't mind admitting. Handsome fella like that, acting like some slip of a gel, no offence."

"None taken," Ana said sourly.

"My point is, everyone's saying he took advantage, but I don't see it. If he could use his beauty and his words to muddle us 'characters' up, why'd he go so far out of his way to hide himself? All I see is someone who tried to help. He helped me, and that's a fact. When all the rest thought I was some juggins in a crown – you included, Miss Regal – Seven actually listened to me. And not to get me on side, before you jump on that," he added, seeing Ana about to pounce. "He didn't agree with me all the time, called me a damned fool more than once in his funny way. But he cared, underneath it all – cared more than I think even he realised."

"I thought that, too. But he was just very charming. That's how they work, Melly says. Make you think they're your friend."

"He was my friend, damn it all," John snapped. "I don't believe a word of what's been said about him. And I think you ought to remember that if it weren't for him, you wouldn't be standing where you are now, face going all purple."

Ana shook her head. "He only got me to come to that Ball to keep you distracted–"

"I'll thank you to note that I'm perfectly capable of working with someone of the opposite sex without becoming distracted."

"That wasn't what I meant. John, please. You must see what Seven really is?"

John pushed himself over to Ana and laid his hand over hers. "With respect, Ana, I think it's you who doesn't see what he really is. You're not a stupid gel, not by a long chalk. So what is it you're trying to prove?"

Sighing, Ana pulled her hand out from under his and ran it through her hair. "We need to stop the Baron, that's all."

"And I agree. Chin up, old sport. We're all on the same page."

"I hope so." Ana shook herself. "So, then. How are we going to get two elves into the Baron's palace? One was bad enough. They're not exactly inconspicuous – Hemmings' ears stick out a mile with that dreadful haircut."

"I've been thinking about that."

"His haircut? It doesn't bear much thinking about."

"Damn right about that, but no. How to get them into Cerne Bralksteld. Come over here." He wheeled over to the window, Ana walking next to him. "See that?"

"What? The tent? That's just the travelling theatre. They come here every year during the spring flings."

"Quite, quite. You ever watch them?"

"Not really. Sindy liked it though."

"I loved it when I was a nipper. Couldn't tear me away. Drove my aunt to distraction. All the costumes, the possibilities. Folks pretending to be someone else, somewhere else. Fantastic stuff, what? Anyone can be anything in the theatre."

Ana didn't answer, but her expression implied she was more closely aligned with Aunt Constance when it came to treading the boards.

"Come on, gel. Catch up," John said. "We've got two elves to hide somewhere no one'll look twice at them. Somewhere that with a bit of help under the table, p'haps, can get into the Baron's Palace unremarked on."

"Good Lord. You're a genius!"

John grinned. "Damn right. Can't believe it didn't occur to me sooner, truth be told. We can get them in the company, pull a few strings and get the company performing at the Palace in the Bralks. Plus it shouldn't cost that much, certainly not near the expense of an official diplomatic party, even if the Baron would give us an audience. Now tell me if that isn't a little bit of terrific?"

"More than a little bit, John. It's perfect! Only..."

"What?"

"Are you going to tell Melly and Hemmings, or am I?"

23

Bea saw Mistasinon before he saw her.

She was walking down the street outside her building, having just popped out for more wine. A mistake, she'd warned Joan and Chokey, but they'd been so busy gossiping about the Academy and the Mirrors and – mostly – Bea herself, that in the end she'd been happy to get five minutes away. There was, Bea felt, some kind of universal law that dictated that when you introduce two separate friends to each other, the only way they can possibly bond is over the sharing of embarrassing stories about you.

Still, it had been a good day – projectile eggs notwithstanding. She hadn't really known what to expect from the Fairies United rally, but the jeering crowds had been close. Joan seemed happy, though. And the GenAm had largely left them alone; a couple of brown suits had come over to push them around a bit, but hadn't made them disperse. A few fae from non-fairy tribes had even shown them some support, including Chokey, who Bea had been delighted to see.

And now she was seeing another familiar face. And, while she told herself she wasn't in any way delighted to see *him*, there was a fluttering in her chest that hadn't been there a moment ago.

She could almost have laughed – you waited ages for one friend-who-helped-you-rescue-a-load-of-Redacted-human-women-and-bring-down-one-of-the-oldest-GenAm-institutions and then two came along at once.

Mistasinon was easy to spot, standing at least a head taller than most tribes, especially those who lived by the wall, where fairies, elves, gnomes and goblins were the majority inhabitants. But even if he hadn't been tall, with skin the colour of ripe wheat, she would have spotted him. The way he hunched over, gripping his satchel, his head down.

She'd struggled for months to work out what he reminded her of, trying to figure out his tribe. But he had none. He wasn't one of them: he was something different.

The Princess And The Orrery

It occurred to her, as he drew closer, that he moved like a beaten animal. Damn it! Would she have made that comparison if she didn't know what he was? No, what he had been, she corrected herself. Hells, he'd seen her now.

"Hi," she shouted.

"Hi," he said, a smile lighting his face before he caught himself and reset his expression to something more neutral.

"What's a blue suit doing in a place like this, then?" she said as he came to a stop next to her.

"Ahhh. Well, you know – have to stay in touch with the common folk."

She grinned. "I see. Keeping your feet on the ground?"

"Exactly. Easy to lose sight of it all from my position."

"Quite right. I've seen your office, don't forget. Very exclusive."

He chuckled. "Assuming you take the word to mean I'm the only person who'd get stuck there, you're right about that."

"I'm not sure what else you'd think I meant. Sooo... I thought you said we weren't to see each other for a while?"

He rubbed his neck. "Well, it's been thirty-four days..."

"You've been counting?"

"Haven't you?"

Bea fidgeted with her bag, clanking the bottles of wine against her leg. "Sure. It's hard not to, when you think about everything that happened."

The words were out of her mouth before she had a chance to think about them – filling the space between them worse than the smell drifting from the open gutter than ran down the length of the street. She'd been thinking about West and the Redacted women, but from the way his expression froze, it was clear he'd taken it to mean what had happened to him.

What West had done to him. Hells, what Bea had done. What she knew.

But what exactly was she supposed to say? *"Hi there, Mistasinon. How's it going? You're looking particularly hounded, no offence, ha ha. How's the singular head working out?"*

"I mean, it's not every day you fight a troll on a rooftop. Hard not to keep track of time," Bea said, following it up with what she hoped might pass for a friendly chuckle. "How have you been?"

"Oh. Well, you know."

No, that's why I asked. "Yup."

"Yes."

He was staring at her. Mortal gods, she was making a mess of this! Why was she so nervous, anyway? She hadn't done anything wrong, neither had he. There was no reason for all this awkwardness.

"What? Why are you looking at me like that?"

"You look really pretty." Mistasinon's cheeks flushed. "I mean, you've changed your hair. It's nice. I didn't mean you don't always look pretty, because you do. Mortal gods..."

Bea, feeling all of a sudden rather pleased with herself, took pity on him. "You don't think it makes me look a little 'cabbagey'?"

A pause. And then he smiled. "Very much so. I thought that was the point?"

"Quite right. I did wonder about dying it red, you know, like a carrot. Experimenting with other root vegetables."

"Ah, yes. What about orange? Like a pumpkin?"

Bea shook her head. "I think that would clash with my eyes. Besides, I've had some pretty bizarre experiences with pumpkins."

"I remember. That was a rather unexpected addition to the Plot."

"A good addition?"

"Yes. A very good addition." His smile faltered. "I, ah, I heard about the Fairies United rally today. I wanted to come down, but I wasn't sure if I should." He gestured towards his blue Plotter's uniform. "If I'd be welcome...?"

"Of course you'd be welcome."

Mistasinon started to speak and then stopped, his eyes fixed above and behind her. Bea spun around just fast enough to see Joan and Chokey diving back from her window.

"Well, you'd better come up, now," she heard herself say. What was wrong with her mouth? Was it trying to give her a heart attack? "I'll never hear the end of it if you don't."

The Princess And The Orrery

She waited, very much not holding her breath, thank you, while he decided. It was just a friendly invitation; a friendly invitation to spend time with friends. Yes. Friends, friends, friends. There wasn't any harm in asking him. And if he said no, she'd not lost anything. Friends turned down invitations all the time.

It was taking him a long time to make up his mind, though, even by his standards. Maybe he didn't realise it was just a friendly invitation. Maybe he thought she wanted to spend time with him, which she didn't. At least, no more than she wanted to spend time with any of her other friends.

Mortal gods, why hadn't he said anything?

"Well? In or out, Mister Plotter?"

"...In. Please. If you don't mind?"

"Darling!" Chokey screamed, dashing across the room to envelop Mistasinon in a hug. "Goodness me, you look positively *frite-ful*! Whatever have you been doing to yourself?" She turned to Bea. "Doesn't he look haggard, Buttercup? Not nearly as handsome as we've grown to find him?"

Bea blushed scarlet, mumbled something, and then busied herself opening the wine. Chokey winked at her new friend, Joan. They had engaged in a speedy conflab on the subject of Bea and Mistasinon and had found that they were both on the same page. Now they just had to get the fairy and the Plotter caught up.

"It's nice to see you again, too," Mistasinon replied, gently disentangling himself. "And, um, Joan, isn't it? Hello again."

"It is! Hello! We've just been talking about how wonderful Bea is, haven't we, Chokey?"

"Oh, yes, absolutely," she replied, ignoring the death stare Bea was throwing their way. "Absolutely wonderful. I should think you'd have to be bonkers not to think so, wouldn't you, Mistasinon, darling?"

Bea practically flew across the room, shoving a glass of wine into her hands.

"We were talking about Fairies United, *actually*," Bea said, as she offered Joan and Mistasinon their own glasses before pouring a large measure for herself. "Joan's been working really hard on it, haven't you, Joan?"

Much to Chokey's disappointment, the little house fairy took the hint.

"It's actually going really well, considering. We've got about forty fairies now, all active members, and we're reaching out to the other tribes. The rallies are working well in terms of getting our name out there, but they're not really ideal for nuanced conversation. Delphine – that's my girlfriend – thinks we should host some kind of get together. Something where we can meet people, explain what we're fighting for. Fairies are just as useful as any other tribe – we can do anything they can do. Just look at Bea. She finished that whole Plot and got a place at the Academy. Without her-"

"Yes, well," Bea interrupted, her tone pointed. "I don't think it's quite that simple, as you well know. Besides, it's you and the others that actually got the whole thing off the ground."

Chokey rolled her eyes. Not that she didn't support Fairies United – she knew two fairies now, after all – but it was hardly the most important topic they could be discussing at this precise moment.

"Did you see Hemmings today?" she asked Mistasinon. "We dropped him off this morning. Gosh, he was so embarrassed, poor lamb."

Mistasinon looked surprised. "What about?"

"Oh, Mama, of course! I did warn you she wasn't to be underestimated, didn't I, darling?"

Bea and Joan exchanged glances.

"What's happened?" Joan asked, her eyes alight with intrigue.

"Oh, darling! You'll never believe it. Mama went off full tilt to the GenAm and practically threatened the entire city if our lovely little Plotter here didn't get Hemmings an apprenticeship."

"Noooooo? Wow! Really?" Joan answered gleefully. "Did it work?"

"Oh yes," Chokey said. "Very well. Isn't that so?"

"Um. Well, yes," Mistasinon replied. "Actually, I suppose you might as well know, since you're all here, that I've arranged for your friend Melly to be Hemmings' mentor."

Bea looked up. "Oh, really? What gave you that idea?"

"Well, I suppose it was Joan, when she approached me about the Redacted women and, well, you know what happened after that. I thought, given what we all know about the GenAm, it would be safer for Hemmings and Melly to be together. Was that wrong, do you think?"

"No, no. It's very sensible. Just good luck getting hold of her," Bea replied. "I've only seen her once since I got back. Apparently, she's too busy working on her Plots."

"That's not really fair, Bea," Joan said gently. "You know she's more scared of the GenAm than we are. She's probably just trying to keep away suspicion. Which we should probably all be doing, to be honest. I haven't been doing nearly as many teeth collections recently."

"She was very helpful with the Redacted women," Chokey offered, confused by the sudden change in atmosphere. "She took them all in and got them to that human woman, Ana, safely."

Bea sighed. "You're right. I suppose I just thought – never mind. The most important thing is to make sure it won't happen again. Mistasinon, I don't suppose you've been able to find out who was behind it?"

Mistasinon fiddled with the stem of his glass. "Not really. I've been busy sorting out the Academy – it is my job," he added, seeing Bea gearing up to interrupt him. "We need to keep things running, for everyone's sake. Besides, West is gone. Her workshop and all the Letheinate was destroyed. I don't really see how whoever it was could do it again."

"We can't assume that," Bea said.

"I'm not saying we should," Mistasinon said. "I'm just saying it's unlikely."

Chokey caught Joan's eye. "Come on you two, let's not have a row. I'm sure we'll find a way to sort it all out – we're simply far too wonderful a gang not to. Especially now we've got our dear little Plotter back, right Joan?"

F. D. Lee

Joan nodded. "If working with Fairies United has taught me anything, it's that we're better together."

Mistasinon put his glass of wine down, untouched. "Like a pack?"

"Well, yes, I suppose so," Joan said. "A team."

Chokey looked over to Bea, who'd gone unusually quiet. She was watching Mistasinon, an odd look on her face. Dear oh dear. This wasn't going right at all. It was clear that an Ogrechoker was needed – thank the mortal gods she was here.

"I say," she said, yawning, "Hasn't it got dark? I really need to get back home before I'm missed. Joan, perhaps you might walk with me? I do so like the local colour, but I'd feel much happier not walking alone."

"Of course," Joan said. She turned to Mistasinon. "It was lovely to see you again. You should come along to the next F.U. event. We're always keen to get non-fairy tribes involved."

"Oh yes, darling! You simply must involve yourself more in fairy matters!" Chokey said. "And I think, in the interests of security for our little gang – our pack, as you say – that you should wait a while before leaving. Let Joan and I get a head start. I'm sure Buttercup will be happy to play host a little longer."

"Oh, yes," Joan said, catching on. "A very sensible idea. Very sneaky. The GenAm doesn't stand a chance!"

They tumbled out the door, laughing their heads off, leaving Bea and Mistasinon alone.

24

"Well, that wasn't at all suspicious," Bea said as the door closed.

Her flat seemed even smaller, if such a thing were possible. She'd never really minded the lack of space before. She'd hardly ever been home anyway, and was well aware she'd been lucky to find somewhere that would accept a cabbage fairy from outside the wall. There wasn't even a divider between her kitchen and living space. The kitchen was a just couple of old cupboards attached to the wall adjacent to her front door, with a stone oven. Then, in the demarcation space, was her old, round wooden table and four chairs, a sofa towards the far left, and her narrow bed on the far right, near the window.

Oh, hells. Why was she thinking about her bed? Now she was staring at it.

Look at something else. Do something else.

Picking up the bottle, Bea sat at the table, grabbed her half-full glass and topped it up. Mistasinon moved to the window. The window by the – *nope. No.*

He leaned against the frame. Bea noticed his knuckles were pressed hard against his skin, whitening the honey-brown of his hands.

"I could get you some herbs if you like. To help relax you."

Mistasinon raised his thick eyebrows.

Somehow, Bea did not smash her head into her kitchen table. Why in the worlds had she said that? She'd have done better to have kept staring at the bed.

"Sorry. I don't mean... You just seem like you've got a lot on your mind."

Oh, mortal gods. Now she was talking about his mind... mind, heads, three heads, Beast. She wouldn't be surprised if he left right now. But no – he was smiling at her, his summer rain smile.

"It's alright, you don't need to look so worried," he said. "It's a very, uh, thoughtful suggestion, but I'd better not. I don't really know what kind of head I've got. Your medicine might not work, or it might make it worse."

A weight Bea hadn't been aware she'd been carrying lifted a fraction. "How have you been? You know, since...?"

"Since I nearly let myself get Redacted by a woman with a death wish? Or since I turned into whatever it is I am now?"

"Gosh. Well, those are very intriguing choices. Can I have both answers?"

He smiled properly then, his hands relaxing on the window sill. "Greedy."

"Impatient, more like. After everything that happened, I've been dying to know. I could never resist a good story."

"Exactly why the GenAm doesn't know what it's lost. You're sure you don't want to rejoin? I could find you a good mentor."

Bea took a sip of wine. She was finding that the further down the bottle she got, the less it burned. "No. I don't understand how you and Melly can carry on working for them."

"Yes, I noticed that. What about Hemmings? Or Joan?"

"What about them?"

"They work for the GenAm, too. Or are about to, in Hemmings' case. Why aren't you cross with them?"

Bea opened her mouth to say she wasn't cross with anyone and instead decided on another sip of wine. She was rather proud that she didn't down the whole glass. There was a chip on the base. Where had she... oh, yes. She'd stolen the glasses from a wedding, a Happy Ever After she'd been Plot Watching. Probably half of her belongings were stolen from weddings or naming days. Nothing matched, she knew that. Her whole life was a hodgepodge of gathered things...

Wood scraped against wood as Mistasinon took the seat next to her. He picked up his untouched glass of wine and took a small sip, his eyes watering.

"Mortal gods – does all wine taste like turpentine?"

"Hah. If it's made in Ænathlin, yes. Did you know that turpentine comes from trees?"

"Ah? No. A garden fairy secret?" He took another sip, this time only wincing. He wasn't really drinking, Bea noticed. Just little sips.

"Not really. But we can get the trees to give us the sap. The other tribes have to take it."

Mistasinon pulled his long legs up so his feet were resting on the bar between the chair legs, and leant on his knees.

He really was ridiculously tall. Gangly. Bea had always imagined the Beast to be a huge, ferocious thing. Mistasinon was more like one of those hunting dogs, the ones with the sleek brown coats that were all legs. Her gaze darted down to where his knees were almost touching hers. She grabbed the bottle and refilled their glasses.

"Anyway, you didn't answer my question," she said.

"You didn't answer mine, either."

She caught his eye. "Fair point."

"Bea..." He put his hand over hers, the way he had the day they'd first met. "I should have come to see you sooner. I wish I had. But-"

Her fingers moved, threading between his. Bea was sure she hadn't meant for that to happen, but he didn't seem to mind. His hand was warm, his skin smooth. The mortal gods knew what her hands must feel like – rough, probably, years of living in the forest giving her calluses that no amount of hot water and scrubbing with stone could shift.

"It's alright," she said. "We all agreed we should wait a while. Let the dust settle. Besides, nothing happened. I mean, well, obviously things happened... West and everything... but nothing happened between us. Nothing that, uh... There's no reason you should feel bad about not seeing me, is what I mean."

She coughed, her throat unaccountably dry. Another sip of wine should ease it.

"Please, let me finish," he said, large brown eyes searching her face. "You told me when you were sick that you liked me. I mean, before you found out that I'd... what I'd tried to do with the genie and then... I mean, you know all about the wishes and the belief and magic, and what I am... And you saved me. You should have let me die, but you didn't. That's why I haven't visited." He pulled his hand away. "I think that's why I shouldn't visit again, either."

"That doesn't make sense."

"Bea, listen. The other two haven't come back, but I don't know where they went. Perhaps they didn't go anywhere. Perhaps-"

"You can't keep running away from things."

"Running away? Is that really what you think? You've got no idea what it's like," he said, a sharp edge cutting through his tone. "Everything comes easily to you."

"Easily? I've put up with years of abuse from this rotten city and your precious GenAm, and that was before I knew what they did to the genies, to those human women – to *you*. I've had to fight for everything I've got."

"And now you have it," Mistasinon snapped, pulling away from her. "All your friends came the minute you asked them. Everyone wants to help you – mortal gods – they want to help you bring down the GenAm. Aside from the fact that it's total madness, don't you understand how precious that is? To have people who'll protect you? Who'll guide you? Who can tell you what it all means?"

She could feel the air between them changing, the intimacy that had filled her small apartment just moments before evaporating. And yet, she couldn't stop herself from answering back, "Tell me what it all means? That's nonsense. And what good has that ever done you, anyway? All your so-called masters have ever done is use you, lie to you, for their own benefit. Now you have a chance to work it out for yourself."

"That's not true – the Teller Cares About Me. You weren't there, you didn't know him." He stood up. "See? I shouldn't have come here."

Bea was on her feet too. "So why did you?"

"I don't know. I was confused."

He walked towards the door. He was leaving her. Just like last time and all the times they'd so nearly managed to navigate the strange space between them, that felt vast and incomprehensible and yet also, paradoxically, close and safe. He was going to leave, and she doubted she'd ever see him again.

She reached out and grabbed his arm.

It shouldn't have worked. But he stilled. She flexed her hand, feeling the tension in his muscles, under his suit.

"Please," he said, eyes wide, the anger in them replaced with something else. "Let me go. You don't understand..."

Bea dropped her hand, horrified. "I... Gods, I'm sorry. If you want to go, it's alright. I won't stop you. And if you... if you really don't want to see me again, I won't try to see you. I promise. I didn't mean…"

She stepped back, no idea how to finish. *If he goes now, you've still got half a bottle of wine. It'll be fine. And tomorrow you can put all this behind you and get on with breaking the world. Which should be easy, in comparison.*

But him didn't go. Instead he took a step towards her, bringing them close again, his hands patting against his legs, his soft, sad eyes searching her face.

"It's just – everything is so difficult," he said. "It's all new and..."

"I know."

"I want to get it right."

"I know. And I'm sorry – I shouldn't have tried to stop you leaving. It just feels like we've been here before, you know?"

"Yes," he replied. "But I like being here. With you."

They stared at each other.

He'll turn around and go, Bea told herself. *And that's fine. This is madness, anyway. He's right: I don't understand. He's a blue suit. The GenAm is in his bones, whatever shape he's in. Whatever they did to him, it was something that even changing his whole physicality couldn't erase.*

West said he wouldn't choose me...

Bea hadn't believed West when she'd said it. Deep down, she still didn't. But then, Mistasinon didn't need another person telling him what to be. He had to work it out for himself. He had to start making his own choices, didn't he? And if he chose to leave her, well, that probably was for the best, anyway.

Yes. He should go. In fact, she wanted him to. She wanted him to-

He leaned down and kissed her, his lips brushing lightly against hers.

It was the most chaste kiss Bea had ever received.

And it was over all too quickly.

Mistasinon pulled back, his eyes wide. "Oh, gods. I don't know why I did that. I've never done anything like that before."

"Never?"

A beat, and then he shrugged. "Is it really that surprising?"

"No, I suppose not."

"Do you – why are you smiling like that?"

"No reason." Bea saw the blush building in his tawny skin and straightened her face. "It's been a long time since someone's kissed me, that's all. It was nice. Thank you."

He stared at her for a moment, thick eyebrows caught in a frown. "Oh. Well. I, uh, I'm glad I could help."

"Me too. So... I mean, are you still planning on going, or..."

"Or?"

"Do you want to try again?"

A smile tiptoed across his face and then settled. For once, there was no rain in it. "Yes."

Bea grinned back at him.

"Good."

25

Hemmings was mesmerised.

He'd forgotten about the uncomfortable hay bale he was sitting on and the chill breeze, now that the sun had set. Even the grumbles of Melly, sitting next to him at the very back of the audience, couldn't pull him out of the theatre's spell.

When the young girl had been sold by her father to the cursed prince, he'd groaned along with everyone else. When she'd broken the rules, dooming the cursed prince to life as a grizzled old man, he'd nearly wept. Then, when she'd undergone various torments to prove her worthiness and lift the curse, he'd actually leapt to his feet and cheered. And now that the play was drawing to a close, the girl and the prince were getting married and a comedy sketch involving a large root vegetable and some very suggestive actions was being performed to the audience's great amusement, he was wiping away tears of laughter.

The play ended, and the actors lined up at the front of the staging area and bowed. Hemmings joined in the rapturous applause, grinning from ear to pointy – and safely hidden under a cap – ear. He flopped back down onto the itchy hay bale, his hands stinging.

"Did you – I mean – that part when the witch tried to eat her and she had to boil her – how did they do that? All that smoke? And then, when the wizened old man changed back into a prince! Mortal gods, and then when the maiden's father cut her hand off and all that red material came out to make the blood. I didn't even realise that humans bled the wrong colour! Have you ever, ever, seen anything so amazing in your life?"

Melly crossed her arms. "Yes. That's one of our stories."

"Excuse me?"

"Oh for – it's one of the old stories, before the Teller."

Hemmings looked for the joke. This was just the sort of thing his sister would say to wind him up. But judging from the way

Melly was glaring at the now empty stage, it seemed she was serious.

"How do you know that?" he asked.

"I've seen it before. Come on, let's get to Ana and John."

They slipped through the crowds hanging around for beer, bread, sugared apples and other post-culture treats. Hemmings spotted one of the actors, the sandy-haired man who'd played the prince, smoking a cigarette and talking to some of the audience. He was still wearing his wedding costume, his face thick with make-up. But there was no chance to stop; Melly was forging ahead like a hot and exceptionally annoyed knife through butter.

Hemmings caught up with her just as she was lighting her own cigarette.

"Stories get retold," he said. "Isn't that the whole point?"

"Yes, but not those stories. They turned the characters against us."

"Everyone was enjoying it." He stopped himself from adding *except you*.

"We'll see."

Melly stalked on ahead, clearly not wanting to discuss the matter any further. They finally reached the castle, entering by a side entrance past a startled guard who eyed Melly with particular suspicion, even though their names had been left on the gate. They left him grumbling about washerwomen, which made no sense at all to Hemmings, and made their way to John's office, where the giant map of Ehinenden lay spread out on the table.

Ana and John stood to one side, talking. Though they fell quiet the moment the two elves marched in, both of them looking slightly guilty.

"What ho!" John said cheerfully. "How were the theatrics?"

Hemmings opened his mouth, but Melly got there first.

"Why did you want us to see it?"

John and Ana looked at each other.

"Ah, well, y'see, we've hit upon something of a scheme, don'tchaknow?" John said. "To get you both into the Palace."

"I see," Melly said through thin lips.

"It's a bit of a ripper, if I say so myself. Jolly clever. Dash cunning. Sly as the ol' fox, in fact."

"Go on."

"Ah. Yes. Well, p'haps the details are a job for my Royal Adviser, what?"

Ana shot John a look over the end of her nose. "Good grief. Alright. We're sending you to Cerne Bralksteld with the theatre. There. It's the best plan we've got, so it's happening. No arguments."

Everyone looked at Melly. The witch stood still as a statue, her long red hair glowing like fire in the lamp light, arms folded across her slender frame. Hemmings realised he was holding his breath.

"How will they get us into the Palace?" Melly finally said.

It wasn't exactly a vigorous endorsement, but it wasn't a 'no' either. Hemmings breathed out.

"It's almost all sewn up," John said. "We've been in touch with various contacts – diplomats, business folk, people of that cloth. The crown still counts for something, eh? And luck's on our side. Calan Mai's only ten days away, which means the festival – bonfires, feasting, fun and games. Everyone celebrates it up here, even them lot. We're financing the troupe and my contacts are getting them on the list of performers for the Baron. Truth be told, it was pretty straightforward, once we'd set to it."

"I see," Melly said. "What's the 'almost'?"

John coughed. "Well, rather, you. Both of you, I mean," he added somewhat arbitrarily. Everyone knew the final decision would be Melly's.

"There's no other way," Ana interjected.

"Theatre and the fae don't mix well," Melly said, pulling out yet another cigarette. It was like her little cigarette case created them from thin air. She lit it from an oil lamp in the wall, and took a long drag. "We tend to get... overexcited. But at least it isn't musicians, I suppose. How will you get us into the company?"

"We've already spoken with the director," John replied. "Ex-money man. I don't think he got much further than the gold we offered him, to speak plain. They're expecting you in the morning." He clapped his hands. "See? All sorted!"

Hemmings noticed Ana and Melly looking at each other. Each seemed to be trying to out-glare the other, but neither was inclined to give voice to whatever was going on. And, frankly, he didn't care.

The play had been one of the most amazing experiences of his life – right up there with the first time he'd written his thoughts down in his journal and discovered that he could work them into something meaningful and, he hoped, one day helpful. The theatre had fanned that same spark. The way the story had unravelled in front of his eyes, the interactions of the actors, the atmosphere of the audience, the smell of the lamps, even the scratchy hay against his palms... it was spellbinding, thrilling, alive in the way an idea was alive, dancing behind his eyes as he tried to tame it. Except this was all playing out in real life, in front of him.

The next day couldn't come soon enough.

Melly helped herself to a glass of water from Ana's bedside table. She noted that her crown was on the dresser, by Ana's covered mirror. Strange that she'd forgotten it. It had been a gift from her husband, long ago. After he'd been taken, she'd worn it every day as a reminder of her choice to bow to the Teller. And to remind her of him and their life together.

Ana came through from the bathroom, brushing her teeth with a piece of frayed hazel and charcoal tooth powder. Black froth in the corners of her mouth. Like blood, Melly thought. Fae blood, at least.

"Come on, then. Let's hear it," Ana said around the stick.

"Hear what?"

Ana rolled her eyes. "Whatever it is that's got you upset about the theatre."

"It's a good plan. Clever, even. And I suspect you'll have Hemmings' eternal gratitude for it."

"And?"

"The story they were performing. It was one of ours. You remember the girl you found? The one who'd been tortured?"

Ana pulled the hazel from her mouth. "Yes."

"It was that story. Well, part of it, anyway. They'd made some changes. But the essence was the same. Stupid father, stupid girl, stupid hero. Hands cut off. Marriage. Blood and bone and, apparently, phallic vegetables."

She pinched her nose. Ana poured herself some water and rinsed her mouth.

"It worries me," Melly admitted. "The whole point of this is to stop those stories coming back. And now you're making them yourselves, and at the thin time."

"The whole point of this is to stop the Baron," Ana corrected, wiping her hand across her face. "The stories are a secondary concern. What's the thin time?"

"Spring. Specifically, the beginning of May."

"You mean Calan Mai?" Ana said. "It's just an old holiday. The whole of Ehinenden celebrates it. Feast and famine, fertility, the river swelling. It's just an excuse to get drunk, eat too much and, aha, sow some seeds for the winter."

"Yes, but it's also the time when belief is easier. The winter is old, and the summer is young. Absolutes. But the spring and the autumn... that's when things change. When you need to be damn sure your fields get planted right or else your harvest will fail. Beltain in the spring and Samhain in the winter-"

"You're in Caer Marllyn. Calan Mai and Calan Gaeaf, thank you."

"Fine. They're all the same, anyway. And they've always been good times for the fae. Humans are a bit more open to belief... to hope and fear, to stories and rituals. Certainty is thin, and the fae creep in. And trust me, if the fae ever do get their hands on this world again, you'll miss the Baron."

"Alright, fine. But what's this got to do with the play?"

"You saw how Hemmings reacted to it all?"

"Not really," Ana said. "He just followed you in and then spent the entire meeting staring goggle-eyed at everyone. It was a bit of a blessing, I thought – at least he didn't try to explain whatever it was he was thinking."

"He wasn't thinking. He's an elf, and you've just given him a group of actors at the thin time, and they're already doing an old story. It's a recipe for belief – the GenAm is bound to notice. And the mortal gods know how Hemmings will handle it. As a tribe, we've never been particularly good at denying ourselves, and we *loved* the arts, back in the day."

"Honestly? From what you've said, I think your GenAm has enough to deal with. They're clearly floundering – the fact Hemmings is even here shows as much. And while Hemmings is quite possibly the biggest berk I've ever met, one thing he didn't seem was cruel, which I guess is what you're so-very cryptically suggesting. Out of his depth, maybe. Self-important, certainly. But not cruel."

"Handsome though? Beautiful?"

"With that hair cut?"

"I'm being serious, Ana."

Ana shrugged. "Yes, of course I think he's beautiful. I've got eyes."

"Would you want to deny him? Hurt him, if you had to?"

Ana opened her mouth to reply, but she must have seen something in Melly's expression that made her pause. She frowned. "Nooo. But I wouldn't want to hurt anyone. I've spent my whole life trying to stop people getting hurt. That's not what you mean, though, is it? You mean *could* I hurt him? If I had to?"

Melly nodded.

"No," Ana said. "I don't think I could. It'd seem wrong, somehow. Like defacing a painting or burning a book. When he's not blabbing on, he's very... I don't know... you just want to look at him. You sort of want to make him happy."

"You see? That's the danger of the fae. We get into your heads, especially at the thin time, and once we're in it's almost impossible to get us out. Gods, we used to work on you as babies..."

"And what? You think Hemmings is going to take over the theatre company?" Ana laughed, shaking her head. "I can't exactly see him treading the boards with an over-sized marrow sewn onto the front of his trousers."

Melly laced her fingers together, stared at them.

"I don't know," she said in a small voice. "Maybe this play isn't anything. It's just... everyone keeps doing things without any idea what went before. Bea, you – even Joan's got herself mixed up in this fairies' rights group. And it's not that I disagree. The fairies have been treated appallingly since the King and Queen gave everything over to the Teller. Everyone has. Including you, and the other humans. But it works. In all the time the Teller's run the city, there've been no deaths, no hunts, no kidnappings." She flexed her hands. "No 'fun'."

The bed shifted. Ana had sat down next to her. "Do you think I'm under your elven spell?"

"I don't know. Maybe."

"You know what I felt when I first met you? Not wonder or amazement. Pity. I felt sorry for you."

Melly looked up.

"There you were, all kitted up in black, that stupid crown on your head, smoking like a chimney, and absolutely terrified," Ana continued. "Bea was on a mission to fix everything she'd messed up – as she bloody well should have been, frankly. But you? You just watched her, getting more and more afraid as she spilt the beans about what you both were, where you're from, the stories and all the rest of it. And then Bea nearly died, and you were crying, panicking. Do you remember? I told you to use magic, and the very first thing you said was, 'I'm not allowed'. And I pitied you. To be so afraid of losing your friend, and even then to be even more afraid of something else? I wasn't mesmerized by your beauty. I just wanted to slap you, to snap you out of it. Which, if you recall, I did."

Melly smiled.

"You said everyone keeps doing things," Ana said. "Maybe one of the things we all keep doing is changing – that's what Calan Mai is about now: change. Perhaps it isn't all going to be as bad as you think. We'll get Seven, and you can hand him over to your Teller, and then come back here and we can be together. We can stop the Baron together. Do good things together."

"Do you believe that?"

Ana put her arm around her, and Melly leaned into her.

"Sure? Why not? Also, by the way, you're not all that beautiful. I mean, yes, you've got that face and body and so on, but you stink like an ashtray most of the time and your hair's too long."

"I want to believe you," Melly said. "But you don't know the fae like I do. You don't know what we're capable of."

"I live with John, and I saw that girl," Ana said. "The one that was tortured."

"Yes. But we can do worse than that. Once... the King and Queen were fighting over a boy. A halfling child. The Queen was friends with his mother, who died. But really, it was just part of their game. The King and the Queen's, I mean. Things got out of hand."

"How out of hand?"

"The King had a servant, an imp called Robin Goodfellow. 'Mischievous' is the word they used, but I see now that he was vicious. He tricked people, drugged them... murdered them. He defiled a corpse, sewed an ass's head onto it and brought it to the Queen as a gift."

"That's disgusting."

"The Queen thought it was hysterical. She even tried to bring it back to life. We can't revive the dead, but elves can heal people, and after a fashion, it works. Worked well enough for them, then. What came back wasn't the same as a living person, but... She thought it was a wonderful addition to their game. Tit for tat. Sent the creature back amongst the humans, used it to interfere with the King's plans. And that was just one of their games. One of their stories. They ruled the fae for almost a hundred years, and they were married much longer than that."

Ana shook her head, scowling. "Alright. But I've never heard that story. It can't be-"

"Of course you haven't heard it! That's the whole point. The Teller put a stop to all that." Melly jumped up from the bed. Raked her hands through her hair. "Now do you see? It's not the Teller or the GenAm that scare me. It's us. The fae. The monsters we can become if we're given the chance."

She waited for Ana to snap at her, to tell her she was wrong. Even to hold her to her bargain. But instead, Ana got up from the bed and walked past Melly to her dresser.

To her crown.

She picked it up and turned it around, studying it.

Melly's breath caught in her throat. She stilled, her hands dropping to her sides. She'd said too much. She'd gone too far. Ana had worked it out. Uncovered her shameful past.

"But the Queen isn't here anymore," Ana said, looking up. "Now it's you, Melly. And you won't let that happen again. Nor would Hemmings. And Bea? Seriously? Can you see her doing anything like that – she'd turn herself inside out worrying about how it was all her fault before she even did the act. That's what I mean. I'm sure that there are fairies and elves and God knows what, who would still make mincemeat out of us if they could get away with it. I *know* there are. You keep forgetting I saw that dead girl, and I've got ten brain-dead women that we're looking after, probably for the rest of their lives. I know, Melly."

Melly's breath bottled in her chest, making her dizzy. A thick lump formed in her throat. She swallowed, trying to think what she could possibly say, how she could defend herself. But there was nothing. No way to justify what she had done.

Ana held Melly's gaze. And then she dropped the crown into the bin. It landed with a *thunk*.

"But there are also fairies and elves and whatnot like you," Ana said. "Ones who have empathy and understanding. You're not the same person you were. Leave her in the past where she belongs."

"Ana, I-"

"I know." Ana stepped forward and took Melly's hands. "It isn't easy. But as long as we're honest with each other, and understand who we both are, we can get through it – Hell, we might even win."

Melly didn't know what to say. Her stomach was still knotted; she desperately wanted a cigarette. Mortal gods, she wanted to run back to her cottage and lock all the doors and hide for another few hundred years.

But... she also wanted to stay. She wanted Ana to put her arms around her again. And she wanted to be honest.

"I love you," she said, gripping Ana's hands.

"Bloody hell," Ana replied, her face taking on the intense blank stare that meant she was laughing on the inside. "Really? Wow. You hid that so well. Oh my. I must have been under some elven spellcraft and not noticed the way you hung around the Palace months after John was healed, *and* took an interest in my work with the slavers, *and* then came to me when you needed help, *and-*"

Melly shut her up with a kiss.
And Ana, being Ana, responded with enthusiasm.

26

Night fell on Ænathlin, not even bothering to apologise for its clumsiness. Why should it? The city hardly noticed, anyway. Ænathlin had never been quiet at night; the nature of its business simply shifted.

During the day, the city moved to the rhythm of the markets and the Mirrors, fae of all tribes hustling and bustling through their tasks. The Fiction Management Executives travelled to and from Thaiana to run the Plots and generate the belief the Mirrors needed to function. Godmothers, witches, perils, companions, helpers and all the other roles the Teller had so carefully devised, all moving endlessly between the two worlds, running stories that ensured nothing ever really changed, for them or for their characters.

During the day, the markets and dragon dens, the pubs and the General Administration were all open for business. The covered market was the central hub of commerce. Step inside, and you would be set upon by hawkers and crafters, tailors and tinkers, bakers and butchers – or, at least, what passed for butchers in a city where meat was a meal few had the stomach – or the items to trade – for. Often, if the fae had meat at all, it was leathery hardtack that needed to be soaked for hours to make it even vaguely edible. Most rarely bothered, and hardly any missed it.

At night, the fae imported everything needed to keep the markets and, indeed, the city running.

The Mirrors, now charged – hopefully – with enough belief, were used to bring in whatever the fae could steal. Night and day ran to much the same time-frame in the Land as in Thaiana, and so the Contents Department sent the brown suits after dark to steal from the characters. Smaller tribes, usually, were given this responsibility. Disappearing through the Mirrors, they would sneak on soft feet or fly on small wings into the characters' houses, picking up as much as they could that wouldn't be noticed.

It was a tricky balance.

Ænathlin needed more than the thieves could ever provide, but if they took too much the characters would notice, and the belief would be jeopardised. Belief, as is well known, only really works when it's hidden in darkness, allowed to ferment in the unconscious parts of the mind; when it is brought into the light, it can be questioned, unpicked, unravelled. Torn and broken. And a whole village suddenly losing its livestock, or a barn being found empty, or a series of houses ransacked, would certainly raise questions.

Worse, though, if the characters realised what – or rather who – was responsible.

The fae could only maintain their precarious balance of the Plots, belief and theft when no one really thought they existed. Oh, the characters believed in the roles the fae created for them, and they would, hopefully, retell some of the stories they ran, but they never really considered that the fae were *real*. They was just part of the story, a rumour from far away, where people were stupid and credulous.

If the characters ever found out that they had been in a resource war for hundreds of years with an entire species, belief would very quickly turn to cold, hard logic.

Although, of course, this seemed to be happening anyway, as the characters grew ever more curious about their world. As they built cities and universities, as they met and spoke and shared ideas and experiences. As they developed their steam engines and mathematics, their art and culture. Less room for the fae and their story formulas.

But still, when the Mirrors were working reliably, Ænathlin did... better. Prices went down, and resources were, if not plentiful, then at least available. Thus, the night-time city was busy with the general rigmarole that accompanied importing. Items came through the Mirrors, were sorted and catalogued, and then sold on, the Grand and the area outside it transforming into a sea of auctions.

When the Mirrors weren't working, when only a handful of brown suits could make the raids, prices, inevitably, went up, dragging tribal tensions with them. The Land relied on the Mirrors.

And now, something terrible had happened.

The Princess And The Orrery

The Head Indexer, Agnes, looked at the shattered Mirror. There was glass and pieces of broken wood scattered all over the floor, almost as if someone had smashed the Mirror outwards.

"But how could this happen?" she asked. "No one would ever break a Mirror. It wasn't long ago they were fixing themselves, and now this. What in the five hells is going on? The Mirrors crack – they don't shatter. Was it just this one?"

"Yes, my Lady."

Agnes looked up from the shards of glass on the floor to the rows of broken Mirrors, all stored – supposedly safely – in the underground Indexical Department. There had to be hundreds of Mirrors down here, ranging from the smaller, more recent ones to the enormous, ancient Mirrors of old: the ones from back in the earliest chapters, before the first fae war.

The chief cataloguer shook her head. "Imagine if this happened at the-"

"Don't say it," Agnes interrupted. "Just don't. It's one Mirror – a small one, too. One of the weaker ones. We need to isolate what caused it to... what caused this," she finished weakly, not being able to bring herself to say the word 'explode'. "Get this bagged up and stored somewhere safe."

"Where's safe?"

"Mortal gods – just get it away from these other ones. I've got to work out what I'm going to say to her."

The chief cataloguer didn't bother asking who 'her' was. There was only one 'her' in the General Administration who could elicit that mixture of abject fear and bitter resentment: Julia, Head of the Redaction Department.

"Tell her the truth?" the chief cataloguer suggested.

"She won't like it."

"Make something up?"

Agnes glared at her colleague. Imagination was not a trait the Indexical Department prized. When you had countless Books to sort and shelve, Plots to record, and broken Mirrors to house, solid and precise thinking was the order of the day. No one wanted to get lost in the spiralling, labyrinthine Index because some fool had decided to get creative with the organisational system.

"Come on, we've got a long night ahead of us," Agnes said.

"Wait – did you hear that?"

"Hear what? We're the only ones here."

"I don't know... it sounded like a tree moving. You know, when the wind blows."

Agnes met this comment with the same level of enthusiasm as the suggestion about making something up. Grabbing her pile of folders, she marched off.

The chief cataloguer paused, ear cocked. Apparently hearing nothing else, she ran after Agnes, leaving the Mirror room behind.

On the floor, one of the shards, still attached to a piece of its wooden frame, twitched and jerked.

An eye appeared in the glass, yellow like bile. And then it was gone.

Stillness returned to the Index.

※

Screaming. The crackle of glass under his paws. The scent of fear, and the chase. The dead, everywhere. His brother amongst them. A river, stretching for millennia, its source lost to the darkness.

His master's voice...

Mistasinon's nose, sensitive as an exposed nerve, flooded his brain with hot, vibrant colour.

Anger, red; guilt, blue; fear, white; comfort, pale green; lust, violet...

He couldn't breathe. There was a vice around his chest, tightening. The colours were everywhere, a thousand clammy hands pressing against his skin, leaving sticky, sweaty trails behind them. Scents, muddled and confused, forced their way inside him, penetrating the dark, hidden spaces where the shadows still lived.

He wouldn't go back there...

He was broken...

His master would punish him...

He wouldn't want him, anyway...

His heart pounded in his chest, faster and faster. Scrambling from the bed, Mistasinon threw himself on his clothes and tore through his pockets, his head screaming. He grasped his salvation, but his hands were shaking, he couldn't undo the lid. He needed to calm down, to breathe – but if he did, he'd only invite the colours further in.

Biting his lips closed, he held his breath until his chest burned, and, somehow, managed to undo the bottle and upend the clear, oily liquid onto his handkerchief.

Cloth against his face. Deep breath.

A bright, hot whiteness exploded across his vision, different from the cold, hard colour of fear. This was like the scorch marks on the inside of his eyelids when he stared too long at a flame: it blinded him, erasing everything else into the bargain. The peppermint burned the tender skin around his lips and nose as he pressed the handkerchief to his face.

Breathe slowly.
Breathe slowly.
Breathe slowly.

The blinding light faded, taking the colours with it. The pain in his chest lessened. The sensation of being touched all over, inside and out, grew fainter until it was nothing but a shameful memory. He pulled the handkerchief from his face. Cracked open one eye, and then the other.

He was staring at a dirty ceiling. Where was he?

Risk a sniff.

Bea. He was in Bea's flat. He sat up, blinking.

"...just happened? Are you alright?" Bea was sitting next to him, her eyes wide in alarm. She was also stark naked, soft and round and beautiful.

He looked down at himself. Oh, no. He was naked, too. He pulled his legs up, trying to hide the hair on his chest and... oh, gods, lower down.

"I... can you pass me my shirt?"

She frowned but did as he asked. He dived into it, managing to pull it closed without revealing too much of himself. When he looked up, Bea had wrapped herself in her cloak and was again sitting on the floor next to him. Her green hair was sticking out at all angles, her cheeks flushed, dark grey eyes searching his face, her lower lip caught between her teeth.

"What happened?" she asked again.

"I... it's hard to explain."

"Are you alright?"

He didn't know what to say. How could he explain? There were no words, none, that would allow him to speak the truth without giving away what he really was. What she had allowed into her life, her home, her bed.

His stomach lurched, guilt and revulsion churning like rotten milk at the thought of his hands on her body, of being inside her, polluting her. He brought his handkerchief to his nose, eyes watering as the stinging menthol hit the back of his throat.

The light blinded him again, but not before he saw Bea's forehead crease. Revulsion? Anger?

"What's on the handkerchief?"

If he could have curled into a ball and shut her away, he would have. He made do with ducking his head. "P'perm'nt."

"Peppermint?"

He nodded.

Thumps and swishes as she got up. Clatters and bangs, odd sounds. What would she do now? Throw him out? He could manage that. As long as he didn't have to see the disgust solidify on her face as she realised what he was.

"Come on, head up."

He pulled his knees closer to his chest, ducking his head into the darkness. Always in the darkness...

A hand in his hair, gentle. Mistasinon's head moved of its own accord, the heat of shame cooled with compliance. Bea was sitting next to him, legs crossed. Her knee almost, but not quite, resting in the arch of his bent legs.

"Hi," she said.

"...hi."

"Try this." She passed him a strip of material, obviously quickly torn from something.

"What...?"

"Sniff it."

Gingerly, he brought it to his nose.

A warm summer day. Cool breeze on his skin. His shoulders slumped, the tension in his back giving way. The churning in his stomach eased. He pressed the strip of cloth to his face, taking a deeper breath.

"It's lavender, with a bit of rose. My mum used to wear it," Bea said. "Peppermint was a terrible idea. It excites the humours. There, is that better?"

He nodded.

"Honestly?"

He nodded again.

Bea's cloak had slipped, displaying an expanse of skin from her neck, across her shoulder and under her arm, the swell of her right breast, still covered, pressing against him, soft and warm. His throat caught. Violet blurred his vision, a dancing frame around his senses.

He pulled his gaze upwards, inhaling the lavender and rose. The violet faded, but did not disappear.

"Everything's alright," Bea said. "Deep breaths. Everything gets too loud, right? And then you feel like you're falling but not falling, all at the same time. Heart running too fast, head humming." Her hand brushed against the bare skin of his thigh, disturbing the fine hairs there. "I'll make us some tea, then you can tell me what happened."

No. She couldn't find out.

He jumped to his feet, one hand holding his shirt closed, the other grasping the cloth she'd given him to his face, offering him some cover. His skin felt like it was shrinking, pulling him inwards, crushing him.

"I have to go."

"What? It's barely morning – what's happening?"

He began pulling his trousers on, not daring to look at her.

"I... I need to go. It's not... I'm not..." *I'm not right. I'm not real. I don't belong here.* He snatched up his satchel, his throat working behind the cover of the cloth. "There's work to do at the GenAm. I have to go. I shouldn't have – I'm sorry."

And then he bolted, leaving Bea sitting on the floor, her pale skin flushed.

Mistasinon hurried out of Bea's building, head down, hand gripping the strap of his satchel.

"About bloody time," muttered the tompte. She was sitting on a jutting brick in the wall of a small alley opposite Bea's building. Still, she allowed herself a brief grin – as annoying as it was to have had to stand sentry all night, the fact she was watching him leave the fairy's apartment first thing in the morning was worth it. And from the look of his creased suit and unbuttoned waistcoat, the Plotter had had a busy few hours. Such violent delights! And she, too, would reap some reward from them.

She fished out her notebook and jotted down the time, just beneath the entries for Joan and a stocky, female dwarf with blonde curly hair and a ridiculously loud voice whom she couldn't, currently, put a name to.

The dwarf was an unexpected bonus that would garner her an extra token or two, in addition to what she expected in return for the news of the development in the Plotter and the fairy's relationship.

Whistling a merry tune, the tompte buzzed off on iridescent wings to meet with her liaison from the Redaction Department.

27

In a tent on the edge of Llanotterly, an argument was erupting. Christopher held up his hands in supplication. He'd been up since dawn, preparing himself for this meeting. In hindsight, he probably shouldn't have bothered going to bed.

"It's not selling out," he said, alarmed to hear the pleading note in his voice. He was the owner of the company, for God's sake. He coughed and set his tone to that of a man in control. Too late, he'd forgotten to rearrange his hands so they weren't literally begging Alfonso to calm down. "It's business. We need the money, Alf. Besides, don't you want to perform in front of the Baron?"

Alfonso glared at him. "You know I do! But at what price?"

"Twenty gold pieces, my lad. That's not to be sniffed at, is it?"

"Oh, and I suppose everything has a price, does it?"

"Well... yes? The tents, the horses, costumes, make-up, scribing, food, drink. Grandmothers' birthdays," he couldn't help adding.

Christopher tugged at the point of his beard, which he kept carefully oiled so it formed a triangle sitting upside down on his chin. He'd never really thought much about his face before buying the theatre company, but had realised soon enough that a short, fat man with a shiny complexion didn't exactly inspire respect in the artists he managed. They all seemed to think you had to dress in black skin-tight trousers and high-necked vests while smoking forty cigarettes a day to fully appreciate the arts – and the amount they drank! No wonder they'd been on the verge of bankruptcy.

He knew the cast still called him 'The Accountant' behind his back, and made little jokes about him using an abacus to try to count the 'art' in each line of dialogue. Mind you, they'd been happy enough to welcome him when he'd decided to buy the bloody troupe, and they never had a problem asking him for extra money to send home for their grandmothers' birthdays.

In fact, Christopher had one night given into type and done some arithmetic: He'd counted up how many grandmothers the company claimed to have, and had been gloomily unsurprised to learn that in a company of ten, there was somewhere in the region of thirty-seven. Alfonso seemed to have five, at the very least.

"And art? Dignity?" the actor demanded. "This play is dreadful. It's not at all what I meant we should be doing. If we perform this in front of the Baron and the nobility, we'll be a laughing stock."

"It's very popular," Christopher countered. "We've been selling out in every town and village. Word's spreading ahead of us. Don't you want us to be successful?"

Alfonso flopped down onto a hay bale. "I'm not trying to make trouble, you know," he said, his accent tumbling more than a few rungs down the social ladder. There was a definite twang of the farm that hadn't been there before. "When I suggested doing a traditional folktale, I thought it would be more artistic. Sensitive – the true lives of normal people. This is bawdiness, plain and simple." He sighed, shaking his head. "Bawdiness and crowns."

"Bawdiness and crowns sell. We've been packed out in the last three villages." Christopher turned beseechingly to Peter, the playwright, who so far had kept his silence. "Peter, can you talk some sense into him?"

"I don't expect so. I agree with him. The play's shite. And what are we supposed to do with a couple of Royal ninnies?"

"Bloody hell," Christopher said. "Not you as well. Look, I just don't see why art has to go hand in hand with poverty, that's all. Besides, I've taken the money. And I'm the owner, thank you very much. So it's done. Now come outside, because they'll be here any minute and I want to show the rest of the cast that we're of one mind."

Alfonso and Peter glared at him.

"Please?"

⚙

"Welcome, welcome!" Christopher said, bowing low to the two Royal ninnies.

They were both dressed in black, though the man's clothes were significantly more ornate than the woman's, except for the cap he wore, which was green check with yellow ribbing and was pulled down low over his ears. They both returned his bow, the woman with a slightly more measured calm than the man.

"Well met," she said. "My name is Melly. This is Hemmings."

"Charmed, charmed. I'm Christopher, the director and financier of this merry band. And this is Peter, our playwright-"

"Ah. So you write the stories?" Melly asked.

"Aye," Peter said, casting a glance at Alfonso. "When I'm given five minutes' peace."

Silence rolled out. Christopher tried to shove it back in again.

"Peter is an exceptional artist, m'lady. He's written all our most popular pieces."

"Has he indeed?"

"Er. Yes. And this is our leading man, Alfonso," he said, pushing the sandy-haired actor forward. "You probably saw him last night? Great talent and a wonderfully generous man. We're like a family here, m'lady."

Melly raised an eyebrow. "Oh? That bad?"

Christopher didn't get a chance to ask her what she meant. The other one, Hemmings, had dashed forward and was shaking Alfonso's hand with near manic vigour.

"I thought you were simply amazing," Hemmings said, his eyes alight in his pale face. "I've never seen anything like it. I've been thinking about it all night, especially the bit where the girl's hand was cut off. Hands could be seen as a metaphor for agency – which the girl didn't have, of course – but did the hero know the girl had no choice in the events that were unfolding, or do you think he was oblivious?"

Alfonso seemed momentarily at a loss. Christopher filed his startled expression away, to pull out the next time the actor was shouting at him.

"My character, the Prince, is only focused on breaking the spell," Alfonso said, rallying. "His super-objective is to release himself from the curse, so for him, the girl is just an additional reward for his suffering."

"Ah, yes, I see," Hemmings replied. "So, rather, you were aiming to recount the metaphorical difficulties the hero faces through the practical debasement of the heroine? She isn't a main character in his story, so he doesn't think about her?"

"Princes don't tend to think about the people they use, though, do they? It's the only part of the bloody thing that's accurate."

"Perhaps," Hemmings replied without, as far as Christopher could tell, any offence taken at Alfonso's impertinence. "It just seems like he ought to? Think about the girl, I mean, and what effect his story is having on her."

Alfonso's brow creased, his eyes darting over Hemmings' face and clothes. "Interesting that someone like you should see it like that."

"Why don't you take his Lordship to watch the rehearsals?" Christopher said, his cheeks aching with the effort of smiling. "I'm sure he'd rather enjoy the play than your, ah, commentary on it."

Alfonso, for once, followed his instruction without argument. Peter pulled his pipe out and began stuffing it with tobacco as the two men walked away. "Bloody brilliant. That'll be another rewrite on the cards, you mark my words."

The situation was escaping him, Christopher realised. In fact, it was probably well over the horizon, having purchased new identity documents and secured passage on one of the O&P steamer ships. He clapped his hands together. "Ah, the theatre, my Lady! Never a dull moment!"

"So I see. And what is my task to be?"

"Your task?"

"Yes, my task. What will you have me do?"

Christopher glanced at Peter, who shrugged his eyebrows and puffed on his pipe. There was no help there. "Well, my Lady, we rather thought you and the gentleman would prefer to, uh, observe and generally get a feel for the life from a distance. Somewhat of a distance, I mean. Distant but not, as it were, absent."

"Not at all, sir. I intend to be very involved. Myself and my companion must earn our keep."

"You must?"

"Absolutely. I insist on it. In fact, I'm also very interested in the play you're performing." She turned to Peter and, pulling out her own cigarette, begged a light off him. "What say you and I take a look at this story you're telling, sir? I'd love to know how you came upon it."

Peter took a puff.

Melly took a drag.

They stared at each other through the rising smoke while Christopher tried not to have a heart attack.

"Alright then," Peter said at last. "Best follow me. It's a bloody thankless task though, I'll tell you now."

The woman offered Christopher another quick bow and left with the playwright. Christopher stood in the morning sun, trying to work out whether that had gone better or worse than he expected.

When he finally turned around, the rest of the company were behind him. More than a few of them were trying not to laugh.

"Alright, alright. Show's over. Get that tent packed up. We've got four more towns before we reach Cerne Bralksteld. Come on, chop chop."

The company yawned, stretched, broke off into little groups for a chatter and a cup of strong tea, and then, finally, started breaking the set.

28

What a wonderful thing the theatre was! Five days had passed since Hemmings and Melly had joined the company, and they had been five of the best days of his life.

He'd watched the rehearsals, reading along with his own copy of the script, which he'd begged off the man in charge. He'd helped prompt the actors when they'd forgotten their lines, dashed around finding missing props, and even been asked to help backstage. How had he never known about the theatre? What had he been doing all his life?

And the humans – they were spectacular. So passionate and committed and fierce. They argued all the time when they weren't on stage, and yet the moment they stepped into the story everything else was forgotten. He could genuinely believe that Alfonso was in love with Beatrice, the woman playing the maiden, even though he had overheard him calling her a 'hack' and a 'scene stealer'. Yet, when they were acting together, it was like they had stepped into another world and somehow swept Hemmings along with them.

No matter how many times he watched them running through the same lines, each performance was better than the last. Beatrice might emphasise a line slightly differently, and Alfonso would change his reply to match it, or Alfonso would stand on a different part of the stage and Beatrice would change her blocking and somehow, with such a small difference, the meaning of the scene would change. It was like watching thoughtsmithing happen in real time, right in front of him. New avenues, new openings, new understandings, were constantly being revealed.

If all the world was a stage and all the people players upon it, Hemmings had spent his entire life the metaphysical equivalent of spear carrier number three: standing at the back, watching everyone else get on with it, distant and removed.

But not, he learnt on the fifth evening, unobserved.

The Princess And The Orrery

The actors had performed that afternoon in a village that was more mud than municipal, and the troupe were in a grumblesome mood. Melly had, like every day before, spent her time either working on the playwright to simplify the story – a task she was succeeding in, judging from the daily changes to the script – or holed away in the caravan they were sharing, filling it with her sickly smoke and bad temper.

Hemmings, consequently, found himself spending time with other people. He'd never minded Chokey's company, of course, and at the Academy he'd become very fond of Bea and her Plotter. But it was a strange thing to be surrounded by so many people and not feel out of place.

But tonight, tensions were high. The company had squeezed only a small bag of copper discs from the meagre audience, which Hemmings took to be a poor show, and they had outright refused to practice that evening on yet another new draft. The small stage had been dismantled in ill-disguised bad temper, the horses fed and watered as quickly as possible, and the whole thing packed up and moved along under a gloomy cloud.

The original plan had been to camp that night in the village before making their way westward towards a larger town – somewhere called Skraq, a name which sat uncomfortably on Hemmings' tongue. But such had been the company's ire over the lack of appreciation of their art, that they'd insisted on leaving there and then. So, they had settled their caravans and tents in a farmer's field, paying three of their precious metal coins for the loan of it and shelter for the horses overnight.

The horses, Hemmings was also learning, often ate and slept better than the humans. They certainly had more comforts than he did, a novel experience in itself. He was currently sitting away from the fire, watching the comings and goings of everyone. For all his new-found sociability, it was harder in the rare moments between performance and rehearsal, when there was nothing going on, nothing for him to do.

He pulled out his pocket watch and stared at the second hand as it ticked around the face, and wondered what Chokey was up to. She'd have known what to say when there was nothing that needed saying. She'd have pulled him into a conversation. Even when he made a fuss, she was always there to make sure he wasn't-

"Not what you're used to, I'll wager."

Hemmings snapped the watch closed. Alfonso was leaning on a prop spear a few feet away, a half-eaten apple in his other hand. It was the first time he'd spoken to Hemmings since their introduction.

"Do you want to play some cards? They're all too sour," Alfonso said, nodding at a nearby group of actors. He didn't wait for a reply, dropping the spear carelessly and then depositing himself on the earth in front of Hemmings. He shoved the apple between his teeth and pulled a deck of cards from his pocket.

"Ka'ff d'teeth?"

Hemmings took a moment to translate around the apple. "Catch the thief?"

"Yub. Sem a'po'at." Alfonso shifted the cards to one hand and pulled the apple from his mouth. "Yes. Seems appropriate. You know the rules?"

Hemmings nodded, an action that made him an immediate liar. But card games were card games – all Chokey's friends played them, so how hard could it be?

Alfonso grinned, and then expertly shuffled the cards with his free hand, flipping and splitting the deck as easily as he flipped and split between characters.

"A bet, to make it more interesting?" he asked, fanning the cards out on the dusty, uneven earth. "My Lord?"

"Ah... I um... I've got some brass buttons and a small bag of salt. Oh, and a half-weight of bone dust my mother gave me."

Alfonso stared at him, the apple halfway to his mouth. "Well... isn't that... mysterious. Bone dust, eh? I was thinking perhaps for coin or matches, at a pinch. Young King John didn't send you out into the wilds with a bag of gold, then, my Lord?"

"Why would I carry gold? It's not much use, too soft and heavy."

"Heh. Either that's the wisdom of wealth or the stupidity of it. We'll play for fun, then."

He dealt a hand for Hemmings and one for himself, and made a show of studying his cards. "So, my Lord, if you don't mind me asking, why did you and your Lady decide to join us?"

Hemmings dropped his cards. Flustered, he tried to pick them up and answer at the same time. Melly had instructed him what to say:

"King John wanted us to learn the ways of the small folk so as to be better able to advise him. He has sent many of our kind to study and to learn the ways of his subjects. King John wishes to be a kind and benevolent ruler."

"Ah. I see, my Lord. And that's why you spend all your time mouthing along with the lines and rushing around doing the backstage jobs, is it? Will you drop or draw?"

"Er. Drop?"

Alfonso shot him a smile unlike any other he'd seen. It made his stomach feel strange. Uneasy. The actor tapped one of his fallen cards and pulled it away. The remainder of his cards now back in his hands, Hemmings focused on the faded print. A few moments passed in silence as they studied their cards.

"The thief in four, my Lord," Alfonso said at last.

"Please don't keep calling me 'my Lord'."

"But the small folk must show their respect, my Lord," Alfonso said, laying a card down between them.

"All people should be equal. There is nothing inherently virtuous about being born into the right family. The ability to look beyond one's advantages is, indeed, the greatest advantage of all."

"Says someone born into the right family. Begging your pardon, my Lord."

"I was adopted, actually."

"Luck and advantage then?"

"I... yes, perhaps. It's hard sometimes to distinguish the two."

Alfonso dropped two more cards and drew another. "Thief in seven. What would you have me call you, my Lord?"

"My name?"

"Hemmings, isn't it? Strange name, if you'll forgive me. But I suppose you're a strange fellow... bone dust in your pockets, dressed all in black – except for that rather astonishing cap – travelling with a band of bawds. Gathering information. Learning the lines of the play. Rushing around to get us props and costumes. You've yet to drop or draw, my Lord."

Hemmings was thoroughly confused and fast realising he was out of his depth. The actor wanted something out of him, he sensed, but he had no idea what. And he was pretty sure he was losing the game. He picked up three cards, entirely unconvinced it was the right move when he didn't understand the rules.

"So you don't mean us any harm?" Alfonso asked, rearranging his cards.

Hemmings pulled back, shocked. "Of course not! Why would you think that?"

Alfonso shrugged and laid down another card. "A couple of swells joining a small-time band like ours with stories about learning the ways of the commoners? What are we supposed to think? Though, I myself wondered if you hadn't perhaps, ah, embarrassed your lady friend...?"

Hemmings took a moment to work out who he was talking about, but when the penny dropped it landed with a clatter. Melly. Of course.

"Oh. Well. Yes. She's often embarrassed by me, I think. We've not known each other very long, but she made it clear pretty quickly she'd rather I wasn't here."

Another long look from the actor met this statement. And then he sniggered. "You are an odd one. But it seems my guess was wrong as well. Perhaps you really are just here to learn the local colour. If anyone needed some help escaping their tower, I suspect it might be you, my Lord. Thief in one."

"I'm not trapped anywhere," Hemmings replied, shocked how much the statement irked him. "In fact, I've made it the focus of my life to ensure my freedom. While everyone else walks around with blinkers on, I see the world and understand it."

"Is that so?"

"Yes. It is."

"As you like. It just seems to me you haven't spent much time outside your castle, that's all." Alfonso handed him three cards. "You're enjoying the play, though?"

"Yes, actually."

"But you have more thoughts? Notes? I've seen you reading the script."

"Oh. Yes. Like I said, I think about things. Thinking makes sense of the world."

Hemmings had no idea why he'd said that, but Alfonso merely nodded. "Ahhh. I get that. Somewhere you can escape to, where no one can find you? Somewhere safe?"

"...Yes."

"But you're not in need of rescuing. Interesting." Alfonso picked up a card, smiled, and then fanned out his hand on the dirt. He had a run of numbers, one, two and three, and then five, six and seven. "Four's the thief and I win the game."

He stood and wiped his sandy hair back from his forehead. His eyes travelled over Hemmings', taking in his ornate black clothing, his expensive shoes with the silver buckles and his checked cap.

"Bone dust and bags of salt. What a character you are. Well, I'm off to bed. See you later, Sunshine."

With that, he returned to the fire, leaving Hemmings with a pile of scattered cards and thoughts to match.

29

Mistasinon waited outside Julia's door. He'd known he'd be invited to see her sooner or later. She never demanded his time – it was always an invitation, which he always accepted. The mortal gods knew how he'd have to respond if she ever dropped the courtesy, nor what she would do if he ever refused it.

Still, he could have done without it. Almost a week had passed since he'd run away from Bea's flat, and the guilt he felt at both his actions and the event that had precipitated them burned hot in his chest.

Maddeningly, his clothes still carried the faint smell of Bea's apartment, a soft undercurrent to the more demanding scents he'd picked up from his day-to-day tasks – tasks which, he could admit, might have taken him longer than strictly necessary, just so he could avoid sitting alone in his office.

The door opened, Julia's dead-headed goblin holding it for him, her large, saucer-shaped eyes staring at nothing. Julia was sitting at her desk, pale green fingers threaded together. Standing in front of her like a student brought in for a telling off was Agnes, the Head Indexer.

"Busy day?" Julia asked, taking in his unusually scruffy appearance. "I trust you managed to get the last of the apprenticeships organised?"

There was no point asking how she knew what was patently Plot Department business. He nodded.

"Good. We can make an announcement, food and drink, perhaps some Raconteurs. I'll have the Contents Department set it up. Show that the GenAm still has a firm hand on the pen. Something which I think we very much need, if I understand my Lady Indexer correctly."

Mistasinon came to attention. "The Mirrors?"

"*A* Mirror. But yes." Julia turned back to Agnes. "My Lady, will you explain the issue to my Lord?"

"My Lady, are you sure? It's very... sensitive."

"Just do it."

Mistasinon understood the Head Indexer's hesitation. It should be Deborah here, the Head of the Plot Department. But she was next to useless, and so Mistasinon had been allowed to join meetings which he wouldn't normally have attended, given his current status. The Heads of the other Departments had voiced concerns, which Julia had summarily dismissed.

Which meant that this had to be something particularly awful if Agnes had found the courage to question Julia.

Agnes turned to him, revealing a large notebook held close to her chest. He knew her to be kind, if a little anxious. A brownie, she was happier in the dark and took great satisfaction in being useful. The Index, buried deep underground, had been a good fit for her, and she'd quickly proven herself loyal and competent.

He remembered the day she'd been brought to the Teller's spire to meet the man himself. She wouldn't remember Mistasinon – or, he supposed, she didn't know it was him that she remembered. People rarely forgot meeting the Cerberus. Back then, the Teller had always ensured he met all his higher-level workers, and Mistasinon had always been at his side.

A lump formed in his throat, which he tried and failed to swallow.

Agnes leafed through her notebook until she found a sheet so covered in scribbles it was difficult to tell what colour it had been originally.

"We found a broken Mirror in the Index a few days ago," Agnes said. "Not cracked – shattered. Like it had exploded."

Icy fingers gripped his heart, freezing him into dumbstruck silence.

"Obviously, we need to know what happened," Agnes continued, apparently taking his silence for interest as opposed to sheer panic. "We know that, of course, the issue with the Mirrors is based on the problems related to affirming the consequent, that is, the fallacy that x, where x is belief, implies, or rather, creates y, in this case, y being the Mirrors, the pathways between worlds. That is, the idea that we'll end up with q if we use x to create y. However, that would need to be seen in terms of x implying y but not y, because we can't really state that y even exists based on the

F. D. Lee

existence of x. We could safely say that x is not q, of course, but I think we all agree on that point, anyway?"

"For the sake of the mortal gods, get to the point," Julia snapped.

Agnes paled. "I..."

Mistasinon somehow found his voice. "Perhaps you might try explaining it again? With a little less alphabet?"

"Ah. Yes. Of course," Agnes said. "Well, in terms of denying the antecedent, that is of course that the inverse is a fallacy, we might reasonably conclude, well, I *say* reasonably, but nothing is certain, that if we accept that the Mirrors rely on belief because they rely on magic, we might also accept that they rely on magic because they rely on belief. But in fact, it's rather like flavoured ice. It doesn't mean it's hot just because more flavoured ice is sold, does it?"

"No?" Mistasinon hazarded.

"Exactly. That kind of thinking leads to several false assumptions based on the nature of x when y is activated, that is, when the Mirrors are used. But then, given the intrinsic instability of y, it's hard to argue what exactly x implies. Possibly that there is, in fact, a w and not a q at all. Or everything is q, of course."

He replayed the brownie's words, trying to make sense of them. Something had to make sense, because if it didn't... If the Mirrors were exploding...

"So something else is affecting the Mirrors? Something new – 'w'? Or something old – 'q'?"

Agnes awarded him an appraising look. "So it seems."

Mistasinon could feel Julia's eyes boring into him. He didn't dare look at her. Instead, he said to Agnes, "New belief?"

"Possibly," Agnes answered, pulling a pencil from behind her ear and making notes on her already overcrowded page. "Or it could be nothing at all. The Mirrors have been cracking for years, perhaps this is just the next step in their degradation. I've had to work backwards, trying to piece it all together from what little evidence we have, which of course means that we need to account for the-"

Julia held her hand up. "Thank you, but I think myself and my Lord are a poor audience for your musings, my Lady. Perhaps we might speak as laypersons? Whatever caused the Mirror to explode, we have a serious problem. Agnes, I suggest you return to your colleagues and continue doing whatever you can to untangle this issue."

Agnes was up and out of the room in seconds, the sweet, apricot scent of relief trailing behind her. Julia left her desk to stand by the window, overlooking the square.

"Why didn't you tell me sooner?" Mistasinon asked.

Julia stared out of the window, her long blonde hair falling down her shoulders, her green hands clasped behind her back.

At last she spoke. "I wasn't sure, my Lord, whether you would *want* to know. You seem to have been... distracted... since your return from the Academy. Of course, I don't mean that as a criticism. You chose a life in the Plot Department, after all."

"Because I thought that was where I could be most use! The GenAm doesn't need another white suit – it needs someone paying attention to the Plots."

"Is that the only thing you've been paying attention to?" Julia asked, still staring out of the window.

"I, uh-"

"You're entitled to a life, my Lord. The mortal gods forbid I begrudge you that." She turned, so her face was in profile. "But do not expect me to wait on your convenience. Besides, you're here now. We need to know what this 'q' is. I was hoping you might apply your unique talents to the problem?"

She let the question hang in the air. *She must know already*, Mistasinon thought. *She knows everything.* So she was asking him to say it. Rubbing his nose in the mess he'd made of his short independence.

"No," he admitted. "I can't hunt anymore. My senses aren't... they're too erratic. Too weak. I didn't pick up on the Mirror exploding – something must have caused it, something I should have sensed."

Was that true? He thought back to the morning in Bea's apartment, when he had been so overwhelmed. He should correct his statement, shouldn't he? He rubbed his neck. Despite what he'd said to Bea, he felt it was very likely Julia had had a hand in Redacting the characters.

The thing was, if Julia had been involved in the fiasco with West and the Leithinate, she'd done it to help the city, to save the fae from losing the Mirrors and being plunged into the mortal gods alone knew what torment. If she had done it, she'd *had to* do it because he'd let the genie escape. Ultimately, everything came back to the choices he'd made.

But he hadn't wanted Bea to know that. So, he'd kept the thought to himself, not wanting to further muddy the waters between them, because he'd thought, hoped, deluded himself, that he might be able to... to be something else. Something better.

Julia was right. He had allowed himself to become distracted. His attention – his loyalties – divided. Another mistake in his never-ending tally of mistakes.

She turned to face him, leaning against the window. "A shame, my Lord. But we will find another way. Assuming you are now suitably focused on the problem at hand. How are you keeping?"

"Uh... well, thank you."

"You don't need to pretend. I know what you are, don't forget."

Mistasinon bit back a bitter laugh. Everything he was, was a pretence. "Yes. But I'm trying to-"

"Trying to be less than you are. I hope that, when you realise I'm right, you won't feel too ashamed to come to me, my Lord. My door will always be open, unlike some."

"What do you mean?"

"Just an observation, my Lord. The truth will come out sooner or later – not just about you. All of it. The Teller's death, the genies. When the time comes, you will need someone who understands exactly what you are. Who can help you. Now, tell me what you know about the Mirrors."

Mistasinon blinked, trying to keep up. His neck ached and his chest was still a stinging pin-cushion of adrenaline-spiked needles. He took a slow, deep breath, catching the faint scent of Bea's flat from his jacket. The sharpness in his chest softened a fraction.

"There isn't anything I haven't already told you. When I brought the first genie to the Teller, he tried wishing for more wishes. She died almost instantly – they have to service the wish or the magic gets them, the same as it does the fae. It just takes longer. The Teller was more careful with the next one. He understood the genies, my Lady, and belief, and stories. But I don't think he ever really understood the Mirrors."

"He didn't understand much, towards the end. Look what he did to you. Never mind, we'll just have to work with what we do know. You and I, my Lord – we are all this city has. We have to be strong. United. Like we once were."

"I don't think I can-"

"No, no. Please. No more whining and self-doubt. I understand what you've been through, Mistasinon. I see you. I always have. Even when you were the Beast, following at your master's heels. The Teller thought you were little more than an exaggerated guard dog. A thing on a leash that he could do whatever he wanted to."

"No. That's not – he cared about me."

Julia raised an eyebrow, but said nothing. She didn't need to. Even Mistasinon could hear the hollow tone of his voice. The doubt, creeping in. Bea had said something similar, hadn't she? That the Teller had used him ill... But what Julia said seemed different, somehow, though he couldn't quite work out how.

"The Teller did, uh, questionable things," he continued, unsure why he was saying it. "But he always told me it was because it was the only way. And he did care about me – he brought me in from the wilderness when no one else wanted me, when everyone was afraid of me. What is that, if it isn't love?"

"Perhaps the Teller did care for you, love you even, in his own way. He saw your talent, your potential, even if he did this-" she waved her hand, taking in his new body "-to you. But now he's dead, and you are what you are. I trust that you still want to avoid another civil war?"

There was no sympathy in her eyes, no confusing expectation. Just the honesty of her interest in him. She wanted nothing from him except that which he could give – to follow commands, and to keep the city safe.

"Of course I do."

"Excellent," Julia said. "This burden has fallen to us, and we must carry it. Oh, and my Lord?"

"Yes?"

"Tidy yourself up. I know how you like to keep yourself neat."

"I... Yes, my Lady. Of course."

Julia smiled.

"Good boy," she said.

Fortune may well favour the brave, but fate laughs in the face of the optimist. Sensible people planned; better people made more than one.

Julia stood in front of the cabinet in her office. She unlocked it and, ignoring the dozen or so jars of chalky, white liquid lined up on the shelves, a safety bar ensuring they wouldn't topple over, she opened a drawer, pulled out a file, and returned to her desk.

The file was fat, much like its real-life counterpart. She read over the information she had gathered on Buttercup 'Bea' Snowblossom. She had copies Bea's letters to the Plot Department, alternately begging and demanding to be given a chance to train as a godmother, and the Plot Bea had completed that had finally gained her a place at the Academy. She had two versions of this, the official one Mistasinon had entered into the Index, with all his little lies and amendments to protect the fairy, and the one she had pieced together herself from various reports, including those of the witchlein who had attacked the Ball.

Julia also had Bea's emergency contacts, written in Mistasinon's messy scrawl, from which she'd divined the names of Joan and Melly – a useful little titbit for some future purpose, she had no doubt. Next were Bea's class reports, none of which were favourable, and, finally, the various other bits of information she'd gathered from her networks. It was this last category that was most disappointing.

While she had amassed a decent amount of information on Bea's life in the city, there was nothing about her life beforehand. She'd learnt that Bea was from one of the nomadic fairy clans that infested the Sheltering Forest, but that was all. It was tiresome. Knowing where someone came from helped you work out their weakness, the best places to apply pressure.

Julia did know one thing, though. The cabbage fairy was vying for control of the Beast, and that simply wouldn't do.

The Princess And The Orrery

Still, the development with the Mirror could be a boon, if she managed it correctly. Uncertain times always called for a strong leader. But it would be easier with Mistasinon at her side. Even in his new form, he was strong, fast. And the label of the Beast would carry him far, even in his new shape. How he'd spent so many years at the Teller's side and yet learnt nothing about the importance of rumour and reputation was beyond her. The Teller, for all his dreary attempts at redemption towards the end had, at least, understood *that*.

Julia closed Bea's folder and turned her attention to the rows of bottles. The last remaining bottles of Letheinate, the Redaction drink West had devised, in existence. Yes. There might well be an opportunity to be found in the latest issue with the Mirrors, and if not... Well, she had options.

Hanging on the inside of the cupboard door was a white suit, cut to Mistasinon's measurements. She was beginning to wonder if she would ever see him wearing it.

Julia got up, returned Bea's folder to her cabinet, and pulled out another, much thinner one. Written neatly along the top was a single word: *'Edward'*.

She smiled. There was always a way to get what you wanted if you had the courage to do what was needed.

30

The first couple of days in the observatory were conducted in barely concealed animosity.

Seven did what Amelia instructed, speaking only when he needed clarification. But there was an undercurrent to their work which pervaded every word uttered between them. When the physical tasks were done, Amelia returned to her reading and Seven was left to his own devices, which mainly involved staring at the ceiling from his new bed or turning circles about the room. As long as he did nothing to disturb her, she was content to pretend he didn't exist.

On the second night, he was roused by a shock of pain, terrifyingly present and then quickly vanished. He sat up and wiped his hands across his face, the sheets sticking to his sweat-stained body. Movement caught his eye, and he spotted Amelia inside the orrery, a dimmed lantern appearing and disappearing as the planets moved. He pulled the pillow over his head and bit into it. When she did whatever she was doing to his piece of necklace again, he was ready for the pain.

By the middle of the week, her midnight tests no longer hurt him. This was not, however, a relief – at least, not psychologically. It signalled a change in his connection to his necklace. Soon, Seven found himself lying awake at night fretting rather than suffering. Amelia didn't seem to notice. She kept working on the orrery long after she bade him finish, and he doubted she was even aware he was awake almost as much as she was.

Still, despite this deeply alarming development, working on the orrery quickly became, to his surprise, tolerable. Amelia kept her promise and had him brought a table and drawing materials, and he was well-fed and watered. During the day, when she had no need of him, he practised his drawing. The atmosphere thawed somewhat. Amelia's instructions developed from snapped directives to more politely delivered sentences, and Seven found himself matching her newly forming civility.

Perhaps, Seven decided on the sixth day, his good fortune was returning. He could keep himself clean and even entertained, and the dull pain of Joseph's second wish never grew more insistent than a heat behind his eyes and, when he wasn't distracted enough to forget it, a heavy ache in his temples. More than that, while the danger of the orrery was ever present – hells, ever growing as they added more fiddly little parts or amended the ones already in place – he was at least in a position to keep abreast of it.

And he was recovering, slowly, from his months of neglect and separation from his necklace. The small piece in the orrery might be shifting its allegiance, but it was still enough to revive him from a shambling corpse to, at the very least, one capable of climbing the orrery without passing out from exhaustion. And as long as Amelia was content to leave him alone, he was more than happy to be ignored.

Which was why he was especially annoyed when, on the afternoon of the seventh day, a high-pitched voice interrupted his concentration.

"Who's that?"

Seven looked up from his drawing to find Amelia peering nosily over his shoulder. On the page was a charcoal sketch of a young man, handsome in a traditional sort of way, with a neat haircut and a rounded chin. He wore a white uniform with an ornate, brocaded collar. In real life, the collar had been gold, but Seven had shaded it carefully to give the appearance of deeper colour.

"No one," he said, pushing the drawing away. "I thought you were occupied? Researching your 'orrery'."

"Barry wanted to know what you were doing."

She moved to his left slightly. Seven shifted to block her view. Too late, he realised it was a feint. She slipped right, snatched up the drawing and jumped out of his reach, quick as any sneak-thief he'd ever met.

"It's very good," she said, studying it. "It looks like that King from Llanotterly."

Seven shot up and grabbed the drawing, scrunching it into a tight ball. "My drawing is none of your concern."

F. D. Lee

"Alright. No need to get worked up," Amelia said, nonplussed. "I was just paying you a compliment. Why were you drawing him, anyway?"

Seven glared down at her, his hands working the balled-up paper. "What interest is it of yours?"

"None. Barry wants to know." Barry stared at them from Amelia's desk, deciding to keep out of it. "Besides, if you're my assistant, I should know a bit more about you."

"And instead of continuing your questions as to where I am from or why I am blue, you choose to interrogate me over a drawing?"

"Well, yes. You chose to draw that King, John Edward of Llanotterly. That is who you drew, isn't it? Why did you draw him? Can you draw me?"

Seven realised he wasn't going to escape the conversation any more than he could escape the observatory. For a brief, mad moment he actually missed the tower. "Very well. Sit down."

Amelia ran back to her desk, grabbed Barry, and returned to Seven's workstation. She took a seat and settled Barry on her lap.

"I never met an artist before," she said as Seven began sketching. "My mum can sing, which I suppose is similar."

"Hfm." Seven didn't care for women who could sing, not anymore.

"So why did you draw King John?"

Seven didn't look up. "I knew him."

"Really? How?"

"We... worked together."

Amelia leaned forward – "Sit still, if you please" – and back again into her original pose. "Were you there when they had the attack? The one at the Ball last year?" she asked.

Seven gritted his teeth and bent closer over his drawing. "Yes."

"Did you meet the Adviser?"

"...Yes."

"You know he was the one who caused it?"

Seven's hand stilled. "Excuse me?"

"That's what I heard. He wanted the throne for himself."

Seven took a sharp intake of breath, like he'd cut himself unexpectedly. So, that was how the General Administration had covered their tracks. Blamed the whole thing on him. Blamed John's death at the hands of *their* ogre on him. Because Seven knew, logically, that John must have died from his injuries... Red blood smeared against the wall, and his body crumpled at the bottom of it...

Of course the General Administration would have lied. In truth, he didn't know why it shocked him. Nor why he felt suddenly so strange; why he had to press his lips together and stare, unseeing, at his drawing of Amelia. Why when he swallowed, it made his eyes burn.

A hand landed on his knee.

"I'm sorry," Amelia said. "I'm very good with sums and designs, but sometimes I don't say the right thing. 'Think before you speak', that's what everyone always used to tell me, back home."

"It is no matter. I simply did not know that is what happened."

"I shouldn't have reminded you. There're things I don't like to be reminded of, too," Amelia said, her voice low and quiet. She shook herself off and then, sounding more like her know-it-all self again, said, "You're very cold, you know? I mean, you feel cold. I'll ask one of the porters to bring you a jumper or something."

"Thank you, but there is no need. My temperature is simply an aspect of who I am."

"Oh. Well, if you say so. You did some good work today, by the way. Under my instruction, I mean. You're not as much of a bother as I thought you'd be. Did you know you're the only boy working here? And I'm the youngest Sister. That makes us quite special, really, doesn't it? How's the drawing?"

She uttered her last question with the guarded excitement of someone who didn't want to seem too eager, too invested. Someone who had been hurt, perhaps, and was fearful of history repeating. Hah. He knew what that was like.

The observation made Seven pause. The observatory was large, full of tools and materials and, of course, the hated orrery – but nothing else. No drawings of family, no mementos of a life outside. Only Amelia, and Barry, and now him.

He looked down at his sketch. He had been drawing her with rotten teeth and squinty eyes, spots and sores covering her face.

"Excuse me, I fear I made a mistake." He folded the paper and slipped it into his pocket. "Let me begin again."

Amelia settled back into her seat. For a while, the only sounds were the two of them breathing, the scritch-scratch of the charcoal, and the gentle whirring of the orrery.

Eventually, the drawing was complete. He passed it to Amelia. She looked at it, then at him, then at the picture again. A smile darted across her face, almost as if it didn't quite know what it was doing there. She jumped down from her seat, took the piece of paper over to her bed, and stuck it to the wooden headboard with a couple of pins.

Then she returned to her desk and her work. Later, when their dinner arrived, she chatted with him a bit about the orrery and the Cultivators. Casual, empty chatter. But he found himself responding, even asking questions and offering his own little bits of conversation. They even wished each other a good night, when they finally fell into their respective beds.

Seven's picture showed Amelia standing at one end of a large, boxy machine with giant cogs and a pipe emitting a vast amount of steam. A conveyor belt went into the machine on one side and came out the other. Amelia's hand was on her hip while the other cupped her chin, a quizzical look on her face. On her side of the machine, bottles of cream sat on the conveyor belt, while on the other side, ice-cream cones came out. Barry was on the ice-cream side, lying on the ground, his mouth open to catch the ice-creams as they fell from the belt.

The caption under the picture read '*Barry fails to communicate that the ice-cream machine is a success*'.

More days passed with gentle uneventfulness in the Observatory, testament to the newly formed peace between Seven and Amelia.

Not that it was something as trite as 'friendship' that sanded down the rough edges of his black mood. Absolutely not. Seven wasn't going to fall for that trick again. He had a plan, and that plan necessitated he gain her trust. And besides, the wish stopped him from performing any of his usual confidence tricks on her, which meant he *had* to allow himself a little amenability with the girl. But showing one's hand was not the same as throwing the game, nor a concession to the skill of the other player.

So the strange discomfort he felt when he rolled out of his bed in the morning to see Amelia already leaning over her books, Barry sitting next to her, was clearly nothing related to concern for her wellbeing. It was, if anything, concern for *himself*, he decided.

After all, if she worked too hard, the orrery might suffer, and then he might suffer. Who in all the five hells knew how Joseph's wish would manifest such an outcome? It could easily kill him for a failure on *her* behalf. That was obviously why he felt unaccountably fretful. Besides, unlike him, she'd chosen to be stuck here, working on the wretched device that now sprawled over nearly two-thirds of the generous floor space.

But still, he felt it... prudent... to query her obsessive timekeeping. So settled, Seven yawned and stretched, making a show of the actions so as not to make her jump, and then padded over to her desk.

"How long have you been working, my Lady?"

"A few hours, I think," she said, not bothering to lift her eyes from her notebook.

"Ah, so?" They had been up until the small hours the night before. "Are you not tired?"

"I don't really need a lot of sleep."

"Nonsense. All creatures need sleep, even I."

"You snore," Amelia said, at last looking up. "I couldn't sleep with you here, anyway."

"I most certainly do not snore."

"Yes, you do. Loudly, too. Huuurrrrnnnnnn huuuuurrrrrrn hurrrrrnnnnn. Just like that."

"I will have you know – oh. I see." Amelia was grinning at him. "You jest."

"Your face!" She burst out laughing. "You looked like a cat having its temperature taken!"

Seven turned to Barry. "Your mistress is exceedingly unkind, sir. I wonder – will you side with me against her?" He cocked his head, listening to an imagined reply from the bear. "What is this?

F. D. Lee

Oh, is it true? I cannot believe such a thing! She does? Burps the entire alphabet, even the 'zeds'?"

Amelia was clutching her sides, laughing so hard she wasn't even making any noise.

"You are quite right, good Barry," Seven continued. "It is indeed very unladylike behaviour. What shall we do about it? Oh no, we cannot do that. Eat all the breakfast? Tis too extreme a punishment."

"Wh-what? No! I'm – I'm – I'm-" But Amelia was laughing too much to speak.

Seven snatched Barry up and darted to the breakfast table, where their morning repast had already been laid out by a porter. He and Barry started snatching up pieces of fruit and pastries made with cinnamon and dark, bitter chocolate, which Seven then made a pantomime of feeding to the bear.

"I think that our Lady does not care for chocolate, anyway. Look how she prefers to toil at her notes than share these sweets with us. Ah, I thank you, Barry," Seven added, taking a pastry from Barry's proffered paw, held deftly in his own nimble blue fingers. He took a large bite, making a show of rubbing his taut stomach in appreciation.

"Mmmm, it is delicious. What luck no one else here wishes to cease their work and eat-"

Amelia, her breath coming in little gasps as she laughed, charged at him. "No! I want some! Barry! Barry! Don't listen to him – he's a snoring old fusspot!"

Seven held Barry and the pastry up high. "Such rudeness! Barry and I are shocked and appalled!"

Amelia jumped up and down, giggling, her hands outstretched. "C'mon Barry! Give me some!"

Seven twisted his grip so that it appeared that Barry had jumped out of his hands to Amelia, the chocolate pastry held in his paws. Amelia shoved the treat into her mouth and chomped, hugging Barry in her free arm.

"See? See? Barry knows who his best friend is," she said once she'd finished.

"Indeed he does." Seven helped himself to a peach. "To be outwitted by a bear! Never would I have predicted such an outcome."

"Barry's a very clever bear," Amelia conceded. "He always helps me with my work."

"And does your work often keep you awake at nights?"

"I suppose so. I dream a lot."

"About the orrery?"

"Mostly. I'm going to be like Naima, a brilliant Cultivator."

Seven made a calculated guess. He almost got it right.

"You are focused on your future, I see."

The mirth drained from Amelia's face. "I can hardly be a Cultivator if I don't work hard." She wiped the crumbs from her fingers. "So, let's get back to it."

31

"It's definitely not meant to look like that?" Joan asked the gathered fairies.

"I don't think so," said Tom, fluttering his wings nervously. He was a flower fairy, with purple and white wings and matching hair.

"Why is it so thin in the middle?" asked Jilly, also a flower fairy. Her wings and hair were bright yellow, like a daffodil.

"It's not very impressive, is it?" added Aida, who, like Joan, was a house fairy and so had no wings or pretty colours in her hair. She did, however, sport a rather large badge on her lapel, emblazoned with the words *'fairy rights are fae rights'*.

They all stared at the cake. It started well, they agreed. It was about four inches high and twelve across. The problem was that the centre of the cake, which was thin and brittle as a biscuit. The cake was not, they felt, going to embolden the citizenry of Ænathlin to join the cause of fairy equality and rise up against an unjust system which institutionalised the hatred of their various clans.

They were practising for the inaugural Fairies United community meet-and-greet, and so far, this was the best they'd managed.

"Tooth and nail," Joan said. "Can we try again?"

Jilly offered a quick stock take of their provisions. They were, unbelievably, in a worse state than the cake. "I don't think so. We can substitute the eggs and the butter easily enough, but we're out of flour."

"It's the oven, I think," said Joan. "Baking isn't like cooking. It's more precise. If something goes wrong with a stew, you can just add salt and spices and it'll come out alright."

"Maybe we could do that, then?" said Tom. "Offer people stew?"

Joan tugged at her hair. "The copiers have already started on the leaflets. I don't think we've got enough to trade for them to start again."

At this point, the cake was positively buoyant in comparison to the fairies' mood.

"How much is it to trade for flour, anyway?" Aida asked. "The Mirrors are working. Most of the time, anyway."

Over the winter, the city had enjoyed a boom in trade, thanks to the Mirrors finally working reliably. Recently, however, there had been a few issues with the giant glass doorways between worlds. None had broken, but rumour was there had been some near misses.

These seemed to mostly involve Fiction Management Executives getting stuck on the wrong side because the Mirrors in the Grand Reflection Station couldn't make a stable connection. It wasn't a problem compared to the Mirrors cracking, but it had resulted in a few 'Happy Ever After' stories suddenly needing to account for the witch and the godmother being found hiding in a cellar long after the wedding.

Normally the GenAm would manage such minor problems, but, coupled with the public fiasco at the Academy, prices were creeping up again. No one was hoarding, not yet, not again. But a handful of months of easy living didn't wash away the memory of what had gone before.

Joan, who thought she knew exactly why the Mirrors were having difficulty and how it was connected to the scandal of the Academy closing, tried not to let it show on her face.

"It'll be fine," she said. "We're Fairies United! There's nothing we can't do, is there? Look how far we've come already! A year ago, we'd have been glaring at each other across a Contents Department waiting room, blaming each other for the fact no one takes fairies seriously. Now we're solving the problem, together. What's a flat cake compared to that?"

The other three fairies allowed themselves to be cheered up.

"I've got a button and some string we can trade for flour," said Tom. "I was going to use it to fix the blinds in my lodgings, but that can wait."

"And I know a baker in the covered market," said Jilly. "He might give us a discount if we take some of the older stuff. We can always pick the weevils out."

"Or we could keep them in," Aida replied. "There's plenty who'd be grateful for a bit of extra protein."

"There, see?" Joan grinned at her comrades. "Nothing can keep us down if we work together. Besides, I'm sure that-"

Just then, her youngest and stickiest sister, Mags, burst into the kitchen, dragging Bea behind her.

"See? I said they weren't doing anything important," Mags announced. "If I was in charge of the fairy revolution, I'd have flags and barricades and songs and all sorts of stuff like that. Whoever heard of changing the world with cakes?"

"Oh, shove off, Mags," Joan snapped, making a dive for her sister, which Mags deftly avoided. "We're engaged in a systematic redefinition of the rights of fairies, not some, some, some stupid theatrics!"

Mags ran to the door, blew a raspberry at her sister and then launched into the song she'd been working on: "Do you hear the fairies sing? Singing the song of angry-"

She just managed to slam the door closed before the wooden spoon Joan had hurled at her made contact.

"Honestly, that girl! I'd wring her neck if she wasn't so bloody squirmy! Anyway. Yes. Hi, Bea. How're things?"

Bea offered her a smile. "Oh, you know. Same as always. Sorry I'm late. How's the cake?"

They all looked at it.

"Oh," Bea said. "Well, you know, these things can be tricky. I've got a recipe for carrot cake at home if that helps?"

Joan smiled at her. She couldn't shake the feeling that there was something wrong. Bea had been hugely active in F.U. since she returned from the Academy, but the last few days she'd been turning up late and generally distracted.

She'd hoped Bea might volunteer what was troubling her, but so far, she'd just been pretending everything was fine. A good friend, Joan thought, would continue waiting to be told what was up. But a good *detective* would try to get to the root of the mystery, and Joan had always wanted to be a detective. It was time, she decided, for a change in strategy.

"Alright, let's leave it for today and come back tomorrow," she said to the other three fairies. "I'll see what I can do about this oven in the meantime."

Five minutes later and the kitchen belonged to her, Bea, and the cake.

"Right then," Joan said, ushering Bea into a seat. "What happened the other night?"

"What other night?" Bea asked, taking on a look of such innocence Joan was positive she knew exactly what she was referring to.

"With Mistasinon, at your flat."

"Oh. Right. I don't want to talk about it," Bea said in the tone of voice of someone who did, in fact, want to talk about it very much.

"But he, ahem, stayed the night?" Joan asked, sitting opposite her. "You know... *Stay* stayed the night?"

"Yes, I know what you meant. And yes, he did."

"And you had a good time?"

"Yeeees," Bea said. "It was nice. No, not nice. It was... good."

Joan watched as her friend miserably ate a chunk of cake. If she hadn't been sure before that Bea was feeling depressed, that confirmed it.

"'Nice' and 'good' weren't exactly the updates I was hoping for," she said gently.

"I'm sorry, Joan. I'll try to do it better next time, just for you," Bea muttered, picking up another bit of cake and chewing it with some effort.

Joan grinned. "So, you want there to be a next time?"

A smile fluttered across Bea's face. She put down the cake. "Yes, alright. You've got me. I don't know; maybe, maybe not. I told him if he wanted to leave, I wouldn't chase after him... but that was before. Urgh. It's too bloody complicated."

"Well, what do you want?"

Bea, clearly determined to end it all, broke off another bit of cake, this time from the biscuity middle. It snapped.

"I think I'd like to see him again," she said, nibbling. "I don't think he knows what he wants."

"He definitely likes you, Bea. It's been obvious from the start."

"He works for the GenAm. How can I possibly have any kind of relationship with someone who does that?"

Bea dropped the cake back onto the plate and leaned back, staring at the wall. "I know you work for them, too, before you say it. But I also know you wouldn't if you didn't have to. And Hemmings would definitely prefer to do his thoughtsmithing, but his family have other ideas, and Melly's always been... well, Melly's always been a bit odd when it comes to the GenAm, admittedly, but I'm sure she wouldn't be a witch if she didn't have to be. But I think Mistasinon actually *likes* working for the GenAm. We had a row about it, at the Academy. I think he sees the GenAm as the solution, not the problem."

Joan reached over and put her hand over Bea's. "Lots of people do, though."

"But most people don't know what the GenAm are capable of," Bea replied, a sharp edge entering her voice. "He does."

Joan got up and wrapped her arms around her friend. "Oh, Bea. I'm sure it's not like that."

Bea hugged her back, but it was half-hearted. "I think he'll always choose the GenAm. He hides things, you know? Not just from me, but from himself. And the GenAm... the things they did to him, and he just ran back to them instead of trusting me, after everything that happened at the Academy. How can he possibly still think they're the answer?"

Joan pulled back, studying her friend's face. "What did the GenAm to do him?"

"Oh. You know. The usual, I suppose. It's not important."

"You know you can tell me anything, don't you?" Joan tried not to sound hurt. "We've been friends for years, haven't we? When have I ever let you down?"

For the first time since she arrived, Bea gave Joan a genuine smile. "I know. It's just... it's nothing. I shouldn't have mentioned it. I'm just cross, I suppose. And my pride's taken a beating. It'll pass."

Joan wasn't at all convinced it was nothing, but aside from torture, she didn't see what she could do to make Bea tell her. Besides, she was already eating the cake voluntarily – there wasn't much else Joan could threaten her with. But she couldn't deny that it stung that Bea wouldn't tell her what was going on.

"What's this?" Bea asked, picking up a sheet of paper. It was a high-quality print of a raised fist, with the slogan '*Ænathlin Again*' printed across the top and, lower down, '*Making our city great again.*'

"Oh. They're turning up all over the centre, haven't you seen them?"

"No." Bea took a closer look. "Whoever made them has a lot to trade, that's for sure – look at the quality of that paper."

Joan nodded, leaning across the table to pick up another of the Ænathlin Again flyers.

"It's a reaction to Fairies United. I'm not sure who's behind it, but they're definitely well organised. They've already got some kind of protest lined up for the day of our community meeting. I went to the Contents Department to see if they knew about it, but I got shut down pretty quickly."

Bea rolled her eyes. "Of course there'd be a protest group. Mortal gods, you'd think we wanted to take over the city and smash all the Mirrors. Mind you," she added with a wink, "If this cake's anything to go by, they might be right to think we've got plans to bring down the city."

Joan punched her on the arm. The two fairies spent the rest of the day trying to bake a flourless cake, with alarming results. Bea seemed a bit more her old self, Joan thought, but there was definitely a shadow hanging around her, one that had been there since she'd returned from the Academy.

32

The troupe had performed four more times since Hemmings' strange encounter with the lead actor, Alfonso. Since then, they'd got into the habit of chatting between rehearsals, always about the play – no more odd little games of cards, which was, of course, a very good thing and not at all the reason why Hemmings felt like he might jump out of his skin every time the actor opened his mouth.

The play had changed again; Melly's influence, no doubt. Hemmings tried not to be annoyed by it, but it was difficult. The characters – the ones in the play, not the humans who played them – were becoming so simple, it was a miracle there was any story left. And yet, the story was successful even so. It was depressing. Hemmings contented himself with thoughtsmithing and scrawling notes on his copy of the script.

Alfonso came off the stage and flopped down next to him.

"What did you think, Sunshine? I think my character is getting worse. And I could have hit the line about my due and just reward better. Do you think I could have hit it better? I think I could have hit it better."

Hemmings went to rearrange his itchy cap, only just remembering in time that he risked revealing his ears. Melly was lucky: her hair was thick enough to easily hide her long, pointed ears. He and Melly were like Alfonso, weren't they? Playing a role. He had to remember his motivation. Melly had been very clear about that. But that didn't mean that his character couldn't be the kind of person who wanted to help others think more clearly, did it?

If Hemmings had ever heard the expression 'casting to type', he probably would have thought it had something to do with metal work.

"You did it very well. It's not you that's the problem," he said, checking his notes. "Your character doesn't *do* anything, not really."

Alfonso shrugged. "He's the hero. He wins the girl."

"Yes, but there should be more to him than that. There's no sense that your character is trapped in a situation outside of his control, torn between his desire to have the curse lifted and his fear of intimacy – he wants to be part of the world, but he doesn't know how to be. The curse ought to be a sign of that, somehow. We should be asking the audience to wonder what caused these fears in the first place. You shouldn't just have people going through the Plot – that is, I mean, the play – without any real reason for doing what they're doing."

Alfonso pulled out his pouch of tobacco and began rolling a cigarette. He had a narrow face, quite plain underneath all the make-up. But when he was on stage, he could twist his features into all kinds of emotions, like he was drawing experiences up from a well inside him.

Hemmings had practised making faces in the small looking glass in his and Melly's caravan, but he hadn't been nearly half as good. And then Melly had caught him and given him one of her sharp looks and taken the mirror away.

The actor lit his cigarette, blew out a stream of smoke, and then chuckled to himself.

"You're right," he said. "He is afraid. The hero grew up in a castle, surrounded by everything he'd ever wanted. He never had to try for anything, it was all given to him. So when it was taken away by the curse, he had no resources. No experience. And then he meets the maiden, and she's used to working hard and sacrificing, and he loves her but he's afraid. It's easier for him to push her away."

Hemmings nodded. "To lose something through one's own doing is a bitter thing – much better to lose it through inaction and avoid the blame. I say, where's Beatrice?"

"Oh, God. Really?"

"Yes. We need to discuss this with her as well. In fact, we should speak to everyone." Hemmings climbed up onto a hay bale and clapped his hands. The cast turned astonished faces to him. "Everyone, let's take a moment to think about the message of our characters. What is that they want? Who are they, in the secret parts of their minds?"

The cast glanced at one another. No one moved.

Slowly, a chubby woman who was playing the maiden's mother in scenes six and ten raised her hand. "Er. I think my character is worried that her daughter's just had her hand cut off and been taken away by a stranger?"

Hemmings awarded her an encouraging smile, forgetting the way it made his scars crinkle. "Excellent, Chloe. Yes. But why do you think she's worried?"

"Er. Because you would be, wouldn't you?"

Alfonso flicked his cigarette. "You might, but I think the point is you have to decide why your character cares."

Chloe shot him a murderous look. "Fine, then. Well, my character only has one child, right? So maybe she was trying for years to have a baby. Maybe she lost some. How's that?"

Hemmings jumped down from the hay bale and bounded over to her. "How does she feel about her husband bargaining her only daughter away to a stranger? That his actions caused her daughter to have her hand cut off?"

"Well... I think she would be pretty angry. But she doesn't show it in the lines... she's frightened of her husband, maybe? I know! She married him when she was very young and didn't know any better, and now she's stuck in the marriage and she can see the same thing happening to her daughter, but she can't stop it?"

"Wonderful," Hemmings beamed. "Perfect. Now, uh, Alwyn, how does the father feel about all this? Does he know his wife is angry with him? That she feels trapped? Or is he oblivious?"

Alwyn looked panicked. "Look, I only joined up to get out of a, ah, difficult situation back home. I'm barely in the bloody thing."

"But the scenes you are in are crucial – the moment when you make the bargain with the old man on the side of the road, that's when everything begins." Hemmings clutched his script to his chest, eyes screwed shut. "You say to him 'Good morrow, kind sir, and wherefore art thou wandering this lonely road? For in truth I am lost and in dire need of assistance – canst thou be the one to aid me?' and the whole thing begins. Why would you ask for help – how does that make you feel? And then to discover that you've been tricked, that your wife hates you, that you've got it all wrong..."

The Princess And The Orrery

He opened his eyes. The whole cast, Alfonso included, was staring at him. Silence reigned.

Hemmings felt his cheeks growing hot. He coughed. "I just mean, every character is important. You all make the story."

Alfonso came and flung an arm around his shoulders. Hemmings tried not to squirm.

"He's right," Alfonso said. "By God, he's right. We are the tellers of truths! This is what the theatre should be – emotion and character – real stories. Not fart jokes and hackneyed, one-note portrayals. No, Beatrice, don't make that face. I'm talking about all of us. We have to be brave enough to really dig into the characters we're portraying, to find their essential truth." He turned to Hemmings. "What should we do now?"

Hemmings thought about everything he'd learnt about running Plots and character archetypes and how the stories had to be told in exactly the same way, over and over again.

And then he decided to do the exact opposite.

"I think you should all get into pairs and decide on a pivotal moment for your characters, a point in their lives that helped make them who they are, and then act it out. No lines. Just... see where the character takes you. And then decide why that happened. What can you learn from them?"

There was some muttering, and then, miraculously, they all started pairing off. The little grove filled with the murmur of intense conversation.

Alfonso grabbed Hemmings' arm and hooked it through his own. "You're coming with me."

"What? But-"

"No buts. We need to speak to the Accountant, right now. Chloe, darling, be a dear and ask Peter to meet us in Christopher's!"

"Oh God." Christopher's face fell as Alfonso barged into his caravan, dragging Hemmings behind him. "How much is this going to cost me?"

F. D. Lee

"Nothing at all," Alfonso said. "But we need to change the play."

"Absolutely not. No. We're performing it in front of the bloody Baron of bloody Cerne bloody Bralksteld in three days! No, Alf. That's my final word on it."

"Just hear me out," Alfonso said. "Hemmings has some wonderful insights into the characters, he's got the whole company reworking them right now-"

"He's done what?!"

Hemmings cringed, but Alfonso didn't seem at all bothered by his manager's increasingly red face.

"Yes, yes, and I think we need to be prepared to work with what they uncover. Just think about it – Ah, Peter! Excellent. Now, just listen to what I have to say, will you?"

Peter trudged up the stairs, Melly behind him. He looked exhausted. He pulled out a chair and slumped down. "What now?"

"The play, of course!"

"Not you as well. I've had it in my ear for days from this one," Peter snapped, waving a thumb in Melly's direction. Hemmings' stomach dropped.

"Yes, the play!" Alfonso answered. "Of course the play! The play's the thing where we'll catch the conscience of the Baron." He paused a moment, looking annoyed. "Damn, I thought that might scan better. Never mind. Don't you see? We have to make it real. We have to show the Baron something he won't ever have seen before, make him think. Peter, didn't you want to do something that would highlight the plight of the slaves?"

"Have you lost your mind?" Christopher roared. He was now almost entirely puce. "Do you want us thrown into the manufactories?"

"Aye," Peter answered Alfonso, glancing at Melly with the look of a man thoroughly harangued. "But apparently stories have to be simple. Predictable. Easy."

"Predictable?" Alfonso replied. "Nonsense! They have to be real, don't you see? Not all this bawdiness and fairies and angels and God knows what coming in at the end and fixing it all. Hemmings is right, it has to be about the characters. About who they are and why they are."

Melly narrowed her eyes. "Hemmings, what exactly have you been doing?"

"Helping us, that's what," Alfonso said.

Melly turned her green gaze on the actor.

Hemmings couldn't breathe. This was worse than the time Chokey had tried to get him to read his poetry aloud at one of their parents' parties.

"Go on," Melly said, her voice ominously flat.

"We need to use the theatre to tell people the stories of their lives," Alfonso said, holding his ground against the heat of her glare. "People have to see themselves in the plays. We can still have Kings and maidens and magic and all that – I'm not mad – but we need to make sure that each and every one of them is real. People have to believe in the characters even if the story is fantastical. Isn't that right, Hemmings?"

Hemmings could hear the blood rushing in his ears. Melly was going to kill him. And then his mother would make a scene, and he'd die of embarrassment all over again.

But... the theatre... the possibilities. The things these humans could do. The truths they could explore, all within the safety of a story. It was the exact opposite of everything the GenAm taught, but then, the GenAm's stories weren't working anyway, so why not try something else?

Thoughtsmithing, but happening in real life on a stage, showing all the different possibilities from behind the artifice of greasepaint and cheap costumery.

He straightened his back and met Melly's glare.

"Yes. It is right. There's so much that can be done. It's like magic."

"Magic?" Melly's voice was like chipped ice. "And what do you know about magic? You stupid child. You have no idea what you're talking about."

Peter lowered his eyes. Christopher looked like he was about to have a heart attack. Even Alfonso seemed taken aback.

"Yes, I do," Hemmings said. He had no idea where the words were coming from. "I've spent my whole life thinking about things. What have you done? Just gone along with it all, from what I can gather."

"Oh, really?"

"Things have to change. The tree has to grow."

"I see," Melly said, her jaw tight. "Aren't I lucky to have you here to enlighten me."

The three humans caught each other's eyes and slowly started inching towards the exit. The subtlety of it was ruined somewhat by Christopher trying to squeeze between Melly and Hemmings, his head ducked below their furious glaring like a thief trying to avoid a tripwire.

"And how many times have you been in Thaiana?" Melly continued once the humans had slipped out. "How many characters have you met?"

"Humans," Hemming corrected. "And it doesn't matter. I know what I'm saying is right."

Melly threw her hands up in the air. "Mortal gods. Put an elf in a theatre and see what you get? Do you think I haven't seen you and that, that fop making eyes at each other? That'll end in tears, mark my words."

"I'm not making eyes at anyone, and even if I were how is it any different from you and Ana? I'm not stupid – there's obviously something going on between you both."

Melly stilled, her eyes narrowing to sharp flecks of emerald. Hemmings was reminded why she was so perfectly cast as a witch. If he hadn't known better, he would have sworn she was hexing him that very moment.

"Ana's different. She knows what we are. She's seen how dangerous we can be. And I know how dangerous they can be to us. I've made my mistakes with the humans, I know what it's like to inspire them and bespell them and bathe in their awe and their love, and it never ends well. If you really want to help these people, the best thing you can do is leave them alone. What do you think will happen if the GenAm gets wind of this?"

Hemmings faltered. "Why would the GenAm care?"

"Because you're interfering, that's why! You're basically trying to run an unsanctioned Plot. That's a Redaction, right there. Bloody hells – all you children, running around with no sense of the past, no idea what you're doing."

"But I can help them make it better. So can you. I'm not saying we should write the story for them. I just think I can help, with my thoughtsmithing."

Melly closed the space between them, so her face was barely inches from Hemmings'.

"No. We're here to get the genie, or have you forgotten? The whole of Ænathlin's safety rests on our shoulders. What do you think will happen to your sister and your – *our* – friends if the Mirrors stop working permanently? Do you think they'll thank you for helping a handful of actors tell a better story? I won't have you drawing the GenAm's attention to us. Is that clear?"

Hemmings held her gaze for all of a second. And then he dropped his eyes and nodded.

"Clear," he said.

33

While Hemmings might have understood what was being asked of him, Mistasinon was completely in the dark. His feet tap-tapped against the stone steps as he descended into the Index, his breath forming little clouds as the air grew colder.

He tried not to think of his previous life, alone in the blackness with only the passing dead for company. He hated the Index. Not for what it represented – it was the embodiment of the Teller's order, his vision for the fae and the stories. His kindness. Without all the Books, safely stored in long aisles that spiderwebbed out from the spiral staircase, the Land of the Fae would have never survived as long as it had.

No, he hated the Index because it reminded him of everything he'd lost whilst, perversely, representing everything he longed to forget.

The note from Agnes, the Chief Indexer, was clutched in his hand. He took a careful sniff of the air, came off the staircase, and followed one of the identical aisles running off the landing, past high shelves stacked with Books. Eventually, he reached her office door. He shoved the note into his satchel and knocked.

It opened a crack, revealing a thin slice of Agnes' face. She looked him up and down and then glanced at the long corridor behind him. Satisfied he was alone, she opened the door just wide enough for him to enter, closed it quickly, and bolted it. Next, she went to a string attached to a small bell hanging from the wall and pulled it tight, tying it off on a hook.

"A precaution," she said, seeing his curiosity. "This string runs down the aisle and, about halfway along, crosses it. If someone comes, they'll trip the string and this bell will ring."

"Ah. Yes. Very clever."

"Necessary, not clever. They'll know they tripped it, but it will give us some time to prepare."

Mistasinon wasn't entirely sure what she meant by that, but he did note the long knife in her belt and the sheen to her brow. His

The Princess And The Orrery

grip on the strap of his bag tightened. "You said you wanted to talk about the Mirrors?"

Agnes' mouth drew into a thin line. "Need to, not want. You and Julia are very close."

The implication hung in the air. Mistasinon thought about how to answer. He could understand Agnes' fear of speaking out of turn to someone she didn't know she could trust. But equally, she obviously did want to talk to him.

"Julia is... she's part of the GenAm. The Teller, *whocaresaboutus*, promoted her himself. She wants what we all want. But I wouldn't say we're close, exactly."

"Why does she include you in everything, then?"

He could lie. Every day, he lied to the people around him. What was he, in fact, but a walking, talking lie? But he'd made a promise to be better. To try to make up for his past. To keep everyone safe.

Whether, at that moment, it was his promise to Bea or his promise to the Teller that motivated him was impossible to say. Either way, he opted for the truth. Or the closest approximation of it he'd yet come to, anyway.

"I used to work with her. But the Teller, *whocaresaboutus*, gave me a choice, and I chose to move to the Plotters. I'm loyal to the GenAm and the city. But if you don't trust me, I understand. You've not said or done anything that I would consider, um, suspicious." He offered her a smile, sweet as summer rain. "I know you're a good person. I can leave now, there's no harm done."

A minute passed, Agnes worrying her lower lip with her teeth.

"No, it's fine," she decided. "You've been good at the meetings. Tempered a lot of things that would have gone too far, otherwise. Besides, I'll have to tell Julia you've been here. It's better to tell her yourself than have her find out. I just wanted to know what to make of you before I say more."

He nodded. "Of course. How can I help?"

"We've been looking into the shattered Mirror. Reviewing the more recent Plots and some of the classified histories."

"Have you found anything?"

"Yes and no." Agnes moved to her desk. Neat piles of paper were laid out like battlements, numbers and letters filling them in a code he couldn't begin to fathom. "As I said before, the problem is the consequent. We assumed a correlation, but it's more complicated than that. Over the winter, we had some success with the Plots, a surge in belief."

"I know," Mistasinon said, remembering the woodshed at the Academy and the cage full of empty-eyed, smiling women.

"Ah, but do you know that the Mirrors began repairing themselves?"

"That's impossible. The Mirrors haven't been repaired in over two years, not since the last genie died."

She gave him a sharp look. "How do you know that?"

Stupid! He was a Plotter, not a Head of Department. He shouldn't know any of this.

"Ah. Well, when the Teller, *whocaresaboutus*, changed my role, he explained it all to me."

Agnes' hand shifted to hover above the knife at her belt. "Why would he do that?"

What could he say? What would happen if he told the truth – but what would happen if he lied? Agnes knew something about the Mirrors, clearly. Something important, which she was worried about sharing. He needed to know what it was. If he kept calm, he'd be alright. He could talk about the Teller, surely, without it all coming back? He had to learn, sooner or later.

Mistasinon steeled himself.

"Because he was dying, and he trusted me."

"Dying?"

"Yes."

"*Was* dying?"

"…yes."

Agnes staggered against her desk. "He's dead?"

"Yes."

"When?"

"Around the time we lost the last genie."

Mistasinon waited, rubbing his neck, taking measured breaths in through his nose and out through his mouth. Bea's cloth was in his pocket, but the few drops she'd sprinkled on it were already fading. It was too precious to use unless he absolutely had to. After all, he doubted he'd ever get it replenished.

"Well. I didn't see that coming," Agnes finally said. "I thought that old bastard would carry on forever."

The weight in the room lifted. Mistasinon found himself laughing, actually laughing, and then Agnes was laughing with him. She didn't care. She wasn't angry or afraid. She hadn't asked why he hadn't saved Teller.

His eyes were watering. Was this madness or relief? He didn't know. But it felt wonderful.

"Julia knows?" Agnes asked at last.

"Of course."

"And the other Heads?"

"I don't think so."

Agnes nodded. "Makes sense. I wouldn't tell anyone, either. So, just us three, then? She knows you know?"

"I was with him when he – when it happened."

"Nasty for you. I wouldn't want Julia knowing anything about me if I could avoid it. But it does explain why she's had you at all those meetings. Alright. The Mirrors started repairing themselves. We didn't know why. I took the information to Julia; she already knew, naturally. She said the Plotters were experimenting with new stories. Said not to worry about it."

Mistasinon heard the distaste in Agnes' voice. It was strange. He'd never heard anyone in a suit even vaguely hint towards a fault on Julia's part. But then, he didn't really have any friends, did he? He'd had the Teller and his other hims, and that had been enough. And whatever meagre bridge he and Bea had built, which he'd since set fire to.

"So, we let it go," Agnes continued. "I wish we hadn't, but you know what she's like. She'd find out. She doesn't understand knowledge for knowledge's sake. She looks for the facts that support what she wants supported. It's all a weapon to her."

"Is that why you hide it, then? In all that language?"

Agnes awarded him another approving look. Mistasinon felt his heart flutter, pleased to have pleased her. Old habits.

"Yes. I never lie, but it doesn't hurt to make it a little harder for her. The Mirrors have been fixing themselves for a while now, we think. Whatever Julia might think about this new Plot, it's not the stories. They can't fix a broken Mirror, only keep the active ones functioning. That's why we used the genies in the first place, and they've been dead – well, dead as long as the Teller, *whocaresaboh*. There's not much point in that, is there?"

"I find it comforting," Mistasinon confessed. "Plus, it's safer to keep the habit."

"Sensible. So, something's been fixing the Mirrors. Or, at least, trying to. And now, one seems to have exploded. There could be a connection, or it might just be blind bad luck. That's the trouble, you see? Sometimes you don't know what the story is until it ends, and we don't really know anything about the Mirrors. Yarnis had some crazy ideas about them, started a war over it – hells, destroyed the Land for it. I need to know more. Reduce the variables. Anything the Mirrors have done that goes against expectation. Can you help me?"

Something tickled at the back of his mind – Bea. Something to do with the Plot she'd run, the one he'd amended to get her into the Academy. Something important.

"I need to look at the Books," he said. "Just the common ones."

"You're a Plotter – you're allowed in the Index. Not that any of you ever bother."

He turned to leave, and a thought occurred to him. "Agnes?"

"Yes?"

"Thank you for trusting me."

The grey-suited brownie smiled. "You trusted me with the truth about the Teller. Let's see if trusting each other proves worthwhile. Besides, it's not like there's anyone else working on the Mirrors, is it?"

※

Amelia sat inside the orrery, staring at the snake-necklace cog. It was still freezing cold and covered in the same clear, thick substance. But whereas before the gunk had clogged the machine, now it seemed to be helping it. It was like the material was oiling the cog and the surrounding mechanisms, making the whole thing work better.

The Princess And The Orrery

She'd tried again to remove the cog, but the gunk held it firmly in place, even when, in a moment of frustration in the middle of the night, she'd gone at it with a crowbar.

It wasn't magic. It couldn't be.

...but while she was certain what it *wasn't*, she hadn't been able to find out what it was. She'd been reading up on various types of metal, but the truth was there was little in the books and journals that she didn't already know – and what she did discover didn't account for the cog, the transparent goop, or the orrery's strange refusal to work without it.

She scooted through the orrery, from the internal platform along the main beams, until she could see Seven through the forest of mechanisms.

He was at his table, drawing. He was a very strange man. He took himself too seriously, that much was certain. But he also took her seriously, too. And he seemed as intent on making the orrery work as she was, and she couldn't deny he'd been useful – they'd got more done together than she'd managed in months on her own.

He made her laugh, too. It had been a long time since she'd laughed.

She scooted back to the central platform and climbed down the narrow ladder, jumped past the spinning planets, and joined him at his desk. Today, he was drawing a pretty cottage, nestled in a forest grove. She leaned over his shoulder to take a better look.

"Is that a coffin in the garden? Why would you draw a coffin?"

Seven turned the paper over, but he didn't seem cross with her for interrupting. "I thought you were checking the day's work?"

"Yes, I was. But I want to ask you some more questions. Why did Joseph bring you here? And how come you know about the orrery when you don't know anything at all about maths or engineering or astronomy?"

"Why does that matter, if my work is well?"

"Because if we're working on the orrery, you should tell me," Amelia answered airily. She'd get to the cog in good time. She needed to warm him up first. "Because we've got a deal. And it's much better to understand everything, or else accidents happen."

F. D. Lee

Seven fixed her with a very long stare. Amelia felt unaccountably uncomfortable. And then he sighed and rearranged himself on his chair so he could talk to her better.

"Ask your questions again, and I will answer them best I can. But might I ask you something first?"

"Alright."

"Why did you come here?"

"Because I want to be a Cultivator. ...And it wasn't very good at home. So, where are you from, really?"

"As I told you, I think of Ota'ari as my home. My kind, though, are from somewhere very far away. A place that no longer exists."

Mmm. That would explain why she'd never heard of any other blue people. The Five Kingdoms of Thaiana spread across the known world, but the oceans went on much further. It wasn't so impossible to think that there might be another country, far beyond the horizon, where the people were blue and had strange eyes. It would explain why he spoke so funny, too, like he'd learnt Ehinen from a book. Besides, what other sensible explanation was?

"Was there a war?" she asked. "Is that why your family left?"

Seven thought for a moment. "Yes. A war. One we had no chance of winning."

"How did you escape?"

"I did not. These events occurred long before I was born. However, my ancestors built, ah, ships. Very fast, very clever ships. My family came here. Others went elsewhere. It was, from what my parents recounted, a time of confusion and desperation. Mistakes were made."

"Where are your parents?"

"Dead, as are all my kin."

Amelia felt a wave of something unpleasant slosh in her stomach. For a moment, all she could think about was the smell of old wood and the darkness of the deep forest. Yellow eyes and the twang of a crossbow bolt...

"Let us not dwell on it. It is done and cannot be undone," Seven said softly, bringing her back to the present. "To your next question, Joseph asked me to work with you because of the, what is the word? Ah, yes. The mechanics of our ships. He mistakenly

The Princess And The Orrery

thought I might know more than you," he added with a conspiratorial smile.

"Ships aren't the same as the orrery, though. Why would Joseph think you could help me?"

Seven sighed irritably. "You have a very singular focus, my Lady. You should be careful you do not ignore the periphery. In answer to your question: heritage, I suppose. I grew up with the stories of our home and the tragedy that befell it, as all refugees do."

"Stories?"

"Indeed. Stories are useful hiding places for things which need to be remembered but not examined."

"The stories my mum used to tell me were just silly children's stories full of made-up things. Cultivators deal in facts."

"And yet, facts come from imagination," Seven said. "You must first imagine a world that is different, in which something has changed, before you can begin to search for the means, the methods, to change it. These two things are not distinct, they are bound on the same thread, the same line."

Amelia frowned. There was some sense in what he said. Was that enough to tell him about the snake-necklace cog? Joseph had told her it was a secret. But then, Joseph had also brought Seven to her, hadn't he? Besides, she could hardly keep working on the orrery if she didn't know why it broke or how to fix it.

And Seven was her colleague, so she shouldn't keep secrets from him.

"Do you know any stories about a... a strange metal?"

Seven leaned forwards, his eyebrows meeting.

"A strange metal that does not behave as it ought?"

Amelia nodded. "Yes. A metal that isn't, perhaps, just in a story...?"

The atmosphere changed, almost as if the air was crowding around them, eager as she was to hear what he would say. When he spoke next, it was slow, like he was choosing his words with care.

"My people did indeed master a very special, very rare metal. It is powerful and can be used for all manner of things. But it is also... ahhh... *gu'lin vut*... like the animal? It is not independent? There is not a word in your tongue, I think."

"Permanent?"

"No, not permanent. This metal is, sadly, not immune to damage. Let me... Ah. You are aware that living creatures carry minerals within their bodies?"

Amelia nodded.

"There are some, like myself, who have a greater quantity of such minerals – were you to cut me, my blood would appear black, for example. This is due to the quantity of iron within it."

"That can't be true – too much iron is poisonous."

"Ah, yes, but too little makes you weak. I dare say that somewhere there is a race of people who have the perfect balance of such things, but 'tis neither you nor I. Still, you have the sense of it. My point, however, is that all things are connected. We all have minerals, metals, within us. The metal of my kind can connect in a similar fashion to flesh and blood, amongst other things."

Amelia thought about the snake-necklace cog, and how it seemed to bleed that thick, clear substance. "You mean it's alive?"

Seven shook his head. "Not in the sense that you or I are alive. It is *gu'lin vut* – attached, perhaps, is the closer word."

"*Gu'lin vut*," Amelia repeated, trying out the strange syllables. "This metal... does any of it exist here, in Thaiana?"

"I think you know the answer, my Lady. Have you not seen it for yourself?"

She looked at the orrery. When she turned back to Seven, he was watching her closely. "I... yes. I think so. Joseph gave me a small piece. I used it in the orrery, but it – you won't laugh at me?"

"I will not."

"It seemed like it was bleeding – it gummed up the orrery, and it wouldn't work anymore, even when I removed it. But then, I cleaned it and put it back, and now the orrery won't work without it, and it keeps producing this thick substance that won't let it go. Has it attached itself to my device?"

"Yes. The orrery will be finished soon, I think," Seven said. He seemed suddenly very disappointed, like he had been waiting for an exciting present only to discover it was a pair of socks.

Amelia reached out and patted his chilly hand, misunderstanding his sudden despondency.

"Don't worry. I'm sure when it's finished, you'll be able to stay at Starry Castle. Naima wants to let boys study here, she did a lecture about it. She wants to invent lots of new things, even things that might stop them using slaves in the manufactories – she says that more minds make more answers." Amelia paused, suddenly nervous. "So, y'know, if you like, we could work on something else together, after this is finished. If you wanted to."

"Yes. I think I shall spend the rest of my days here."

As quickly as her nerves had come, they disappeared. She knew why the orrery had broken, or at least had some sense of it. True, it wasn't the most reliable information, but it was a starting point. Plus, her new friend wanted to stay in Starry Castle.

She grinned at Seven.

"Good. We'll be like *gu'lin vut* too, a proper team," she said. "I'm never going to leave here, either."

34

Hemmings sat on a hay bale in the early afternoon sun, his delicate chin resting in his hand.

He was in a quandary. Some choices could be made slowly, adjusted and perfected by the weight of experience. And then there were choices that hammered against the cool restraint of patience like a woodpecker with a grudge. Choices which demanded attention and had to be made within the context of the ever-shifting *now*, or else they would make themselves and damn you to the consequences.

After a morning of careful thought, he had reached the conclusion that he was currently facing the latter type of choice. Unfortunately, that was as far as he had got.

He understood why Melly was so anxious about the play and the risk of drawing the attention of the GenAm and its Beast to their endeavour. Of course he did. She needn't have gone and mentioned Chokey – the thought of something happening to her made him feel sick.

Indeed, from that first nasty little piece of imaginative fodder, he'd made a meal out of picturing Chokey, his mother, father, and baby sister all stood on the Redaction Block in the main square outside the GenAm, standing proudly – as Ogrechokers would – while some jobsworth in a white suit placed an Eraser to their forehead.

The GenAm needed to change. Of that he was certain. Redaction was vile, one of the few things that made him genuinely angry. To strip a person of their thoughts, their choices, their history... it was unconscionable. And to wield such power with impunity but without foresight or guidance, as the GenAm did, was, surely, evil.

It was a strong word, and Hemmings didn't care for absolutes. But what other word fitted? He'd tried a few: misguided, reactionary, overzealous... but those were excuses. As difficult as it was to admit, thoughtsmithing couldn't provide him with any other way to view the situation. Some things were just wrong.

And Melly thought she could do something about it, with the genie. Stop the Mirrors breaking. If that was true, wouldn't it also mean that the GenAm wouldn't be able to resort to such measures? If the Mirrors worked properly again, there wouldn't be any excuse for the Redactions and the curfews, the Beast and the informers. The GenAm were able to exercise such devastating control because the city was afraid of losing what little it had.

Or so it seemed. Hemmings was also aware, in a dim kind of way, that the Teller had had control of Ænathlin for many hundreds of years, and Melly had said they'd had the genies back then, too. But the Redactions and the Beast had also been around for that long. The history books were vague, focusing only on the Teller's extraordinary accomplishment in creating the General Administration, the Four Departments and the Plots. The saviour of the fae, the fixer of the Mirrors, the writer of the Plots. One person's voice, one person's vision of the world...

Hemmings sighed and shifted his chin from his right hand to his left.

A shadow fell across him.

"Alright, Sunshine. Budge over," Alfonso said in an accent Hemmings hadn't heard before – all long 'r's and rounded 'a's. The actor sat next to Hemmings, shoving the elf over with his narrow hips. "You've been sitting here for hours with a face like a slapped arse. I can't concentrate on my lines."

"You sound different...?"

"Ah, well. Sometimes I remember who I am. So what's got you all in a tizzy?"

What should he say? He obviously couldn't explain himself to a human, but thoughts were always better shared. And besides, Alfonso was his friend, wasn't he? That was why the actor always seemed to seek him out, obviously.

"I'm just thinking about the play," Hemmings settled on. "About storytelling. Did you know that telling stories began as a way to create better social harmony?" He didn't mention that the society in question was the fae and that the harmony benefited only them. The omission stuck in his throat, scratching like dry air.

"Makes sense," Alfonso replied with a shrug. "Easier to tell someone what to do if you aren't really telling them."

Hemmings' gawped at him. "How do you know that?"

"It was the same where I grew up. Had to be this, had to be that, 'cause everyone was this or that. No one knew any different. It's part of the reason I left."

"That's exactly why it matters – the play I mean. We could show people a different way to be. Show them something that reflects real people and real problems. We could find a new truth."

Alfonso leaned back on his arms, staring at the company going through their scenes. "Not with you sitting over here on your lonesome, we can't."

"But... Melly... it's not that easy..."

Alfonso put his hand, briefly, on Hemmings' knee. "Who's she to you, anyway?"

"I don't know how to explain it. My teacher, perhaps? She certainly thinks she knows more than me."

"Is that so? You don't strike me as a person who thinks his opinion isn't worth knowing. You were loud enough with your ideas before."

"She said that if we change the play too much, some people might take notice. Bad people."

Alfonso thought for a moment. He had long, narrow eyebrows, currently drawn together in a frown, above dark brown eyes. Hemmings tried not to stare.

"You can't please all the people all the time. And maybe there's some that ought not to be pleased," Alfonso said, finally. "S'up to you, Sunshine."

He stood in one movement, spinning on his heels and dropping a low bow to Hemmings, just like he did at the end of the play. When he spoke next, his accent had returned to its carefully modulated tones. Hemmings couldn't help wondering which version of him was the act.

"But I know what I would I do if I thought I had a chance to change the tale." Alfonso held out his hand, a challenge glittering in his eyes. "So, are you going to sit there feeling sorry for yourself or are you going to get up off that hay bale and help me make some God damn art?"

The next part of the day came with even more surprises. Alfonso dragged Hemmings to the costume and props department, a slightly grandiose term for what was, in fact, four large wooden trunks. The actor then proceeded to tear through their contents until he pulled out a pile of clothes and a violin.

"What are we-" Hemmings began, before an even more pressing question made itself known. His hand shot up to cover his eyes. "Why in the five hells are you getting undressed!?"

"There's no room for modesty in the theatre, Sunshine. If we're going to change the play, we need money," Alfonso stated, the unmistakable sound of a grin in his voice. "The Accountant will never let us do it if the coppers are at stake. We need to fund this next one ourselves, prove we can do it better."

Hemmings was in a state of total befuddlement. "I should give him the bone dust Mum gave me?"

"Good God, no! Don't mention that to anyone – it's beyond weird," Alfonso replied, chucking some clothes at him. "Get changed into these. It's time for you to step out of the wings and into the lamplight!"

That had been ninety minutes and one horse ride ago. Now they were standing outside a restaurant in one of the towns that Christopher had decided wasn't worth performing in, their schedule being too tight. Alfonso had dressed in a slightly worn suit, added some glasses, and found a case for the violin. Hemmings, mortified, had scooted off to get changed in private, telling himself it was because he didn't want Alfonso to see his long, elfin ears, even though they were still hidden under the garish cap John had given him.

The restaurant looked very well-to-do, Hemmings thought. The menu, written on a chalkboard and hanging from the outside wall, boasted no less than four different dishes, all of which listed their ingredients! It was a far cry from the meals back home, where it was generally considered better not to ask what you were eating.

He was, therefore, entirely astonished when Alfonso regarded the menu with a sneer.

"Good thing we don't need to raise much money. If this town ever had one horse, it probably died of starvation. Right then, this is the plan. I'm going to go in and put on the performance of a lifetime. You just wait under that tree, alright? When I come back out, I'll tell you what to do."

Hemmings had no idea what was going on but did as he was told. How in the worlds had he got himself into such a mess? Melly would be furious. He hadn't seen her since their row, which he was certain meant she was brewing up another invective to hurl at him.

He wasn't thinking properly. That much was becoming very clear, very quickly. Mortal gods. And what was Alfonso doing? The day was spilling away; the company was due to perform in a few hours. Even with a horse and only two of them on its back, they'd be hard pushed to get back in time. It was one thing to try to change the play, but another thing entirely to cause its cancellation due to the absence of the lead actor.

...but maybe that wasn't such a bad thing? Now he was alone, Hemmings couldn't help doubting his earlier resolve. All of this was too new, too strange. He suddenly wanted nothing more than to go home, where his books and his journals were. He wanted to see Chokey and his family. Hells, he'd even go with Chokey to one of her parties, a show of desperation he'd never expected to encounter.

Melly was right. He'd got in too deep. Something about the theatre had struck a chord within him, but perhaps it was a note best left unplayed. He felt like he'd been under some kind of spell, lulled into behaviour that he would never, ever have dreamed of had he stayed at home.

Stuck in a tower... But what was wrong with that, anyway? It was a very fine, comfortable tower; much better than most other elves ever got. Oh dear, he was really making a mess of everything, wasn't he?

"Y'know, this is the second time I've come upon you today looking all morose. If I didn't know you were under Royal decree

The Princess And The Orrery

to uncover the real lives of the downtrodden classes, I'd think you didn't want to be here."

Hemmings started. Alfonso was back, already rolling a cigarette.

"That went very well, if I do say myself," he continued, leaning against the tree. "Now, normally we'd leave it a few hours but time's pressing. Luckily, I don't think that barman would know the difference between a sheep and a goat with cotton wool stuck to it, so we should be safe. We'll give it half an hour, and then you're up."

"Look, I was thinking and-"

Alfonso turned his head slightly, so he could look at Hemmings and still see the restaurant. "Come on now, don't be boring. The hard part's done. Besides, don't you want the full experience – living the life of the travelling nomad, relying on your wits to secure your next meal, yadda, yadda, yadda?"

Alfonso spoke with almost exactly the same tone Chokey used when she wanted him to do something he didn't want to do. The only difference was, Chokey very rarely combined her wheedling with a wink and a smile that made Hemmings glad the actor wasn't giving him his full attention. His resolve wavered.

"What do you want me to do? I don't mean to say I will," he added quickly.

"Fair enough. All you need to do is go in there and offer that man a few gold pieces for the violin-"

"But we haven't any gold pieces?"

"It doesn't matter. He won't accept. Then I'll head back in there and either come out with the money we need for the show or with the violin. Hah. Thief in two, if you like."

"I don't follow."

"So, I went in there, bought some wine and some food, and then made a show of having left my purse at home. I offered the violin as collateral while I run home and get my money. You go in, offering more than the thing's worth. Say you're a collector or whatever. If he takes the deal, he's a thief, right? If not, when I go back in, he'll offer to buy it off me, less the cost of the meal no doubt, in order to sell it on to you. I take the money and leave the violin."

Hemmings couldn't believe his ears, points and all. "That's disgusting," he cried. "You're tricking him into trading for something that has no value."

"It's bloody unoriginal, is what it is. But we don't have time for anything better. And that violin does have value, thank you very much. If he gives us a few silvers for it, he won't be out of pocket, and I doubt we'll shake even that much out of him."

"Well, what about the company? It's their violin, isn't it?"

Alfonso glared at him. "You think I'd steal from my family? It's mine. I brought it with me when I left home. I just happen to think the play is worth more. Look," he said, returning his attention to the restaurant, "If this goes off right, that man will just be getting what he deserves, which means what we're doing is, if anything, the moral action. And if it goes south, well then, he's a good man and we've just proven it, which must also be a good deed, mustn't it?"

Hemmings ran the statement back in his head. "That shouldn't make any sense."

"But it does, right?"

And so, thirty minutes later, Hemmings found himself inside the restaurant, repeating the lines Alfonso had quickly taught him to the bemused and then surprisingly cagey barman. He did not offer to sell the violin to Hemmings there and then, instead making an arrangement for Hemmings to return later.

Alfonso's next turn was even quicker. He was in and out of the restaurant in less than ten minutes, conspicuously absent a violin. He shook a small coin purse at Hemmings.

"Let's go make Christopher an offer his accountant's mind can't refuse," he said with a grin. He dropped the purse into Hemmings' hand and then reached into his jacket, pulling out a bottle of wine. "And it seems our barman was slightly more on the up-and-up than I gave him credit for. While he did grossly underpay me for the violin, he did throw in this bottle of white. So, now we can celebrate or commiserate tonight's performance in style!"

35

Melly, meanwhile, stalked through the forest, stamping her feet against the dry floor, kicking up leaves as she went.

The forest didn't complain, or if it did, she couldn't understand it. Melly didn't have the talent of talking to plants. Every tribe had their gifts, and for the elves, it was the ability to heal. Although, unusually for an elf, she'd learnt how to communicate, after a fashion, with the Sheltering Forest. But then, she'd lived in her little cottage for hundreds of years, and the Sheltering Forest was a fae place, different from the stark simplicity of the human world. Here, the forest was just so much wood and leaves.

The animals, though, sensing her anger and perhaps remembering, in a distant way, the cruelty of the elven, kept their distance. Birdsong and insect chatter fell silent as she approached and for a time after she passed, creating an unnatural vacuum in the soundscape of the trees. Even the deer avoided crossing her path, something which – had she been in a more receptive frame of mind – might have upset her. As it was, she was about as receptive as a block of wood at the bottom of a deep hole in the farthest reaches of the darkest cave on the remotest island. Simply put, she was not in the best of moods.

That stupid bloody elf! Melly fumed. Though with glum self-awareness, she had to admit she could just as easily be swearing at herself as Hemmings. She'd known bringing him into the theatre was a bad idea, and yet she'd still done it. Now she'd have to contend with his sulking, which would no doubt affect the humans, too.

Melly knew what happened when humans got in the middle of elven disagreements. To say things got messy was to suggest that the Rhyme War had been a minor disagreement or that the Mirrors breaking was a mild inconvenience. Humans just weren't capable of keeping a level head around elves. It was how they were made – how both tribes were made, as far as Melly was concerned.

Certainly, Ana and John were different: sensible, cautious, curious. *They* might be able to see past the beauty and thrill of pleasing an elf, but that was no reason to assume that the rest of their tribe could. Gods, even Melly was guilty of falling into her character. Less than a year back in the world, and here she was trying to usurp a crown, romance a human, *and* fight a genie. And she had the benefit of age and experience – what did Hemmings have? A head full of ideas and a life spent cosseted in one of the wealthiest families in Ænathlin.

He meant well, she could see that. But elves got caught up. They tinkered and played and were fascinated by things. And humans, well. They gave the elves plenty of things to tinker and play with, for good or – most commonly – for ill. Fascination is a wonderful thing, right up to the moment when it shifts into obsession. There was, Melly felt, a reason why the word had once meant 'witchcraft'. And the humans were very quick to take sides, and quicker, then, to spill blood.

What was Hemmings thinking? Her instructions had been clear: don't get involved. And what had he done? Infected the whole bloody cast with his ridiculous ideas! And after she'd spent all that time getting the story back under control!

That whole camp was a disaster waiting to happen. Which was why she was leaving it. One elf was one too many in an environment like that, two might as well be a declaration of war. She'd known it, and she'd ignored the lessons of her past. So, after much deliberation and many, many cigarettes, she'd decided the best thing she could do was to leave Hemmings to it and get on with the real task. She'd find a way into the Palace when she got to Cerne Bralksteld – and she'd make better time than the company, who moved at a snail's pace even without stopping at every town that had a population made up of more than five surnames.

When the genie was returned to Ænathlin, she'd come back for Hemmings. For now, she just had to hope that there'd still be something to come back to. So decided, she tracked through the trees, not paying attention to where she was going. Until suddenly she wasn't in the forest anymore, but on the outskirts of a small village, encircled by a dry-stone wall. A sign stuck into the earth proclaimed it to be Skraq. The theatre was due here that evening,

The Princess And The Orrery

but she'd be long gone before they arrived. If she travelled all night, they'd never catch her up.

It wasn't much of a place. Maybe a hundred houses, all huddled together inside the wall – a wall which, compared to the one that encircled Ænathlin, might as well have been a circle of salt for all the protection it offered. They hadn't even laced it with iron, which might at least have kept them safe from the fae. As it was, she could hardly imagine it withstanding a good push from a strong man, let alone a raging troll.

See? The humans had forgotten the danger the fae posed. And with every reason. They hadn't had to worry for hundreds of years, not since the Teller took control. If the fae regained their taste for the blood and the bone, for the *real* stories – of fear, of anger, of cruelty, the ones that sharpened belief to a razor's edge on the whetstone of survival – they'd find no resistance in little villages like this one.

Power like that would destroy the fae. It had been too long, and they were different now. There were more of them, for one thing, and tribal allegiances had shifted and changed as a result of so many living shoulder to shoulder in Ænathlin. Oh, she didn't doubt that their lust for a story remained; Hemmings' giddy reaction to the theatre proved as much. She was simply terrified that if the GenAm lost its stranglehold on the city, the resulting 'freedom' would lead to all-out war. Tribe against tribe; fae against human; human against human.

The fae would win, of course. Humans were soft, fragile things. But it would be a hard battle. The humans had changed as well, as Ana had said. Not all of them would bow easily. For all their current lack of belief, they'd remember the iron quick enough when their kith and kin started disappearing.

As much as she hated and feared the Teller, she had to admit he'd been deviously clever. He'd given the fae a substitute for the thrill of the story in his simple, sanitised, repetitive Plots, just enough to sate them but not quite enough to put the fire in their blood. But the Mirrors were breaking, and the GenAm were attempting ever more risky avenues, like Redacting characters, to keep it all together...

Melly wiped her hands over her face. They needed the genie. Then he could wish the Mirrors working again, and they'd have some more time to come up with a solution. It was the only way.

"Hey, miss, what're you doing out here?"

Melly looked up, confused. A man was leaning against the drystone wall, watching her curiously. He seemed, understandably, somewhat taken aback to find a beautiful, red-haired woman in a tatty black dress standing outside his village, having some kind of argument with herself.

Melly drew herself up to her full height, radiating regal importance. "That is absolutely none of your business."

"Fair enough," the man said. "Only it seems to me you're in a bit of a tizz."

"Nothing could be further from the truth," Melly retorted. The validity of her statement was undermined, unfortunately, by the way her voice cracked. What was wrong with her?

The man eyed her, impassive. "Come on then, let's get you a cup of tea."

"I don't want a cup of tea."

"Aye, well, that's as may be. But you look like you need one."

Melly had no idea what she was thinking when she actually walked through the opening in the wall. Perhaps the fact that everyone around her was losing their mind had finally caught up with her, and she'd decided to do the same thing?

Her eyes shuttled left and right as she followed the man through the village, but no one paid her more than the cursory glance her stature and dress demanded. Her ears, the most visible sign of her otherness, were safely hidden under her thick red hair. She was more slender than the average human, her proportions slightly longer despite her shorter height, her skin paler, but such was her beauty and her pride that they likely didn't notice the incongruencies between her tribe and theirs.

"Here, sit down," the man instructed, guiding her to a cushioned bench outside a little stone cottage. A small garden led up to the bench, but there was nothing stopping Melly getting up and walking away. Against her better judgement, she sat.

"Tea, eh?"

She nodded. The man disappeared inside the cottage. She straightened her skirt. Around her, village life continued. Humans hustled and bustled about their day, unaware there was an elf amongst them. There were some fruit bushes growing in his garden, flowers still attached to their branches, green berries slowly forming behind their leaves. Spring was a wonderful time for plants, Melly knew. She grew her own, back home.

"Here we go," the man said, emerging with two steaming cups of tea. A little girl followed with a third. She looked at Melly from behind long brown hair and with a weariness that no child should ever wear.

"Thank you," Melly said, taking the cup. She couldn't think of anything else to say, so she took a sip of tea. It had too much sugar for her taste.

"We don't believe in ignoring people in trouble, here. My name's Josh, and this is Giss," the man said, nodding towards the little girl.

"Well met. I'm... Mildred."

The humans exchanged a sideways glance.

"That's a lovely name," Josh said politely.

Giss flopped down on a wooden stool and watched Melly over the top of her drink, the steam rising up to dampen her little face.

Melly took another sip, trying to think of something to say without a Plot to help her. She'd only ever really spoken to Ana and John as herself.

"So, what's wrong?" Josh asked.

"Nothing."

"I wondered if you were an escapee. You don't need to worry if you are, we won't turn you in, will we Giss?"

Melly looked blankly from Josh's friendly concern to Giss, but the girl just stared back her, offering nothing.

"Escapee? From where?"

"From the Baron," Josh said. "You don't need to put on an act. I can't imagine what you've been through, but you can trust us. Tell her, Giss."

"You're safe here. For now," the little girl said, sounding so tired it made Melly shiver despite the warm cup in her hands and the gentle sun on her face.

"What do you mean?"

"You can't run from the Baron," Giss said. "He'll catch us here too, he's going to catch the world. I keep telling them. They don't listen."

"Don't mind her, she's got no faith, have you, Trouble?" Josh said, pulling Giss into a hug. Melly noticed that, although she didn't protest, Giss' body was stiff as a branch.

"You know Ana – King John's Adviser?" she asked Josh.

"Aye. Knew her before she got her airs and graces, too. I was in her camp."

Melly nodded slowly. "The one she set up to help escaped slaves."

"He burns people underground," Giss said, matter-of-factly. "My mum got done by the steam. She died."

Melly had no idea what to say. The GenAm used older orphans a lot, sure enough, but only because they tended to be more willing to be in a story, and there was no one to care about them if the Plot went wrong. There was no script that dealt with a tired child recounting the gruesome death of her mother.

"Giss," Josh said, "Why don't you pop inside and see if you can find some cake?"

The little girl looked from him to Melly suspiciously.

"I'll be ok, Giss," Josh reassured her. "I'm not going anywhere."

Giss gave Melly a warning look, but trotted into the cottage.

"She was born in the manufactories," Josh said. "I don't know how she got out, she doesn't talk about it. I don't think she remembers, which is probably a blessing. I found her in the woods over near Llanotterly. I'm a poa-, er, a hunter – was, anyway. There I am, up before the lark, see some funny tracks, follow them a half mile or so and she drops on my head, screaming her little lungs out. She was ready to kill me, even made a blade with a stone. T'was sharp as buggery," he added warmly. "I took her to Ana's camp and ended up staying. That was about a year ago. Then we came here."

"You took her in after the camp closed?" Melly asked. When Ana had become Royal Adviser, one of the first things she'd done was set up a formal system to care for the escapees, finding them

The Princess And The Orrery

homes in Llanotterly and the surrounding villages. She'd even roped in her sister, Sindy, who had set up a medical centre of sorts.

"That I did."

Melly was impressed. "I've, uh, met Ana a few times. She says the Baron is a dangerous man."

"Aye. The Baron won't notice one. But right now, there're probably near a hundred escapees spread over these parts. Small beer compared to the numbers still in the manufactories, but the Baron doesn't look kindly on people stealing his property."

Melly felt the revulsion curdling her face. "Why don't you just move on? Take Giss and get away?"

"And then what? It's only in Caer Marlyn now, but it'll be Marlais next. And after that Sausendorf, and then it'll be Dirkbrock and The Six Points... the Baron won't stop."

"No," Melly said. "I don't think he will. I know the type."

Josh took a sip of his tea, watching the villagers going about their day. "Aye. Well. We'll find a way to stop him, I reckon. Ana's a smart one, and she's got the King's ear now."

Giss returned with a plate piled high with biscuits. She shoved it under Melly's nose. "We didn't have any cake," she said. "You can have a biscuit."

"Thank you." Melly smiled, took a biscuit, and laid it on her knee.

The little girl's eyes followed the food, her mouth moving as if she were chewing. Josh rested his hand on her shoulder. "There's plenty more, Giss. Look, see? You've got a whole plate full."

"There wasn't any cake."

"Because we haven't made any cake. We can make one later, if you like. Take a slice to the players this eve. You remember the players are coming through?"

Giss nodded. "Can I have a biscuit?"

"Just one. You know the rules about sweets."

Giss already had a handful of biscuits pressed against her mouth. She shoved them in before nodding again. "'es," she mumbled.

"Mmm. Go on then, best be getting back to it." He looked at Melly. "You feeling better now, miss?"

Melly took the hint. "Yes, thank you. Thank you, Giss, for the biscuit."

The little girl didn't reply.

Melly bowed to Josh and Giss and made her way back through the village. She had every intention of continuing on to Cerne Bralksteld, but she couldn't shake the way the little girl, Giss, had watched her with wide, wary eyes.

He burns people up.

Melly didn't know much about children, but she was pretty sure they weren't supposed to be silent and scared. They weren't supposed to be so afraid of losing food they resented someone eating a biscuit.

Somehow, instead of leaving the village, she found herself outside the pub. She rummaged through her sleeves and, after a few false starts, uncovered a few copper coins. Praying to all the mortal gods it would be enough for a glass of wine, Melly stepped inside.

36

"Chug, chug, chug, chug!!"

Melly picked up the tankard and downed the apple juice. It tasted sweet and faintly sharp. She slammed the tankard down next to all the rest with a satisfying *thump*, casually picked up her cigarette and took a long drag. She shot a thin smile at the old woman sitting opposite her.

The bar fell silent.

And then, like an eruption, a great hollering cheer broke out. Men and women grabbed each other, bemused, beaming faces meeting equally bemused, beaming faces. This was it, they all seemed to understand – this was the thing they'd tell their grandchildren about.

"But... but..." the old woman said, staring wide-eyed at the empty tankard. "That were my special brew. I 'ad that one cooking for over six weeks..."

"It was very tasty," Melly conceded.

The old woman fixed her with a look that spoke of absolute defeat. "Tasty? That were about one step down from rubbing alcohol – I've sold that brew to that woman over Llanotterly way what runs the clinic, so's she can use it to send folks a'sleep a'fore she fixes 'em up!"

Melly licked her lips. "Have you got any more?"

Each person in the pub leaned back and then, slowly, forward. The old woman looked like she was going to faint.

And then, from behind the bar, the Landlady emerged.

She was probably somewhere in her fifties; Melly found it tricky to judge the exact age of humans. Usually, the ones she encountered were only babies – ready for her to start the Plot off with a nice, dramatic cursing – or they were in their mid-teens, and far too drippy to bother with beyond the obligatory mild peril she was charged with delivering.

F. D. Lee

This woman, however, looked anything but drippy. She carried a dark terracotta bottle stopped with a cork sealed with a generous amount of wax.

The old woman left her seat; the Landlady took her place. The terracotta bottle was placed on the table between her and Melly.

"You done alright so far, I'll grant," the Landlady said with a nod of her head. Professional to professional. "But this is of my own making. I use it to clean the pipes. This one has been sitting under my bar since summer a'fore last."

The bar *oooh*-ed. A comedian at the back started humming a funeral march.

Melly took another drag on her cigarette.

"This ain't cider," the Landlady continued. "Ain't scrumpy, neither. This one 'ere, this is made from elderflowers and plums. You game, then, Mistress?"

Melly stubbed out her cigarette and leaned forward, meeting the woman's challenge eye-to-eye. "I was just thinking I could do with a change."

If the atmosphere in the bar had been thick before, it was now positively gelatinous. Not unlike the liquid, in fact, which glooped from the terracotta bottle into the small glass the Landlady produced.

In obedience to all the laws of Narrative Convention Melly had ever known, as the last drop slid from the lip of the bottle, the light from the setting sun caught it, causing it to shine orangey-red with mythic foreboding.

The Landlady pushed the glass to Melly.

The crowd grabbed each other's hands. Partners hugged each other close. Everyone watched, unblinking, as Melly picked up the glass and sniffed. Was it their imaginations, or did they notice a slight creasing of the red-headed stranger's forehead?

Melly lifted the glass to her lips.

Paused.

And drank it in one go.

No one moved. No one spoke. Quite probably, no one breathed. It was perhaps hard to say whether this was entirely down to the tension in the room – the air was already growing in alcoholic potency through the sheer fact that the bottle had been opened, and some of the patrons had early starts the next day.

The Landlady scrutinised Melly as if it was only now occurring to her that there was a room full of witnesses, should things take a turn for the macabre.

Melly blinked. A single bead of sweat appeared on her smooth, pale forehead and trickled down her face.

The Landlady was looking decidedly less self-assured.

Melly burped.

"That was lovely," she said, grinning at the Landlady. "The best one so far – I think I actually felt it going down."

The Landlady glared at her. And then burst out laughing. "Well, you're a hardy one, I'll give you that. 'ere, Jacob, get us some ale and one of 'em potato pies," she yelled across the bar before turning back to Melly. "What's your secret then? You got a gut of iron?"

Melly laughed. "No, not iron. I'm just tougher than I look."

In fact, in comparison with the Ænathlin-made wine she was used to, this stuff had been like watered down fruit juice. But, and here was the strange thing, she'd enjoyed herself all afternoon. The challenges had been set and she'd bested each one in turn, but nothing worse than another sickly-sweet drink had come of it.

The people here were friendly, proud, and welcoming. Not at all like she remembered the humans being.

Maybe Ana was right...

A pint of ale was plopped in front of her, and the conversation began to bubble up as everyone started retelling the story of the mad stranger with the iron stomach. It was already being embellished.

"So, then," the Landlady said, taking a drink, "You passing through?"

"I'm travelling with the theatre."

"Is it? Well, I'm glad to hear it. You're not exactly gonna do wonders for my reputation if you stay," the woman said with a deep chuckle. "You're an actor, then? I heard you lot were debauched. Always fancied a bit of debauchery, as it goes."

"It gets quite tiring, after a while. You like the theatre, then?"

F. D. Lee

"Aye. What's not to like? All 'em whoopsies up on stage making arses of themselves? Great stuff. Plus, it keeps the kiddies quiet for a night. And the pub does well afterwards."

The potato pie arrived. Melly helped herself to a slice. "You don't worry about... I don't know... people getting strange ideas?"

"All ideas are strange to someone. Look, when I first took over this bar from my husband – God rest his soul, blah, blah, blah – it was a dirty old place with a handful of tinkers and rag 'n bone men drinking half pints and pissing on the doorstep. My husband, he didn't like change. S'way it's always been, he'd say, so why make it new? Anyway, when I finally got my hands on it, I got Jacob in to do the cooking, cleaned it up, put in some new furniture, that sort of thing. Now look at it."

Melly did so. And, indeed, the pub was full of people, all chatting and laughing around wooden tables or leaning against the bar. The windows were thrown open, pretty flower boxes wafting in the scent of spring on the breeze – almost, but not quite, overpowering the smell of sweet alcohol that surrounded her particular table. It was, truthfully, a wonderful space, and Melly said as much.

"Thank you," the Landlady said. "It took some doing, but it was worth it. So, then. You gonna stay for another?"

Melly checked the clock. She had an hour or two until the theatre was due to arrive. She could still be out and away before they caught up with her. Besides, there was something else playing on her mind.

"I think I will, yes," she said. "I was wondering, as well, if you could tell me anything about Cerne Bralksteld and the manufactories...."

37

As she stumbled out of the bar, leaning on Kathy the Landlady for support, Melly was prepared to admit she might have made a minor miscalculation.

They meandered through the dusk towards the field where the theatre company had set up their makeshift stage. Melly tried not to pay too much attention to the ground, which seemed to be moving under her feet. She probably should have eaten a second pie. Still, with only a few hiccups and one rather large pratfall that saw Kathy land bum first in something soft and, likely, bovine in origin, they made it safely to their destination.

"I'ma sid'down," Kathy said, landing with a flump on one the hay bales towards the back of the seating area. Melly, only slightly better for wear, took her seat next to her new friend.

Around them, the seats filled up. Lanterns hung on crooks to light the way. The cast's caravans were set in a semi-circle behind the stage, a wooden platform about fifteen feet wide, with curtains branching off its sides for the actors to hide behind while they waited for their cues or to quickly change into new costumes. The area directly in front of the stage was lit with bright hurricane lamps, their dampeners turned so that the beams of light landed solely on the actors. One of the company was walking around the audience, selling programmes and treats; another was playing a string instrument – a guitar, Melly remembered. She'd liked human music, once. Liked the musicians, too.

She was just drifting into memory when she saw Josh and Giss.

"Hey, hey, over here!" she found herself yelling. She coughed and tried again in a more civilised tone. "Josh, Giss, would you like to sit with us?"

Josh looked a little surprised, but came over anyway. Giss hung off his arm, staring at Melly warily.

"I didn't expect to you see here, Mildred," Josh said.

"Mildred? So that's your name! Hah! Mildred!" Kathy guffawed. "I'd never have guessed that."

F. D. Lee

Melly blushed. Names were important. You should never give out your real name. But for some reason, right now, her carefully tended paranoia seemed silly, childish even. Josh and Giss took up the hay bale next to them.

"You been taking care of our guest, then, Kath?" Josh said in an altogether far too knowing tone.

"Aye."

"Cider?"

"Aye, and scrumble and Vori schnapps."

"God above," Josh said, turning worried eyes onto Melly. He waved his hand in front of her face. "How many fingers am I holding up?"

"Three," Melly said, grinning.

Josh opened and closed his mouth. Then he laughed. "Well, either Kath's gone soft, which she ain't, or you're tougher than you look."

Melly bowed her head. The field spun slightly but recovered its equilibrium.

"She's with the theatre," Kathy said, as if that explained it.

Giss sat forward on her seat. "Are you really?"

"I am," Melly said.

Giss' eyes widened. "Wow."

Melly was about to reply when Alfonso appeared on the stage. Under the warm glow of the lights, he looked entirely different. When he'd been throwing his weight around earlier, he'd struck her as wholly unremarkable: slight and plain, with slicked-back hair and plucked eyebrows and a chest puffed-out with self-importance. But now... now he was something else entirely. His whole demeanour was changed. He seemed larger, somehow. Not in stature, not as such, but in presence. She couldn't tear her eyes from him. It was almost... magical.

The audience clearly agreed. Silence fell, and the space inside the lanterns filled with a sense of happy concentration.

Alfonso bowed, and the play began.

The Princess And The Orrery

Hemmings watched the audience from the wings, chewing on his handkerchief. Even in the half-light, there was no mistaking that straight back and shock of fox-red hair. Melly was watching.

Ohgodsohgodsohgods. She was going to kill him. He knew it. What had he been thinking? Had he been thinking? He'd always prided himself on his ability to see his way past things. Whenever the bullying got too much, or the loneliness when Chokey was busy with her friends, he'd always taken comfort in the fact that, for all and everything, he had something the rest of them didn't: a brain. But in a handful of days, it had deserted him. Alfonso had said he needed rescuing from his tower, but right now Hemmings felt more like he'd been kidnapped.

His and Alfonso's version of play was going magnificently, the actors performing wonderfully – there were a couple of stumbles over their new lines, but nothing serious. The audience was enchanted. He could feel it, the power of the story washing over them. The energy tingled against his skin. The feeling that everyone was experiencing something, together, and yet making it their own.

When the father died, the audience drew back in horror. When the Prince, played with such depth and sensitivity by Alfonso, lamented his curse and the choice he had made to bring it upon himself, more than one person reached for their hanky. When Beatrice, playing the maiden with the missing hand, stood up in the second act and demanded her freedom, the audience cheered and hollered and applauded.

And yet Melly sat, stony still, throughout it all. Even when the little girl next to her jumped up on her hay bale, her fist raised, and yelled something Hemmings couldn't hear, Melly didn't even twitch.

Hemmings continued chewing his handkerchief.

※

Applause erupted all around her, near deafening.

F. D. Lee

Giss grabbed Melly's hand and pulled her down, so her ear was near Giss' mouth. "Did you see it, Mildred? Did you see the girl fight back?"

Melly nodded. "Yes, Giss, I saw."

"It was amazing. She bashed that old monster on his head, and then she told them all off, and then the Prince came and they went to the castle, and they found the cure and then the Prince was all better and-"

"Yes, I saw it, too. You liked it then?"

Giss beamed at her. "Yes. I liked it a lot."

"Why?"

The little girl pursed her lips. "Because it was good," she finally said.

Melly nodded. She patted Giss on the head and then slipped away from the lights and the noise. Kathy and Josh didn't notice, they were too busy having their own conversation about the play.

The moon was up, but it was still warm. She came to the edge of the field and stood by the hawthorn row. The field beyond was lain with barley, shining almost white in the pale light, its thin, feathery stalks swaying gently in the breeze.

Someone coughed, politely.

"You changed the play," Melly said, not bothering to look around. There was only one other person present who could move so quickly and quietly.

"Yes," Hemmings said.

"After I expressly forbade it."

"Yes."

Melly sighed and turned to him. He looked extremely anxious. She couldn't help feeling rather pleased. Old habits.

"Why did you change it?"

Hemmings sighed. "Because it's better this way. You can't stop stories. And you shouldn't keep them the same. They need to change with the people who have to hear them."

Melly thought about Giss and Ana, and the manufactories in Cerne Bralksteld which they both, in different ways, represented in her mind. "Yes," she said.

"Yes? You mean you agree with me?"

The Princess And The Orrery

"Yes. I do." She took a breath. In front of her, the barley swayed. "You have to understand that everything I told you before is true. That hasn't changed. The GenAm, the Mirrors, the genie, none of that is different. But... Ana told me that perhaps people have changed. I think she was right. The humans need stories, but they don't need ours. They need their own. And you saw that before I did."

"I... thank you."

"Yes, well," Melly said, folding her arms. "We still have a lot to do. And I hold to the fact that we need to get you away from all this as soon as possible, especially that Alfonso. Elves and theatre don't mix at the best of times, and I'd bet my crown he's got designs on you."

Hemmings' eyes darted up to her head, and Melly remembered suddenly that she'd watched Ana throw her crown away. But instead of drawing attention to its absence, he said, "Alfonso and I are just friends. I know why we're here, what we have to do."

"Mmm. Good. And well done with the play. It was very entertaining."

Melly held her hand out, her expression impassive. Hemmings looked down at it, startled. And then he took her hand in his and shook it.

38

"Yes! It worked!"

The orrery glided smoothly, the latest planet settling easily into its new arc. There were seven planets now, each one moving through its revolution in a complicated dance, looping around the central pillar and over and under each other. Well, all except the black planet, which moved more ponderously on its trajectory, like a cart horse pulling a heavy load.

Amelia grinned at Seven, creating a somewhat kaleidoscopic effect as the dirt and grease clashed with her sunny-brown complexion.

"As you predicted it would," Seven replied. Considering what they'd achieved, he looked remarkably gloomy. He'd been in a mood all day, and yesterday, too.

"So, who taught you about astronomy, anyway?" Amelia asked, grabbing Barry and padding over to join him where he was sitting, morose, on the floor.

"Many people, one way or another. Though some knew not what they were saying. The language did not exist, then, to describe what it was they wanted."

"That doesn't make sense. How did they know what to say?"

Seven rested his elbows on his knees, his forehead against his knuckles. "If one knows how to listen, words are not necessary."

"Naima says that listening is the first step to knowing."

"Hmf. You admire her greatly."

Amelia fiddled with Barry's ears. "She takes me seriously. Even though she calls me 'little princess'. Which I'm not, by the way. My parents are Counts, which makes me a Right Honourable Lady."

Seven looked up. "Ah, so? It is a Baronet here."

"I'm not from here." Amelia shifted, crossing her legs like Seven, and set Barry between her thighs. "I was thinking about how cold you are. Did you know there are some plants and animals

The Princess And The Orrery

that actually thrive in the cold? And they say it can be a sign of pregnancy."

Despite his air of gloom, he smiled. "I assure you, I am not pregnant."

"Ha, ha. Sailors use the cold to desalinate seawater, too. The salt crystallises when the water freezes. There are lots of things cold can do, in actual fact. But it shatters steel. A lot of metal can't function in the cold. And people, too. We die in the cold."

"Not always," Seven countered. "The people of Voriias have learnt how to survive in the bitterest of climates."

"Exactly! So, you see, I was thinking maybe your people come from somewhere beyond Voriias. We don't really know what's past there – the Republic doesn't explore, and the O&P haven't found a way to get a boat up past the ice flows. What do you think of that?"

"Nothing at all," Seven said, getting to his feet. "You have your new planet. I am going to bed."

Amelia stood with him. "I was just saying, that's all. I don't see why you're in such a foul mood – don't you realise how lucky you are to be here?"

Seven looked down at her, his pretty face blank. And then he shrugged. "It matters not what I think. None of this matters."

"Well, if that's how you're going to be about it, I'll ask Joseph to send me someone else to help with the orrery-"

Seven doubled over, gasping, his eyes screwed shut, teeth bared.

"...Seven?"

He fell to his knees, his arms wrapped around his stomach. A low groan emanated from between his teeth.

"What's happening?" Amelia cried. "Seven? Seven?"

Still struggling for breath, Seven tried to right himself.

The orrery groaned, the planets seeming to strain against their mechanisms.

Amelia spun around, her attention torn between him and the orrery.

"Our work..." Seven breathed, his voice thin and alien. "Too much for me... Rest..."

"Of course. We haven't stopped all day, and you're very old," Amelia said with all the confidence of one barely into double figures. "Do you need something to eat? Water?"

"Just... rest... you... work... please..."

Amelia dithered for a moment and then nodded. "Alright. Let me help you."

They managed to get him to his bed. Seven lay absolutely still. Amelia sat next to him, her heart pounding, at a loss for what to do. She suggested summoning Naima, but Seven just grunted and shook his head. In the end, she poured him a glass of water and offered him little sips until, eventually, the tension in his face eased and his body relaxed.

Behind her, unnoticed, the orrery slowed ever so slightly, for a split second holding the planets in alignment.

A crackle of energy forked across the black sphere, gone in the blink of an eye. The planets resumed their normal rotations.

Mistasinon's head shot up from the Book he was reading, an animal sensing a predator.

He closed the Book and brought himself to his feet, moving slowly. The long, Book-lined corridors of the Index stretched out as far as he could see. But Mistasinon wasn't using his eyes to locate the source of his unease.

He reached into his pocket, fingers closing around the scrap of material Bea had given him, then lifted his head so that his nose was high, and sniffed.

Nothing, except the smell of old paper and leather and, one floor below him, someone sweating as they shelved the latest additions to the Index.

He closed his eyes and took a deeper breath, letting the world flow over his senses, flooding him.

Boredom, frustration from the worker below...
Mould and oil and binding material...
Concentration...
A half-eaten sandwich...

The Princess And The Orrery

Hunger...

And nothing else, except the Books. He shook his head, releasing the scrap of material in his pocket. It was probably just a trick of his nose, like the way it decided on a whim to flood him with sensations and then, at other times, to barely work at all.

Nevertheless, he put Bea's Book back on the shelf and then carefully picked up the papers he'd taken from his satchel: his own scrawled, handwritten account of her Plot. He'd been cross-referencing his notes with the official copy he had submitted to the Index, looking for the thing that had tickled his mind.

Pulling his satchel onto his shoulder, he followed the corridor to the circular stairwell that bisected the Index and trotted down the stairs, following his nose until he came upon a goblin. She was sitting on a pile of Books, eating.

The goblin looked him up and down, taking in the colour of his suit, and quickly swallowed her food.

"My Lord?"

"Er... Hello. I was just wondering if you're the only person down here?"

"Yes, my Lord. Just me. There's not many to put away."

"Ah. Yes. And you didn't, um, I don't know, sense anything just now?"

The goblin blinked her large, round eyes at him. "No, my Lord. Just you."

Mistasinon turned and looked behind him. The corridor was reasonably well-lit, though for obvious reasons the Index discouraged open flames. Still, covered lamps lit the way at wide intervals, working on low wicks hidden within thick glass. He could just about make out the staircase – but then, the goblin had better eyesight than him.

"But you didn't see anyone else?"

"No, my Lord."

"And there's no other way into the Index?"

She gave him a funny look. "No, my Lord. Just the staircase."

"Yes. Of course. Sorry. I'll leave you to your meal – oh, one last thing, if you don't mind? Are you hungry?"

The funny look evolved into one of outright confusion. "Yes, my Lord – that's why I'm having my lunch."

"Yes, of course. Thank you. I'll leave you to it, then."

Mistasinon walked away, pausing at the staircase for another sniff. He picked up nothing that couldn't be accounted for.

He really was going mad – he could have sworn that, for a fraction of a second, he'd picked up the odd, sparkling scent of magic. But then, his nose was hardly reliable, was it? And he was studying Bea's Plot, his version of which was rife with mentions of the genie. No doubt reading about Seven had awakened some latent memory that one of his other hims had been carrying and which, now he was alone, he'd forgotten he knew.

He stood, undecided, on the stairwell.

Magic might seem to appear and disappear in the blink of an eye, but it had a strong smell. It *pervaded*. Hah. Bea had stunk of it when she'd visited his office after seeing the genie, when she'd thought he didn't know what was happening. The Mirrors, too, when they were working properly, carried the faint smell of magic. But there hadn't been any significant amounts of magic in Ænathlin for years. It had gone with the genies.

He shook his head. He'd let his mind wander, and it had taken advantage of its freedom to team up with his nose and play tricks on him. It occurred to him that it could even have been one of his other hims. Did one survive and two die, or were they still inside him somewhere, taking their revenge? The thought made him shudder, though he wasn't sure whether it was the idea that he wasn't alone in his mind, or the possibility that he was, that upset him.

Well, assuming it was just him, he'd have to learn to keep an eye on himself. Yes. He was a person, now. Not a real one, maybe, but some approximation of it. He allowed himself a little smile, pleased he had managed to reason through the strange, momentary confusion that had overcome him.

Perhaps, with practice, he really would get control of himself and his senses.

Mistasinon walked back to the shelf with Bea's Book, away from the hidden room at the bottom of the Index where the broken Mirrors were kept, feeling something that might, under a gentle light, have been pride.

The Princess And The Orrery

Deep in the darkness of the Index, a small, seemingly inconsequential piece of wood and glass flailed across the floor, twitching and jumping, clattering and banging.

The wood spasmed. Groaned. The grooves along its surface split open. The creature wiggled free, birthing itself in sap and splinters.

Barely an inch long, it was neither snake nor octopus but something in between. Six tentacles, sticky with their own liquids, eagerly tested the environment, some pressing against the ground while others tasted the air, small circular sensory features on the ends of each muscle opening and closing. Tiny, serrated teeth snapped as it worked its beak-like mouth.

A tentacle pressed against a shard of glass, cut itself, and retracted back into the creature's tubular body in shock. Too late. For something so small, the cut was mortal.

The whole process lasted less than a couple of seconds, but as the creature lay dying, it used the last of its energy to transmit what it had found back to its hive, its power pulled into the vacuum it had pushed through to arrive.

Confinement. Darkness. Pain.
Not here. But close. Soon.
The way is opening.
Find the path.

Any planet is home if you take it.

39

The weeks had not been kind to Joseph. His illness had flared up again, forcing him to his bed, subsisting on a diet of thin soup and thick, white bread, the only things that didn't aggravate him. But it was a hardship he was used to bearing, and it gave him some peace to read.

He'd hoped that Naima might visit him. It was a new and exciting thing to have a friend, but he supposed she was busy organising the Cultivators. She'd kept to her word and not visited Amelia again, according to the girl's hastily written reports. The genie, too, seemed to be performing his task well. Joseph was certainly pleased with their progress, which was the central matter.

It was all falling into place. Strange, really, to think that the thing which had plagued him as a child had become his biggest asset. Without his illness, he never would have become so isolated, never been permitted the freedom to focus on the hidden truths of the stories he'd devoured as a child. Hell, his father would have seen to it that all his books were taken away if he'd not written him off as a dead weight.

Joseph had learnt to wear his loneliness like a cloak, sheltering him from the rumours and abuse his disease heaped upon him. Within the Palace walls, his brother had seen to it that people steered clear of him by spreading lies about his habits and interests – lies other people were only too happy to believe of the quiet, intense, skeletal man he had become, who sat wreathed in smoke and always smelled of medicine, who walked with a cane and disappeared for weeks on end. Who had developed hobbies and obsessions to fill the time that should have been spent with other people, learning how to become a person himself.

What a difference it would have made if he'd had someone to join him in his mock battles, to share his love of folklore and figure painting, to sit with him when he was in pain and alone.

But it wasn't to be. The second son of the Baron was afforded every doctor money could buy, but the treasury had never stretched so far as kindness. Joseph, for his own part, saw himself in the characters in his storybooks; the hero, trapped in a curse with only his guile and determination to save him. But where those stories ended with the hero magically restored, Joseph had set his sights on a far grander ending:

A cure for everyone.

"It's about time."

The Baron glared from his golden seat as Joseph entered the throne room of the Imperial Palace, leaning heavily on his cane.

The room was long and cool, with high pillars every few yards designed to intimidate and, more practically, to support the ceiling. Huge chandeliers swung from that same ceiling, lit by candles and oil lamps day and night against the constant threat of darkness. In any other space, especially at this time of year, the heat would have been unbearable; however, inside the canyon, all those flames did was lift the room to a mild fifteen degrees.

The Baron's attendants tutted and scowled at Joseph. Chattering sycophants. They reminded him of the tales of talking monkeys, screeching and gibbering, never saying anything of value. When he, Joseph, was finally in power, he'd have each and every one of them sent to the deepest, darkest part of the manufactories.

Ah, no, Joseph corrected himself, *when I am in power, I won't need to send them anywhere.* The thought cheered him immeasurably.

"Apologies, brother," he said. "I was busy working on-"

"Don't tell me, let me guess." The Baron grinned beatifically at his attendants, patting his swollen belly. They giggled and nodded, encouraging him with whispered compliments and feigned curiosity. "You were working on a spy hole in the lower quarters, so you can watch the scullery maids undressing?"

A chorus of laughter from the monkeys.

Encouraged, the Baron tried again. "No, you were hiding in the steam-mat to imbibe the air for your 'health' – and steal some unwashed knickers from the pile?"

The monkeys howled their amusement.

"Aha, no! I have it! You were in the stables, in the mistaken belief that the smell of the manure might cover the stench of your-"

"You're very funny, brother. I'm sure you'll be remembered for your wit."

The chattering monkeys fell silent.

"Better than being remembered for being a sickly, whiny little freak who gets his kicks playing with dolls," the Baron shot back, biting his lower lip and curling his upper lip to reveal his teeth – an expression that was, locally, the height of rudeness. Joseph ignored it.

"Soldiers, brother, not dolls. You wished to see me?"

The Baron heaved himself out of his chair and made his way down the steps leading from the throne to the floor, his enormous, stockinged thighs rubbing together in a manner that made Joseph repress a shudder. His fingers twitched, tightening on his cane. If only he had one of his modelling knives in his hand instead!

His brother arrived at Joseph's side and slung an arm across his shoulder, his breath hot against his skin. "Preparations for Calan Mai are underway. Fire, feasting and maybe a little bit of the other 'eff', too, if you catch my meaning."

"I think I understand, brother, despite the subtlety."

The Baron's brief camaraderie shrivelled and died. "Watch your tongue, Joe, or I'll have it pulled out where others can keep a better eye on it. It's caused me enough trouble already. Hence this quiet word we are now engaged in."

"Yes?"

"This festival's my favourite, Joe. The weather's picking up, winter's on her heels. Food, drink, the bonfires – even got some theatrics set up. I *was* looking forward to it. And then what should come to my attention, do you wonder, while you've been in your bed?"

"I have no idea."

"Well, you're about to. I've been getting grief from that woman you were obsessed with last year. Listen to me, Joe. Listen very bloody carefully. I don't really care what you get up to. All the time you spend on your own with your weird little hobbies. But this time you've caused me some trouble." The Baron didn't even bother lowering his voice. All the monkeys could hear him, and they snickered. Joseph turned slightly, so he didn't have to look at them.

The Baron continued, nonplussed. "God knows why, but it seems she's rather stuck on you. Normally I'd tell her to count her blessings and be glad you're not interested anymore, but this is a diplomatic matter."

"I honestly have no idea what you're talking about."

"Didn't I tell you to listen? She's coming to my festival, without her husband. Threatening all sorts of nonsense if she ain't invited – all because she wants to see you. Now, whatever it is you've got going on with her, I want it sorted, understand? I won't have you embarrassing me with your... well, just with yourself."

"I don't know what woman you're talking about. I've never-"

"Like I said, I don't care what you get up to, as long as we can cover it up. But this one's a Countess. Even I can't shove her in the manufactories and be done with it, or so I've been advised. Good God, man – a Countess? A creepy little weirdo you are, Joe, but I never took you for an idiot."

Realisation dawned.

Joseph's mind spun. Not a Countess. *The* Countess. Amelia's mother. So, she'd finally found a way to force his hand. God damn it! How had he let that happen?

But he knew. He'd been relying on the wish, thinking he was untouchable. He supposed he couldn't blame the genie for this, tempting as it was. And the irony of it! It was almost funny. That it would be her who caused him this new problem. He had to get this back under control, and quickly.

"Ah. Yes. I know the woman. I did try to keep this away from you. I can only apologise."

The Baron smacked his lips, the sign he was trying to gather a thought in his thick head. "To be honest, the whole thing's given me a bit of a laugh – but I won't be laughing if you show me up, got it?"

"Got it."

"Just stick to the help, or get yourself a woman from the Scree if you must," he said, referring to the cluster of houses built into

F. D. Lee

the foot of the cliff face, right in the narrow point where the canyon petered out, where there was low light and rising damp.

"Wise words, brother," Joseph said, his voice measured. Only the tapping of his fingers against his cane betrayed the rage inside him. It was no good. He could stand it no longer. He had the genie, he had the orrery – well, almost, but the genie would get it working if he wanted him to. Such was the genius of his wish. And wasn't there some poetry to the idea of rising to his true station on Calan Mai? The seasonal change, heralding the rightful ruler...

Yes. It was time.

But first, he had to maintain the facade of inferiority.

"Brother, I am sorry to have caused you this problem. Perhaps I could do something to make it up to you?"

The Baron snorted. "I treasure my ignorance on the things you do, locked up in your rooms with your dolls and children's stories. No, thank you."

"Please. Let me give you a gift. A device the Cultivators have been working on for me for more than two years. A wonderful device. It's bound to impress everyone. You know how jealous all the neighbouring rulers are of our technological advancement."

The Baron rubbed his chins. "Mmm. True."

"It's a marvel of the modern age. Steam-powered. Mathematically divined. Beautiful – polished wood and brass."

"Oh, very well then," the Baron said, as if he were doing Joseph a favour. "You can present it to me between the theatre and the bonfire."

"Thank you, brother."

"Yes. Well. Go get on with whatever it is you do all day." The Baron looked him up and down, his lip curling. "Makes my skin itch spending so much time with you. Father always said you were contagious."

Joseph bowed and made his escape. He hobbled through the lamp-lit corridors of the Palace, his cane leaving small circular welts in the plush carpets. When he arrived at his official office, he wrote a short note to Naima, demanding she meet him in an hour... no, two hours... And then another to the snotty cow of a Countess, telling her he would meet with her at the festival, as long as she promised she wouldn't make a scene or try to interfere prior. Hell,

The Princess And The Orrery

not that it would matter much if she did, but he'd prefer things to go smoothly. He wanted a show, after all.

Joseph took a moment to read his letter back. And then, on a whim, he added the promise that she could have the thing she wanted, the thing they'd bargained for. It wouldn't matter once the orrery was working.

In the privacy of his rooms, he allowed himself a wide smile, revealing his narrow, worn-down teeth – damaged from countless bouts of sickness and failed attempts at treatment. He still remembered the stinging, fizzing medicine his so-called doctors had foisted on him as a young man, given in the hopes of burning away the rot inside him... and how it had burned. But it didn't matter. The past was done. It was the future Joseph was looking to.

Soon everyone would finally see the real him.

40

There was a knock at the observatory door.

"We are expecting company?" Seven asked, wiping his brow.

He was laying across the orrery's newest planet, fiddling with the adjustments. There had been a bit of a row over it; Amelia saying he wasn't well enough to go climbing the device. He'd argued back, Amelia eventually throwing her hands in the air and saying that if he hurt himself, that was his choice, though he'd been aware of her eyes on him like a hawk the entire time he was up there.

Probably worried he would do something to damage the machine – if only he could. But it was too late. The piece of his necklace had found a new home in the orrery. Or an old home, he supposed. Now his only chance of escape lay with getting his hands on the remainder of his necklace, a near-impossible task. He doubted very much Joseph would give it up willingly.

"What? Oh, no. I don't think so," Amelia said, watching him through a glass and metal device of her own design. "You need to tighten the A6 again."

"I have tightened it, thrice. It is as tight as it is able to be. Are you not going to see who is without?"

"Without? Without what?"

"The knocker." Seven slid down from the planet. "It might be an important guest."

"Nothing's more important that the orrery. Besides-"

The door opened. Naima stepped into the room.

"-they'll let themselves in, anyway," Amelia finished.

"My favourite gaoler, finally come to call on us," Seven said, not bothering to keep the bitterness out of his voice. "You are in luck, Madam, for you find us both at our leisure and able to receive visitors."

"Ignore him, he's in a bad mood," Amelia said to Naima. "He won't tell me why."

Naima turned her attention to Seven, quick as the snake she was. "You'd better not try anything. I won't have you... upsetting... Amelia, understand?"

"What are you talking about?" Amelia said.

"Our warden believes I mean you harm," Seven replied. "The irony of which astounds even I."

It was intriguing. Naima cared for the girl's safety, at the very least. Her spike in anger had come with a very real need to get the girl away from him, amplifying a low-level and ever-present desire to keep Amelia from harm's way. Why then did she allow Joseph such control over Amelia's fate? Was she so stupid as to be blind to what the man was?

And what did he care, anyway?

"Oh, no," Amelia said. "Seven's my friend. He's just not feeling very well. Anyway, we should have the orrery finished soon."

"That's what I need to talk to you about," Naima said, her eyes still on Seven.

"Why are you staring at him like that?" Amelia asked. "He's vain enough as it is."

"It is not vanity if it serves a purpose," he said. "I have found it extremely useful to be thought beautiful."

"Huh. If you say so. I'm never going to bother with stuff like that. I'm definitely not going to get married or have children."

"You may very well have the right idea, my Lady. Love has certainly offered me no kindness."

"See? And you're sooooo pretty, too." She grinned at him. "You should use what's inside your head, instead. You're quite clever when you want to be."

And Seven, he knew not why, found himself a little cheered. He even chuckled. "Attend as I hang my oh-so-pretty head in shame at my misguided attempts to best you."

Amelia burst out laughing.

Naima stared at them. "You... you're joking with this mon- this man?"

"Why should she not?" Seven snapped, his levity dissolving as quickly as it had arisen.

"I can think of more than one reason."

F. D. Lee

"Ah, yes. I remember well the kind of things you think of. It seems we both know what you are prepared to do to see these thoughts actualised. I wonder if you would be so confident if-"

The wish clawed at his stomach – not attacking, but warning. Amelia watched them both, an anxious look on her face.

"...if you were to visit more often, and see how hard we are working?" he concluded, softening the edge in his voice. "Do you not think the orrery is looking fine?"

Amelia relaxed. The wish retreated. "Yes, do you like it?"

"It's very impressive, Amelia," Naima said. "It's the orrery I need to talk to you about, in fact. It won't take long."

"A splendid suggestion," Seven said, wanting nothing more than to get rid of this woman – why he had let her comment get under his skin was anybody's guess, but it was certainly better that she left. "Barry would no doubt like some fresh air."

Amelia pursed her lips. And then she picked up the toy bear and brought him over to Seven. "No. Barry wants to stay with you. He can keep an eye on you."

"Ah, so? Then I thank you, Barry. And you, too, my Lady. We will take good care of each other."

Looking over her shoulder at him, Amelia allowed Naima to lead her from the room. Seven sat crossed-legged on the floor, idly running his fingers through Barry's soft, thick fur.

He had to be more careful. Why had he allowed himself to argue with Naima, and in front of Amelia, no less? The girl had already forced too much from him, and now he was volunteering his own exposure over some snide comment from a woman too stupid to realise she'd crawled into the lion's cave expecting to find shelter.

But then, if Naima was staring at the lion, Seven had already been devoured.

Joseph's second wish was, he had to admit, a clever one: *Happiness*.

Everything Seven did had to ensure Joseph's continued happiness. And, by all the gods in all the worlds, the wish bound him perfectly, blocking intention and action, omission and neglect. Currently, what Joseph wanted to make him happy was the orrery. After that... who knew?

The Princess And The Orrery

But it was now Seven's bound duty to keep the man happy. Anything he did that might negate that would see the wish broken, and the retribution of magic upon him. His fingers tightened in Barry's fur, squeezing his fat tummy. In front of him, the orrery turned, the black sphere casting its relentless shadow.

Perhaps he was worrying about nothing. Joseph couldn't know what the original *es'hajit* were designed for, couldn't know what a surge in power would invite. And even if he did, the chances of anything coming from the black planet were a million to one.

And yet, long ago, they had come...

He needed his necklace back. It was the only hope he had, and even so, it was not guaranteed it would offer him enough protection to find a way out of Joseph's wish. How could he have allowed it to be taken from him in the first place?

But he knew the answer, of course. In a moment of weakness, in a moment of *belief*, he had thought he could trust a human. That The Woman was different. That she loved him for what he was, not what he could offer her.

Belief – it ought to be too horrendous to be embarrassing, but nevertheless it was.

He should have known better, that was the truth of it. After all, the duplicity of humankind was one of the first lessons the genies had ever learnt.

When they had first arrived on Thaiana, refugees from their own world, they had sought shelter, offering help and protection in return. Offering their gift. They hadn't known, in the beginning, that they had no way to refuse, only that they could mitigate the power of the wish, channelling it through the connection the *gu'lin vut* made between them and the wisher, so that it wouldn't kill them outright.

But the humans had realised their weakness quickly enough.

It didn't take a genius to work out how badly that ended. Only the stories of the limitation saved them, and then only because they rarely survived multiple wishes in quick succession. Only because the genies learnt the necessity of manipulation, of ensuring that most people very rarely wanted more than three wishes.

F. D. Lee

The genies may well have grown cruel, but only because the humans had taught them so decisively what they were capable of when they could get exactly what they wanted.

He watched the orrery, feeling suddenly heavy and tired. Was it simply the genies' fate to die? Perhaps Amelia's *es'hajit* was the inevitable ending for the last ever genie. The circle finishing its loop.

But he didn't want to die. He never had. Noble as it was to sacrifice himself, he didn't have the courage. There had to be another way, a loophole in Joseph's wish. Seven was a genie, gods damn it. He might be alone. He might be a coward. But he was still himself.

Something tickled his hand. Seven pulled his eyes from the orrery. There, resting on the curve of his thumb, was a tangle of his own hair. Shaking it off, he reached up to touch his scalp, gently running his fingers through his tousled curls. When he pulled his hand away, strands of hair were woven between his fingers.

Whatever he was going to do, he needed to do it fast.

41

Amelia followed Naima through the busy corridors of Starry Castle.

It was always full of hustle and bustle, the other Cultivators dashing to and fro, often trying to navigate around each other from underneath huge piles of manuscripts and notebooks. There was a particular smell to Starry Castle, an amalgam-like mess of a hundred other little smells all bundled up together: old paper and odd alchemical scents, stodgy food cooked *en-masse*, candle wax and the sweet scent of heated metal.

Naima brought her to the canteen, a vast open space with long lines of wooden tables and a kitchen that could be seen through a wide serving window. The Cultivators went up to the window and chose from selections of pre-plated food which were kept warm atop candle-lit heating trays. It was impossibly hot, even with the windows thrown open and giant fans spinning on clockwork mechanisms. The days were getting longer, the sun taking advantage of its turn in charge of the skies.

Long, hot days were rotten luck for the chefs, replacing meals on an endless cycle. It didn't matter what time it was – a Cultivator could walk into the canteen at 3am and choose from breakfast foods or snacks or even a full-on roast dinner. No one kept proper hours in Starry Castle – you worked to the task, not to the time.

And yet, it was still worse for others. While all this industry went on, slaves cleaned and washed-up, peeled and primed, stirred and sorted. Even in winter, it was hot, tiring and thankless work. In the summer, it was torture. The chefs shouted and bullied, and the Cultivators huffed and puffed if they had to wait. Slaves slept in short shifts in an old stable block transformed into dormitories, behind the kitchens. In the heat, the acrid stench of horse urine rose up from the brickwork to clog their noses and seep into their lungs.

But it was better than the manufactories. Almost anything was better than the manufactories.

"Do you want some juice? Tea?" Naima asked, ushering Amelia to a table.

"I want to talk about Seven, since we're here. I think he's sick, he keeps having these funny turns. My brother got sick, and we had to get the doctors in for a whole month to get him better. He had the 'enza, and we all thought he was going to die, but the doctor said we caught it early enough. You have to catch these things early, the doctor said."

Naima took a seat. She had the hunted look that grown-ups got when they were trying to hide something but hadn't managed to get their faces in order. Tricksy, hippity-hoppity little lies darting into the shadows under eyes and hiding in the deep lines in the sides of mouths. Amelia had seen it plenty of times.

"He seemed fine to me," Naima replied. "Sit down."

"How do you know he's not sick?" Amelia demanded. "People get sick, and then they die."

"Amelia, please. Sit down."

"Get him a doctor and I'll sit down."

"Sit down, Amelia. I am your superior, and you will do as I instruct."

"Fine." Amelia pulled a chair back and threw herself down heavily, folded her arms and glared at Naima. "Happy?"

"Delighted. Now, listen to me. Seven isn't going to die. He's not... Amelia, you must realise that Seven isn't like us?"

"Just like all the slaves? I thought you disagreed with slavery? Besides, Seven's alive, isn't he? He eats and sleeps and uses the toilet. How much more similar to us does he have to be?"

Hah! She'd got her there, Amelia could tell.

"Well, yes," Naima said, tangling her hair in her fingers for a moment, before she noticed and stopped. "You're right about the slaves, and I know Seven isn't a, a, thing... But what he is – I mean, he isn't... I don't think you need to worry about him the way you are."

"He's my friend. Like you. I'd worry about you if you were falling over and fainting. Wouldn't you worry about me?"

"Of course I would-"

"Well, then." Amelia fixed Naima with a very hard stare. "What's the difference?"

The Princess And The Orrery

Naima fell silent. Amelia waited.

"Seven works for Joseph," Naima said at last. "Joseph won't let anything happen to him."

"Does Joseph know he's sick?"

"Oh, yes. Definitely."

Amelia considered. Joseph was the Baron's brother and very powerful. And he'd made sure that Amelia could join the Cultivators – he'd sorted it out with her mother, personally. And he'd introduced her to Naima, who was usually very clever even if she was behaving stupidly right now. So, if Joseph knew Seven was unwell and he wanted Seven to be able to work for him, it stood to reason that if Seven was *really* sick, Joseph would make him better.

And yet, despite the logic of this thought process, Amelia didn't find it at all comforting.

"If he knows he's sick, why is he making him work? Is Seven a slave as well? Is that it?"

"Not a slave, no," Naima said slowly. "More like... indentured. Do you know that word?"

"Of course I do. My father has heaps of indentured people who work on the farms and so on. Ground tenants, freeholders, all that."

"And your father expects them to work? To pay their taxes, even when they're unwell?"

"Well... yes. I suppose so."

"It's the same kind of thing, then," Naima said, but she didn't sound particularly convinced by her own argument.

Amelia was almost entirely certain it wasn't the same at all. If only she'd paid more attention when her father had been banging on about state business. Now she had to think about it, there didn't seem to be a whole lot of difference between the slaves here and the people back home in Marlais.

True, they weren't forced to work, not as such. They could choose to leave. But where would they go? To another Kingdom with the same rules. Wherever the peasants went, Amelia realised, they all had to work the fields or create produce, providing coin or goods in return for their houses and access to the land and the protection of the armed men and women her parents, or people like them, employed.

If they got sick and couldn't work, what happened to them? Or what if they wanted to study, as she did? The truth was, Amelia had no idea.

"People always have masters, Amelia," Naima said gently. "My father was an Officer in one of the standing armies in the Six Points. He was a good man, kind and straightforward. But he expected his soldiers to do their job, to follow orders."

"I s'pose so," Amelia said. It still didn't seem right. But Naima's next question shunted the thought from her mind.

"So. You and Seven are friends, then?"

"Yes," Amelia said. "He doesn't really understand what he knows, which can be a bit annoying as it takes ages to get at the important information, but he's very hard working. I think he's quite kind, actually, but he gets embarrassed about it and then has to have a huff."

"But he hasn't... I don't know... put ideas into your head?"

"Yes, obviously he has. That's the whole point of him being my assistant, isn't it? To help me have new ideas about the orrery. Why are you being so weird about him?"

Naima shook her head. "It's nothing. I'm glad you're getting on."

"He's funny, too."

"Funny?"

"Yes – he makes me laugh. He's easy to tease, too, but he laughs at himself. I like him a lot. We're a team. *Gu'lin vut*, he called it."

Naima opened her mouth, then closed it. Shook her head again. "Well, I'm pleased. I was worried because I've not been able to visit you, but it's good that nothing's happened. Now listen, I didn't bring you here to talk about Seven. You know the spring festival is nearly here?"

"What's that got to do with me?"

"Joseph would like the orrery finished by then. He has a lot of important people visiting, there'll be music and theatre and dancers and food. It should be a lot of fun."

"It sounds like more politics to me. But he wants the orrery there?"

Naima smiled, though it seemed to Amelia that she'd forgotten to tell her eyes to match her mouth. "Yes exactly. He wants to show it off, I think. Can you have it finished in time?"

"I don't know. Maybe. We've got seven planets now, but it doesn't feel finished yet. I should ask Seven." She stood up, pushing her chair under the table. "I won't get it finished wasting time here."

"Wait. There's something else..."

"What?"

"When I tell you, I want you to remember that while you are staying here, you have duties to the Sisterhood. I don't want any upset."

"What is it?"

Naima took a deep breath. "Your mother's coming to the festival. She wants to see you."

42

"Uh, m'lord, beggin' your pardon, but I don't think that's such a good idea."

Mistasinon paused in the middle of the reception to Bea's building. The gnome who worked the desk was eyeballing him, a cloud of reddy-brown fear swirling around his head.

"I'm sorry?"

Ivor fidgeted, like his lower half was trying to abandon his station but his top half wasn't allowing it. "On your way up to see her Ladyship?"

"I'm here on business, yes."

Some strange theatre played out on the stage of the gnome's face. It included all the major actors – eyes, eyebrows, lips and teeth – and also had parts for some newcomers, including the ears and cheeks. It was a virtuoso performance from all involved and conveyed very fully the difficulties Ivor was currently experiencing speaking to an Official General Administration Blue Suit.

"S'not my place to tell a suit what to do. You come and go however you like, m'lord. I'm just saying she ain't her best self. Been in a foul mood since – for a couple of days. Might be better if you, er, you didn't see her, no offence."

"I need to ask her some questions," Mistasinon said.

"Like I said, ain't my place to say you can't, m'lord. Just... well, she ain't working for the GenAm no more, and I ain't sure why you're coming 'round. Seems t'me like maybe your, uh, your responsibilities are finished."

Ivor's eyes bulged. The stench of fear was thick and heavy, but the gnome nevertheless held his ground. "She don't mean no harm, m'lord. She don't deserve no harm, neither."

"I understand. I won't... It's just business." Mistasinon paused. "You're a good friend."

He left the gnome in his cloud of fear and made his way up four flights of dark, sticky stairs. A hobgoblin appeared from his flat, took one look at Mistasinon's suit, and darted back inside.

He reached Bea's door and knocked twice. Some muffled swearwords greeted him about two seconds before the door opened and then Bea was in front of him.

"Ha. Hello, Mr Plotter."

"Um. Hi."

"What are you doing here?"

He rubbed his neck. He'd been planning what to say, and now he couldn't remember a single one of his carefully composed lines. "I need to speak to you. About the Mirrors."

"The Mirrors. Of course."

"It's important. I wouldn't have come if-"

"-if it wasn't important, sure. Spit it out, then."

"Er. Can I come in?"

She stood for a moment, glaring. Then she gave a curt nod and beckoned him in.

Nothing had changed – though why he thought it might have done was beyond him. Her bed was made, though there were some clothes scattered on her tiny sofa. The only new additions were a near-empty bottle of wine on the kitchen table and a large pile of papers next to it.

He walked over to the table; they were leaflets, emblazoned with large, cheap print:

Fairies United
Law abiding ~ Plot enabling

PUBLIC MEETING

The Quill and Ink
Double Fortune Lane

all fae WELCOME to join
Refreshments served

F. D. Lee

'Fairy rights are Fae rights!'

"Well?" Bea said. She had closed the door and was leaning against it, arms folded.

He looked up.

"I... I wanted to talk to you about your Plot. The one you worked on with Sindy."

"Alright. Sit down, then."

He took a seat at the table, but Bea didn't join him. Instead, she rummaged in her cupboards. Mistasinon's heart sank. She couldn't stand to be near him. But perhaps that was better? Easier. Safer. Although he would have been hard pressed to say who he thought it was safer for.

But in fact, Bea was just getting another bottle of cheap, vinegary wine and a second glass. The smell, sharp as knives, made him blink. She plopped down on the chair next to him and poured out the last of the old bottle into her glass before opening the new one, topping herself off and pouring one for him.

The sediment at the bottom of the glass shifted and spun as he picked it up. Muddy and confused, just like him. He took a sip, this time prepared for the sharp heat.

"So, then-" Bea burped into her fist. "-'xcuse me- the Mirrors?"

He blinked. "You're drunk?"

"Only a little. Garden fairies are made of strong stuff, or so I've been told. All the cabbage soaks up the booze. Besides, it's my business. I said, didn't I, that if you didn't want to see me, I'd respect that – seems to me the courtesy should go both ways, but I guess the GenAm is more important, right?"

"The Mirrors are the most important thing. They always will be."

She stared at him for a moment, her expression unreadable. And then she took a gulp of wine and waved her hand, a signal to say what he'd come to say.

He looked at the door. The gnome had been right. The best thing to do was leave. But he was here now, and he did need to ask her about her Plot. Yes. So he had to stay a little longer. He'd ask his questions and then he'd go.

The Princess And The Orrery

"Your Book, the original one, said that your heroine ran away and you got her back. I thought it was odd at the time, but everything else... other things took over."

Bea pursed her lips. "You mean when the GenAm attacked a room full of people with an ogre and a horde of witchlein, that kind of 'took over'?"

"Yes."

"When people died? When John was injured for life? When Llanotterly lost all its standing because the King – that's John, remember – hosted a Royal event that turned into a bloodbath?"

"...yes."

"Right. Just checking. Y'see, when you say something like 'things took over', it makes it sound like no-one was responsible. There's always someone who's responsible."

"Bea, that wasn't the plan. I explained-"

"Yes, yes. You wanted to get the genie. You wanted him to help you find some mythical tree that'll solve all our problems. The GenAm wanted to torture him to death. I remember. And that didn't work, so then they started Redacting humans. The Teller Cares About Us, though, so the fae'll be fine. The GenAm only do what they do to keep us safe, right? *You* only do what you do to keep people safe. Stupid of me to ever think it was anything else."

"It's not that simple – please, Bea. I know you're angry with me. I know I shouldn't have left the way I did. I shouldn't have kissed you or... But you don't understand-"

"Just ask your questions," she said, taking another gulp of her wine.

Mistasinon's mind was blank. And then he remembered his lines. "I remember your Book, the original version, had something in it about you rescuing Sindy, but there's no record in the Contents Department of you coming in through the Grand. How did you get to her?"

"I didn't go through the Grand. I used a normal mirror. Sindy's mirror."

He shook his head. "Look, I can see you don't want me here, but this will take longer if you don't tell me what really happened."

"Hah. Right. Whether you believe me or not, that's what happened. Seven used magic to travel, that's where I got the idea from. I just sort of remembered what it felt like when he moved me and did the same thing."

"Magic kills. The genies are stronger than the fae, but even they die, eventually. Are you sure that's what happened?"

"Yes, I am, actually." Her tone dripped with anger. "And for your information, it did. The magic, I mean."

"What? I don't – I didn't mean – what did the magic do?"

She glared at him, her eyes dark grey and full of challenge. "It killed me. Sindy and Melly brought me back."

The world, usually so full of sounds and smells, colours and contradictions, was suddenly small and silent, except for a ringing in his ears.

He didn't know how it happened, but the next moment, he had her hands in his, gripping tight.

"Are you serious? You died? Why didn't you tell me? Mortal gods, Bea – I can't... What if you'd been alone? What if they couldn't save you?"

She pulled her hands out of his. "And what do you care?"

"What do you mean, 'what do I care'? Of course I care! You'd have gone to the Shadow Land! Bea, the Shadow Land, where... where... the Shadow Master! Bea, I'd go back there and never leave rather than see you spend one second in that place."

He dug his nails into his neck, if only for the tangy, familiar scent of blood in a world that was so suddenly empty.

Bea chewed her lip, her gaze fixed on him with such intensity he thought she must be reading his mind. In all his life, he had never felt so seen.

"It's alright," she said, something softer entering her voice. Not friendship, but not the hard anger of before. "I'm not going to the Shadow Land. And, for what it's worth, I'm not going to try travelling by magic again any time soon."

"Do you promise?" he asked, urgent as an arrow loosed from a bow.

"Yes."

"A bargain made?"

"Yes. A bargain made." She wiped her hands down her face. "Mortal gods. This is too much. Why did you come here, really?

You could have worked it out, couldn't you, from my original Book?"

"I had to be sure."

Bea raised her eyebrows. "I don't believe you. You keep hiding things. All the time. I don't know if it's a trick you learnt to survive when you were the Beast or what, but I've had enough of it."

"How can you say that?" He drew back so sharply his shoulders hit the back of the chair. "You know everything about me. You know what I am. You saw it."

"It? What 'it'?"

He was on his feet before he knew he'd moved. Shame boiled under his skin. Was she really going to make him say it? But then, maybe that was why he had come here. To make sure she knew. To close the book on them, once and for all.

"The Beast. You saw it. Me. Us."

Bea stood too. "What? At the Academy, in the woodshed?"

"No, not in the woodshed. Mortal gods!" He heard the bitter anger in his voice and had no idea whether it was directed at her for making him say it, or at himself because there was something to say. "Here. The other day. After we – you saw *it*."

Bea's face was a picture of incomprehension. And then, slow like the sludge of time in the Shadow Land, he saw her understand.

"You mean when you couldn't breathe? That wasn't the Beast. Why on Thaiana do you think that?"

His hands clenched. He wanted to leave. To run back to the Teller's tower and never, ever come down again. But he couldn't move.

Around Bea there was a cloud of colour. She was angry, anxious, afraid – but behind that was a strange, new shade he couldn't name. It was somewhere between pink and peach and smelled of summer and cosy evenings and contentment. Of long, white sandy beaches and green hillsides. Of little wooden houses with cattle grazing outside. Of a fireplace with a cushion by the hearth, just for him, where he could curl up and sleep for hours.

It was a lie. The promise of a life that would never be his. And it was so much worse than the stench of anger and fear or the crippling, gut-wrenching loneliness that had always been the textures of his life. The cold, and the dark, and the dead.

And he knew she was right. He had to tell her the truth. He had to burn the lie, burn it to ashes, before he allowed himself to believe it.

"Maybe what happened the last time I was here wasn't the... the Cerberus. But *I* was." He swallowed, his throat dry. "I thought that losing the other two gave me more control. That I was better. But I'm not."

Silence.

Then Bea sat down, gesturing for him to do the same. "Did you think it would go away by magic? That you'd just wake up and everything would be better? Easier?"

He hesitated and then sat.

"No. Yes. I don't know. I thought... I thought it was behind me. That I was in control."

"Alright, but how many of those, uh, moments have you had since you drank the Letheinate stuff?"

"Just that once – but I had them before, and when they happen, I don't know where I am, what I'm doing. I can't be trusted, don't you see?"

"But that's the thing about trust, isn't it?" Bea said. "You don't get to demand it. You have to show people trustworthy behaviour, and then they give it to you. It's a gift, not a request."

"What do you mean?"

Bea sighed. "I mean it's not up to you how people feel about you, only how you behave. You have to show them you're worth it."

A weight fell on him. "I see."

"No, I don't think you do. Mortal gods. Look. I like you. Like you more than as a friend, you understand? I know you're messed up, and you don't understand who you are or even *why* you are. But I'm not exactly perfect either, and I like you, and I don't know what to do about it, because I can't – I *can't*, you understand – support the GenAm, and I can't fix you, either. All I can do is like you, but you have to like me, too. I won't waste my time on someone who's going to run out on me."

"I know."

"I hope so, because all this backwards and forwards... It's stupid. It's a waste of time. I know that this 'thing' between us will probably end badly. But, I mean, it can't be as bad as what's happening now, can it?"

Mistasinon knew about Narrative Convention. He knew about Fate. He knew how amazingly stupid it was to say that 'things can't get any worse' or, even more dangerous, 'it has to get better'.

That was the problem. She didn't understand what he was. She never would, not really. One day, she'd realise he'd told her the truth. And then it would all be taken away from him.

Only good dogs are rewarded. Bad dogs get the stick.

He knew all this. And yet he said, "No, probably not."

"Do you like me too?"

"Yes. Since I first met you."

Bea nodded.

"So, then. You have to decide if you trust me, too."

43

"I won't go." Amelia stormed into the observatory. "I won't and you can't make me."

She threw herself down on her chair, picked up her pencil, and started scribbling notes. Her hunched-over back was like a brick wall, blocking any further conversation. Naima stood in the doorway, completely confounded. Even worse, the genie was sitting on the floor, staring in shock at Amelia.

He turned and fixed his empty eyes on Naima. Was there an accusation in them?

"She's upset," Naima found herself saying, entirely pointlessly given the abundance of evidence.

"And what is it that has upset her?" The genie rose to his feet and walked towards her.

Naima swallowed, ignoring the twinge of warning in her stomach. It was so tempting to just step backwards, through the door, where that thing couldn't follow. But she couldn't leave, not with Amelia in such a state.

She needed to get control of the situation. She should have done so some seven months ago, when Joseph brought her to the tower. Hell, she should have done something two and a half years ago, when Joseph had first brought Amelia to Castell y Sêr, demanding she be given the space and resources for the orrery.

"She'll be alright," Naima said, not sure who she wanted to convince. "Let her work through it."

The genie stopped in front of her, his featureless eyes regarding her with keen intensity. How was it that he made her feel like a rock magnified under one of her glass microviewers?

When he spoke, his tone was soft with sympathy, soothing as a cool pillow against her skin after a long day.

"You would feel so much better if you unburdened yourself. Have you not been carrying such weight, for so very long? Come. Lighten yourself."

"It's Calan Mai in a few days, the spring festival. The Palace is entertaining. Her mother's coming."

Seven frowned. "And this has precipitated such upset?"

"They don't get on," Naima found herself saying. "Amelia never answers any of her letters. She hasn't been home in all the time she's been here."

"Then why force her to attend?"

Naima felt the words on her tongue, tickling, trying to be said. Good God, she actually *wanted* to tell this creature about her concerns. About how she was so far out of her depth she couldn't even see the shore anymore.

"You're doing something to me," she hissed, stepping sharply back. "Get out of my head."

The genie smiled thinly. "Our master has ensured I cannot 'get into' your head, as you are well aware."

"I don't believe you."

"You have borne witness, have you not, to what befalls me if I disobey him? Madam, think what you will of your own intentions, I care not. But you must, surely, realise that Joseph's-"

His grip on his stomach tightened, his knuckles turning his skin icy blue. He swayed, but caught himself before he fell.

"I cannot speak on this," he said through gritted teeth. "The orrery will be completed, and my master will be happy. This is my only focus."

"Wait, no – you were talking about Joseph. What were you going to say?"

The genie leaned forward, like he was sharing a secret. "Amelia tells me you are gifted with great intelligence."

"Yes? And?"

"I have yet to see you use it. Perhaps you might begin?"

"Begin? Begin where?"

"At the beginning, of course."

And with that, the genie turned his back on her and went to Amelia, pausing only to pick up Barry on his way. Naima stood, anger and embarrassment colouring her cheeks, burning her throat.

The genie placed Barry on Amelia's desk and then leaned over and said something to her. The girl paused in her writing, then nodded and whispered something back. Seven said a few more words that Naima couldn't hear, and then he straightened.

Amelia spun round in her chair. "Fine," she said. "If I have to go to this stupid festival and see my mother, I will. But Seven's coming with me."

"Well, my Lady," Seven said after the door closed behind Naima. "Will you not tell me what the issue is with your parents?"

Silence.

"I thought we were a team. Confidants. Alas, I see I was mistook. A shame, as I would have dearly liked a friend. I have had but few."

Silence, but a slightly different kind. A listening silence.

"In truth, I never saw the world the same as my kind," he continued. "They wished for everything to be static. Stagnant. It never appealed to me. And then, of course, they died."

The pencil stilled in Amelia's hand.

"It has been perhaps two or three years since the last of my kin passed," Seven said. "I forget. It is easier, I think, to push such things away – a trick I think you also employ. 'Tis better not to dwell, or so I thought. But now I am alone, and I find I wonder whether I am... whether I should have appreciated them when I was able. Whether I might have done something to help. If I could have helped avoid the fate that befell them." He shook his head, surprised at the turn he had allowed the conversation to take. "Ah, well. But they are dead and here am I, alive and without a friend in all the worlds."

Amelia put her pencil down but did not look up. "I'm your friend."

"How can I be your friend if you will not tell me what so troubles you?"

"I just don't want to see Mum, that's all."

"I am to accompany you. I thought that resolved the matter?"

Amelia lifted her head. "I'm glad you're coming. I wouldn't go at all, otherwise." A pause. "How did your family die?"

The Princess And The Orrery

"It is a long story. I am not sure how much I can tell of it, but I will try."

Amelia moved so she was sitting cross-legged on her chair. Seven lifted himself up to sit, likewise, on the desk. He picked up Barry and set him between them.

"Now we have a story-circle," he said, offering her a wink. "I have told you already we were refugees, that we travelled here looking for a safe haven." So far, so good. Joseph's wish had not ignited. Seven kept his eyes from the orrery, lest Amelia somehow make a connection between his words and her device. "We were but few, even then. Still, we settled. Made lives for ourselves. Until, let me see, until our illness was discovered."

"How can you discover an illness?" Amelia cocked her head. "I mean, didn't you have it already? What was there to discover? I guess this is the illness you have now? Is that what gave you the funny turn?"

Seven smiled. "So many questions... The illness I speak of is indeed the same as that from which I am currently suffering. As to its discovery... we did not have it in our homeland. It came upon us when we arrived here. Fortunately, we had a way to manage the sickness. Not a cure, but a salve, if you will. It kept us relatively safe, and what the salve could not accomplish we learnt ways to manage."

"So did this illness kill your family?"

"Yes and no. Someone placed my family in a situation where even their protection was not enough to save them."

"Who?"

"You would not believe me. In truth, I find it hard to believe myself."

"Yes, I will. You can tell me. If you want to." Amelia rested her chin in her hand, fixing him with a look that warmed his chest. Something familiar, friendly. A feeling he wasn't sure he wanted, but could absolutely remember.

"Very well. A three-headed monster hunted them down and brought them to its master, who killed them. There? Did I not say you would disbelieve me?"

Amelia's eyebrows shot up. "That sounds stupid. But... well, you're blue, and I would have thought the idea of a blue person was stupid not long ago, as well as a metal that could join itself to a machine. It's important to pay attention to the evidence." She poked his knee. "Besides, I'm your friend, so I have to believe you."

"I... thank you."

"You're welcome." Amelia smiled at him. "Let's do some work on the orrery? I feel better now."

They worked for the rest of the afternoon. Seven did as he was told, but he was slower than strictly necessary, and when Amelia asked him for his thoughts, he tried as best he could to skirt the answer. He couldn't lie to her, couldn't misdirect her, not where improving the orrery was concerned. But if he was slow, vague, helping but not, as such, helpful, Joseph's wish did not strike him down. It was hardly the complex verbal dance of the genies, but it was something.

Still, by the mid-afternoon, they had, despite his efforts, managed to attach the eighth planet to the device.

44

Mistasinon let his head fall against the pillow. Dusk was settling outside, that strange yellowy-blue light that only spring could bestow. He rolled over, resting on his elbow, and allowed himself a long, deep breath in through his nose.

Around Bea, the soft cloud of colour, somewhere between pink and peach, remained. If only he could show it to her, the way the scents mingled and danced. Usually a threat, right now they were beautiful.

"What are you smiling at?" Bea asked.

"I can see your smell."

She fixed him with the same expression one might make upon discovering half a maggot in their apple.

"That's disgusting."

"No, no. You don't understand. It's you. You're everywhere."

"You're not making it any better, you know." She pulled the blanket over them, probably in the mistaken belief it would make the colour disappear. "So... was it, uh, was it the smells that upset you the other day? That's why you had the peppermint, wasn't it?"

"Yeeees. Yes. It's like... the smells are always there, but sometimes they're more there. Sometimes, I can tell how people feel, what they've been doing. Even where they've been, if it's recent. When there was three of me, it was even stronger. We could see so much. Magic, even – have I told you that before?"

Bea shook her head.

"Really?" Tentatively, he rested his hand on the dip of her waist – she didn't flinch! Emboldened, he ran it along the round swell of her hip. "I want to tell you everything. You really like me?"

She rolled her eyes. "Yes, really. Can't you tell if I'm lying, then? Mortal gods, that's creepy."

"No, not exactly," he said, watching the way her hair curled around her face. Everything about her was soft and warm, heavy and safe. Gentle.

F. D. Lee

Well, perhaps not everything, he conceded as she jabbed him in the shoulder.

"Go on, explain it to me, then."

He caught her hand, dropped a kiss on her knuckles – a kiss! She giggled! "It depends on how you're feeling. If someone thinks they're lying, for example, I might be able to tell – but if they believe they're telling the truth, they smell like the truth."

Bea frowned, confused.

"Like I said, it's not as easy now I'm just me," Mistasinon sighed. "People think smells are passive, that they just float around. Well, I mean, they do just float around. It's... um... It's like the way you feel affects your body, you know?"

"Sure. Like when you're angry or upset and you really, really need a glass of wine."

"I'm not sure – really?"

"Well, I was joking. But yes, sometimes. For me, anyway. Carry on."

He closed his eyes, trying to think how to describe something that was, to him, as much a part of the world as the sky above, and just as subject to change. How could he translate all that possibility into words?

"Alright," he began. "If you're afraid, your blood pumps faster. You sweat. Things change inside you... I can't explain it properly. I don't know what happens, exactly, only that it does. When someone's scared, it's like an explosion. It fills them up and comes out through their skin, and because it's a fear explosion, they smell of fear. I can see the smell. It's white."

Bea frowned. "What about other things, then? I mean, you can't have just... seen... fear, right?"

"Um. I suppose fear is just the one I know best. Not many people were pleased to see me. You were, though. When we met. You were excited, nervous. And I think you thought I was handsome?"

"What! Oh, mortal gods." She buried her face in the pillow. She only had one. They were having to share. It was amazing.

A muffled question rose from the cotton. "How do you know that?"

"I didn't, then. I just thought it was strange. But you were strange, so I assumed that's how strange people smell. But now I know, I think, what it looks like."

Bea groaned. "This is awful. I'll be a week in the bath."

"Please don't."

"Yuk. I'm not going to stop washing," she said, lifting her head. "Tell me something else about you. Something nicer."

I don't really have anything nice to tell, he realised. But he wanted to make her happy. He wracked his brains. "Ah. Well. My brother, Orthrus, used to live with a farmer on a hill-"

"This is the brother you traded your freedom for? The one who died?"

"Yes... yes. The hill he lived on was by the sea – the smell was wonderful. When the sun was on it, it was like freedom, turquoise, bright as an oil lamp turned up high. And then, another time, I was, um, looking for someone, and I had to go to this little place in Ehinenden. There was a field there, full of flowers. We wanted to stay there, all three of me. We hardly ever agreed, but we did then. We never, ever wanted to come back."

"But you did," Bea said. There was a new note in her voice, something small and sad.

"Well, yes. Of course. The Teller needed us. Where else should I have gone?" He rolled onto his back. "Those were good smells."

"Tell me about your brother," Bea said, wriggling so she could rest her head on his chest.

A warning quivered in his stomach. His breath stilled, shoulders tensing. But she didn't seem to mind the dapple of hair that covered his skin, a shameful remnant of his true self that the magic hadn't been able to change, only mute. Like his sense of smell, his speed, his strength.

You're still the Beast, deep down, a voice whispered in his head. *In the parts of you that explode.*

"My brother was a good boy," Mistasinon said, speaking a little louder than strictly necessary. "He only had two hims, not like us. But he was bigger than us. People always think I was huge, you know, but why would we be? You can't chase people if they can see you coming from miles away. The Shadow Land was full of places for the dead to hide. Heroes were always trying to break in.

I needed to be fast and strong. Not big. The Shadow Master didn't like it when-"

Bea turned her head and kissed his jaw. "You were talking about your brother."

"Oh. Yes. Sorry. He worked for a farmer. Helped him with the cattle. He... Oh. Oh, no."

Bea shot up, her eyes searching his face. "What is it? Are you alright?"

"No, no," Mistasinon said, jumping out of bed and pulling on his trousers. "My shirt? Where's my shirt?"

"By the table – what's going on? What's happened?"

He stumbled over to his shirt, doing his trousers up as he went. "The Mirrors! Sound! I can't believe I didn't – how could we have not noticed? How could I have missed it?"

Bea was out of bed too, the bedspread wrapped around her. "Know what? What are you talking about it?"

"My waistcoat? My jacket?" He froze, eyes scanning the room. "My bag! Where's my bag?"

"It's fine, it's all here, look." She picked up his bag from the sofa. "Just calm down. What should you have noticed?"

"The Mirrors! When I was... when you were at the Academy and I, we, my other mes I mean, used a Mirror. It showed me where our brother used to live."

"So?"

"So I could hear the seagulls!"

Bea stared at him. "That's not possible. Mirrors don't pick up sounds."

"Exactly!" Mistasinon exclaimed, grabbing his satchel and throwing the strap over his head. "It shouldn't be possible, but it happened! Something unusual – another variable – Bea, don't you see?"

"Slow down, I've got no idea what you're talking about. Besides, you can't just go running off. Where are you going to go? The GenAm can't be trusted."

Mistasinon paused, trying to do up his waistcoat underneath the bulk of his satchel. Stupid! He took the satchel off and started again. "I met with the Head of the Index, Agnes, and she asked me to find out if the Mirrors had done anything strange. That's why I was checking your book. You travelling by magic is one thing, but sound? Sound is extraordinary. So I'll go and tell Agnes."

Bea grabbed his arms, halting his frantic dressing. "Listen to me. You're over-excited; if you go running through the GenAm now, dressed in blue, diving into the Index, people are bound to notice."

"Oh. Yes. You're right."

She led him over to the sofa and sat him down. "Let's just try to think, alright? How could a Mirror pick up sound, anyway?"

"I don't know. But... yes... I remember when I got lost in the Shadow Land, I heard a sound – a drumbeat. West said she heard it, too."

Bea bit her lip, thinking. "Yes. When Seven moved me with magic, I heard it. I used to have nightmares, after the attack on the Ball, and there was always this drumbeat there. You think the music is important?"

"It has to be. It led me to Tartarus."

"Tartarus?"

"The place below the Shadow Land. Or within it. Time and space weren't fixed there. I was upset, lost, ashamed, angry... I just wanted to go home. I followed the sound down and the next thing, I was in the Land of the Fae. That was during the War."

"The War? The *Rhyme* War? You've been here since...?" Bea trailed off. "Mortal gods. We really don't know anything about each other, do we? How come you've lived so long?"

"I don't know. When there was three of me, we didn't age at all. Honestly, I never really thought about it. Our parents were gods, so I suppose that kind of thing didn't apply. I don't know if it's still true, now I'm like this." He searched her face for any tell-tale signs of anger, of disappointment. The ones he'd learnt to watch for in the Shadow Land and had never quite forgotten. "I didn't mean to mislead you. I've been myself, like this, for nearly two years."

But Bea had apparently got stuck on another awful detail. "Your parents were *gods*?"

If she'd looked shocked before, now she seemed downright flabbergasted. Mistasinon had never told anyone this before, but in hindsight, he realised he could have led into it all a bit more gently.

His breath quickened. White flecks starting bleeding into the edges of his vision, spotted with bursts of hard, icy blue.

He reached into his pocket, grateful he'd managed to get his waistcoat on, pulled out his cloth and sniffed it. Bea's eyes followed the action, but she didn't say anything.

The colours receded. He pulled the cloth from his face and tested the air. Nothing happened. Tentatively, he took a deeper breath, and then another. It had passed.

Bea raised a questioning eyebrow. "Everything alright?"

"Yes. Sorry. Um. Do you want me to... should I leave?"

She laughed. "Leave? Mortal gods, no."

"You still like me?"

"Like you? I'm bloody fascinated. A cabbage fairy and a god? Imagine what the anti-intertribalism lot would think if they found out, let alone the fairy-haters. Come on then, spit it out. I want to know how I ended up dating a god."

Dating! Mistasinon couldn't have stopped the smile splitting his face even if he'd wanted to. How was it possible to feel so happy? He was telling her about the Cerberus, about everything that made him wrong and different, and she still liked him.

"To be honest, there were a lot of gods where I'm from. It wasn't really anything special. Oh, but my grandmother was probably a tree. I always thought that was interesting."

"A tree? How did you end up a three-headed dog-thing, then?"

"Um. Well, we didn't have tribes the way you do, here. Things didn't pass down so neatly. Can we go back to the Mirrors?"

"Fine, but just be warned – I'm going to want to know more about all this. So, the music is important, that's what we're thinking? And something is affecting the Mirrors, but we don't know what."

He grabbed her hands. "Yes, but if we can find out what it is, maybe we can use it. I can keep my promise – keep everyone safe. Stop another war. Save the-" he stopped himself from saying *'save the GenAm'* "-save us all. Bea, we could really do this!"

She grinned at him, grey eyes sparkling. "If we can find out what it is – mortal gods. We could stop it all. No more fear. No more control. Oh, Mistasinon! I really think we can. But..."

"What?"

The Princess And The Orrery

"But we have to be careful. Someone in the GenAm isn't playing by the rules – look what happened with West. You can't trust them. And I don't think you should go rushing off to the Index, you're too noticeable. We need someone on the inside – what about Chokey? She needs an apprenticeship, doesn't she?"

Mistasinon baulked. "You can't be serious? Look, I like Chokey, I do. But she's not exactly subtle."

But it was too late. Bea had that look, the one he'd come to recognise as her I've-made-up-my-mind-so-you-can-either-agree-with-me-or-you-can-be-wrong face. Not for the first time in their relationship – relationship! – he wondered if it wouldn't be easier to just bundle her up and lock her in a room for her own safety.

"Fine," he said. "I'll set up a meeting."

"Good," Bea said, smug in victory. "Let's go back to bed."

45

A new day dawned and with it a new problem.

When things go wrong, it is a natural instinct to try to trace the mistake back to its origin. To pull at the loose thread, hoping that, somehow, what went wrong might magically be untangled and made well. But which thread should eager fingers grasp at? Go back to the beginning, the genie said. But when all is said and done – and nothing that is said can ever be entirely undone – finding the true beginning of the end is never easy.

Naima, for example, had grown up in a sprawling barracks with a beautiful sweeping garden and tall trees where birds nested and sung to each other in the spring, but she had always found it overwhelming.

She hadn't minded the soldiers as individuals, but it had made her realise she didn't want a life spent trying to ignore the noise and confusion that invariably came with large groups of people. She wanted to be able to study the world in quiet contemplation. To learn about the earth and the rocks, to know where they came from, what they were made of, what their purpose was. To uncover the secret history hidden beneath her feet.

And so, at eighteen, she had made her way to Castell y Sêr. That had been thirty years ago. But it had also been the beginning of the story that had brought her to this point, where she was inextricably tied to a madman and taking snidely given advice from a genie.

"I expect you're wondering why I've asked you here?" she said to the woman in front of her.

"I'm always happy to help if I can," Kamala said.

"And very pleased I am to hear it. I need your anthropological expertise."

"*My* expertise?"

"You're surprised?"

The Princess And The Orrery

Kamala looked like she was trying very hard not to say something rude. It was quite possibly one of her least successful endeavours.

"I suppose I didn't think that a Sister of your stature would ask for the help of a fourth-year Cultivator, that's all. Especially given the fact you rejected my report."

Naima moved around her desk and perched on the edge. "Yes. And I'm truly very sorry about that. All I can say is that I've since realised my mistake, and I hope that you can forgive me."

"I... Well, I mean, I can understand why you didn't believe me, I suppose. I questioned myself as well."

Naima ran her hands through her curls. "Questioning is never a bad thing, but in this case, the mistake was mine. We have to recognise our errors, Kamala, or else we're doomed to repeat them. Did you know, when I first came here, it was organised very badly? There was a lot of good work being done, but it was all isolated. And then one day we had a death. More than one, actually. It was the fault of a young alchemist, trying to refine dissemination powder – you know, the kind they use to dig into the rock?"

"Yes, I was born here. I grew up listening to the explosions."

Naima nodded. "Well, this Cultivator wanted to create a powder that would make the dissemination of the rocks more precise. She wanted to reduce the number of slave deaths. So she did what all Cultivators are trained to do, and experimented. Day and night, for the best part of three years. And then she struck upon a solution – a new mineral powder. She tested it, of course. Small experiments in the laboratory, all very positive. She took it to her more senior alchemical Cultivators, who were, naturally, extremely impressed. They set up a demonstration to display their discovery in the main courtyard. All the Sisters were invited. This was fifteen years ago. Do you know what happened?"

"The Cultivator made a mistake, and when they tested her dissemination powder outside of the laboratory, there was an accident. She died. Lots of Sisters died."

"That's a rather sanitised version, but yes." In fact, the woman in question had been submerged in an extremely toxic, fast-spreading alchemical foam. She'd died melting. "Do you know the mistake that this Sister made?"

This part of the story was famous in Castell y Sêr, so it was hardly a surprise when Kamala said, "She used a mineral that reacts badly to the high levels of salt in the air outside. When it was combined with other ingredients and then heated, it caused the reaction. That's how you-"

"Yes." Naima held up her hand. "That's how I rose so quickly in the Sisterhood. I worked out the issue with the mineral."

Kamala was leaning forward now, hanging on every word.

"But it isn't that simple," Naima said. "Any of the geologists could have told Celia that the mineral was dangerous, but they didn't know she was using it, and Celia didn't bother to ask. She thought it was an alchemical issue, quantities and heat diffusion and so on. She thought that as long as the base reaction of the mineral components was the same as the ones traditionally used, they'd be the same in all conditions. It was an ignorant mistake, and she paid for it with her life and the lives of others."

"I see," Kamala said. "That's why you make sure we all work in different departments before specialising."

"And why I'm not embarrassed to admit when I don't know something or when I've made a mistake. We learn through testing and trying, through studying and thinking – but mostly, we learn through sharing. And I need you to help me learn, Kamala, and quickly. Please."

Kamala nodded, squaring her shoulders.

"How can I help?"

"I need to know about the Ball last year, the one with the monsters. I re-read your report, but I need to know exactly what happened, everything you remember. I need to know how you felt."

"I was scared, Sister," Kamala said. "Scared for my life."

Naima stood up and clasped her hands behind her back. This was it. "I can only imagine, and I'm sorry to make you think on it. But I mean before that. The blue man you mentioned... did he make you feel anything? Did he – and this is going to sound strange, but I want you to answer seriously – did he make you think about things you wanted? Or needed?"

The Princess And The Orrery

Probably someone else would have laughed or, at least, asked for clarification. But Kamala sat quietly, thinking. Naima forced herself to stand still.

"No, Sister," Kamala said. "But the whole attack was very strange, even so. I've thought about it a lot, in fact. What were the creatures that attacked us? I even went to the zoology department, and you know what they're like."

Only the fact that her father had drilled into her the importance of maintaining a firm appearance stopped Naima from shuddering. The zoology department always made visitors feel ill at ease. It was something about standing in a room with hundreds of pairs of glass eyes staring down at you.

"What did they say?"

"They thought I was winding them up, like you did."

Naima gave a glum nod. She'd received the same response. Status only went so far amongst the Sisters, and asking coded questions about genies and other childhood monsters was well beyond the border of reasonable questioning, even for her.

"But it wasn't just the, er, monsters that were strange about the Llanotterly massacre," Kamala said.

Naima threw her a questioning look. "What else?"

"In anthropology, we study social interaction and norms. And something I still don't understand is why the Baron's brother was there. I mean, of course, it's not my place to say he shouldn't have been... but it was hardly an event worthy of his attention. And he ignored all the other guests, even the King. He only spoke to the Count and Countess of Marlais. It was highly irregular – very rude. I think if it hadn't been for all those deaths, Llanotterly would have had every right to be seriously offended."

Naima's heart beat faster. The tips of her fingers tingled, and she was suddenly very, very awake. "It sounds like you're saying that his Lordship only attended the Ball to speak to the Count and Countess of Marlais? You're quite sure?"

"It certainly seems that way to me."

"Do you know what they spoke about?"

"No, Sister. I only observed him talking to them. He was speaking to both the Count and Countess, and then the Countess excused herself and went to talk to the King's Adviser. His

Lordship shared a few more words with the Count and then left. About fifteen minutes later, the monsters attacked and the Adviser and the Countess disappeared."

None of her father's training could stop the shock taking hold of Naima's expression. Her mouth fell open. "The Countess of Marlais is the same one that hasn't been seen since the Llanotterly Massacre? The one who ran off with the King's man?"

Kamala nodded. "Er, yes, Sister. I thought everyone knew? It was all anyone was talking about, last year."

"I was… distracted around that time," Naima said, her mind spinning ahead while her mouth managed to say, "Thank you, Kamala. Your insights have helped me a lot."

Kamala made the proper goodbyes and left. Naima sat down on her desk, her hands gripping the edge of the table, the tingle in her fingertips spreading to her chest.

Her gaze turned to the pile of unopened letters sent by Amelia's mother for the last two and half years. The most recent had arrived just a few days ago. Just a few days before Joseph had summoned Naima and told her that both the orrery and Amelia had to be at the Baron's festival. That Amelia's mother would be attending.

The answer was in front of her, Naima knew it. All the pieces were laid out – and now, finally, some of them were starting to fit together. She just had to work out what picture they created.

She'd never understood why Joseph was so obsessed with the orrery. Why would anyone think about anything else if they had a genie at their disposal? Joseph had made one wish the night the genie arrived, and that had been that the creature could not leave without his permission. Since then, she knew he'd made another wish, but had no idea what it was. Nothing had changed, after all – but now, Naima was wondering if it had, and she just hadn't been able to see it.

What had changed was the orrery. It was almost finished, thanks, no doubt, to the genie's help.

Start at the beginning, the genie had said. But what was the beginning? She'd thought it was the genie's arrival in the tower, but now she thought the story started much earlier.

Joseph's behaviour had never made sense. When she'd recovered from the shock of her first meeting with the genie, she'd assumed Joseph would wish for his health, or for the death of his brother, or money or love or youth or power – wasn't that what wishes were for? But instead, he'd kept that thing locked up for months, doing nothing with it until the orrery had broken. And even then, he'd put it to work instead of wishing the device mended or even completed.

Amelia's orrery. Amelia, who was suddenly intricately connected to the arrival of the genie and the events in Llanotterly, where the mysterious Countess had gone missing at the Ball. The very same Ball that had provided Joseph with the genie, where the only people he spoke to were the Count and Countess of Marlais, Henry Guilliam Ghislain and Maria Sophia Ghislain, the latter of which, Naima now knew, had been instrumental in getting the genie for Joseph:

Amelia's mother.

F. D. Lee

46

"A grey suit? Darling, you can't be serious?"

Bea set her expression into one she hoped conveyed her seriousness very, uh, seriously. "I know it's not what you wanted," she said. "But it... it's important. Mistasinon?"

He rubbed his neck and leaned forward on the table. They were in Chokey's living room. She had her own living room! Apparently, Hemmings did too – or so Chokey had said as she'd led them through a spacious hallway and up a wide staircase to the sixth floor. Each floor had opened onto tastefully decorated landings with more doors leading into even more rooms. The place was massive. No wonder Chokey hadn't found the Academy's winding corridors and high ceilings intimidating.

Under different circumstances, Bea was certain she'd have felt completely over-awed by such surroundings. As it was, she just felt sick. When she'd suggest Chokey for the job, it had been in the safety of her flat, buoyed-up by the prospect of perhaps, finally, getting at the GenAm. But now she was actually here, asking her friend to do something very dangerous and unable to tell her entirely why, the idea had lost a lot of its sparkle.

"We need someone working with the Indexers," Mistasinon said. He didn't seem any happier about the conversation than she was. "There's trouble with the Mirrors and Bea and I, well, uh, we think we might be able to do something about it. But not on our own."

"Darling, there's always trouble with the Mirrors. What in the worlds makes you think the Index can do anything about it? That's the Teller's, *whocaresaboutus*, job. Or the Redactionists. Besides, you know what those grey suits are like. They're so *frite-fully* bookish. I'm sure they couldn't possibly want me."

"But you're the best person for the job," Bea said, ignoring the little voice that reminded her Chokey was the only person for the job. That she was putting her friend in danger.

"Gosh, darling, why ever do you think that?"

The Princess And The Orrery

This was a bad idea. Maybe she could join the Index instead? But no, that wouldn't work. Bea was too infamous in the GenAm, between her public acceptance into the Academy and her status as the fairy who nagged and complained to get it. There was no way she could work as a secret go-between for Mistasinon and the Head of the Index.

Bea and Mistasinon looked at each other. He hadn't wanted her to come, but she'd insisted. If they were going to ask Chokey to get involved in this, she thought it was only right that she be there. But now Chokey was sitting opposite her, grinning hesitantly, and all their vague explanations counted for nothing. The truth was, she was putting her friend at risk. Was she going to send Chokey off, without her fully understanding why, to potentially be labelled an Anti or, worse, Redacted?

Mistasinon was watching her closely, his thick eyebrows drawn together, nostrils flaring slightly. The mortal gods knew what he was smelling – seeing – right now. She didn't care.

Choice. That was what was important. People had to be able to make their own choices.

Bea put her hand over Mistasinon's, turned to Chokey, and told her all about her Plot, and Seven, and the music and the Mirrors and the magic – everything except what Mistasinon had been, and was now.

✦

"Golly," Chokey said when Bea had finished.

"Yes." Bea squeezed Mistasinon's hand. He'd been silent throughout, but she'd felt his gaze on her all the time she'd been talking. He didn't squeeze her hand back. She let him go, and his hand moved to grip his tatty satchel. She forced her attention back to Chokey. "I know it's a lot to take in. I'm sorry I didn't tell you sooner."

"I simply can't believe it." Chokey turned her head between the two of them. "Darlings, you're honestly telling the truth?"

"I'm afraid so," Bea said.

"The two of you have finally got together?"

F. D. Lee

"I – what?"

Chokey burst out laughing. "Oh, your faces! I do wish Hemmings were here. Have you told Joan?"

As was so often the case when talking to Chokey, Bea had the confusing sense that she was coming into the conversation halfway through. "About the genies and the Mirrors?"

"No, you goose! About you two!"

"Er... Yes, sort of. Is that really the most important thing?"

Next to her, she felt Mistasinon stiffen.

"Well, no, I suppose not," Chokey grinned. "But it is pretty important news, all the same. Now then, about these Mirrors and the Index. I should think I haven't much choice, now I understand the full scope of the situation. Mama won't be best pleased, but I can knock her into shape. At least I'll be working with the Head Indexer, that'll cheer her up."

Bea pulled herself together. "You mean you'll do it?"

"Well, of course I will. What are friends for? Besides, this sounds terribly thrilling! And I haven't much else to do, have I?"

"You can't tell anyone anything Bea's told you," Mistasinon warned. "It's vitally important we keep a lid on things."

Chokey rolled her eyes. "And here I was about to announce it at the next bash. Honestly, you're being a dreadful killjoy. If we're to be working together, you really are going to have to lift your chin a bit."

"Oh, thank you," Bea said. "You won't have to do anything dangerous, I promise. Just ferry messages. And if it seems like anyone might have got wind of the scheme, we'll pull you out."

"Oh, I shouldn't worry about that. Mama will be trying to undo the whole thing anyway, I've no doubt. If I need to bow out, it'll be easy enough." Chokey clapped her hands. "Gosh, this is exciting! Working in the shadows to control the fate of a nation! So, when shall we three meet again?"

"There's the Fairies United community meeting coming up," Bea suggested. "We could all meet there? Mistasinon can claim he's there on behalf of the GenAm, you know, to make sure we're not threatening the Plots or some such nonsense, and you've already been seen with us, Chokey, so it shouldn't raise any suspicion-"

"Well, no more suspicion than an Ogrechoker hanging out with fairies already raises!"

"Er. Yes."

"Perfect! Now then, tell me again about when you first met..."

Bea and Mistasinon walked through the wide streets in the centre of Ænathlin, away from Chokey's townhouse. Bea had always had very mixed feelings about this part of the city, but now she was grateful for the distraction.

It was all tall, beautiful old buildings and pretty cobbled streets. Clean and safe, with ornate gas lamps keeping the darkness at bay – and with it, the type of 'excitement' that tends to come at the end of a knife and the offer to relieve you of your possessions. The kind of excitement Bea and the other fae who lived by the wall could never really avoid, no matter how hard they tried.

Ænathlin's inner circle always elicited in her a tight, hot feeling, like she'd swallowed a balloon full of boiling water and it had got stuck somewhere between her mouth and her stomach.

The inner-circlers had everything; or, at least, everything Ænathlin could offer. The GenAm didn't really pay attention to them. Sure, they had to follow the Teller's rules, but even those were often treated with a kind of grudging acceptance rather than as the iron strait-jacket they tended to be for those who lived out by the wall. Everything was easier for the inner-circlers, and it made Bea angry.

And yet she couldn't help wishing she was one of them. That she could walk through the streets without having to ignore whispered slurs about fairies and not-so-whispered jokes about cabbages and farts and 'oh, what's that dreadful smell?'

Rather like the way she was walking now, in fact.

It had to be because she was with Mistasinon – or, more precisely, with his blue suit. Fae nodded to him as he passed and moved out of his way. No one tried to spit on him or told him to go back where he came from. And he had no idea! He was just marching along beside her, scowling.

F. D. Lee

They arrived at the covered market near the Grand. Bea's flat was further out, where the streets grew narrower and less welcoming, while the GenAm was behind them, along open lanes and cleaner, safer streets. Mistasinon came to a stop, shrugging his satchel strap back onto his shoulder.

"I need to go back to the GenAm," he said.

"Why are you so upset? Is it because I told Chokey about everything? I won't apologise. She has every right to know what we're asking her to get involved in."

"Yes, I agree." He glared off into the distance, his thick eyebrows meeting in the space above his nose. "Anyway. I'd better-"

Bea was having none of it. "Or is because Joan and Chokey know about us?"

Mistasinon glowered a moment longer and then deflated.

"No. Yes. I don't know." He sighed, turning to her. "That's not a very good answer, is it?"

"Not really."

He dithered, and then said, "Look, it's like this. When you bleed, you bleed black. When humans bleed, it's red."

"Yes?"

"When I bleed..." He brought his hand up to one of his satchel buckles and, before Bea could stop him, scratched the soft skin of his palm against the prong. It was only a graze, but it was enough. Spots of blood appeared against his tan skin. "See?"

Bea took his hand and inspected it. It was the strangest thing: Mistasinon's blood was two colours. Red and black – not blended or mixed and yet together, like oil and water in the same saucer. Some of the spots were mostly black with red dappling, some the other way around, and some were an even mixture of the two.

She looked up at him. What was she supposed to say? Was this a bad thing? It was certainly... different. But she didn't understand what it was meant to signify.

He must have read her expression. "I'm the – I mean, I was..." He shook his head. "We don't know what I am. And the more you involve yourself with me, the more you... connect yourself... It's like with Chokey, don't you see? You don't know what you're getting involved in."

"That's ridiculous. You're you. It's not like I didn't know '*you know what*' before we got together. I mean, sure, I guess if we'd slept together when we first met or something, then maybe you'd have a reason to worry, but that's not the case."

"You know that's not what I mean," he said, pulling a handkerchief from his pocket and wiping his hand. "I'm thinking about what happens next."

"What is it you think will happen next?"

Panic darted across his features, quick as a minnow. When he spoke, there was an edge of desperation in his voice.

"I don't know – that's the point! But if something does happen, if people find out what I am and that you and I are... You're already too closely associated with me, professionally. Imagine if they found out!"

They were drawing the attention of the surrounding fae. Bea grabbed his hand and pulled him past the Grand and the market, down a couple of narrowing streets until she found a small, makeshift plaza created from the walls of the surrounding buildings. They weren't alone; space was at too much of a premium for even somewhere this tiny to be without its uses. There were some brownies with clothes laid out for sale on the floor, a gnome next to them selling tin, bone and other miscellaneous items, and a smattering of bystanders casually picking through their wares.

Still, it wasn't as busy as the market, which was probably the best they could hope for in the middle of the day and the middle of the city. At least they could duck into the corner, the other fae seeming more than happy to give Mistasinon's suit as wide a berth as the space allowed.

"Listen to me," she said, trying to make her voice quiet and firm at the same time. "I made my choices. All of them. It wasn't you who got me involved in this mess, and it wasn't you who decided to keep me involved once the truth was out. Everything I've done has been my choice. It was my choice to save your life, too. And it was my choice to tell you I like you."

"That's not what I mean-"

"I haven't finished," Bea said. "I'm not going to pretend we're not together. I'm not worried about who you are, Mistasinon, I'm not. I'm bloody worried about a lot of things, but not that. If people find out, we'll deal with it, somehow. But I'm not going to pretend I don't like you in the meantime."

She reached up and brushed her hand against his cheek. "You can't be afraid of yourself. I'm not afraid of you."

Mistasinon made a little sound somewhere between a sob and a sigh. And then he smiled.

"I'm not afraid of you either, by the way. Even if you did kill an ogre and fight a troll. Just so you know."

"Oh, really? What about the time I drank unboiled water from the well on Carter's Lane?"

"Mortal gods. But no, still not afraid. Besides, I once ate a sausage from that vendor near Tannery Street. By choice."

"Really? That just seems a particularly masochistic way to commit suicide. I, however, once drank in an elf pub by the wall. So I think of the two of us, I've earned the right to be feared."

Mistasinon laughed. "Yes, yes, you win. Here I stand, shaking in terror at your bravery and stupidity."

"Hey!"

"Why in the worlds did you drink in an elf pub, anyway?"

Bea grinned. "Well, I'd only been in the city a couple of weeks, and..."

Unnoticed by either of them, a little tompte watched them leave the plaza, writing in her notebook as she did so.

47

Of course, deciding to do something and then actually doing it were very different things.

Naima tugged at the hood of her cloak. She was pretty sure she'd lost her mind. If Joseph found out, she'd be in the manufactories quicker than she could blink. He wouldn't care that she was the daughter of an important man. That much was plain as the nose on her face, given the person she intended to visit.

She felt sick to her stomach, her limbs heavy as she slipped out of Castell y Sêr and through the gardens, trying hard to look inconspicuous. At least Cerne Bralksteld was the kind of place where people didn't tend to look twice – a city where no one knew your name and didn't care to find out.

The sun warmed her head through her hood, threatening to agitate a headache she'd been ignoring for hours. Summer was still a way away, but spring was a time of change, wasn't it? The chill of winter one day, the heat of summer the next. Unpredictable.

She tried to walk in the shade, but the canyon floor was, at its widest point, some three miles across and with the sun directly above her, there were few shadows. She should have come out later in the day. She should have thought this all through properly.

She should have been cleverer.

'I have yet to see you use your intelligence'. That was what the genie had said. It stung, a scorpion hiding under her shame and embarrassment at having been so stupid. Worse, at having been caught out in her stupidity.

She had always been clever; it wasn't exactly a bruised ego that hurt her now. It was more like a betrayal. Something she had relied on had let her down, abandoned her when she needed it most.

Or, perhaps, she had abandoned it…

The wide streets narrowed as she drew closer to her destination, nestled in the part of the canyon where the walls closed in. At least here the shadows lengthened. Her clothes were sticking to her skin, sweat turning chilly as she began to cool down.

F. D. Lee

Naima had been surprised to discover this was where she needed to go. When she'd checked the records, she'd been directed to a townhouse near the bay – not as expensive as those built up high into the canyon walls, but not cheap, either. Most visitors of class owned houses near the water. Outsiders tended to find living between the canyon walls oppressive.

And if they thought the mouth of the canyon was claustrophobic, with the high walls looming above them, they would have hated the Scree. The streets narrowed to thin avenues barely wide enough for a horse and cart, the buildings huddled together for space, long and thin like skeleton fingers, and it was always dark – a permanent twilight, with oil lamps burning twenty-four hours a day.

But this was where she was supposed to be. The townhouse had been a dead end – an uppity servant informing her in a nasal, Marlaisian accent that her mistress had not been there in months. Naima had returned to her office, at a loss. The Countess had to be in Cerne Bralksteld.

Naima, naturally, realised the absurdity of her stubborn insistence. But she couldn't resign herself to defeat. Not after everything. So, she'd sat down with a cup of strong tea and done some thinking.

It had been the letters to Amelia that had, once again, tipped her off. With a twinge of guilt, Naima had broken the seals and read through them. Most of them were bland, but the more recent ones were very carefully written.

It had occurred to Naima that these letters were slightly too careful, the way that you can tell when someone knows they're being listened to and adjusts their speech accordingly. But every now and again there were little scraps of colour to the text. Stories about a tree house her father had apparently made for her, and how Amelia and someone called Julian used to have dinner parties there, and Amelia saying that one day she would buy Julian his own house.

Naima had dashed to the public library and the census information. A flight of fancy, perhaps, or perhaps the strange magic that occurs when one finally starts thinking in the right way... Either way, she had checked the records for a property owned by Julian Ghislain and, as the Marlaisians would say, *voilà*.

And so Naima found herself standing outside a tall, narrow stone house in the Scree. Built into the bottom of the canyon, it jutted, nondescript, a few feet from the wall. The bulk of it went who-knew how far into the stone. It would be damp and cold. Not the kind of place one would expect to find anyone important. The rock houses weren't specifically reserved for the poor but, generally speaking, the lower into the stone they were situated, the lower the class of the inhabitants. The houses higher up the cliff face got more sun, warming the stone to counter the natural chill of living almost entirely inside the rock. Moreover, their proximity to the plains made it easier to run chimneys through the strata, which meant fireplaces – another means of chasing away the damp and the cold.

But this was where her investigation had brought her. Naima adjusted the hood of her cloak once again, and knocked.

What felt like hours stretched by, each moment giving her a chance to walk away from it all and pretend she didn't know something was terribly wrong. Ah – but she'd known that for a long time, really, hadn't she? Known and turned a blind eye, her silence paid for with donations to the Cultivators and promises of a happy ending. Her father would be ashamed of her if he were still alive.

The door opened just wide enough for a face to peer around it. Naima was met with a pair of bright blue eyes set in skin the colour of milk, framed by ebony hair. Lips red as fresh blood formed a thin line in an almost painfully beautiful face.

"Who are you?" the Countess of Marlais, Maria Sophia Ghislain, demanded.

Naima introduced herself, but it was only when she gave her title that Maria Sophia's expression changed. The wary annoyance slid off her face, her eyes widening and her lips parting into an 'o'. She grabbed Naima and pulled her inside.

The hallway was much nicer than Naima had expected – but she should have guessed that the nobility, even in hiding, would live well. Oil lamps cast a warm, cosy light, making it hard to judge the

Countess' age, though Naima suspected she was in her late thirties or early forties, slightly younger than herself.

A thick rug ran the length of the long corridor, protected from the cold stone by a layer of rush matting. There were paintings on the walls showing a family: Maria Sophia, Amelia – perhaps two or three years younger than she was now – a handsome man with thick dark hair and olive skin, the Count, judging from his similarity to Amelia, and a younger boy with much paler skin, black hair and a wide grin.

"You're a Cultivator?" Maria Sophia's words came out in a gasp. "My daughter – Amelia – do you know her?"

"Yes, my Lady, that's why I'm here."

Maria Sophia waved her hands in front of her like she was trying to fan a fire into life. "Did she read my letters? She sent you here?"

"...no, my Lady. I, uh, I found this place myself."

"But then... If she didn't send you... Does she even know I'm here? Oh, God. Please, is she safe?"

"I... think so."

"You *think* so? Is she or isn't she?"

"Yes, she is. For now. But my Lady, I must speak with you."

Maria Sophia pulled back. Flickering shadows danced across her face.

"You need to leave. This place is for Amelia to find, no one else." She put her hands on Naima's shoulders and pushed. "Go, now. Get out. Out, out, out!"

Naima grabbed her wrists, planting her feet on the floor. "Stop it! My Lady, please – I'm here to help."

"Help? If he finds out you're here – he's got Albelphizar, God knows what he'll do. Oh, oh." Maria Sophia stopped pushing against Naima, her whole body slumping. If it weren't for Naima's grip on her wrists, she would have collapsed. "You stupid woman. If Amy's safe, why would you come here?"

"Because I want to keep her safe!"

Maria Sophia stared up at her with wide eyes. After a moment, she nodded.

"You said Joseph had Albelphizar?" Naima asked, releasing her grip. "Do you mean the genie, Seven?"

The Princess And The Orrery

Maria Sophia shuddered. "I hated that name the moment I heard it. Yes, Albelphizar is the genie. If you know that, what in the name of all things decent brought you here?"

"Because I need to know what the hell is going on."

"You mean you don't already?"

Naima hesitated. Whatever she'd been expecting, this wasn't it. The woman was a nervous wreck. How she had given birth to a child like Amelia was anyone's guess. If Naima said too much, the Countess was just as likely to fall to pieces as tell her what she needed to know. She had to tread carefully.

"I know that Joseph captured the genie from Llanotterly and that he's using him to build a device. And I know Amelia is mixed up in it all somehow and you are, too. I want to help Amelia. But I need to know what I'm dealing with."

Maria Sophia choked out a bitter, ugly laugh. "What you're dealing with? He's a monster. A vile, evil thing that should have been killed at birth. If I had any hope I could do it, I'd kill him myself with my bare hands and bathe in his blood."

"The genie? I knew it!"

Maria Sophia shot her a pitying look. "Not Albelphizar. Albelphizar is just a teenager stuck in the body of a God. I'm talking about Joseph."

48

Conversation is, as Amelia would say, a tricksy bunny. Sometimes you prepare yourself to chase it all over the garden and then, sometimes, it just wanders up and sniffs your hand.

"How do you know Seven?" Naima asked.

Maria Sophia had brought them to a small, windowless sitting room: comfortably appointed, but not lavish. Like the hallway, lamps burned in fixtures on the wall and a thick rug took up most of the floor. There were some books on a shelf, a coffee table and a couple of sofas. The only extravagance was the four or five occasional tables, each cluttered with more paintings of Maria Sophia and her family.

Naima tried not to stare at Amelia, smiling brightly in each one. If it hadn't been for the resemblance to her father, Naima would never have believed it was the same girl who'd been living in her observatory for the past two years.

Maria Sophia shrugged. "We were lovers."

Naima nearly choked. "Excuse me?"

"Oh, don't look so shocked. You've seen him, haven't you?"

"Yes, of course – but he's... He gets inside your head. How could you...? Oh, God. Did he-?"

"Trick me? No." Maria Sophia crossed her legs, drumming her fingers on her knee. "It's hard to explain, but he didn't trick me, didn't force me. That's not who he is. Not how it works. Look, obviously he's upset you somehow. Tell me what happened."

Naima chewed her lip. But if she was going to find out the truth, she had to be prepared to ask – and answer – difficult questions. She could only hope that the warm, soft light from the lamps went some way towards hiding her discomfort.

"I could feel him in my head. Like a boil, filling up. And then it burst and everything I'd ever wanted – needed – came flooding out. Stupid things; a doll I'd begged my mother for as a child, a soldier who'd left me to return to war. But bigger things too... More money for the Cultivators. Better equipment. More time."

Naima dropped her head. "More recognition. I didn't realise all the things I wanted for myself. How... materialistic and *common* my dreams were. Fame, power – to be the creator of a legacy. I'd always thought I was happy just working, finding answers. And then, suddenly, it was there in my head – in my whole being. This need to be respected, to be known as the one who raised the Cultivators up. To be the one who made people grateful for us."

"Ah. He made you realise, underneath it all, what drives you?"

"Yes."

"And you didn't like what you discovered?"

"No."

Maria Sophia frowned. "I'm sorry that happened to you. I thought better of him."

"Well... He might not have been exactly... That is to say... He wasn't in the best of states when it happened."

"Oh. I see. Joseph, I suppose?" Maria Sophia dropped her head, a flash of guilt visible for a moment on her face. "I knew he'd hurt him. I'd hoped... I don't know... I'd hoped Albelphizar would be able to escape." She looked up. "I didn't want any of this. I didn't have a choice."

"A choice about what?"

Maria Sophia threw her gaze at the wall. "If I tell you and Joseph finds out, he'll stop me from seeing Amy. It's taken me over two years to get this close. Why would I give that up for your curiosity?"

Naima leaned forward, closing the gap between them. "Because Joseph's up to something, my Lady, and I think Amelia is caught up in it, her and her orrery, and the genie. We must help each other."

Maria Sophia bit her lower lip, her forehead knotted in a frown, still glaring at the wall.

"Please, my Lady," Naima said, hating herself for pushing but knowing she had to. "Tell me what you can. And then you can see Amelia at the Calan Mai festival – hell, if we can work out what Joseph is doing, perhaps she could even go home with you."

"Home?" Maria Sophia let loose a bitter laugh, turning to look at her at last. "Joseph won't let her come home. Oh God, it's all such a mess. I thought if Joseph had Albelphizar, he wouldn't need Amy anymore."

"I don't understand. What did you do?"

The other woman shot her a look so full of hatred Naima recoiled. And then something even worse happened. Maria Sophia's face crumpled. She wiped her eyes, tears spilling down her cheeks.

"My daughter has been trapped in that building of yours for two-and-a-half years, and the best I've been able to do is hand a genie over to a lunatic, and I still haven't got her back. And now you're saying that something even worse is going to happen and it's all my fault."

Maria Sophia crumpled in on herself, her shoulders heaving as she sobbed into her hands. Naima looked around for help, but there was none – they were alone. Hesitantly, she knelt down by Maria Sophia and patted her shaking shoulders, making what she hoped were soothing sounds.

Somehow, it worked. Maria Sophia's sobs turned, slowly, to whimpers and then to sniffles. Finally, she looked up, her bright blue eyes shining in the lamplight, and took a deep breath. "Thank you. I'm fine. Go back to your seat, please." For all the authority of her words, there was a quiver in her voice. "You can help Amy?"

"I want to try, yes."

"And Albelphizar?"

"I... yes. Yes. We have to get him away from Joseph. Joseph wished him a prisoner, I saw that happen, but I think there's more to it. Another wish. And... they hurt him, don't they? The wishes?"

Maria Sophia nodded. "It's strange. The genies can't refuse a wish, but they can usually control it. They have this special metal that helps them – Albelphizar's was a necklace. The stories say a lamp, but I suppose each genie had their own tastes. Anyway, they can't refuse a wish, so they try to get them finished quickly, or, better, to make the reality of the first wish so horrendous nobody ever tries for another."

An ugly sound of revulsion escaped Naima before she could stop it.

The Princess And The Orrery

"Yes, well," Maria Sophia said, fixing her with the kind of look only a mother could give: sympathetic, certainly, but also a little bit annoyed. "I know what he did to you was wrong. I won't defend him. But you said yourself he was in pain. That's the thing, you see. He can't really help it. You spend enough time around him and you just end up wanting things. Most of the time, I don't think he has any control over it. None of the genies had, from what I understand. And people took advantage of their inability to refuse. Is it any wonder they found a way to protect themselves?"

Naima hung her head. "No. I suppose not."

"It's not your fault, either. He shouldn't have done that to you," Maria Sophia replied, a touch more softly. "Anyway. Albelphizar and I were lovers, a long time ago. That's how I learnt that genies were real. Genies and more: dwarfs and fairies and elves, all of it. God, the things he told me. But anyway, the thing with Albelphizar is that it was all new to him. I meant it when I said he's a teenager, really. He'll tell you he's hundreds of years old, but genies live for thousands of years. I'm thirty-seven now, and I met him when I was eighteen. I grew up faster than him."

Maria Sophia took a deep breath, brushing her hands down her thighs like she was trying to rub dirt from her dress.

"I didn't mean to hurt him," she continued. "But I was young; I didn't know how to break it off. So I left him. I mean, I *left* left him. I had a chance to go without having to face the music, without having to tell him that... well, anyway, I'm not proud of it. I ran away with Henry, got married. Had children. I didn't even really think about Albelphizar until... until after Julian, Jules, died."

"Julian?"

"My son."

Naima's gazed pulled back to the pictures dotted around the room. The little boy with the mop of dark hair and the wide grin.

"I'm sorry," she said. It was stupid, but what else could she say?

"Thank you, I suppose. It was a messy business. Amy blamed herself. She was only ten, it wasn't her fault."

"Why would she blame herself?"

"There was an accident. Henry likes to hunt, and Amy wanted to impress him. She was always tinkering with things... even as a very young girl, she'd take things apart and put them back together again. Well, she got hold of one of his crossbows, God knows how, and decided to improve it. And Jules, you see, he loved his sister. Followed her around like a puppy dog. When she snuck out to test the bow, he snuck out with her."

Maria Sophia's voice flattened. Her eyes closed. "She went into the woods. Didn't know he was following her. She wasn't thinking, she just wanted to test her crossbow. Make Henry proud. But there are wolves in the Athenine forest, and Amy... she was only small, only ten years old. Only a baby herself. She shot one and turned and ran. She didn't know Jules was there until she heard the scream."

"Oh, God. I'm so sorry. Poor Amelia. And you, your husband..."

Maria Sophia opened her eyes. "Yes. It was a tragedy. I lost my baby boy, and then I lost my little girl. Amy couldn't bear the guilt. She couldn't stand to be around us, in the castle. Everything reminded her of Jules. And then, one day, she announced she was coming here. She'd heard about your Cultivators and written directly to the Baron. I don't know how Joseph got hold of her letter, but he did. He invited her here, and the next thing I knew, there was a coach outside and she was leaving."

Maria Sophia drew another deep breath. "I know it sounds ridiculous, but we thought it might be better if she did go, just for a little while. We thought she needed the space and the time. But she never came back – about six months after she left, we got a letter from Joseph saying he was keeping Amy indefinitely."

"But Amelia can leave any time she wants to. Joseph told me..." Naima trailed off, cold realisation freezing the words in her mouth.

"I expect I can imagine what he told you. That we were cruel? That she was in danger from us?"

"Something like that," Naima admitted. "I'm sorry. But Amelia wanted to stay with us, and it seemed to add up and-"

"Amelia is a child, running away." Maria Sophia gripped her knees. "She probably gets that from me. I ran away from my home, too, straight into the arms of a man I didn't understand. I don't know – maybe if Joseph wasn't involved, I would have let her stay with you. I know she doesn't want to come home. But she's my daughter, and I have to protect her even if she doesn't want it.

Joseph is evil. Pure evil. I knew it the first time I came here, trying to see Amy. He said he needed her to build something for him, and I said that surely anyone could build whatever it was, and he said no. Only Amy. That there was something special about her, that she had *magic* in her blood. I don't suppose you can imagine what I felt then?"

Naima stared at her, horrified. "You're not saying Seven is her father?"

"What? No, of course not. Amelia's twelve – I thought you Sisters were supposed to be good at maths? But I spent a lot of time with Albelphizar. A lot of... well, you know. Is it so hard to believe that something might have, ah, rubbed off on me?" Maria Sophia shrugged. "Or maybe not. Maybe Amy is just extraordinary. I always thought she was. The cleverest little girl in all Five Kingdoms, that's what I used to tell her. But it put Albelphizar in my mind."

"And that was two years ago?" Naima hadn't meant it to be an accusation, but Maria Sophia stiffened, her knuckles whitening to the colour of paper.

"Believe it or not, I didn't just hand a genie over to that maniac without thinking about it. Amy was writing to us. She sounded happy enough. And then the letters slowed down. When she did write, she said Joseph was annoyed she was taking so long to build her thingy – the orrery? And then the letters stopped. Everyone knows what you people are like. The slave pits. The cruelty. The obsession with being the best. I wasn't left with any choice. So a year ago, I came here and met with Joseph in secret. Told him I could get him a genie. You know, I expected him to laugh at me? But he just sat there, watching me squirm and suffer with those hateful eyes of his. And then he agreed. If I got him Albelphizar, he'd let Amy go."

"That's what happened in Llanotterly."

Maria Sophia nodded. "It wasn't actually all that hard to find Albelphizar. I had a whole Kingdom at my bidding, and anyway, I think he wanted me to find him. So Henry and I went to the Ball, met Joseph, confirmed Albelphizar was real – you know what it's like when you're close to him, even if he's trying to hide what he is, you know something's not right – and that was that. It should have been easy, but there was this attack. I wished myself and Albelphizar to Joseph. He was waiting for us, it was all planned out. Albelphizar was sick with the wish and easy enough to lock up in irons. Joseph brought him here, and that was it. I never got Amy back."

Naima pinched the bridge of her nose, trying to take it all in. "Seven's with Amelia-"

Maria Sophia shot forward on her chair, relief flooding her face. "Albelphizar is with Amy? Oh, thank God. He'll keep her safe. He'd never allow a child to get hurt, I know it. Oh, oh, thank God." Tears pooled in the corners of her eyes and ran down cheeks stretched in a smile of genuine gratitude.

It took all Naima's strength to say what she had to say next.

"I think… yes… I think he's trying to help Amelia. But, my Lady, I'm sorry… but I'm not sure how much help Seven can be. Joseph has them both working on the orrery. I think that was Joseph's second wish. To make the orrery work. Or make them both make the orrery work."

The smile slid from Maria Sophia's face like she'd developed an allergy to happiness. "If there's a wish involved, there's nothing Albelphizar can do. What is the orrery, anyway? Why is it so important?"

"I don't know, but he's planning to unveil it at the Calan Mai festival."

"Listen to me," Maria Sophia said. "If Joseph has Albelphizar working on that thing, it's dangerous. I have no doubt of that. You have to find out what he wants from it, and you have to stop him. Albelphizar will help you. He's not a monster."

"But how? Joseph has control of him."

Maria Sophia pressed her hands to her head. "I don't know. If only there was a way to get Joseph or to separate him from the necklace… But he'll be surrounded by guards – besides, I'm no swordswoman, and you don't strike me as one, either. We'd be dead before we got close."

"Then we need a way to get close to him with a weapon no one will expect. My father once said that the best way to beat an enemy was to have the battle won before they even realised it had begun.

The Princess And The Orrery

God! I've been so stupid – I've been playing politics instead of playing Cultivator."

"What are you talking about?"

Naima took a deep breath. Was she really, seriously going to suggest the idea that had just formed in her mind? If she did, there'd be no going back. Not because Maria Sophia could force her to see it through – after all, only Naima had access to the old reports. Either she did it, or no one did. No, what would be irreversible would be her understanding of herself. If she gave voice to the idea, she'd be the kind of person who was *capable* of giving voice to such an idea.

…but didn't she know that already? Wasn't that what the genie had shown her? That she was ruthless, career-driven, selfish? The kind of person that would keep a child away from her family to further her own ambitions; who would condone the torture of a living creature for the same. Saying she was doing it for the Cultivators was an argument that no longer bore scrutiny.

Naima had wasted seven months trying to ignore the truth. She knew that deep down. As much as she wanted to comfort herself that she'd raised her voice against Joseph, she hadn't actually done anything until today. Now she was sitting in front of Maria Sophia, it was impossible to hide from the reality of what she'd allowed to happen.

She leaned forward. "I have an idea how to stop Joseph, once and for all…"

49

It was the day of Calan Mai, and it was, perhaps typically, raining.

Hemmings walked alongside the caravan, breathing in the thick, earthy smell of the rain on the cobblestones. Ænathlin didn't get much rain. Ænathlin didn't get much weather at all, really. It was sticky in the summer and chilly in the winter, but that was about it.

It was a small place, with small ideas.

Cerne Bralksteld, however, was vibrant and rich and colourful. The streets were laced with people, shops, craftworkers, printers, alchemists, homeopothecaries, and all manner of businesses with interesting names and strange items in their windows which he didn't recognise but instantly wanted to know more about.

He idled as much as he could, falling behind the caravan more than once when something caught his eye. He'd been particularly fascinated by a shop that sold nothing but glass – figures and mirrors and bottles and lamps and strange, twisting sculptures stained in rich, deep reds, bright, aqua blues or shiny, translucent yellows.

Back home, glass was an extreme luxury. If a window broke or a bottle shattered, more often than not it was replaced with some kind of wooden counterpart. Hells, even he couldn't trade for new glass in any substantial amounts, and the Ogrechokers were one of the wealthiest families in the city. A few years ago, Chokey had gifted him his pocket watch with the glass face, which he treasured. The mortal gods knew how much she'd traded for it.

But here they were selling similar watches and other trinkets for just a couple of their little metal coins. A quick word with one of the cast members had informed him such things weren't even considered all that valuable. "Tacky muck" had been the exact phrase she'd used. Hemmings hadn't cared; he'd swapped his only coins – two dirty brass ones he'd picked from the road as souvenirs – for a glass fish for Chokey.

And the food! Mortal gods, the food! He'd swear he'd seen at least forty different restaurants in the dozen or so roads they'd

The Princess And The Orrery

travelled along; there probably weren't forty restaurants in the *whole* of Ænathlin. Sweet smells of garlic, onion, frying tomatoes and the tangy, clean scent of a plant he now knew was called 'basil' drifted in the air, mingling with the smell of the rain and the sea.

But it was the chocolatier that ruined him.

The shop window was a painting made up of a thousand little brush strokes rendered in small squares and ovals of shiny white, brown, black, pink, and yellow chocolates, some dusted with crushed nuts, others decorated with whole pieces of fruit or snowy, powdered sugar. Surrounding the tasteful displays were sugar flowers, their petals so thin they were almost transparent, and spiderwebs of spun caramel. It was a masterpiece in minimalist decadence and pre-portioned indulgence.

The smell was maddening, making his mouth water and his throat dry all at the same time. He could only stare, mouth slightly open, at all the wonderful things on the other side of the window.

Hemmings was getting the hang of the human's barter system: a two-hour performance, with three or four hours of rehearsal and the rest of the day spent travelling and setting up and striking the stage, equated to two or sometimes three small copper coins from each audience member, depending on where they wanted to sit.

The numbers handwritten on discreet cards next to the chocolates were much higher than '2' or '3', though they certainly did contain two or three numerals, separated by a small dot.

"Alright, Sunshine."

Hemmings couldn't tear his gaze from the window. "Isn't it wonderful?"

"Eh. It's chocolate, that's all," Alfonso said. "Rots your teeth."

Hemmings felt he had more than enough teeth to risk it. "The smell... mortal gods, the smell. I think I might have died."

"Don't the rich have chocolate coming out of their ears? That's rather disappointing. I'd set on being the mid-life crisis of some grand old Duke and living out my autumn years in the lap of luxury."

Hemmings pulled his gaze, with some difficulty, from the window display. "I don't understand?"

F. D. Lee

"I mean, I would have thought young King John would have had all the chocolates you could ever want," Alfonso said, leaning against the glass. "What's the point of being rich if you can't have what you want?"

Hemmings remembered his character. Thank the gods Melly was far ahead with the caravan, a plume of smoke marking her location. "Oh. Yes. Well, Melly and I were only staying there briefly. We probably missed the... er... chocolate course at dinner."

Alfonso raised an eyebrow. "You're pretty, but you're certainly strange. Right, then. Wait here."

Hemmings opened his mouth to ask what was going on, but Alfonso had already darted into the shop, spitting on his palm and sweeping his sandy hair back from his face.

Outside, he'd been Alfonso. But as soon as he passed through the door, he became someone else. He straightened his back but curved his shoulders over, like a person who spent all day at a desk but knew they had to stand up properly. He clasped his hands in front of him and rearranged his features into a genteel sneer, his nose lifted ever-so-slightly upwards, so he was somehow looking down on everyone else, even though he was, in reality, rather short.

It shouldn't have worked. Alfonso was wet and still wearing his travelling clothes, the hems of his trousers muddy and his shirt dusty, but somehow he managed to make himself appear like someone extremely important and not at all used to waiting around.

The effect was instant. The woman behind the counter came forward, moving like a yacht across the floor. She dropped a curtsy which Alfonso returned with a stiff bow. Hemmings couldn't hear what they were saying, but he assumed it was introductions. Next, Alfonso pulled a piece of paper from his pocket and waved it airily under the woman's nose, too quick to be read. His expression was that of a man who was slightly bored, like he was engaged in a necessary evil, a task that had to be done but was bothersome, nonetheless.

The woman frowned, said a few words back.

Alfonso shrugged, tucking the paper back into his pocket. He glanced around the shop and said a few more lines before turning to leave.

The woman stood for a moment, face blank, and then stepped quickly after him, reaching him just before he got to the door. A few more turns were exchanged, and then she bustled over to the counter and – Hemmings nearly swooned – began putting a small selection of chocolates into a little white box. She tied it off with a ribbon and handed it to Alfonso, who didn't seem at all pleased to receive it. He once again offered the woman a stiff bow and walked out of the shop.

"Quick, follow me," he hissed as he passed Hemmings.

Hemmings looked back into the shop, and then again at Alfonso, who was already quite far down the street. Grasping his cap to his head, making sure his ears were safely hidden, he dashed after the actor.

He found Alfonso sitting on the edge of a fountain in a small square, a couple of streets away from the chocolatier. The company were nowhere to be seen.

"What are you doing? Where's Melly? What just happened?"

Alfonso produced the little white box with a flourish. "Getting you your chocolates, what else? And don't worry about the rest of them, look see? They've set up in the tavern over there."

Hemmings turned. There was indeed a large tavern on the corner with stables built onto the side, in which he could see the company's horses. The caravans had to be further back, hidden by the wall.

"Come on, sit down," Alfonso said, patting the space next to him.

The rain landed in warm, fat drops into the fountain's pool, almost like music. Alfonso's hair was loosening, the water stronger than his spit, and his clothes were sticking to his skin.

Hemmings hesitated, but Melly was, presumably, inside the tavern. She couldn't be cross with him for dallying if he was only just outside, could she?

He perched on the edge of the fountain, next to Alfonso. The stone was warm, wet and actually rather refreshing after the long walk down the cliffs. Alfonso held the box in the palm of his hand

and, with some ceremony, lifted the lid, careful to protect the contents from the rain. Inside were four chocolates resting on thin textured paper. They glistened, shiny and dark and brown.

"Go on then, I'm not a butler. Not today, anyway."

Hemmings looked up at him. Carefully, he picked up a chocolate and put it in his mouth.

Mortal gods and all the five hells. It was *amazing*.

The chocolate melted across his tongue, thick and warm with the texture of cream and the taste of bitter almonds and over-ripe cherries. Hemmings groaned.

"Good, huh?"

"Mmm-ffffmmm."

Alfonso laughed. "Glad to be of service."

Hemmings couldn't speak. There was no way he was going to swallow the chocolate. How had he ever thought he'd lived before tasting something so divine? Even the rain seemed to complement the flavours, warm drops of it running off his cap and down his collar, cooling his skin. It was like his whole body was open to sensation, feeling and tasting the world for the very first time.

He didn't think he'd ever been so happy in all his life.

The last of the chocolate slowly melted on his tongue, but the taste remained.

"I don't know what to say," Hemmings said. "Why did you do that? How did you do that?"

Alfonso put the box between them and leaned back, so he was resting on the heels of his hands, his face up towards the sky.

"That was nothing – easy as pie. Or chocolate torte, perhaps. It's all about believing it, Sunshine. If you believe in the characters, other people will, too."

"But she just gave it to you?"

Alfonso turned to Hemmings, blinking away the rain. "Sure. I told her I was a food inspector and there'd been complaints. She didn't buy it at first, but I just said it was up to her, but that my report was due today and I wasn't about to go in front of the Baron for her sake. He's got a reputation for enjoying the finer things, has the Baron. She changed her mind, sensible woman, and now you have chocolates. You can have another one if you want. They're for you."

The Princess And The Orrery

Hemmings wavered for a moment and then shook his head. "I'll have one later."

"Suit yourself. They'll keep for a while." Alfonso closed the box and handed it to Hemmings. "Put them away, you don't want them to get wet. Hah. *Vive l'amour et d'eau fraiche.*"

"What does that mean?"

"Nothing really. Just reminding myself that you'll be leaving us. We've arrived in Cerne Bralksteld, haven't we?"

"Oh. Yes."

Hemmings had somehow completely forgotten the whole reason he was with the theatre in the first place. How was that possible?

"So, what is it you and the scarecrow are doing here, really?" Alfonso asked. "It's not exactly usual for a King to ask us to educate two how-do-you-dos on the ways of the common man."

Hemmings fiddled with his cuffs, trying to think of an answer that wasn't actually the answer. Like so often recently, he was at a loss. Thoughtsmithing was all about finding the truth, not masking it. And he didn't want to lie anymore. Not to Alfonso.

"I can't really talk about it."

Alfonso nodded sagely. "I suspected as much."

"Excuse me?"

"You're on a secret mission, right?" Alfonso threw him a look that was equal parts humour and melancholy. "You're not like the rest of them, not you. Not some toff spending the season 'experiencing' life."

Hemmings must have looked as confused as he felt.

"The moment I saw you both, I said to myself, here are two folks on a quest," Alfonso explained, warming to whatever role he'd started playing. "Off to rescue some beautiful Princess, no doubt, who you'll end up marrying and having a dozen fat, screaming babies with. I will say, though, I don't think Melly's cut out for the role of godmother."

Godmother... Hemmings felt a wave of guilt. He was supposed to be helping Melly save the Mirrors and prevent a civil war. Doing his part to keep the tree alive, to make sure Chokey and Bea and Mistasinon could lead long, happy lives. And instead he was sitting in the rain, eating sweets and feeling miserable about leaving a bunch of humans and their little theatre behind.

"So, am I right?"

Hemmings blinked, the rain dripping down his face, getting caught in the scars on his cheek and pausing there before reaching his jaw and falling onto his lap.

"Right about what?"

"Rescuing a Princess?"

"Oh. Um, not really. It's just as I explained. No secret mission, no Princess." He looked over at the tavern, where Melly was probably waiting for him. "We all have our roles to play, I've learnt."

Alfonso brightened, though Hemmings had no idea why. As far as he was concerned, the world had just darkened, like the sun had been plucked from the sky.

The actor shuffled up on the fountain bench, so he was sitting very close to Hemmings.

"Sometimes we can change our role, though," Alfonso said. "I mean, when I left the farm, I left because all I could ever be was one person, with one life. Now I get to be all kinds of people."

"I suppose so," Hemmings said. "But it doesn't always work like that. Not everyone has that freedom."

Alfonso kicked his feet against the edge of the fountain, frowning. Whatever brief cheer he'd felt seemed to have disappeared. Hemmings was just about to get up and go when Alfonso reached up and held his chin, his fingers brushing against the scars on his face.

The aching heaviness in Hemmings' chest lurched, falling until it landed in the pit of his stomach and settled in a hot, tight knot. Alfonso's fingers on his cheek were minute jolts of lightning, frightening and almost painful, bringing to life the damaged nerves with a crackle of unexpected sensation.

Alfonso smiled, shades of sadness in the brown of his eyes.

"Well, I suppose I can change my role, then. Just for you. Did you know the phrase 'one-night stand' comes from the theatre?" He brought himself still closer to Hemmings. His accent had shifted again, dropping into a low, soft wave of thick rolling vowels and short consonants that reminded Hemmings of the smooth, bitter chocolate. "Used to mean a single show. And if it's

The Princess And The Orrery

a good show – spectacular – maybe it doesn't matter if it only happens once?"

Hemmings managed to nod.

Alfonso's hand drifted to his cap, his fingertips brushing against his earlobe. Hemmings flinched, the thought of the human uncovering his long, pointed ears like a knife cutting through him, but Alfonso's hand moved past his ear and came to rest on the back of his neck.

"Once then, but with feeling," Alfonso whispered before pulling Hemmings forward and pressing their lips together.

The kiss was hot and sweet, and tasted of rain and chocolate and, faintly, the tobacco Alfonso smoked.

Alfonso pulled back, his eyes dark and heavy-lidded. He nodded towards the tavern.

"Encore?"

Hemmings opened his mouth to answer when the sky exploded.

F. D. Lee

50

Naima entered the observatory, viewing the growth of the orrery with a mixture of joy and horror. It was now at least thirty, if not forty, feet high, with nine planets revolving around its centre. She knew, sensibly, that it was something to be afraid of. That whatever Joseph's nefarious intentions were, they centred around that machine and the genie who was, even now, adjusting some intricate part of it.

And yet...

It was still beautiful. Mesmerising. The marvel of the cogs and clockwork and engineering that powered the planets' journeys was breathtaking. How could something so wonderful, so indicative of human advancement, be so terrible?

And then she thought of Celia and what had befallen her, and shivered.

"Our guest returns," Seven said, wiping his brow.

Amelia's head poked out from inside the orrery like a rabbit tasting the air. "Oh. Hi."

It wasn't the enthusiastic greeting she was used to, but perhaps that made what she was about to do easier? Naima wondered if her father had nursed himself with similar thoughts before he sent men off to die on the battlefield. It was a part of him that she'd never been wholly able to reconcile herself with; the man who was her father and the man who was responsible for the lives and deaths of hundreds of soldiers.

Ironic, really, considering how things had turned out. She could only hope that, once the dust had settled, history would see what she was about to do as the right thing. Maybe it would. Probably it wouldn't.

But she had to fix what she had allowed to happen, and if that meant ruining her name and her reputation, well, so be it. All she could hope for now was that her actions didn't damn the entire Sisterhood along with her. Which was why she needed to be seen to act alone.

The Princess And The Orrery

"Amelia, it's the festival today... I'd like to, ah, give you something."

Amelia made a face. "I don't want anything – well, except not to go, but I suppose that's out of the question. Do you know if my mother's arrived?"

Naima managed to turn her choke into a cough. "I don't know. Come on, we don't have much time."

Amelia rolled her eyes, but to Naima's great relief she disappeared and then appeared a few moments later at the bottom of the orrery, jumping between the gently moving spheres and skidding to a stop.

"Will this take long?"

"No," Naima said. "Not long at all. Would you mind waiting outside? I'd just like to talk to the ge- to Seven, alone."

Amelia turned a questioning face to the genie. "Seven?"

The genie jumped down from the top of the device, landing neatly. He shrugged. "It makes no difference to me, my Lady."

Naima held her breath. But it was fine. Amelia picked up her toy bear and, shooting her a suspicious look, marched to the door.

The minute she stepped through, two porters grabbed her and carried her away, kicking and screaming at the top of her voice.

Naima spun around, her hands already up in supplication, to find the genie in front of her, his face a mask of fury, his eyes as dark as the midnight sky. She had no idea how he'd moved so quickly or so quietly.

He lifted his fist-

"Wait! Wait!" Naima cried. "I'm not going to hurt her!"

Seven lowered his fist. "You will forgive me, Madam, if I question such a statement."

"Please, just listen. They're taking her to my office, that's all. To keep her safe. To keep her out of the way."

The genie's eyes narrowed, calculating, before fluttering closed. His body went rigid, his hand clasping his stomach as a long hiss escaped through his teeth. Naima didn't know what to do – he was obviously in pain, but it was also clear that whatever he was doing was deliberate.

So she waited, watching him with growing anxiety. A minute or two later, he opened his eyes, his hand still clutching his abdomen.

F. D. Lee

"Very well," he said. "I believe that you believe you intend her no harm. Why?"

"Can we sit?"

Seven thought for a moment and then nodded. He grabbed a chair, placed it in front of her, and sat on his bed with a heavy thump. Naima hesitated and then took the chair he had provided.

"I want to talk to you," Naima said. "To speak honestly. But I also understand, that is, I believe, it may be difficult for you to talk to me."

He gave a slight nod, but said nothing.

"I need to talk about why you're here," Naima continued. "And about Amelia, and the orrery."

"I would rather not discuss such matters."

"And yet we must, if we're going to find a way out of this mess. Can you tell me the nature of Joseph's wishes?"

Seven shook his head.

"I thought as much." Naima sighed. "But the wish must be strong – no, don't worry, that wasn't a question, just a thought. I apologise. I'll keep my thinking to myself. It can't hurt you, can it? If I think?"

"I... suspect not. I cannot control the content of another's mind. Influence it, perhaps, but not control."

"Will you try to influence me?"

The genie leaned forward, resting his forearms on his thighs. "A sensible question. I wonder who have you been speaking to, that you are suddenly in possession of such guile. Joseph? You should not trust his counsel, for he leads you astray."

"What do you mean?"

"'Try' is such an amenable verb, so wonderfully open to corruption."

"Fine. Will you influence me?"

A pause. Seven shook his head. "For as long as I believe you intend to help Amelia? I will not."

She supposed that was fair enough. Naima set her shoulders back and lifted her chin. This was it.

"We both understand, I think, that we have a problem. Or, perhaps, problems. One of them is the orrery. The other is you. It's clear to me that Joseph has plans for the device and it seems that

The Princess And The Orrery

you are integral to both his intentions and the orrery's functionality. I would like to know what and why, but I also suspect that whatever Joseph has wished for prevents you from answering me – that's why you accused me of stupidity."

"My Lady, I accused you of nothing – you have provided evidence enough of the fact. I know how well you Cultivators love evidence."

Naima winced. "I deserve that, I know, and more besides. But I think you care for Amelia and her safety, and I hope that you will continue to do so, should the need arise. I've been told that your magic hurts you, and I've seen it's so. I don't understand what Joseph has wished for, but I'm going to – no, wait. I think perhaps it's better for you if you don't know. Let me say this, instead: I'm aware of the situation."

"You have been aware of 'this situation' since its inception. You must forgive me if I retain my scepticism."

"You'd be a fool to trust me, I know that. But I don't think you have much choice?"

The genie stared at her, his face giving away nothing. Naima resisted the urge to duck her head.

At last, he said, "I did not expect this conversation."

Naima allowed herself a quick smile. "I don't think I did either, to be honest. Magic and wishes and genies… it beggars belief. But here you are, and here I am. I should have accepted the truth that first night, when you crawled inside my mind."

"When I sought to defend myself," he corrected sharply.

"I… yes. My father had a horse once, when I was younger," she said, surprising herself. This wasn't relevant – it certainly wasn't helpful to her plan. But now she'd started she found she couldn't stop, that she wanted him to understand she wasn't a completely terrible person.

"He'd ridden it too far, too fast. Have you ever seen an exhausted horse? All the red foam around their mouths where the bit has cut, eyes wide, nostrils flaring? Welts down its flanks from the whip. It's a terrible sight. Anyway, I wanted to give it some water, but whenever I tried to get close to it, it lashed out. Biting, kicking. I think it thought I was going to hurt it. I'd only wanted to help, but the horse scared me – scared me so much I wouldn't go near any horse, not for years." She paused. "You reminded me of that horse, the very first time I saw you, in the tower. I suppose I just didn't remember all the details until the other day."

"Am I supposed to feel sympathy?" Seven sneered. "I saw your mind, Madam. I saw the things you crave, and I saw little difference between your desires and our master's. You tell a sweet tale, I allow, but it is no justification for kidnap, imprisonment or torture."

"No, it's not. I just wanted… it doesn't matter." She pulled on her resolve, wrapping it around her like a cloak. "I just wanted you to know that I'm trying to address my actions."

Seven glared at her. Naima was about to speak again when he started drumming his fingers against his legs. "I will admit," he began, looking anywhere but at her, "That my response at that time was, ahh, overzealous. I was not in control of myself."

"I… thank you."

He shrugged, almost like he was embarrassed. "Yes. Well, if you seek to keep Amelia safe, you have my support – though I must confess I am not sure what else I can provide. I am bound to my master's desires, not mine and certainly not yours."

Naima got to her feet. "Understood. I'm afraid I'm not here simply to remove Amelia from the situation. There's someone else who needs to speak to you. Someone I suspect you won't want to see. I'm asking you, please, to keep in mind the bigger picture. We… well, we thought it was better you find out now, rather than at the festival when you might – when your reaction might jeopardise our plan."

"Who is this person?"

Naima made her way to the door. Only when she had her hand on the wood did she turn back.

"Amelia's mother," she said as she exited. To her shame, a wave of relief washed over her as she stepped aside and let Maria Sophia into the observatory.

51

Magic roared in Seven's ears, tearing through him as he stared at The Woman while she watched him from the door with a guarded expression-

In the Grand Central Station, all the Mirrors went, momentarily, black...

The broken Mirrors in the Index groaned as their wooden frames expanded, like old doorways in damp houses...

Mistasinon sat alert, head up, in his tiny office deep within the labyrinth of the General Administration...

Far, far away, yellow cephalopod eyes watched with eager anticipation as the gate swung open, the pathway visible...

Seven bent forward, his hands caught in his curls, and willed the instinctual burst of magic back down inside him. Sickness clawed at his throat, his stomach a tight knot of cramping agony, the cannonball in his head slamming into his skull. And then, predictable as the dawn, the tingling sensation of pleasure tripped across his ragged nerves, swirling and blending with the pain until it was impossible to tell where one ended and the other began.

Against the torment in his skull, he tilted his head backwards, drawing deep breaths in through his nose and out through his mouth, his jaw chattering in tiny, desperate movements with each exhalation-

The connection broke, and the Mirrors in the Grand resumed their normal working.

In the Index, the sound of wood suffering faded to nothing.

Mistasinon unfroze with a shudder, reaching for his scrap of cloth.

The monsters screamed in frustration as the gate swung closed again.

The pain was like the pounding of a thousand drums, but Seven refused to keep his hands pressed to his skull. Instead, he straightened his back – a wave of nausea – and carefully crossed his legs, resting his hands on his knees.

"You're bleeding," Maria Sophia said, a note of something he refused to believe was concern in her voice. She pulled out a handkerchief from her sleeve, spat on it, and moved towards him. "Here, let me-"

"No!"

The cry was more sound than word, exploding out of his mouth before he could stop it. Maria Sophia stilled, halfway between the door and his bed, the orrery spinning to her left, and stuffed the handkerchief back into her sleeve. Seven quickly wiped his mouth and nose with the back of his hand and resumed his pose.

"I'm not going to hurt you," Maria Sophia said. "I just want to talk."

"You... you're Amelia's mother?"

Maria Sophia took a deep breath. "Yes."

Outside, clouds gathered above Castell y Sêr, the rain pattering harder against the roof, changing tone as it hit either glass, copper, or tile.

Seven swallowed, the magic inside him scratching him like a forgotten prisoner in a dark and dismal cell desperately trying to claw his way out.

The orrery picked up speed.

"It was all a trick, then? Since the first, I have been taken for a fool by you. But to use a child to manipulate me..." He spat, a thick glob of black blood landing heavily on the stone tiles. "Bah. I should have expected such. Spoiled, nasty, cruel animals you are, each and every one."

"It's not like that, Albelphizar. Let me explain."

The Princess And The Orrery

Maria Sophia took a step forward and then froze as an arc of lightning shot across the orrery. The device groaned, the planets moving faster, straining the mechanisms.

Joseph's wish grabbed Seven, wrapping itself around him, crushing him. For a moment he couldn't see or hear anything, his body and mind caught in the competing currents of his own primal reaction and the wish's demand for his capitulation. Nothing was allowed to endanger the orrery, including himself. The whole universe was a raging ocean funnelled to a needle-point of screaming pressure that pinned him to the bed.

Thunder rolled, the sky darkening, rain lashing against the observatory. A bolt of lightning shot from the sky, earthing itself on the copper roof-

The gate swung open, the pathway clearing...

Deep inside the orrery, lightning crackled in the transparent gelatinous matter that bound the snake-necklace cog to the machine. The planets responded, picking up speed-

Hungry, heavy bodies tumbled and crawled over each other, racing for the narrow opening...

Seven dug his fingers into his scalp, focusing on the pain that was his own creation-

The gate slammed closed, sucking its power into itself, and the monsters howled and screamed and raged...

Seven blinked, his mind jarred and discordant as a bell rung with a hammer. He pulled his hands from his head, wincing at the tender spot already blossoming on his temples.

The orrery slowed down. The magic faded, the wish pulled back, leaving Seven only pain and the memory of raw, bruising pleasure.

Maria Sophia stared at the orrery. It was turning perfectly normally, only a faint smell of tin in the air.

"Is it... that can't be normal?"

Seven blinked, realising she had no idea what had occurred. Of course, something strange and frightening had happened when the orrery picked up speed, but the battle had been fought and won – or lost, perhaps – within him. He ran his hands through his hair, shaking out his curls so they fell across the sore spot on his forehead. He was too distracted to notice the fine blue strands that came away with his fingers.

"Leave here," he said, his voice for once hoarse and ugly.

Maria Sophia spun round, a quizzical look on her face. "What just happened?"

To his horror and exhaustion, Seven realised he had to protect the orrery.

"There is a... a component of Amel- of your daughter's devising within the machine which regulates the speed of the revolutions. It is perfectly normal. I do not pretend to understand it."

It was a weak lie, one that should have been instantly challenged. But Maria Sophia clearly had too much on her mind to examine it closely. She was staring at Amelia's bed, visible now she had passed the orrery.

Seven watched, his mind scattered, as she picked up Amelia's pillow and breathed it in, her shoulders tight as her hands gripped the soft material.

Seconds tripped by into minutes as Maria stood with her face buried in the pillow. Finally, she pulled away, moving stiffly. There were black smudges on the pillowcase and under her eyes. Hugging the pillow, she stepped slowly towards him until she was standing by the chair Naima had used.

"May I?"

"No. You may leave, however. And take your-" He was about to say '*daughter with you*' but he remembered the wish. "-your explanations with you."

Maria Sophia ignored him, taking the seat Naima had recently occupied.

"We have to talk, whether you want to or not. I don't want... this... to happen in front of Amy."

"Ah so, Amy is it? And yet when she speaks of you – if she does so at all – it is only with distaste."

Maria Sophia fixed eyes bright with hatred on him, her hands knotted in the pillow. "You really are a... I came here to apologise to you!"

"Apologise? And where do you intend to start?" He began counting off on his fingers. "When you allowed me to believe you loved me as I loved you? Or when you left me for another, hiding your deceit within the premise of a story? How grateful you must have been that I shared with you what the General Administration are, how they use their little tales to trap and control people. When I gave you the lie you would use on me. Or perhaps you might begin your apology with a more recent insult? Shall we start instead with the fact you handed me over to a madman, or that you used your own daughter to manipulate me?"

Seven spoke quickly, anger fuelling his words. It was only when they had left his lips that he realised the danger he had placed himself in. He stiffened, waiting for the wish to punish him again, but Joseph, it seemed, did not care what Maria Sophia thought. But he had to be more careful.

"I would never, ever do anything to place Amy in danger," Maria Sophia retorted. "And I certainly didn't want her to get caught up in all your lies and glamour and fakery. You were supposed to take her place, God damn it."

Seven took a deep breath, struggling past the spark of anger and magic that ignited within him until it was, if not small and distant, at least weaker and more manageable.

"Take her place? And how, pray, did you imagine such an event? I am to become a twelve-year-old snake, am I? Such a thing is not impossible, I suppose, though your route towards it leaves much to be desired."

"For God's sake Alb, just listen for once in your life! Not everything is about you." Maria Sophia leaned forward, speaking with a new urgency. "Joseph kept her from me. Kept her here – away from her family and friends – and I had to get her back. You said yourself he's a monster. What was I supposed to do? Let him have my only child? What would you have done, honestly? So I bargained you for her. I did it and I'm sorry. But I would do it again, in a heartbeat, to save my little girl."

Seven bit his tongue, refusing the heed the small voice in his head that had the temerity to suggest that he might, possibly, understand her.

"If what you say is true, why not wish for her return? You had me, had my necklace."

Maria Sophia rolled her eyes. "Oh yes, and you would have granted that wish, would you? Without twisting it somehow to punish me for leaving you? And even if I had, Joseph would have got her back. He's next in line to rule Cerne Bralksteld, the most powerful place in the whole of Ehinenden, you idiot. What are Henry and I to do against someone like that? All he'd have to do is have a quiet word with the O&P, suggest they stop supplying our traders and our whole county would starve in less than a year, and I *still wouldn't have Amy*. That's always been your problem – you spend all your time looking at the thing in front of you, and never actually see what's happening around you."

"I seem to recall that the *thing* in front of me was your lifeless body. I thought you dead, stolen from me by a story. And then I discover it was not theft I was the victim of, but duplicity. You claim I would not have helped you, as if I had any reason to offer you my aid."

Maria Sophia slapped the back of her hand against her forehead in mock alarm. "And so it begins, the Albelphizar tale of woe. Look, I know I hurt you. I know I handled it badly. But what did you expect? I was eighteen! I was running away from my stepmother – a woman who, since you remember everything so perfectly, had spent my entire life telling me I was nothing. That I was useless, and disgusting, and selfish."

"A remarkably astute assessment, I am come to realise," Seven snapped.

"That's a low thing to say. But it proves my point."

"And what is that?"

"That you were no better than my step-mother. She abused me and called it love, too."

Seven recoiled, the tendons in his neck straining as he sought to overcome his shock. "Abuse? I never abused you. I never hurt you. I loved you."

"You loved what being in love made you. Not me. If you had, you would've seen how unhappy I was. How broken. All that time we spent together, and you never wondered what kept me awake at night. Why I would cry for hours on end. When I tried to talk to you, you just dismissed it. Said that now I had you, I had no reason to be in pain. God, how I frustrated you! And in the end, I realised that I was nothing more to you than I'd been to my step-mother: a pretty young woman. But where she saw my beauty as a threat, you saw it as an endorsement. Neither of you ever saw *me*."

"That is a lie!"

Maria Sophia gripped the pillow tighter. "Is it? Tell me then... when's my birthday? What's my favourite food, or music, or colour?"

"I do not – it has been too long. Minor details," Seven said, ignoring the splinter-fine crack her words scratched across his certainty. "I doubt you know such details about me."

"You never told me your birthday. Your favourite food is that sweet, almond pastry they make in Ota'ari. You like choral music." She waved a hand at his tunic and trousers. "White is your favourite colour because you think it complements your skin. But yes. Anyone might know those things – although you didn't. Try this. How did my real mother die?"

Seven opened his mouth to answer and realised he didn't know. The crack inside him widened.

"Really? You don't remember? Because I remember how your family died. Let's try another one, then." Maria Sophia spoke slowly and clearly. "What was my step-mother's name? I know I told you. I told you about her over and over."

And with that, the crack became a canyon. He fell into it, engulfed in darkness.

He didn't know. He could remember, vaguely, her talking about it. But he'd been nursing his own grief, and with it ignoring his guilt at running away when the Teller and his Beast came for the genies while he hid in a cave, refusing his magic so he wouldn't be found.

"I don't mean to hurt you. I never did," Maria Sophia said quietly, firmly. "But you didn't love me any more than I loved you. We weren't capable of it – not the kind of love we each needed. You said at the Ball that you've been dead for the last fifteen years, because you'd been without me. That our love is the very earth itself, and nothing will ever compare to it. That isn't love, Alb. That's obsession. And I didn't have the strength, back then, to fight it. So I ran away. And I'm sorry, because I understand now that you can't hide from things, not if you want to heal them."

She paused, her blood-red lips a thin line. "But I was broken in so many pieces back then. I couldn't think for believing I was everything she had brought me up to believe I was. And then you came along... this beautiful, sad, strange man, and you told me I was the universe and everything wonderful within it. That I had saved you. And for a long time, for all the years we were together, I thought that was what love was, because it was the opposite of everything I'd been taught hatred was. When I realised it wasn't, that it was just as damaging, I didn't know how to escape, except to run away again."

The darkness splintered, shards of it flying around him, ripping into him, tearing him to pieces. He couldn't think, couldn't breathe.

"Get out," Seven hissed.

Maria Sophia got to her feet. "I'd hoped you might understand, that time and distance might have matured you – softened you, at the very least. I'm sorry, Albelphizar, that it hasn't, because I can't imagine what a lonely, hollow life you must lead if you haven't learnt your own faults and how to live with them. But understand this: Amelia is my daughter. She's my *baby*. I would give up a thousand genies for her safety. I'd give up my own life in a second, too. I've apologised for a lot tonight, but I won't ever apologise for that.

"I've said what I came here to say. I needed you to know before you saw me at the Calan Mai festival, because I will not let anything stop me getting my daughter back, not again. I'm asking you, Albelphizar, not to stop me."

Seven was only half aware of her leaving. When he finally felt able to move, the first thing he noticed was that she'd taken Amelia's pillow with her.

The Princess And The Orrery

Pah. What did he care, anyway? Maria Sophia was a liar and a thief – not content with stealing his necklace and bringing him to this place, she now seemed bent on taking his certainty, his legitimate and justified anger and pain.

Her visit only confirmed what he'd always suspected: that humans were nought but nasty, greedy, horrible little animals, crawling all over this world with their petty wants and selfish desires.

...But John had been different, a voice in his head whispered. He'd treated him as a friend and a confidant. Trusted him and wanted nothing but his advice and friendship in return.

And what of Amelia?

She had asked for nothing from him; had been kind to him and seen him as a person, just as John had done. She'd called them a team. Had worried over him.

So what? Two humans in all the world that had shown any level of decency? How did that tip the scale in their defence? No. He would find a way to get his necklace, to escape the wish, and let them all live with the consequences of their trivial, cheap desires. Let them deal with the orrery and whatever it wrought upon them.

And yet... and yet...

Damn it and damn himself – he could not abide it.

There was a sickly, clawing, poisonous treachery inside him, and he could not escape it. It was the same thing that had made him stay longer with John than he ought to have, that had convinced him to try to help Ana and her refugee camp, that had stayed his hand when Bea had tried to ruin his plans with her hot, needy anger and her ridiculous sense of entitlement. The same thing that had lured him from the safety of his cave when Maria Sophia had been attacked in the forest, whatever she thought to the contrary.

He was grown into a fool. When had that happened? And what could he do, anyway? Maria Sophia had spoken like all he needed to do was stand back and let her take Amelia away from the orrery. But the wish wouldn't allow that, surely, and how could he possibly go against it?

It occurred to Seven, in a strange sort of way, that if he really did try to stop what was happening, he would die.

If he were a good man, wouldn't he allow his own death – break the wish, take the consequences – to warn them all of the dangers the orrery presented? Give up his life, his chance for revenge, for freedom, to save the world... to save Amelia?

It was a question he had no answer to.

52

Hemmings ran into the tavern. Melly was sipping a glass of red wine, sitting slightly apart from the rest of the cast.

Ignoring the shocked faces of the patrons, he grabbed Melly by the sleeve and dragged her into the street.

"What in the five hells do you think-"

"Look," he said, pointing up at the sky.

Heavy, black clouds were gathering above the city. But, beyond the canyon walls, the sky was as bright and blue as any spring day after a rainfall.

"That can't be normal, can it?" he asked. "I've only ever been in Thaiana once, but..."

"No," Melly said, glaring at the sky. "That isn't normal."

A bolt of lightning flew from the clouds, fast and angry, and landed somewhere in the middle of the city.

The two elves stared at each other.

"The genie," Melly said. "He's here."

"Can we find him?"

They looked at again at the sky, but already the clouds were dissolving, the sky turning from angry purple to dark blue, to yellow... a bruise, healing.

"Blast it all," Melly said. "Ana said he was working for the Baron, but the Palace is up there, look, in the wall. The lightning hit the city, somewhere over there."

"Someone must have seen it?"

"Probably, but there must be a million people living here. We can't ask them all."

Hemmings looked at the fountain, where Alfonso was staring up at the sky. He dashed over to the actor.

"Did you see that?"

"Hard not to."

"Do you know where it hit?"

"Looked like it was somewhere near the Artificers, where the Psychiarium and the Cultivators are. Why?"

"Can you take us there?"

"We've got to rehearse-"

"Alright, can you tell us how to get there?"

Alfonso, looking very confused, gave Hemmings the directions. Hemmings turned back to Melly, when Alfonso's hand landed on his arm.

"You're off on your quest, then?"

"Oh. Yes. But-"

"No need for 'buts', Sunshine. I understand. Off you go." Alfonso sounded cheerful enough, but his eyes didn't meet Hemmings'.

Again, Hemmings wished he could explain everything, but Melly was glaring at them, her foot tapping the cobbles. He waved at her, hoping she'd take the hint and turn away.

He stepped forward and placed his hands on the actor's face. Hemmings was average height for an elf, but Alfonso was short for a human; standing, they were almost the same height. When he leaned forward and kissed him, it felt like they had been designed for each other.

"I'll come back, I promise," Hemmings whispered, once they'd broken apart.

Alfonso nodded, his face for once unreadable.

Hemmings wanted to say more, but there wasn't any time. So instead, he pulled away and joined Melly. They made their way towards the area where the lightning had struck, Hemmings giving instructions when needed.

Melly, thankfully, didn't try to speak to him.

Mistasinon was halfway down the corridor when he heard Chokey's voice. A moment later the door to Agnes' office was opened by the very same dwarf. She grinned at him, her blond curls tied up in a bun on top of her head, her new grey suit sitting handsomely on her stocky frame. Her sleeves were rolled up, her hands black with ink stains. She had a smudge on her cheek.

"Hallo, hallo! Come to join us in the depths, darling?"

The Princess And The Orrery

"I need to check the broken Mirrors. Something's happened."

Chokey stood aside. Agnes was by her desk, a large Book open in her hands. She looked exceptionally frazzled; her expression was some miles distant of friendly and accelerating.

"Close that door!" Agnes instructed. "What do you mean, 'something's happened'?"

Mistasinon pulled the door closed and tried to order his thoughts. He had to be careful; he couldn't really explain that he'd been sitting in his office reading through old papers of the Teller's when he'd been overwhelmed by the stench of magic. Well, not without having to explain a lot else, as well.

"I think we should check the broken Mirrors. I, uh, I was reading a passage, and it mentioned something about... um... forces... like waves at the ocean..." Mortal gods, he should have worked out what he was going to say before he ran down here.

"That doesn't make any kind of sense, darling," Chokey said, jumping up to sit on the desk. "Why don't you sit down and try again?"

"There isn't time – look, can you take me to the Mirrors or not?"

Agnes shook her head. "Not, I think, my Lord. The whole point of you lumber- giving me this assistant was so that you wouldn't need to come down here, drawing attention. And now here you are, demanding to be taken to the broken Mirrors. No, my Lord. Only the very highest members of the Index are allowed in that part of the Index, and certainly not a Plotter. The walls have eyes and ears and notebooks."

Chokey looked absolutely riveted. "Gosh, well, why don't Agnes and I go down and see what's what? I'd love to see all the broken Mirrors, you hear such wonderfully spooky rumours about them. I must say, this job is turning out to be much more exciting than I thought it would be. I bet Hemmings isn't having nearly as much fun."

Mistasinon and Agnes stared at her.

"What?" Chokey said. "I bet he isn't, that's all. Anyway, so why don't we go off exploring and then I can tell you what we find at the Fairies United meeting tonight, just like we planned?"

Agnes folded her arms. "I find myself in agreement with the dwarf, my Lord."

Mistasinon ran his hands through his hair. He wondered for a moment if he was still strong enough to rip the bell-rope from the wall and use it to tie them both up, but he probably wasn't, and even if he were, he'd still need access to the Mirror room. While he had his lock picks in his satchel, the Mirror room was famously protected by a coded locking mechanism. Besides, he was almost certain that tying people up wasn't something his new self would do.

And there was still the chance he'd imagined it...

No, he was certain he'd smelled magic, a great burst that quickly disappeared. It wasn't a scent one forgot. On the other hand, it also wasn't the kind of smell that simply vanished, like it had been sucked down a drainpipe.

Mortal gods, what was he supposed to do?

"Come on, darling," Chokey said, offering him a smile. "I promise I'll tell you exactly what we find."

Mistasinon's shoulders sagged. "Fine. Yes. Alright."

Agnes walked past him and opened her office door. "Good sense prevails. Now, I suggest you go back to your reading and, for the mortal gods' sake, try not to let anyone see you leave."

Mistasinon nodded. As he walked back through the Index, he couldn't shake the feeling that he'd made a terrible mistake.

✲

Amelia sat in Naima's office, beyond infuriated.

How dare she lock me up like some naughty child? Amelia pulled open drawers, ransacked them, and slammed a long metal file onto Naima's desk. *After everything I've done – even agreeing to go to the stupid festival where I'm bound to see Mum,* she fumed, a small hammer for chipping away at delicate rocks joining the file.

And I don't even want to see Mum anyway, Amelia confirmed, grabbing a scarf from Naima's coatrack. *And even if I did, it's not*

The Princess And The Orrery

the point. She kelt down by the door and carefully positioned the scarf underneath the crack at the bottom.

I'm a Cultivator. I know I am, even if she won't say it, so I shouldn't be locked away, she seethed, wiggling the file into the keyhole.

It's my orrery and I should be there when it gets unveiled. Me and Seven, and I bet she hasn't invited him either. Amelia brought the little hammer down hard on the end of the file, slamming it deep into the keyhole.

I'll show her she can't lock me away, Amelia concluded, pulling the scarf out from under the door, the key resting on it.

She marched back to the observatory, ignoring the startled faces of the Sisters as she stomped past them. She pushed open the observatory door and saw Seven sitting on his bed, his head in his hands.

Amelia hurtled across the room, landing in his lap with her arms around his freezing cold neck.

"She locked me away," Amelia said, hot, angry tears running down her cheeks. "Can you believe it? Locked me away! Just because we got the orrery working and Joseph and everyone will know it was us. I *hate* her."

She felt his hand land hesitantly on her back, and then, slowly, his arms around her, returning her hug. They stayed like that until she had stopped crying.

"You are being overly dramatic," Seven said at last, gently pulling back so she could see his face.

"No, I'm not. I'm being exactly the right amount of dramatic. She's the one that made all that fuss about us presenting the orrery."

Seven shook his head. "I am come to think that-"

Whatever he was about to say was cut off by the creaking of the observatory door. Joseph entered.

Amelia stepped away from Seven. Joseph was leaning heavily on his cane, his breath laboured. But it was the thing around his neck that caught her attention and held it like hooks in her eyeballs.

Around Joseph's neck was a scarf tied tight over something a few inches wide, opening at the front, above the dip in his collarbone. The scarf was bulky, wrapped multiple times around the thing it covered, but Amelia knew what it was.

She glanced at Seven. He, too, was fixed on the object around Joseph's neck.

"He's wearing the rest of the *gu'lin vut-*" Amelia whispered, but Seven hushed her, pulling himself with some difficulty to his feet so that he was standing in front of her. Amelia went to duck around him, but his hand landed on her shoulder, squeezing it gently.

"Stay here, please," Seven said to her, his eyes still on Joseph.

"It's time," Joseph said.

Seven stumbled forward, almost like he was fighting against his body. Amelia wanted to help him, but Seven lifted his hand in a stopping motion as if he'd known what she wanted to do.

Joseph pulled a book from his pocket, opening it at a marked page. He showed it to Seven.

"This is what I want," he said, pointing at the page. "Is this what you have made for me?"

"Yes, my Lord," Seven said.

"And it's ready?"

"Yes, my Lord. But it will not end the way you wis-"

Joseph held his pale hand up. "Hush, now. Let's not, not after we've worked together so well. I have your necklace with me; my understanding is that its proximity will make things easier for you, correct? Just a 'yes' or a 'no' will do."

"Yes."

"Fabulous. Right then, let's go make a happy ending. Take us and the orrery to the Palace garden, please."

Seven pulled back, a look of panic on his face as his eyes darkened to black, strange white flecks spinning within them.

"Us, my Lord?"

Joseph tutted. "Myself, the orrery, you. Who else matters?"

Seven bowed his head. "No one, my Lord."

The hairs on Amelia's arms rose as her skin prickled with the sudden drop in temperature. She opened her mouth to demand to be taken. But she was too late.

Seven, Joseph, and the orrery had vanished.

53

Melly and Hemmings turned the corner onto a crowd of people.

It wasn't a mob, but it certainly wasn't a friendly gathering, either. There was a sense of confusion and excitement – the kind of excitement that comes from the type of people who are always on the lookout for the next opportunity to cause trouble. It was not, Melly sensed, a good place to be.

Which meant that they were in exactly the right place.

She slowed her pace and pulled herself inwards, minimising the space she took up. She elbowed Hemmings in the ribs.

"Blend in," she hissed.

The other elf looked momentarily confused and then did his best to copy her. The effect was rather like watching an over-dressed raven trying to fit in amongst a group of pigeons. It would have to do.

Melly eased her way through the crowd until she managed to get to the front. They were outside an old, red-brick building with a green tile roof, a large glass and metal dome rising from the centre. It hardly seemed the place a genie would hide – from what Melly remembered, genies preferred grandeur and comfort.

The genie's apparent divergence from the tastes of his kind was not her immediate problem, though, nor even the crowd. All around the building was a high wall and, in front of them, a large metal gate – iron, she suspected, from the pricking of her thumbs – which was very definitely closed.

"What happened?" she said to the man beside her.

"Cultivators at it again, no doubt. We're waiting t'see what'll happen next. Might be we get an explosion."

Melly paused. "You want an explosion?"

"Nah. I mean not really. Well, depends how big it is, I guess. But if there is one, I wanna see it. My dad was there when that one of theirs melted all those years ago," he concluded with no small amount of envy in his voice.

"And you want to...? Never mind." Melly refocused. "So, this is where the lightning struck?"

"Yup," he said. "Shame about the copper roofing – the whole place might've gone up otherwise. Still, those clouds look angry enough. Might get another shot, eh?"

He waved two pairs of crossed fingers at Melly. She nodded slowly and stepped away.

"We're in the right place," she hissed to Hemmings. "But I don't know how we'll get in."

"She might know," Hemmings said, his eyes fixed on a point away from the general rabble.

Melly followed his gaze. A young girl stood by a side gate, clutching a toy bear, watching the crowd warily.

"How did you spot her?"

"Perception is curated by expectation," Hemmings said in a needlessly sanctimonious tone. "If you look for something you expect, you'll invariably see it, even while others perceive something else. You have to look harder, and see the truth that is really there." A pause. "And hope other people will, too."

She thought of the kiss she'd witnessed between Hemmings and Alfonso, and the way the actor's expression had changed during their brief conversation, and decided not to press the point.

"Well, let's go talk to her, shall we?"

They fought their way through the press until they reached the little girl who was scanning the crowd. She paid them no attention at all until Melly spoke.

"Are you from inside?"

The girl turned dark brown eyes on her, filled with more scorn than Melly had encountered in a long time.

"Obviously, yes. I'm a Sister."

"Ah, yes, of course," Melly said, shifting gears. "Is it your sister you're looking for? Or your brother, maybe?"

The girl shook her head. "They don't allow boys in, and I don't know where Naima is and I don't care. I need to find my friend. He left me but, actually, I don't think that he meant to. I don't see why he would leave me behind, anyway. Something's up, I'm sure of it. He's been taken to the Palace, so I'm going there… or I'm trying to. I didn't expect all these people. Look, what do you want?"

The Princess And The Orrery

"We wanted to get inside," Melly said, giving up trying to understand what the girl was talking about. "Can you let us in?"

"You can go through here, but there's nothing going on inside. I don't know why all these people have turned up, but I wish they'd go away. I need to find my friend."

Melly was about to thank the girl and go through the gate when Hemmings put his hand out, stopping her.

"Do you need help finding your friend?" he asked the girl.

The little girl frowned, her grip on the stuffed bear tightening. "No... yes. Maybe. Naima locked me in her office and then I got out, but when I got back to the observatory Joseph turned up and took Seven. Well, I mean, they disappeared. How is that possible? And he took my orrery, and I don't know why but I think he's going to do something bad with it and-"

Melly dropped to her knees, her hands on the girl's arms. "Seven? You know Seven? The genie?"

"The what?"

Melly licked her lips, and tried to speak calmly. "You said your friend was called Seven. It's a very unusual name. And I'm looking for someone called Seven. He's a very... unusual person."

"You said 'genie'. I heard you. I'm not doing anything until you explain exactly what you're talking about."

Melly could feel the situation slipping away from her. In her desperation to see the whole thing finished, she'd spoken rashly. She turned to Hemmings. "Can you do something? Explain to her why it's important she helps us – I'm sure you've got something about trees or the essential nature of the universe or whatever ready to be unleashed?"

Hemmings knelt down in front of the child.

"This is Melly, and my name's Hemmings. What's yours?"

"Amelia. Hemmings doesn't sound like a real name."

"It's actually Orlyn," Hemmings said with an embarrassed shrug. "But my sister kept on saying I could never answer a question without 'hemming and hawing' and I guess my name just changed."

The girl, Amelia, considered. "My mum calls me Amy. But now I'm a Sister I think Amelia is better."

"It's a very pretty name."

"Orlyn is pretty, too," Amelia allowed. "But Hemmings is alright."

"Thank you."

"How do you know Seven's a genie?"

"Well, because we're elves, so we know when someone's a genie."

Horrified, Melly kicked his shoe. Hemmings ignored her.

Amelia edged forward. "Elves aren't... how do I know you're an elf?"

Hemmings made a show of looking around, and then, very quickly, lifted his cap, showing his long, pointed ears. Amelia inched forward, her eyes darting over his ears. Hemmings sat very still. Melly held her breath.

"Why do you want to find Seven?" Amelia asked, her inspection concluded to her apparent satisfaction.

Hemmings replaced his cap. "We want to, ah, take him home."

"Back to Ota'ari?"

"Back to our home."

Amelia shucked her toy bear under her arm. "He doesn't have a home, and anyway he lives with me now in Starry Castle. Except that Joseph's got him. He's taken him and my orrery to the Palace. I want to rescue him, but... I don't know if they'll let me in without Naima." Her voice dropped, landing in a small and frightened place. "I don't know what to do."

Hemmings stood and held his hand out to her. "You don't have any reason to trust us, but we can get you into the Palace. We can help you find your friend."

Melly tried very hard to look trustworthy. She was well aware that her blood-red hair and tatty black dress screamed 'witch'. Thank the mortal gods she'd given up the green face paint.

Amelia seemed unsure, no doubt instilled with the advice not to go anywhere with strangers, and there were few people stranger than Melly and Hemmings. Maybe it was their elven glamour or the way Hemmings spoke so softly and gently, but Amelia nodded, although she didn't take his hand.

"Alright," she said. "But we need to be quick. I'm worried about Seven."

The Princess And The Orrery

"So are we," Hemmings said. "But I'm sure we can find a solution. There's nothing so bad that a good bit of thinking can't resolve it."

Chokey was, for once, speechless.

The broken Mirrors towered above and around her, running for what seemed like a hundred miles into the darkness of the Index, their cracked and splintered surfaces showing fractured reflections of herself. The ones further away were humongous, looming like old teeth in the mouth of some great monster, the light from Agnes' lamp no more than a hazy discolouration. The ones closer were smaller, like the ones in the Grand, but no less unsettling for their familiarity.

"We need to check them," Agnes said, picking up a lantern from the wall and lighting the wick before covering the flame in its glass bell jar.

"What exactly are we looking for?" Chokey asked, lighting her own lantern.

"Anything unusual. You go this way, I'll go that way."

Chokey swallowed. "I'm not sure we should split up. There was this witchlein at the Academy who went off on his own and-"

"We don't have time to do it together, not if something really is wrong. It's just the Mirrors, Dea'dora, and they're all broken. Nothing can come through them."

Chokey looked up again at the lines and lines of Mirrors, each one showing a broken version of her anxious expression, the cracks in the glass and the light from her lamp changing her into some kind of horrible stranger, her features all in the wrong place.

"Um. Alright," she said, pretty sure that she didn't really believe it was.

Agnes nodded and started walking through the Mirrors on the right, leaving Chokey with the ones on the left.

She stepped forward. Strange shapes followed, stalking her in the fractured world of the Mirrors. It didn't make her feel any better that those shapes were, seemingly, herself. She held her

F. D. Lee

lantern up and made her way into the maze, pausing every now and again to aim her light into the darkness to check the shadows for... well, for something unusual, whatever that meant. Quite frankly, she wasn't entirely sure she could pinpoint what *was* usual, anymore.

At the Academy, all her lessons had focused on the Plots and the characters and the various roles the GenAm had instated. There hadn't been any history lessons, at least not beyond the fact that the Teller had devised the perfect Plots and stopped the Mirrors from breaking.

A story which, as she walked through rows and rows of cracked Mirrors, seemed a little incongruous with her current reality. But then, Buttercup and Mistasinon had told her about the genies, and how the Teller had used their wishes to make the Mirrors better. It had all seemed rather far-fetched at the time...

She approached one of the Mirrors, a spiderweb of fine lines working their way out from a tight formation from the middle of the glass to a loose network at the edges. What must it have been like when all the Mirrors were working? To have had access to Thaiana whenever one pleased, to come and go and have fun and not have to worry about anything?

She brushed her fingers against the glass, careful to avoid the cracks, the reflection of her hand becoming increasingly disjointed as it rose to meet her fingertips.

Buttercup said the genies died for the Mirrors, all but one of them. That in the space of his Chapter, the Teller killed pretty much an entire tribe. Chokey hadn't liked that. She was used to people who thought they were entitled to anything and everything, and they were invariably rotten bullies. The trouble was, as Hemmings often said, that people were very good at thinking they deserved more than anyone else, so everyone ended up bullying everyone. Well, Hemmings put it more complicatedly, but that was what he'd meant. Sometimes Chokey wondered how Hemmings got through the day, he was so caught up in his own head.

She pulled her hand away from the Mirror. That was the real problem – everyone tried to make everything more complicated than it needed to be.

The Princess And The Orrery

It didn't really matter whether Yarnis had broken the Mirrors, or if it had happened during the Rhyme War, or even if Yarnis had started the war to get the Mirrors or whatever else people said had happened. Just like it didn't really matter if the Teller thought he'd had a good reason to kill all those genies. If something bad happens, you put it right. Simple.

Anyway, there didn't seem to be anything 'unusual' down here – well, apart from the hundreds of broken Mirrors but, apparently, that was usual. There were definitely more of them than the GenAm let on. And the ones at the back were huge, as tall as her townhouse. Maybe even bigger. What manner of things had come through those Mirrors, back in the day?

It was all terribly spooky, Chokey decided – but quite exciting as well, in a scary sort of way. Much better than sitting around the house waiting for the next party.

She was about fifty feet deep into the network of Mirrors when something crunched under her boot. She was standing on broken glass. She lifted her lantern above her head, spreading the pool of light as far as it would go.

All around her, the ground was covered in glass and bits of wood. The Mirrors in front of her were... well, they *weren't*, in fact.

If the ones earlier had reminded her of old teeth, these ones had been smashed by a nasty punch to the jaw. The bases were still largely intact, but the Mirrors were little more than jagged shards and splintered wood, with a fan of sparkling debris on the floor around them.

Chokey's first thought was to run away, but she caught her breath. This was definitely unusual. She took a moment to count what remained of the frames – ten Mirrors in all were nearly completely destroyed. She looked around to see if there was anything obvious that could have done such a thing, but other than her reflections, there was nothing.

Right, then. Definitely time to go and find Agnes. Chokey made a mental note of how far into the maze she'd wandered and then headed back to the entrance – not quite running, but certainly not walking, either.

F. D. Lee

Behind her, unnoticed, a shape swam across the damaged surfaces of the unexploded Mirrors, a tubular muscle that stretched and contracted as though pushing through water, its head made up of a tangle of searching tentacles that pressed against the inside of the glass.

Searching for a way that was strong enough.

54

Seven, Joseph and the orrery appeared in the Palace garden, whereupon Seven promptly threw up.

Joseph waited until the noise had died down. "Has it come through correctly?"

Seven, grunting with the effort, pulled himself up and lurched over to the orrery. He ran through all the checks Amelia had taught him, his nausea waning until, an hour later, he felt quite well. Better, in fact, than he had in months.

His necklace hadn't abandoned him, for all that they had been kept apart. Seven could have wept with joy. Now, if only he could wring the neck of the man wearing it and take it back…

The man in question was sitting at a garden table, watching him patiently.

"Nothing amiss?" Joseph beckoned him over.

"Nothing, my Lord."

"You understand what I want to use the orrery for? I would hate to think your answer was in anyway misleading."

Seven sighed. "Yes, my Lord. I understand your intentions, and my answer reflects the same."

"Nevertheless, explain to me what you understand."

"I understand that you are aware of this device's true purpose. I know not how you discovered it, as we sought to bury the knowledge many hundreds of years ago. And yet, such things are never truly lost. The stories, I assume, betrayed us?"

Joseph nodded. "Do you know, everyone who will attend this festival, my brother most of all, thinks I should never have lived? I had no friends as a child, only doctors. And then Mother died, and I was left with my brother, my father, and my disease. With the stories people made up about me to cover their guilt, their superstitions. But my life has not been a sad one. I've been blessed with plenty of time for reading, for example."

"Ah. This is how you discovered us. I will admit, my Lord, that you are the first such person to have done so."

F. D. Lee

Joseph covered his mouth, the apples of his cheeks lifting in a smile. "Now, another question – no lies, please, you know how I feel about that." He gestured to the wrapping around his neck which kept Seven's necklace from touching his skin. "Will the orrery work as I want it to, with the necklace here?"

"The orrery will work, my Lord."

"Excellent. Come, sit with me. There's nothing to do now but wait, after all."

Seven obeyed, the wish offering him no choice – indeed, encouraging the action. Joseph was happy, and the wish was, currently, satisfied. It brushed soft fingers against his skin, tracing whorls of gentle pleasure across his aching muscles.

Had there ever been a place where the genies could control their reaction to the strange power of desire? He wondered what it had been like for the ones that ended up in the fae world, or the other planets their reckless escape had taken them to. Did they suffer as he did, caught between agony and bliss, a slave unable to refuse? Or were they living free, somewhere far away?

If there were any genies left anywhere in the worlds, he hoped they suffered as much as he did.

"You seem troubled," Joseph said. The man's pale eyes were fixed on him, his hands folded neatly in his lap. "I suppose you worry for your future?"

Seven managed not to laugh. "My future is set, my Lord."

"Yes, it is. But you must be pleased to know it will be in the service of improving many thousands, if not hundreds of thousands, of lives?"

"I do not know what you would have me say, my Lord. The specifics of whatever wish you make are, to me, inconsequential."

"Ah. You worry it will hurt you? I am given to believe your kind enjoys the pain?"

Seven winced. "I worry, my Lord, that it will kill me slowly, and worse besides. When we created these devices, it was not out of curiosity but desperation. An act born of fear of something worse. Many died, but the *es'hajit* fulfilled its purpose, giving us the strength we needed to-"

He caught his breath, the wish making a fist inside him, punching his organs: so delicate was Joseph's perception of happiness that anything that threatened to reshape it was a challenge.

Joseph, either unaware of Seven's discomfort or uncaring, settled back into his chair. Although the sky was still grey, the rain had long passed, and the afternoon was warm, colouring his pale skin. "We'll wait until after the performance, when everyone is settled, and then we'll unveil ourselves. You said I'm the first person to discover the truth – how many masters have you had?"

"A handful, only. My parents raised me to be wary of such things."

"I've never thought of a genie having parents, though I suppose it makes sense. You didn't just pop into existence, then?"

"No, my Lord."

"And do you have children?"

"No, my Lord. Procreation is not the same for our kind as it is for yours." He thought for a moment of Amelia, and her mother hugging her pillow close. "Truthfully, I am glad I do not."

"A shame, really. Imagine what we could accomplish if there was another one of you." Joseph yawned. "I'm afraid I'm feeling worn out – a busy morning. You will stay with me while I sleep. If anyone comes, hide us. I want us to have no contact with anyone until I instruct you otherwise. Is that binding?"

"Yes, my Lord."

"Wonderful." And with that, Joseph closed his eyes and drifted off into sleep.

Hemmings guided Amelia into the tavern, his hand on her shoulder.

He had absolutely no idea what he was doing. Just a short while ago, he'd barely even spoken to a character, and now he was kissing one and helping another find a genie. Of course, it was also the same genie he and Melly had to find, but that didn't stop the strangeness of it all.

For want of something better to do, he went to the bar and exchanged a couple of discs of metal for three beers and brought them back to Melly and Amelia.

"I'm not allowed beer," Amelia announced as he put the drink in front of her, before taking a huge sip. She pulled a face and spat the liquid back into the glass. "Yuk. Why would anyone drink that?"

Hemmings looked to Melly, but she just shrugged and pulled out a cigarette.

"Smoking's very bad for you," Amelia said. "I've seen drawings of what it does to your lungs."

"My lungs are my own business," Melly replied, but she put the cigarette back into its case. "Now then, Amelia, what can you tell us about Seven?"

The girl shifted uncomfortably, giving some vague replies that didn't really make any sense. Something about a machine and a man named Joseph who'd taken Seven and her machine away. When she'd finished, Melly was drumming her fingers on the table.

"We need to get him... home... quickly, I think," she said to Hemmings.

"Seven lives with me. We're a team and we're going to invent all kinds of things together. I didn't know he was a genie, but it makes sense, actually."

"It does?" Hemmings asked.

"There's a thing called *gu'lin vut*," Amelia said. "I thought genies had lamps, but metal is metal, I suppose. Actually, a necklace makes more sense because they can wear it all the time – I wonder how Joseph got hold of it? Do you think Naima knew he was a genie? I bet she did and she didn't tell me."

Melly stared at the girl, a look of total confusion on her face. She shot Hemmings a glance and then focused her attention on her beer.

Hemmings, taking the hint, tried to find a foothold in the conversation. "Naima is your sister, you said? I've got a sister."

"Yes, you said," Amelia replied. "But Naima's not my real sister. She's my Sister – that's what Cultivators call each other. There's lots of Sisters at Starry Castle, but only one boy, well, only one boy and one genie, and they're the same person. That's an odd sentence, isn't it? Anyway, look, you said you could get us into the Palace, right? How?"

"We're friends with the theatre company performing there this evening," Hemmings said, not entirely sure how accurate the word 'friend' was. "We can all go in with them."

"They're performing at the festival?"

"Yes."

"Mmm. Well, that will have to do. I was going to try to find my mum – she's here too, somewhere. I was supposed to see her today. But I don't care if I don't. So we'll go in with the theatre."

"Yes, exactly," Hemmings said. He was getting the hang of talking with Amelia. It wasn't actually much different from talking to Chokey, except he got the sense Amelia listened more closely than his sister did. "We'll all go together and find Seven."

Melly stood up. "A bargain made. Now, if you don't mind, I think I'll leave you two to... to make friends. I need to think."

She picked up her cigarette case and the remains of her beer and headed outside. Hemmings asked Amelia what she would prefer to drink and went to the bar to get her the requested glass of water – surprised that it came out of the pump clean, without even any very small wriggly things in it – and returned to the table.

"So, what's it like being an elf, then?" Amelia asked.

"I'm not sure... I've only ever been an elf. I suppose it's like anything when you don't really fit in."

"Why don't you fit in?"

Hemmings sipped his beer. "Well... of course, the nature of most creatures is to look for a group of some kind, isn't it?" He thought about Alfonso. "After all, what is a life spent with only your thoughts to keep you company?"

Amelia considered. "I'd say it was a pretty good one. If you're by yourself, you can't hurt anyone."

"Perhaps. But understanding is built on a rocky foundation of trial and error. Build it on the solid stone of certainty and that construction will be such that nothing ever alters it. Stasis is the anathema of thought."

"But ideas can't grow at all if they're always being pulled and pushed by different forces, can they? You have to look at the facts."

"But facts are only facts for as long as they remain unchallenged," Hemmings countered, surprised to find he was enjoying himself.

Amelia took a sip of water. "Yes, I suppose that's true, too. Did you know in the psychiarium they used to take out women's wombs because they thought they were driving them mad? That's why it's called 'hysterical' when someone gets upset. That was a fact, once. It's not anymore. But even so, you still need facts, don't you? Otherwise you could believe anything. I wouldn't have believed you were an elf or Seven was a genie if I didn't already have facts to support it."

Hemmings couldn't help the traitorous thought that said Amelia might have a point, at least partially. He considered the way the characters didn't just believe in the stories anymore, or the roles the GenAm prescribed for them. How they had shifted from a fear of the darkness to wondering what hid inside it.

Still, you certainly couldn't take facts as the final conclusion – people could find facts for anything if they tried hard enough. Facts were corruptible. But so, too, was belief.

It was all so wonderfully complicated! For the first time since leaving Ænathlin, he felt like he understood something again, even if that thing was the familiar pleasure of a thoughtsmithing problem.

"And then, there're the facts that surprise you," Amelia continued. "Like Seven being in pain all the time. He said it was an illness, but now I think it has to be something to do with being a genie. Y'know, when we were working on the orrery he had all these funny turns. It must be to do with the *gu'lin vut*. You'd have thought a genie could control something like that, wouldn't you? What's the point of being a genie if it makes you sick?"

Hemmings put down his glass of beer. "Made him sick? What do you mean?"

Amelia licked her lips. And then her expression crumpled, and the whole sorry story came pouring out. Hemmings could only listen, wide-eyed, gripping his drink tighter and tighter as she told him about the genie and his illness and the things she was now certain had caused it.

When she'd finished, Hemmings settled her down, then managed to rustle up some food, paper and pencils from behind the bar and left her drawing and eating a sandwich.

He went outside.

Melly was leaning against the tavern wall, smoking and scowling.

"We need to talk, right now," Hemmings hissed, grabbing her arm and pulling her into the stables before she could protest. Once they were safely ensconced in an empty horse box, Hemmings turned on her, his fury as fast and threatening as a fin coursing through still waters.

"How *dare* you not tell me?"

Melly looked genuinely baffled. "What on Thaiana are you talking about?"

"The magic hurts the genie," Hemmings said through his teeth. "It *cripples* them every time they use it. You knew, didn't you? You knew, and you still want to deliver him to the GenAm to fix the Mirrors with his wishes. Mortal gods damn it – it's murder!"

"And what else would you have us do?" She sounded like she'd been expecting this conversation. In fact, she almost seemed relieved. "What's your solution?"

"I don't know! But it's not murder."

"Well, that doesn't help anyone, does it? Come on, you're supposed to be the brains. Think of an alternative!"

Melly glared at him, challenging him to answer. Hemmings' anger circled inside him, looking for something to bite.

"Well? Nothing? No clever little speech?" she spat. "Either we sacrifice him or everyone else. Come on, then. Choose."

"No. I won't let you push this onto me. It's not a question of '*murder or...*' It's never '*murder or...*' The moment you start that argument, you legitimise the choice."

For a moment, he thought she was going to slap him. And then she seemed to deflate, flopping down onto a three-legged stool. There was a curry comb in a box on the floor next to her. She picked it up and tapped her fingers against the little metal teeth. All her grandeur had evaporated, leaving her pale and tired, her red hair falling across her shoulders.

"Oh, really?" she said, picking horse hair out of the comb. "Such an easy declaration from someone who would never feel the effects of his morality. I know all about you – that Plotter told me what your mother pulled to get you on this bloody journey. When the last Mirror finally cracks and we have no way to get into Thaiana, it won't be the Ogrechokers who suffer. It won't be you or your sister who get caught up in the fights over the last mouldy loaf of bread. It won't be the Ogrechokers watching their children starve and their homes looted. Your kind will do exactly what they did last time: shore up and wait it out until the next Teller comes along with the next disgusting idea to bring about order. Then you'll slink and slime your way down from your townhouses and step back into your lives as if nothing happened."

Hemmings' face darkened in disgust. "That's not true. Chokey and I would never, ever watch people suffer if we could stop it."

"Oh, well, hooray for you both," Melly sighed, teasing out the last few strands of hair from the brush. "Care to make that promise for the rest of the inner-circlers?"

To his chagrin, Hemmings realised he could not. "Then we have to find another way to save the Mirrors, one that doesn't involve torture and murder – mortal gods, how is this even a conversation?"

Melly finally looked up. "And we circle back to the beginning again. What way, Hemmings? Seriously? How do you fix a problem like this?"

He didn't know.

His anger sunk back down into the depths, pulling him with it.

"Because we've got about two hours to find an answer," Melly said, standing. "Otherwise I'm taking the genie back to the GenAm and all the gods and you, too, can damn me for it."

55

Maria Sophia sat in her living room, the lamps burning low. She had to get ready, but she couldn't find the courage to lift herself from her chair. If Naima's plan failed...

Amelia's pillow was clutched to her chest, her head resting on it. Was she making a mistake? How had she let it all go so horribly, unforgivably wrong? She had lost both her children, one to death and the other to her own inability to protect her. To comfort her.

The pillow was stained dark with her tears. And yet still more came, like a disease her body was vomiting out.

Her step-mother had been right. She was useless, selfish, an empty vase, nothing more than something pretty to look at. She should never have run away, certainly never tried to raise children. One dead, and the other lost.

How could she ever make it right again, even if they were able to finally remove Joseph? What if Amelia fought her? What if Amelia told her it was all her fault? That she was everything she knew, deep down, she was? A coward. A brat. A waste.

In the flickering lamplight, Maria Sophia wept.

Naima's hands were slippery with sweat thanks to the leather gloves protecting her from the chemical powder she was mixing.

She doubled-checked the formula again, praying that her alternations were correct, that the original process had been recorded accurately.

The Cultivators never threw anything away, even their mistakes...

Chokey led Agnes and two other senior members of the Indexical Department back through the Mirrors, until they reached the circle of exploded glass and snaggle-toothed frames.

A frantic and complicated argument began as they tried to account for what could possibly have happened.

Julia listened intently as the other imp told her about the events at the Academy and the cabbage fairy.

When she'd finished, Julia laced her fingers together and pondered. In the corner of her eye, she could see her locked cabinet and the secrets it housed. The white suit, waiting for its owner. The bottles of Letheinate. The folders, brimming with information.

Clothes can be altered when they need to be, she mused. *Plans, too. Especially plans. All it takes is the right tools…*

She rose and held her hand out across the desk.

Carol, the other imp, had studied with Bea at the Academy. She was, Julia felt, exactly the right amount of angry and stupid to be useful. There was a moment of hesitation, and then Carol shook Julia's hand.

Bea and Joan set up neat rows of chairs in *The Quill and Ink*, bickering good-naturedly about whether they were over- or underestimating the number of fae who might turn up for their Fairies United meeting.

They'd decorated the walls with cheap woodcut prints of their leaflets, along with other posters that detailed all the useful jobs the fairies did. The other fairies were setting up jugs of weak beer, a small selection of snacks, and three rather dense looking cakes. It was meagre fare, but it was something.

Every now and again, Bea glanced at the door, waiting for Chokey or Mistasinon to arrive.

The Princess And The Orrery

Mistasinon was alone in his tiny office, poring over the documents the Teller had left him, the ones he kept safely in his satchel, looking for something – *anything* – that could account for the sudden burst and disappearance of magic in the Land.

He had to keep his promise.

Seven sat, stood up, paced, and sat again, ineffectual as a dream, while Joseph slept peacefully beside him.

Pale, spindly slaves hustled and bustled, setting up the Festival. Round tables of food and drink appeared on the green lawn, little islands of indulgence. A stage was being erected at the other end of the sweeping balcony, and bonfires and tables set up in the space in the middle. Around Joseph and Seven, for reasons the slaves couldn't fathom and yet, somehow, couldn't ignore, the grass remained unburdened with festive accoutrements.

Seven rested his chin in his hand and stared at the orrery, hating it with all his being, trying to ignore the voice that whispered to him, *you don't know what to do...*

Melly smoked, her hand shaking as the cigarette travelled to and from her lips.

Hemmings hung around the bar, nursing another pint of beer. He'd taken off his frock coat and his cravat, and was now staring at his pocket watch.

He felt like a fraud.

A hand landed on his shoulder, making him jump.

"I didn't expect you to come back," Alfonso said, unease flickering across his features.

But Hemmings was too distracted by his own misery to properly register the brief look on the other man's face. He flew to his feet and wrapped his arms around Alfonso and held him as tightly as he could.

On the other side of the tavern, oblivious to the display at the bar, Amelia turned over a new piece of paper.

She concentrated on her designs, long tallies of complicated sums running like rain down the margins and empty spaces, as she tried to work out a way to separate the *gu'lin vut* from the orrery.

She definitely was not thinking about the fact she would soon be at the festival, where her mother, the person she had robbed of their baby boy, would be.

56

The Calan Mai festival had finally begun.

Naima moved through the crowded Palace garden, growing increasingly frustrated. It was proving almost impossible to find Joseph. She'd expected him to be plainly visible – or if not him, then Seven. But so far, nothing.

What wasn't difficult to spot was the orrery. The balcony that housed the garden was shaped in an elongated half-circle, about sixty feet long, the rounded edge extending over the city below. At one end was the orrery, at the other a stage, with all the other distractions filling the space between. The Baron was holding court in the centre, his throne set in the midst of a congregation of food, drink and entertainments. Guests and attendants were clustered around him, no doubt being sure to pay their dues before sampling the other delights of the festival.

And yet, there was something unsettling about the whole event. Too much food, too much wine; too many smaller entertainments, as well as the theatre, the bonfires and the orrery. It was impressive, certainly, to behold the artificial garden, so high up the cliff face, covered in distractions and indulgences while below them the city clustered, its tall, thin buildings stretching up like children trying to pretend they were old enough to join in.

All around, dancers threaded ribbon around poles, musicians played in little orchestras, acrobats and jugglers performed sideshows. Lords and Ladies, Counts and Countesses, Kings and Queens and all the other titles that the Ehinen people seemed to bestow upon themselves without thought for the overall sense they made, mingled shoulder to shoulder.

And amongst it all, slaves wandered, heads lowered, plates held out in front of them. They were pale, willowy veins threading through the body of the festival, connections to the true heart of the city. Naima thought about her long-held dreams that would, if her plan was successful, never come to fruition: to innovate the manufactories and, perhaps, find a way to make everything work without slavery; to modernise the Cultivators and their antiquated admission policy; to be remembered as someone who had done something worthwhile.

To be important. To be recognised. To lead, as her father had done.

Well, if she did pull off her scheme, she supposed she would, at least, be remembered. Perhaps that thought would comfort her when the Baron threw her in the manufactories?

"Joseph's not here," Maria Sophia said for the twentieth time. "You were wrong. You were wrong and I'll never get my daughter back."

"The orrery's here and Seven's missing from the observatory. Joseph's here, too, somewhere. Trust me."

Maria Sophia gave an angry sigh. "And you're certain Amy's safe?"

"Yes."

"And you've got the powder?"

"Yes."

Maria Sophia went back to searching for Joseph, much to Naima's relief. She dipped her hand into her pocket, feeling the glass vial of powder resting there. What she hadn't explained to Maria Sophia was how risky her plan was – not in terms of the Baron's inevitable revenge for murdering his brother, but rather in terms of how drastically wrong the whole thing might go.

When Celia had released the very same powder all those years ago, it had been a massacre, the toxic foam poisoning everyone present. If Naima's own methods were wrong, if she'd made even the smallest mistake, she'd kill everyone here.

So she had to hope she hadn't made a mistake.

※

Melly was also having no luck locating her quarry. She'd expected the genie to stand out like an exceptionally well-manicured and bejewelled thumb. But there were so many bloody humans here! It was like a hive.

The Princess And The Orrery

She'd left Hemmings and the child with the theatre, reasoning it made more sense for her to find the genie alone and then decide on the best way to capture him. She'd even presented herself to the Baron, on the suspicion that the genie would have found a way to ingratiate himself at the top. But all she'd seen was a particularly repugnant man surrounded by a swarm of giggling lackeys. She hadn't hung around *there* any longer than she'd needed to.

If this had been one of the old blood-and-bone stories, the Baron would have had the narrative equivalent of a red cross drawn on his forehead, and all the better for it. Sometimes even she could admit that the old tales had had the right idea, especially when it came to dealing with people like that. It amazed her that the humans couldn't recognise such an out-and-out villain when they saw one.

Or perhaps they could, and they just didn't care. The Baron was rich and important, and his city prospered. Wasn't that how the heroes' stories ended? Not the heroines', which were about submission and marriage and humility. The ones the Teller had devised for the men.

Mug an old lady for her secret trinket? Sure. Kill a humble woodcutter to steal a sword? Go ahead. Murder a witch and marry a teenager? Perfect. The stories didn't care how the hero got there, as long as he was confident and the Kingdom survived. The one true ruler heals the land, and all is well. The Teller's plots never left space to question the *how* of it.

She remembered Giss' matter-of-fact warning: *he burns people underground.*

The thought made her clench her jaw so tight her teeth hurt. Mortal gods, from what Ana had told her of Cerne Bralksteld, she was probably standing above one of their hellish manufactories right now, as she shoved her way through crowds of shocked faces, horrified to be so poorly treated in such fine company. The humans' stupidity really was unfathomable.

Or was it?

Melly slowed her march back towards the theatre.

The fae should have been expert in spotting a nasty bastard at fifteen paces, but they'd let the Teller take control. Let him build the General Administration, with its cold, hard rules and institutionalised hierarchies, in exchange for quiet and security. Hah. Not even in exchange for the opulence surrounding her now.

They didn't even have the excuse of being corrupted by the Plots.

The fae all knew what the stories were. How they trapped the characters to harvest belief. Certainly, it wasn't the same as working to death in forced labour… but it wasn't freedom, either. And she couldn't stop herself from thinking that their stories had almost certainly gone some way towards allowing all these people to distance themselves from the horrors that were happening literally below their noses.

So was it fair to blame the humans for doing the same thing the fae did? Hell, at least slavery was an obvious barbarism. Slavery could be seen and fought, as Ana was doing. Belief pretended to be on your side, making it a much more elusive opponent.

And she'd promised Ana she'd help stop the Baron, once she returned the genie to Ænathlin. But if she returned Seven to Ænathlin, she'd be continuing the cycle, wouldn't she? Gifting the fae a bit longer to weave their stories, to manufacture their beliefs… To create consent for monsters like the Baron to exist…

She looked at all the people dressed in fine clothes, eating rich food and drinking expensive wines, talking about expansion and growth and markets as the slaves drifted past them, unnoticed. Unremarked upon.

No. It was too late for second thoughts. What was happening here was a human problem – they had free will, they could make their own choices, just like she'd done. And they could live with them, too, just as she had to.

She would find the genie, and she would make him return to Ænathlin. He wouldn't have any choice.

After all, all she had to do was make a wish.

※

Hemmings stood in the wings with Amelia as the play began.

"I want to go to the orrery," Amelia said, shifting from foot to foot. "Seven's bound to be there. I thought you wanted to find him."

"I… Melly's out there. She'll find him. You and I can wait here. The sensible person holds tight to patient thought, evaluating all courses before committing themselves to action."

"Sounds to me that the sensible person probably never gets anything done," Amelia muttered, but she stopped fidgeting and, as far as he could judge, resigned herself to watching the play.

"Just stay close to me," Hemmings said, wondering if she was right. "There's a lot of people out there."

Amelia grunted non-committally. And then the play began.

Hemmings mouthed along to every line. Even Amelia seemed relatively distracted; she watched quietly, hugging her toy bear. For an hour, everything melted away. The argument with Melly, his anxiety over the genie's fate, his confusion about the morality of what he was engaged in. He watched Alfonso weave magic on the wooden boards, and felt his troubles ebb like the soft waves of a gentle river against the bank: at some point the water would join the vast turmoil of the ocean, but not now.

Thank the mortal gods he'd seen Alfonso at the pub, even if they hadn't had any real time to talk. Hemmings was certain, when he finally did get a chance to explain, Alfonso would understand. Would wait for him to finish his quest.

The play – shortened to make room for all the other entertainments – entered the third act. Alfonso and Beatrice met in the centre of the stage, ready to declare their love for each other now that the curse had been lifted and the Kingdom restored. The hero would ask the heroine to marry him, and a wedding scene would wrap the play up to rapturous applause.

But it didn't happen like that.

Instead, Alfonso sat on a bench. He began talking to the audience, his voice pitched in that perfect balance which allowed him to speak softly and yet be heard all the way to the back-most seats. Within the story, the speech represented the character's inner thoughts – a conceit, Alfonso had explained, to help the audience follow along.

F. D. Lee

Except these weren't the right lines. The play had changed again.

"*My quest is at an end, so doth seem,*" Alfonso said, looking dolefully at the sky.

"*The night hands me all my dear'st dreams.*
Yet the stars look on me and weep,
Knowing they of my gentle deceit.
But first to finish the tale begun herewith
And thus from my love, free'd, shall I slip."

The audience let up a soft groan as the last line landed like a sigh over them. Beatrice entered from the opposite side of the stage, running up to Alfonso and reaching out to take him in her arms. But he shied away, instead producing a white box tied with a ribbon, hidden behind some set dressing. Apart from its size, it was almost exactly the same as the little chocolate box still sitting in Hemmings' coat pocket, next to his pocket watch.

Beatrice took the box with great solemnity, and opened it to reveal not a ring, but a thin crown. The Prince's crown. Alfonso's crown. She held it up high, so the whole audience could see it, before tucking it safely in her costume. The two actors pressed their hands together, palm to palm, and stared into each other's eyes.

They were supposed to be getting engaged. Instead, Afonso's Prince seemed to be… He seemed like he was… Like he was letting Beatrice's heroine go…

Hemmings reached out to lean on the edge of the proscenium arch, his legs no longer guaranteed to keep him standing. It was their scene, their moment, mined for the theatre. He couldn't hear Beatrice over the thunderous roaring in his ears. He watched, aching all over, as she made a show of her lines until Alfonso stepped up to her, grabbed her face in his hands, and dropped a long kiss onto her lips, breaking only to deliver his lines.

"*I shall return again to mine love,*
So swear I on the stars above."

Beatrice, white box in hand, skipped gaily from the stage and then, safely in the opposite wing, turned to watch.

Alfonso faced the audience, his body shifting from that of a proud hero in love to a man shaken and afraid. Hemmings was so close he could see the sweat streaming down Alfonso's brow, how his make-up was smudged and running; his costume was soaked, staining his neck and armpits. His narrow chest rose and fell with emotion.

Outside the boundary of the fourth wall, the audience leaned forward to a person when Alfonso spoke:

"And the firmament curse upon my oath,
"For it is nought but bad faith troth.
T'aint the quest leads me thither and yon,
But the fear of being scorned upon.
And so I leave, ne'er to face the consequence,
And the fates can curse me for my cowardice."

Alfonso paused. Looked out into the audience. And then he took a stage knife from his sleeve, stabbed himself and fell to the boards.

The curtains closed. The audience sat in shocked silence.

Alfonso pulled himself up, wiping his brow behind the safety of the curtain. Beatrice stormed up to him, her face a perfect tomato, all squishy and red with anger.

"See? I told you, didn't I? No one wants an ending like that – you've really done one over on us now, Alf. We'll never work the toffs again-"

From behind the curtain, a thunderous noise erupted, so strong the curtains shook and shivered. Alfonso and Beatrice quickly took their final poses as the curtains lifted. The rest of the cast ferried onto the stage to receive their applause, shoving Hemmings out the way.

Hemmings, stiff as stone, tapped Amelia's shoulder. She turned to him, her face wet with tears.

"He left her – why did he leave her? I never thought... Why did he do that?"

The words came from some part of himself that was, miraculously, still alive. "I don't know. But we should go and find Melly."

"But you said we should stay here-"

"I know," Hemmings said. It was funny. The words were coming out normally, in the right order and with the right meaning.

How was that possible when everything inside him was broken? "She might need our help. Come on."

They slipped out of the side of the stage, unnoticed by the actors as they stood under the lights, basking in the applause.

57

Joseph awoke with a start, Seven's hand on his shoulder.

"The play has finished, my Lord."

For a moment, he didn't know what was going on. And in that brief second, he was vulnerable. A middle-aged man, ill and tired. Then he righted himself, the cold severity returning to his eyes. He pulled himself up with his cane and positioned himself in front of the orrery.

"Reveal us. Make them look," he instructed. "I want them to see me."

There was a moment of tension, a strange tingling on his skin. Then they were visible, the shock and startled gasps of those nearest them evidence of the fact.

Seven darted inside the orrery, appearing a few moments later right at the top, standing proud like a soldier on a narrow platform that encircled the central column. The nine planets spun over and around him, framing him, drawing attention to his ethereal beauty. It was, Joseph realised, even more perfect than he'd dreamed it would be.

The crowd's chatter lowered to a murmur, their attention fixed on the unexpected sight of a beautiful, blue man scaling such a strange and wonderful creation. Joseph watched in delight as, like a wave rolling towards the shore, more and more heads turned to see what was happening.

And that was before Seven spoke.

"Ladies and gentlemen, Kings and Queens... Your Grace the Baron of Cerne Bralksteld." His voice, deep and musical, carried across the garden, brushing softly against the ears of the guests like the tempting fingers of a lover. "Pray silence for the honourable Lord Joseph David John, Earl of the Golden Rock and the Motshy Fields, brother to his Grace the Baron of Cerne Bralksteld. Pray silence, please... pray."

A hush descended. Even the entertainers and the slaves paused in their duties to stare. The actors on the stage were taking their exit, and those who had hung around to the very end of the performance began to pay attention to what was happening at this end of the garden.

Joseph shivered with pleasure and nervous excitement, his stomach quivering. They *saw* him. He wasn't some sickly whelp hidden away in his bedchambers. He was a man to be listened to. To be seen.

And he hadn't yet even begun.

"I am here today to present my brother, the Baron, and the citizens of this fine city a gift," Joseph said, moving directly in front of the orrery. His voice seemed amplified, carrying easily; the genie? Or his own excitement to finally be nearing the end of his journey?

"I beg your favour as I present it to you. This orrery was designed by our own Sisterhood of Cultivators, with of course the gratitude and patronage of the Baron."

Joseph bowed his head towards his brother, who smiled magnanimously at the crowd.

"And with it, I hope to show you all something amazing. Things have been... difficult lately, I know. Our neighbours don't always appreciate the good work we do. The benefits our industry provides to the whole of Ehinenden." He shrugged like a little boy caught with his hand in the cookie jar. The audience tittered, and then laughed more confidently. "It can be extremely difficult to shoulder the responsibility of improvement; the temptation to bite off more than you can chew can be hard to resist – just ask my brother."

Real laughter greeted this. The Baron smiled, but Joseph clocked the way his face reddened and his hands tightened on the arms of his throne.

Joseph's heart soared.

"Still, I shouldn't tease. My brother has done the best he can with the tools he has. Luckily for us, we have others at our disposal." He gestured grandly at the orrery. "And a great and brilliant future before us, when I take control."

Some people laughed, not yet catching up to the seriousness of his words. His brother rose from his seat like a fart in a bathtub,

The Princess And The Orrery

round and unwelcome. But there was nothing he could do. Joseph was in control.

Happiness rippled and popped inside him, like someone had filled his veins with sherbet. How long had he waited for this moment? God, if he could stretch it out for infinity, he would. But he didn't need to waste his last wish on it. He didn't need his last wish at all, in fact. He had beaten the genie, beaten his brother and his father and all the doctors who had said he'd never be anything more than an invalid, and he'd done it with only two wishes.

Any lingering doubts that he was truly the hero disappeared with the realisation of what he had accomplished.

The planets began spinning faster. The engine inside the orrery whined, screamed, and then fell silent; and yet, the planets continued to fly past each other. The wind rose, the taste of salt and the smell of seaweed hitting the back of Joseph's throat, the folds of his coat dancing in the air like excited children.

The Baron was signalling to his guards. Those nearest him began whispering to each other, realising something wasn't right. But the guests nearest the orrery were mesmerised, ignorant of the growing furore behind them.

Joseph pressed his cane into the grass, leaning on it so he could shout above the whirl of the orrery. "Seven, you know my wish. You must fulfil it."

It was time to be a hero.

"The thing that will make me happy – happier than anything else in the world – is for the people of Cerne Bralksteld to be happy to serve me, and me alone," Joseph announced, telling the world as much as he was instructing Seven. "Their joy will be in the service of my own. Not slaves, but willing subjects – a city of eighty thousand souls, all content, all at peace, all satisfied with my rule. I am the one who will heal this place! I am the one that brings happiness to the land! I am your TRUE and RIGHTFUL KING! THIS IS WHAT I WANT! THIS IS WHAT I DEMAND!"

Lightning danced across the orrery. Bright bands lashed themselves around Seven, lifting him into the sky so that he hung fifty feet in the air, crackling white and blue electricity running from the top of the device, through him and into the churning clouds overhead.

F. D. Lee

Music filled Joseph's body, a beautiful rhythm harmonising with the deepest, most intimate parts of him. An endless, perfect melody he'd known all his life and yet never heard before. The universe, singing to him, lulling him, soothing him.

Even the genie's screams didn't ruin the music.

58

Maria Sophia grabbed Naima. "We're too late! Can't you hear it? We need to run! It's-"

The drumbeat was the patter of rain against a windowpane, the gentle tum-tum-tum of nature warming up...

Amelia shoved her way through the packed audience, desperate to get to Seven. She had to reach him before-

The beat sped up, the crash of waves against the rocks, the roll of thunder on a hot day...

Alfonso stood dumbstruck on the stage, watching the bizarre display at the far end of the balcony: the huge device spinning faster and faster, and the Baron's brother giving some speech about God knows what. Where was Hemmings? He needed to-

Music everywhere, inside them all, reaching deep into their hearts and pulling...

Christopher looked up from his glass of celebratory brandy, noticing for the first time that everyone was staring intently at something. He set his drink down and tried to see what all the fuss-

The universe was made of music, an echoing beat that began with the heart and reverberated in swelling waves through the blood, ebbing gently at the guests' fingertips and toes, softening them from the inside out...

The Baron dropped his arm, his pointed finger relaxing, his hands unfurling. He looked at his brother anew – how had he ever mistaken the man for a weakling? What an unforgivable ass he'd been all his life; and yet, he felt at peace, relaxed and content... It was like there had been a contraption inside him, pulling him tight, twisting his heart and his guts, and suddenly it had broken and everything was as it should be. He could breathe. All the anger and resentment and guilt boiled away like milk in a hot pan, leaving nothing behind but residue.

The Baron looked around at the hundreds of guests crammed onto the balcony and saw that they were undergoing the same cosmic experience. People were laughing, smiling, hugging each other – even the slaves were being embraced as kin. It was... perfect.

All across the city, people stopped what they were doing as the music reached them, easing through their barriers to untangle the knots inside them, loosening their muscles, emptying their minds...

Joseph had done this. It was all thanks to Joseph. His little brother! And what had he, Philip, ever done to deserve such forgiveness, such happiness? Nothing. Nothing at all. He saw it plainly now; his ineptitude and avarice and his selfish need to be the strongest, the most important. To be *needed*.

But he wasn't needed. Joseph was. The truth was there on the faces all around him.

Philip stepped down from his throne and made his way through the people of Cerne Bralksteld, stopping only to hug and be hugged in return, until he finally reached his brother. He realised he was crying, the tears hot in his eyes, saltwater pooling in the edges of his wide, glorious smile.

He took his brother's hand and kissed it.

"Joseph... I was so, so wrong. All these years... everything I said to you, about you. I was wrong. You have never, ever been weak. It was me. I was afraid – afraid of you, afraid of change, afraid that people would realise I don't know what I'm doing. When Mother didn't kill you as a baby, I thought it was because she loved you more than me. Because she knew, deep down, that you would be better than me."

"Brother-" Joseph began, but Philip shook his head, his hands landing on Joseph's shoulders.

"...that you would be better than me. And she was right. You are better than me. Better than all of us. You've saved us all."

Joseph wiped away a tear and rested his hands on Philip's shoulders. And then, to Philip's amazed delight, his brother stepped forward and hugged him.

"All I ever wanted was for us to be good brothers," Joseph said, his breath warm against Philip's ear. "To be friends. I longed for you to visit me as a child, when I was sick. Ha... as a grown man, too."

"I'm sorry, I'm so sorry."

"Hush. It doesn't matter now," Joseph said, pulling away. "I've brought us to our happy ending, Brother. But you know what must happen next?"

Philip realised that he did. The knowledge settled in him with a certainty he'd never known before, and he felt another wave of bliss at its realisation.

"Of course, Brother. Nothing would make me happier than to give you what you deserve. To make up for all the years I failed you."

Philip spotted one of the Palace guards gazing, enraptured, at Joseph. He marched over to him, hugged him, took his knife, and returned to the orrery.

"Do you forgive me, Brother?" he asked, his mind a cloud of fog and music.

"I do, of course I do. This moment – I cannot tell you what it means to me. My only regret is that... well, you understand. Are you happy?"

Philip nodded vigorously. "I am, I am. I don't think I've been so happy in all my life, all because of you. You've saved me, Joe. Saved all of us. Thank you."

Philip took the knife to his throat and, pressing the blade deep into his flesh, tore it across his windpipe. Blood fountained from the wound, the air in his lungs adding little bubbles to the stream. It hurt, in a perfunctory way. But the music softened it, and the delight on Joseph's face was worth any amount of pain. Satisfaction warmed his soul as surely as the blood pouring from his neck warmed his skin, cascading down his body so fast he didn't have time to register his own death. Only the purity of his gift to Joseph mattered.

The old Baron of Cerne Bralksteld collapsed onto the grass, a smile on his face.

The new Baron knelt down and closed his brother's eyes. The earth clogged with blood beneath his slippered feet, but Joseph felt it was important to be with his brother a little longer. The image mattered, the handing over of responsibility, freely given with love and happiness.

He held the pose for a minute before he pulled himself up with the help of his cane and stepped away. When he looked up, the crowd was watching, calm, relaxed.

"There can only be one hero at the end," Joseph announced. "My brother understood that. He was a great man, but his time has passed. Now we must look to the future. Cerne Bralksteld is the greatest city in the Third Kingdom of Thaiana, perhaps in all the Kingdoms. But we are in danger of reaching our peak. The slaves are restless, unhappy. Who can blame them? We have treated them poorly, not recognising all they do for us."

The audience nodded. Some even took the hands of the slaves nearest them, or wrapped their arms around them. The slaves' faces were wet with tears as they embraced their captors in return.

"This situation has for many years made me incredibly sad." A groan from the crowd, anguish at the thought of Joseph's torment. "As has the disrespect shown to our great institutions – the museums, the Cultivators, the hospitals, the banks. We have taken them for granted, living off the success of our structures without recognising the hard work that goes into maintaining them. But no more – do you agree?"

"Yes! Yes! Yes!" the audience shouted, some raising their hands in the air, others clutching their chests, some standing in still contemplation, their eyes wide as they finally understood.

"But now I am happy," Joseph said. "I am happy because you are happy. Slaves – do you not want to work for the betterment of our society?"

The slaves in the crowd cried out that they did, a hundred voices in languages from across Ehinenden and further away.

The Princess And The Orrery

"And my colleagues from industry, do you not want to work for the prosperity of Cerne Bralksteld?"

Yet more cries of agreement.

"My dear friends from the Palace, from our fine city, are you not eager to do all that you must to make Cerne Bralksteld the centre of the known world?"

A roar of approval, so loud it drowned out the whirling of the orrery, which was now spinning so fast the planets were a blur. In the distance, storm clouds gathered over the ocean.

Joseph had never been happier. People *cared* about him. His vile, bullying brother was gone. He'd beaten the genie. It was every just ending he'd ever read about, and it was even better than he'd imagined.

And then the pain came.

59

Hemmings clutched his ears, falling to his knees. The noise... Mortal gods, it was pulling him to pieces, filling every space inside him like burning oil – between his teeth, in the cracks between his bones, in the connections in his brain. He retched, his back arched and his stomach convulsing, but all that came up was spit and flecks of black blood.

His arms shook and collapsed; he hit the grass with a heavy thump, his teeth catching his tongue, filling his mouth with the iron tang of blood. And still the pain grew. The drums, the sound: it was crushing him.

I'm going to die.

Pressing one hand to his stomach, he tried to pull himself forward with the other, towards the blurry shape of Amelia. Blackness filling his vision... passing out...? No. Blood in his eyes...

"Am... Am... Ame..."

Could she hear him? Noise, noise everywhere. Drums, horrendous and enveloping, smothering him. She wasn't... why was she standing there?

"Plea... help... Am..."

The shape that might have been Amelia stepped away from him, unconcerned. Hemmings' hand wavered and dropped. He lay, slumped on his side, his arm outstretched to the girl as she walked away from him.

He had to do something, but he was so weak. He hurt *so much*. The drumbeat was getting louder, the weight heavier. He blinked again, clearing the blackness from his vision only for it to return, hot and thick, rolling down the planes of his face.

He closed his eyes. The pain was hot and hard. He could feel it bending his bones, crushing his organs. He gritted his teeth, his mouth thick with blood, and pushed his mind above the agony, small, wet gulps bubbling up from his throat. He lifted himself up into the topmost part of his mind, imagined himself as a tiny boat on a raging ocean, and concentrated everything he had left on healing himself.

For Hemmings, his elven talent for healing had been a thing he pulled on every now and again when his dwarven family forgot their strength: when his mother hugged him too hard or when, much younger, Chokey's play fighting had got out of hand. He was unpractised... his little boat was no match for the storm.

Please, please... I can't... Chokey, please... Mum...

Images of his family burned the inside of his eyes, drying his throat in spite of the blood from his bitten tongue and bleeding gums. His baby sister, fat and naughty and always, somehow, sticky. His father, kind and bemused, never quite sure what to do with the elf in his family but always, always welcoming.

Chokey. His sister and best friend, another world away. He'd never see her again. Never be able to tell her how much he loved and needed her. How truly amazing she was.

Mum.

He wanted his mum. He was dying, alone and in pain and there was nothing he could do. He wanted her arms around him, the tickle of her hair against his chest and the soft smell of paper and ink that she carried with her.

Mum...

He didn't remember being found in a bag at the Grand Reflection Station. But he remembered her, when he was very young, hugging him close when he'd been lost and alone. Telling him that he was home, and loved, and wanted.

The pain crashed over the bow of his meagre boat, dragging it into the darkness. Sinking him.

And still the drums roared...

...And then it eased.

His fingers twitched, his eyes opening. Everything hurt, but it wasn't the splitting agony of before. There was a hand on his face, wiping away the blood. He blinked again, the world blurring and then snapping into focus.

Melly was sitting on the grass next to him, her hands on his face, her mouth a thin line. There was blood on her, too, around her eyes and mouth and nostrils, but it was drying.

"Melly?" he croaked.

She pulled her hands away. Closed her eyes, took a deep breath, and then toppled forward, her head landing on the grass next to his.

The two elves lay, looking at the dark clouds gathering above, their breathing ragged.

Finally, Melly spoke. "We need to get to the genie. To the machine. Can you move?"

Hemmings swallowed, the taste of blood still on his tongue. He could sense the weight and the noise, still. But it was outside of him now, pressing against his skin but no longer crushing him.

"You saved me?"

"Of course I saved you," Melly said, some of her old sharpness returning.

"How?"

"I'm older than you. Stronger. Plus, I haven't spent my entire life lounging around *thinking* about things."

Hemmings managed a smile. No matter how bad things were, if Melly could afford to be sour there had to be some hope. "How did you find me?"

"You were the only person here not enjoying themselves. Easy to spot amongst this lot."

"What?"

Melly heaved herself up onto her elbows. "Take a look."

All around them humans were smiling and hugging each other, seemingly oblivious to the horrendous, steady drumming and, at the other end of the balcony, the high wail of the orrery. Amelia was nowhere to be seen.

"They're like children," Hemmings said. "Look at them... so happy."

"Children can be nasty little buggers. When we did stories for the young ones, mortal gods... it was always the blood and the bone. *Cough, cough, cough, the song is not enough, cough, cough, cough, off we go to God...* that was one of the children's Plots, way back when. But I take your point," Melly added magnanimously. "It's the wish, it must be. Magic."

"Magic can't do this," Hemmings said. "The Teller, *whocaresaboutus,* banned it because it's too weak-"

Melly gave him a long, hard stare. "You really believe that, after everything I've told you? When you can see – feel – all this? Come on, Hemmings. You spend all your time thinking. Well, now something's really happening and you're going to have to keep up if we're going to help all these people. Can you stand?"

They helped each other to their feet. Something was happening up by the orrery – the Baron was talking to the man who'd given the speech.

"You're right about one thing, though." Melly's gaze fixed on the orrery. "Magic this strong isn't normal. It has to be that machine. Right then, time to put your new acting skills to good use."

Hemmings blinked. "What?"

Melly turned to him, a wide smile stretching across her beautiful, bloodstained features, her red hair whipping in the rising wind, her green eyes bright with furious intent.

"It's time to get happy," she said.

And so Hemmings found himself grinning like a loon, following Melly through the crowds of delirious guests, allowing himself to be hugged and clapped on the back as he went, ignoring the fact that his broken heart was beating at a mile a minute.

It was not, in fact, all that different from the parties Chokey insisted they attended.

Seven had no idea where he was anymore.

All he knew was the pure, perfect agony of the magic, magnified a thousand-fold by the *es'hajit*. Below him, the planets spun faster and faster, the drumbeat at the centre of the universe louder and louder. His heart, weaker and weaker.

And then it was over. The cord of energy holding him in the air returned to the orrery, dancing from planet to spinning planet.

Seven fell to the ground, landing in a crumpled heap.

60

Something was wrong. Joseph dropped his cane and grasped his neck, the cold burning through the layers of cloth wrapped around the necklace.

This shouldn't be happening. The wish ensured his happiness, but the necklace was growing ever colder, the material crisp and brittle as he clawed at himself, trying to prise the thing from his body without touching it.

He stumbled and fell, his hands at his throat, panic filling his veins.

Bea turned to Joan.

"Do you hear that?"

"Hear what?"

"I don't know… like a drumming sound?"

Joan shrugged. "There's Ænathlin Again protesters outside. It's probably them."

Bea chewed her lip, listening. She could hear the protesters outside, shouting some nonsense about reclaiming the city, but there was something else. Something underneath it. Mortal gods, was she finally going mad?

Ignoring Joan's worried expression, Bea went to the window and pulled it up. On the street below was a crowd of protesters – bloody hells, at least sixty of them! How had they managed to get so many people on such short notice? They were making a din, but no one down there was playing a drum.

Bea clenched her fists against the window pane, closed her eyes and concentrated.

Outside: the protesters shouting and, behind that, the general noises of the city which, if she were honest, didn't sound that much different from a group of angry fae, just less organised.

Inside: Joan, breathing next to her. Chairs being placed on the floor. Plates clattering.

Inside her: drumming.

The noise was *inside* her. Below her heartbeat, and yet just as much a part of her. A steady rhythm beating out a melody that had haunted her dreams for months during her time at the Academy.

The melody of the universe, the song of the Redacted women, the music of magic.

Oh, no...

"It's not Ænathlin Again. I know what it is," Bea said, her eyes snapping open. "I've heard it before. Joan, I'm sorry, I have to go. I have to find Mistasinon."

"Wait, Bea, we're starting-"

But Bea was already pounding down the staircase, her heart hammering in harmony with the faint thumping of the drums only she could hear: a tune she'd heard on the day she died.

Outside *The Quill and Ink* were the protesters, all carrying banners and shouting at anyone who passed. At the front of the horde was Carol. Her golden eyes narrowed when she spotted Bea.

"Cabbage mother! A fairy and an invader – you're not even from the city!" Carol raised her voice, performing for the crowd: the crowd that was now gathering around Bea.

"This is exactly what we've been talking about," Carol continued, a smile playing on her lips. "All these fairies, gathering like rats, trying to steal our city, our rights, our Plots. Destroying our heritage. The Teller Cares About *Us*, not them."

For a moment, all Bea could do was stare at Carol, the music still playing, half-heard, in her ears. She shook her head, trying to dislodge the sound, and attempted to push her way through the protesters, but they shoved her back so hard she landed with a thump against the pub door.

"Carol, for the sake of the mortal gods, let me through," Bea demanded, eyeing the closing circle of anti-fairy protesters.

"Tsk, tsk, Buttercup. We've as much right as you to be here. More, since we're doing our civic duty to protect the city." She stepped forward, so her face was inches from Bea's, and hissed, "I told you I'd get you, cabbage mother."

F. D. Lee

Bea opened her mouth to scream at Carol when a bolt of lightning rent the air, bright white and blinding, landing somewhere in the middle of the city.

"Get it off me, get it off me, get it off me!" Joseph screamed.

Three of the nearest guests, the wish compelling them, began scrabbling to remove the necklace. They were quick and clumsy, pulling at the cloth and exposing the metal below, their hands grasping it until their fingers turned red, then blue, then white and, finally, black. Only Joseph's fervent desire not to die kept them careful enough to ensure that the metal never touched his skin.

"Wrap it up, wrap it up," cried a shrill voice. "You're going to kill him!"

Joseph's eyes swivelled to see Amelia pushing her way through the crowd.

"Stop!" he instructed through clenched teeth. The guests paused; Amelia came to a sudden standstill.

"It's joining itself to you," Amelia said. "You need Seven. Please, trust me. I know all about it, I promise."

"Do as she says," Joseph said.

Fumbling, the guests replaced the bandages, keeping the necklace balanced in such a way that it didn't touch his skin; but even so, his neck was turning red. Amelia turned to Seven, lying forgotten on the grass. She knelt beside him and shook him.

"Seven, wake up. You have to help Joseph. Now, Seven."

The genie didn't respond. Amelia pressed her ear to his chest, her eyes screwed shut. "He's... he's alive, but..."

"But what?" Joseph cried, his voice thick with pain and fear, neck straining to avoid contact with the necklace.

"I don't know. He's alive but I don't think he's... here..." She looked back at him. "I don't think we can save you."

61

The wish battled with the strange confusion over what would best make Joseph happy, and the pull of the es'hajit *and the strength it offered. But that strength was also fuelling Joseph's agony and despair…*

Joseph had to be happy. That was all and everything, the ultimate sense in a world that refused to be sensible. He wanted his people to love him and care for him, the wish knew. He wanted to be valued and seen, as he had never been valued or seen. He wanted to matter. To have meaning and purpose.

To feel loved.

The es'hajit *made it possible to enthral the people of Cerne Bralksteld, to satisfy the wish in a way that Seven, with or without his necklace, would never have been able to survive.*

But something was happening to Joseph…

The wish was in flux. It stormed inside Seven as it sought a resolution, pulling him apart atom by atom, cell by cell, as it did so.

62

Amelia had never felt so unhappy in her life.

When Jules had died, her misery had been a dark and narrow tunnel, a labyrinth that always led her back to her guilt and shame. There had been no escape, only endless traipsing around in the blackness, continually returning to the centre and the knowledge that it was all her fault. The orrery had saved her. The darkness still surrounded her. She was still caught in the loop. But the orrery had given her a reason to stand still, to stop returning again and again to the centre, where her grief waited.

As she watched Joseph blinking away tears as the guests tried to keep the necklace away from his skin, she realised that her misery over Jules was nothing but a weak imitation of true anguish.

She could hardly breathe for fear of something happening to Joseph. And yet, in a strange way, she knew that what she was feeling wasn't, exactly, her own emotions. It was like she was hiding under a blanket, and while the material covered her from head to foot so all she knew was the feel of it, it wasn't actually *her*.

So when the orrery shuddered and groaned, she spared it only a momentary glance. When Naima pushed her way through the crowd with her mother – her mother! – in tow, Amelia registered some element of surprise and anxiety, but they were muffled under the thick folds of her fear for Joseph's wellbeing.

When her mother landed next to her, enveloping her in a desperate embrace, Amelia burst into tears, burying her head in the old, unforgotten scent of her skin and perfume. Maria Sophia's hand moved up to her hair, carding through it the way she'd done when Amelia was young.

"Is Joseph going to die?" Amelia sobbed.

"I don't know, my darling," Maria Sophia replied, her voice cracking. "We can only pray he will not."

Amelia held her mother tighter. "I can't believe it. I can't believe he's going to die."

The Princess And The Orrery

A shadow fell across them. Melly and Hemmings stood over her, a look of confusion on Hemmings' face. He crouched down next to her and put his hand out to touch Seven's unconscious body.

"So that's a genie," he said quietly, like he didn't understand what was happening.

"I thought he'd help us save Joseph," Amelia cried, her voice wet and thick. "I thought he was my friend, but he doesn't care. He's just going to lie there while Joseph suffers and dies."

Hemmings frowned. "I don't think he's exactly 'lying there'. Melly?"

The other elf wiped her hand over her mouth pensively. "He's not dead, at least." She looked back at Joseph, who was making short, high whimpers, like a wounded animal afraid of revealing itself to the hunter. "We'll wait for that one to die, break the wish and then-"

Amelia hurled herself at Melly, hitting her hard in the stomach, sending them both flying. She rained down blows on the elf, years of anger and pain erupting from somewhere deep and dark inside her, in defence of the only person who mattered: Joseph.

"Stop!" Joseph screamed, his eyes bulging in his narrow face.

Amelia stopped instantly, the anger still burning, making her fists itch.

"You two, come here right now," Joseph ordered. "You're not – my wish hasn't – why?"

"It probably will eventually," Melly answered, untangling herself from Amelia and stepping over to him. "You'll be dead before it does, though."

"You're not human?" Joseph asked.

Amelia seized her chance to make him happy. "They're elves! They told me – they showed me their ears and everything. They're here to get Seven and take him home."

Melly glared at her. She didn't care. Nothing was as important as helping Joseph. If Seven couldn't do anything, maybe Melly or Hemmings could.

"If you don't help me, these people will kill you," Joseph said, careful to keep his head up. "Their very purpose is to see me satisfied."

F. D. Lee

Melly's green eyes narrowed. "They might try, but the necklace will kill you before they succeed, and then the wish that binds them will break. All I need to do is wait."

"I know the secret of iron! If I die, so will your friend!" Joseph caught the attention of two big men. "Grab that man, the one in black," Joseph ordered, his eyes pointing to Hemmings.

The two men grabbed Hemmings' arms before he could react, shoving him to his knees. They were grinning with pride. Amelia grinned back at them, hope swelling in her chest. Joseph knew what he was doing – of course he did, he was a brilliant, wonderful man. The world wouldn't let such an important person die. And Melly – ha! – she was at a loss now! That would teach her to threaten Joseph!

"You've got iron? Good," Joseph said to the men, his neck straining to keep his chin up. "Hold it to his skin."

The first twisted Hemmings' arms at what had to be a painful angle behind his back. The other man rummaged in his pocket and pulled out a set of keys, rolled Hemmings' sleeve up and pressed one of the keys to his skin. Hemmings let loose a high, breathy wail, his pale forearm starting to redden and blister.

"Wait!" Melly cried, one hand reaching out to halt the man, the other towards Joseph. "Wait. I'll help the genie. Let Hemmings go."

"How can I trust you?" Joseph demanded.

The elf's expression tightened in disgust. "I give you my word. A bargain made. If you know anything, you'll know the power of that."

Amelia leaned forward, barely breathing, as Joseph tried to decide what to do. It was agonising. He had to agree, he *had* to. The material binding the necklace was beginning to steam, the cold radiating from it condensing in the air.

"You don't have to trust them," she heard herself say.

Joseph's eyes turned to her.

"We all love you," Amelia said. "Honestly, we do. If they try to trick you, everyone here will get them. Iron, you said, right? We'll, we'll, we'll iron them to death if they betray you. Won't we?"

Maria Sophia leapt up from Seven's side. "Yes, we'll kill them dead."

Naima stepped forward and pulled something out of her pocket: a glass vial with a grey powder within it. "And if that doesn't work, I'll use this."

"See?" Amelia implored. "We'll protect you, Joseph. But you have to let them fix Seven, or else the *gu'lin vut* will kill you." A sob escaped her. "I don't know what I'd do if you died."

Joseph blinked, unable to nod. "Yes. A bargain," he said to Melly. "Save me, and your friend is safe, too."

Amelia dragged Melly back to Seven, almost shoving her to the ground next to him. "You'd better not try to trick us," she hissed.

Melly rolled her eyes and then rolled up her sleeves. She placed her hands on Seven's body and closed her eyes. Amelia chewed her lip, waiting.

Waiting, waiting, waiting. It was unbearable. The elf didn't seem to be doing anything, just sitting there, eyes closed, like she was listening intently to music. Like her mum used to when her dad played the piano and she sang along. Jules would try to sing, too, but he always got distracted.

Amelia held her hand out to Maria Sophia, who took it and squeezed.

A green light appeared at the tips of Melly's fingers, dull at first, flickering like a candle flame struggling against its own wax. The elf swayed, her fingers digging into Seven's flesh. The light grew brighter, extending up her arms to her elbows. Melly's head lolled forward, and then she brought herself onto her knees and leaned heavily on the genie's chest.

The green light started to drain from her arms, spreading out over Seven. The more it channelled its way into him, the steadier his breathing became.

"It's working," Amelia shouted at Joseph, her voice bright with excitement. "It's working!"

Seven's eyes fluttered open. They were different, though, from the eyes she knew: no longer blue, but entirely black and flecked with little, glowing white spots, like stars in the night sky. The green light was almost entirely drained from Melly's arms and, with each passing moment, Seven seemed more aware.

Melly didn't appear to be doing very well, though. Her skin had taken on a waxy sheen, and Hemmings was yelling something about her not being able to withstand the magic for much longer. Amelia didn't care. Every ounce of her was focused on Seven's improvement so that he could save Joseph. When Melly fell forward and collapsed on top of him, Amelia just got up and moved around her so she could keep her eyes on Seven.

Happily, the green light still glowed between their bodies, so Amelia didn't need to worry, even when Melly began to cough and shudder. Somewhere in the back of her mind, Amelia knew her detachment was unusual; she wasn't even curious when the elf tilted her head upwards and whispered something to Seven, nor when Seven replied in a language she'd never heard before. It was like the sound of people talking at the far end of a long room. It didn't matter.

And then it was over, just like that. Seven blinked, the starry blackness of his eyes appearing and disappearing, and eased himself up. Gently, he set Melly down on the ground, where she lay panting, strange black stuff running from her nose in a steady stream.

Amelia grabbed Seven and pulled him, stumbling, over to Joseph. "Get the necklace off him, it's hurting him. You have to help him."

The storm was rolling inland, the thick taste of thunder filling the air. Amelia hopped from foot to foot as Seven placed his hands on the necklace, carefully taking it from the people who had been holding it away from Joseph's neck.

"Seh... Seh..." Joseph's words were little more than bites of sound through the chattering of his narrow teeth.

"Hush, my Lord." Seven seemed steadier now; his hands barely trembled as he slowly unwound the cloth covering the necklace, revealing the head of the snake. Its eyes were leaking the same clear, oily substance the cog had suffered from before Seven had joined Amelia in the Observatory.

"Is it too late?" she asked, trying to quell the rush of fear that tingled through her.

"I fear it is so," Seven said, not taking his eyes off the careful work of separating the cloth from the necklace without letting the metal touch Joseph's skin. "Though I suspect we are speaking of different outcomes."

The Princess And The Orrery

Ten minutes passed, though Amelia had no sense of them bleeding away. All she could do was watch, her lower lip caught between her teeth, as Seven painstakingly worked to remove the necklace. The orrery was still spinning at a rate that should have alarmed her, clouds gathering above it. A crackle of lightning jumped from the high, black sphere into the sky, like it was searching for something. But no one paid it any attention. All human eyes were focused on Seven.

A hand fell on Amelia's shoulder. She looked up to see her mother standing next to her, her eyes fixed on Joseph. Finally, Seven could reach behind Joseph's neck and pull the hinge of the necklace, opening the gap between the head of the snake and the stub that had been its tail, and remove it.

Joseph slumped forward, his body heaving as he sucked in great lungfuls of air. Seven, meanwhile, held the necklace his hands, staring at it as if he'd never seen anything so beautiful in his entire life.

Amelia jumped forward, wrapping her arms around Joseph, tears of relief pouring down her face.

"Are you alright? How do you feel? Do you need anything? It was the necklace, you see, it tried to attach itself to you. But you're alright now, aren't you? Aren't you? I helped, did you see? We all helped! And now we can-"

Joseph shoved Amelia, sending her flying backwards. She landed on the grass. Her mouth opened and closed, but no words would come.

I've made him angry.

"This is your fault – you didn't warn me about the metal! You knew – you said you know all about it!" Joseph spat, his hands at his neck, gingerly feeling the blistered and raw skin. "After everything I've done for you. All the help I've given you, you almost let me die."

"No, no," Amelia said, stunned. "I didn't – I mean I knew about the *gu'lin vut* but not that it would-"

She didn't get to finish. With his other hand, Joseph ordered the men who were still holding Hemmings to drop him. "Throw her over the edge, put her in the fire, I don't care, just get rid of her!"

F. D. Lee

Moving was like trying to swim in a ballgown. Maria Sophia felt the weight of the wish in every step she took, trying to keep her in place. She was submerged, the very air her telling her that Joseph was the victim, that Amelia had betrayed him and nearly killed him.

He's going to murder my child.

The wish rallied. Amelia needed discipline. If Maria Sophia had been a better, stronger mother, Amelia wouldn't have killed her son. Poor Jules, just like Joseph. Never given the opportunity to be everything he was destined to be.

He's. Going. To. Murder. My. Child.

The pressure of the wish bore down on her, the drums beating faster and faster in her ears: It's not Joseph's fault. Amelia hurt him, she's to blame. Look at him, poor man. Look at what he's been through. Look how good he is, how kind, how *nice*. All he wants is for everyone to be happy. Don't you want to be happy?

No.

Maria Sophia screamed and threw herself forward, shoving past the startled men, landing in a heap next to Amelia. She cradled her in her arms, dropping tears and kisses onto her head. Amelia struggled against her, spitting furious words Maria Sophia couldn't hear over the roaring of the drums, furious at being scorned.

Pain rocketed through her. Maria Sophia ignored it, focusing on the one essential truth: Joseph wanted to kill her child. She'd let the wish kill her before she allowed that to happen.

And still Amelia fought against her, scratching her, kicking her, biting her. Vile, poisonous words spilled from her lips as she struggled to give herself over to the mob forming around them. To make Joseph happy.

Maria Sophia screamed at Seven over the roar of the drums and the wail of the wind:

"I can't stop them! Please – take Amelia away! Please!"

Seven stared at her, his eyes black and full of stars. Maria Sophia knew what he was feeling was a thousand times worse than the vice-like pressure crushing her as she resisted the magic. He was no help. She tightened her hold on Amelia, shielding her from the blows that had started to rain down them.

With a scream, Seven charged at Joseph, landing heavily against him, clamping the necklace back around Joseph's neck.

They disappeared.

63

They were standing on the highest platform of the orrery, by the frozen cog.

The atmosphere was bitter, a mixture of the cold emanating from Seven's necklace and the cog, and the hard lump of fury inside him. Seven swayed, sharp talons of Joseph's distress scraping across his mind, his stomach shuddering and pitching – but he caught hold of Joseph, shoving him backwards, onto the cog.

The orrery flashed blinding white, so painfully bright that even when Seven closed his eyes, they stung like vinegar had been poured into them. For a moment there was nothing but pain and the feel of Joseph convulsing under his hands.

When Seven opened his eyes, the inside of the orrery was alight with jumping sparks of electricity, dancing from bar to bar, rod to rod, planet to planet; a seizure made real. It was beautiful, in its way. In the same way that Seven himself was beautiful: incandescent, sharp, otherworldly – and utterly unforgiving.

"Welcome, my Lord," Seven began, his voice laden with the effort of speaking. But the orrery was giving him some measure of strength. This was not, however, entirely welcome news.

The device was also powering the wish, and he had just brought it more of the *gu'lin vut*. For how long the fragile balance would remain between it aiding him and giving strength to the very thing that was harming him, Seven had no idea. No matter. He didn't need long.

He leaned forward so his face was inches from Joseph's, his teeth bared. If these were to be his final moments, he intended to make them count.

"How does it feel to be so undone?" he spat. "So vulnerable? Does it hurt, my Lord? Not your body – I see well enough that it does – but your soul? You have lost your power over me. How, you may wonder? Let me enlighten you."

The Princess And The Orrery

Joseph's head thrashed as he tried to keep the necklace from making contact with his throat. All his effort was in vain; the necklace was locked fast, pulling against his neck as it tried to reach the cog behind him. Joseph's skin was already turning black, blisters forming and bursting, weeping clear liquid that pooled and crusted on his jutting collarbone, malignant trails of tears that evoked no sympathy.

"You were winning, my Lord. The *es'hajit* is a success. And perhaps you might have won, even with the mistake of trying to wear my necklace. Until you threatened Amelia. How *dare* you? A monster I am, for I have done monstrous things. I have tricked people into going against their better judgement, against their best interests. I have promised the world and delivered nought but shame and misery. I have exposed the best amongst your kind to their greed and selfish desires, ruining them beyond repair."

Seven's fingers dug into Joseph's skin-and-bone arms, the only thing keeping him from being pulled backwards. Their eyes locked.

"And you, you weak, spoilt, vain little man, bested me."

His legs shaking with the effort of keeping his balance, Seven tightened his grip on Joseph. He was only vaguely aware when his nails began to separate from his fingertips, fluttering like leaves to be caught up in the spinning mechanisms of the orrery. He was close enough to smell the sweat and fear on Joseph's skin.

"Until you presented me with a choice that I could no more hide from than the sun might hide from the sky. Tell me, my Lord... how does it feel to die the villain? *Are you happy now?*"

Joseph wheezed and spluttered, frost pulling his skin taut, the tears in his eyelashes crystallising as they formed. His mouth opened and closed, a popping, guttural sound escaping his throat, his eyes as red as his bleeding gums, his skin blistered and peeling. He was wholly exposed to the process of *gu'lin vut* as the necklace sought to rejoin its lost piece, to return itself to the orrery and channel the power crackling and jumping around them. The sticky gunge continued to weep from the necklace, caking his body.

The genie and the man: locked together in their deaths as lightning danced and sparked across the orrery, the planets whirling around them, the drumbeat that held the universes together thumping in tandem with Seven's pulsing heart.

And then, suddenly, Joseph grabbed Seven.

The drums grew faster and faster, the beat impossible to follow, a blurred continuum of sound with no juncture or division. Joseph's grasping hands found their way into Seven's hair, his fingers twisting into the once-tight curls. Clumps of Seven's hair detached from his scalp without even a twinge of pain, the roots simply giving way.

Seven had no strength left to resist the pull towards Joseph's face, and the thought that the last thing he would ever see would be that wrecked and twisted visage made him want to burst out laughing. After so many years spent hiding from the Beast, so many lovers, so many palaces and prisons, vast cities and one-horse towns – what an end he had brought upon himself!

And yet he had no regrets. He didn't want to die, even now, but what life was left to him, anyway? Alone in the world, trapped by the restless, wanton promise of his magic and the sweet, sharp pain that came in its wake. Unloved and incapable of loving. At least, in his final moments, he had saved Amelia. Shown Maria Sophia that she was right to trust him with her daughter's life. He hoped that it would be enough to undo the pain his selfishness had caused her, and that Amelia would live a long and happy life.

Were he able to make a wish, if the strange manifestation of his power allowed for such a thing, he would have wished the girl every genuine, true happiness it was possible to experience. Not the kind Joseph longed for, but the happiness that came because life had shaped it and made it empathic and joyful, resilient and kind.

Seven felt almost peaceful, the core of himself centred in a moment of calm amid the raging whirlwind of pain. It would be alright if he-

"I... one wish... left..."

Joseph's words were wet and weak, slipping past his lips between the dry, hard gulping of his frozen throat. Seven tried to pull away, but Joseph's hands gripped his head, aided by blood and ice and the sticky, clear substance of the *gu'lin vut*.

The Princess And The Orrery

"One... I wish... wish... no more pain... please... no pain no more... pain..."

Seven stared at him, hardly able to believe the words, thin as they were.

"You wish me to end your pain, my Lord?"

"....es.... yes...."

Oh, there was a *lot* of room in a wish like that. Did Joseph realise his mistake, or was he too far gone to know what he'd asked for? His words were a gift, a prize Seven had given up all hope of ever winning.

Seven grinned.

The new wish layered itself onto the old one, squaring it and strengthening it, the two demands combining into one desperate push, one Seven would not have been able to resist, even within the orrery. Even if he had wanted to.

Moving his arms was like trying to lift a barrel of lead underwater with only a mouthful of air. But somehow, he managed to bring his hands up to the tarred and frozen remains of his necklace, resting on the ruin of Joseph's neck.

Seven gripped the snake's head and the remains of its tail and forced them together.

There was a moment of resistance, and then a strange, dry sound that was neither paper ripping nor ice cracking but something in between.

Joseph's eyes met his, a flicker of something like realisation in them. Seven held his gaze, not knowing what the man saw reflected in his star-filled eyes.

Splinters formed on Joseph's frost-rotted skin, quickly running to fractures, before transforming into a network of fractals that suddenly gave way under Seven's hands. A weak, simple sound accompanied the moment Joseph's neck snapped, as if it were nothing at all.

His hands fell from Seven's body, leaving him hanging inert from the necklace, like a puppet nobody wanted to play with anymore.

It was over.

The wish left silently, discreetly, taking the universe from Seven's eyes as it did, returning them to their endless blue.

F. D. Lee

For the first time in months, Seven's mind and body were his own again. Someone was laughing. It took him a moment to realise it was him. And to think, he'd almost given in! Almost done the stupid thing and died a noble death, like some ridiculous hero in a storybook.

Seven yanked the necklace open again, grabbed Joseph's broken neck and flung him away, smiling a thin but satisfied smile at the sound of his captor's body hitting the spinning rotor arms beneath. He was going to get his gods damn necklace back and then he was going to get the hells away from all these people.

The orrery resisted. Snaking threads of the thick, clear substance oozed over his hands, trying to pull the necklace back. But it had nothing on a three-hundred-year-old genie that had almost died, been imprisoned and tortured, *and* nearly forced into playing a gods' damn hero.

Grunting and swearing, legs braced against the platform, Seven fought the orrery, the clear, viscous substance wrapping itself around the snake, drawing it towards the cog. The muscles in his arms and legs, already worked beyond endurance, burned. Seven's mind was empty, his whole being centred on retrieving his necklace. White spots danced in front of his eyes, his teeth grinding together as he strained.

The *gu'lin vut* was stronger than him. All he had on his side was the fact that the connection hadn't had long to form, Joseph's wish disrupting it. Grunting, Seven walked his legs up the central column until he was horizontal, his whole body held in place by the cog's growing connection to his necklace.

Seven opened his mouth and screamed, pulling so suddenly that his legs straightened and his arms flew over his head, the necklace once again in his possession.

Now he just had to deal with the fact that he was falling backwards, towards the spinning rotor arms.

He closed his eyes and pictured his old cave, the place where he'd been safe and happy and alone…

The Princess And The Orrery

64

The pathway had opened; but it was closing again.

The creatures swarmed together in a shifting mass of tentacles and muscle as they battled each other to pass through before the way was lost, the power they relied on fragmenting like dreams in sunlight, lost in the confusion like tears in rain. Like the genies before them, they had no idea where the pathway led, only that it would take them away from the world they had raped and emptied.

All the monsters knew was hunger and the need to keep moving, to keep pressing into the unknown – an instinct that had been stymied by the genies' flight and the consequence of their machines. Highways large enough for such beings to traverse, routes that had been open for millennia, had slammed closed at the sudden, overwhelming thunder of the universe; the music that guided them turning discordant and fractured, reduced to its most basic components and then split across time and space.

That had been the monsters' only mistake, when they had come for the genies' world: they had shown them that escape was possible. When the few remaining genies had fled with the help of their *es'hajits*, they had closed the way behind them.

Until now.

The strongest should have been the one to make it through. But the way was narrowing, moment by moment, and the frantic crush only served to block the biggest monsters. But one, smaller and quicker than the rest, pushed between the writhing bodies, lashing its tentacles onto anything it could, pulling itself toward the narrowing crack of freedom. There was no plan, not in the sense that other organisms, evolved on different worlds to survive different conditions, would have understood it. You might just as well ask a bird why it flies or a cat why it kills.

The small monster slipped, squirmed and squiggled past its larger kin, reaching the gateway as it sealed, the blinding white of potential salvation pulling it forward, the drumbeat – a bare and brutal shadow of the music that had once played – tugging at its synapses, urging it onward.

The monster reached the gateway and, as the light became nothing more than a slit in the universe, it pushed itself into the unknown, trusting only that the music would guide it to a place it could feast on.

65

Hemmings had passed through exhaustion and into a strange, blurry land beyond its horizon. As such, he didn't really know how to react when the humans holding him suddenly dropped their arms, stammering apologies like they'd been caught trying to sneak into a dragon's den and were hoping to talk their way out of it.

Hemmings offered them some feeble platitudes and then waved them away. He staggered over to Melly, who was lying on the grass by the orrery, her hand across her face. He dropped down beside her, his long legs stretched out in front of him.

"Urgh," Melly grunted.

"I couldn't agree more." Hemmings looked down at himself. "My mum is going to murder me when she sees the state of my trousers."

Melly burst out laughing. No, *guffawing*. Her whole body was shaking, her face hidden in the crook of her elbow. And then Hemmings was laughing too, like his life depended on it. He didn't even know why. He wasn't happy. In fact, he was pretty sure he'd never been more *un*happy, whatever his poetry might say to the contrary. He was exhausted, his shoulders were throbbing from having his arms pulled behind his back for so long, the iron burn stung like salt in an open wound, and he still felt sick from the magic. And yet, he couldn't stop giggling.

Everyone was waking up. The horrendous drum beat had stopped as suddenly as it had begun. Amelia was hugging the woman who had dived in to save her, who now had a look of startled delight on her face. A tall, black woman was watching them, grinning from ear to ear. Even the orrery was slowing down.

"Well, that wasn't what I was expecting," Melly said, once she'd stopped laughing. She winced, pulling herself up into a sitting position.

Hemmings passed her his handkerchief. "Are you alright? That seemed very... intense."

"Hah. That's one way to describe it." She spat on the handkerchief and started cleaning the blood from her face. "I've no idea what was happening to the genie, but it *felt* like he was being torn apart from the inside out. I've never had to heal anyone while their body fought against it before."

"But you're alright?"

Melly paused her makeshift ablutions. "Probably. I doubt I'll be much use for a while. But we'll be home soon. I can rest then."

Hemmings exhaustion returned in a lump. "You still want to take the genie back to Ænathlin?"

"Yes, of course," Melly said. "But you'll be pleased to know that we reached an agree-"

She was cut off by an eruption of screams.

Naima stared in frozen horror at the orrery. High above the other eight planets, the black orb continued to spin on its arc, fine blue bolts of lightning crackling across its surface. The air smelled of thunderstorms.

But it was what was inside the sphere that made Naima's heart beat wildly and the blood rush through her veins.

The black planet seemed no longer to be made of wood and brass. Instead, it was like a glass bauble filled with black smoke which shifted and billowed, changing second by second from grey and transparent to black and opaque. And within the smoke, something was *moving*. A shape, shadowy and sinister, undulated inside the orb, ghosting through the miasma.

Then, from the smoke, a fleshy, wide tentacle appeared, pressing its suckers against the inside of the orb. Testing it. Impossibly, the orb seemed to bend outward under the pressure, distorting as if it were made of some malleable substance and not solid wood.

Around Naima, voices rose in panic as people became aware of the presence inside the sphere. Someone threw a rock at it, hitting the planet dead on. But the surface contracted with the impact, rippling and falling inward before springing back into shape, the

The Princess And The Orrery

rock flying out to land with a thump and a scream somewhere in the distance. It didn't even leave a mark on the black planet, and within moments the tentacle was back, pressing at the inside of its surface. The only difference was that now, wherever the tapered end of the wide arm pressed, the planet stretched and bulged outward.

People edged away from the orrery, their steps hesitant, until those closest found the ones behind them blocking their way. A seam of aggression and panic began threading its way through the guests.

The stampede started with pushing, then shoving, then punching. It was like watching a landslide, Naima realised in stupefied dismay: one innocuous pebble tripping down the ragged edge of the cliff and then, seemingly from nowhere, everything was boulders and dust and terrible, crashing urgency.

Naima had witnessed landslides before. The first thing to do was not panic. The second was to get as far away as possible, making absolutely certain not to get caught in any flash floods. It seemed logical that the same advice would apply here, with the heaving mass of stampeding guests a pretty good replacement for the dangers of drowning in a bursting river.

Instead, she ran towards the orrery.

Seven arrived inside his cave, his legs buckling. He dropped his head between his knees, his breath cold and quick against his teeth, and waited for the giddiness of magic to subside. It was uncomfortable, but compared with what he had suffered in Cerne Bralksteld, it was nothing.

He'd done it. Joseph was dead, the wish with him, and Seven had his necklace back. It was damaged, certainly, and would offer him less protection than it had before – protection that had never, truly, been comprehensive to begin with. But having now experienced the agony of being without it, Seven was prepared to re-evaluate his concept of 'bearable'.

When he felt he could stand without falling, he eased himself to his feet. The cave was… smaller. The walls seemed to loom over him in a way he didn't remember them doing. His old bed was still there, the wood damp when he brushed his fingers over it, the blanket mouldy and stagnant smelling. He pulled it back and reached under the bed, pulling out a strongbox.

He paused.

No one knew where he was.

He could stay here, recover… disappear again.

The bargain he'd made with the witch as he lay dying meant nothing to him. He owed the fae nothing. Let their Mirrors break – he would stand in the ruins of their world and laugh. Amelia had her mother back, and Naima and the Sisterhood to keep her safe and busy. She would recover well enough if he never returned. And Maria Sophia was no longer his guiding star, his obsession. He understood, now, what they had been to each other. Let her have her daughter and her husband – he wished them every happiness. He was free.

His thoughts jumped to the orrery, the planets spinning ever faster, lightning and magic crackling across them. The *es'hajit* ripping a path between worlds…

No. The wish was done. The threat passed. He'd *felt* the magic fall away from the device. They were safe. And, as long as he focused only on himself, so was he.

Seven stared at the strongbox, but his thoughts bounced to Joseph, his loneliness and anger. His desperation to be loved, to be valued. Joseph had been forced into his cave by his father and brother, and had created a story for himself to justify his suffering. Perhaps, if Joseph had had friends or a family who loved him, if he hadn't been shut away with his pain and his loneliness, he might actually have been the saviour Seven knew he had so desperately wanted to be.

He shook his head. The world was full of possibilities, the gods knew. Whatever Joseph might have been, there was no denying what he had become.

Seven had no such excuse, if excuse it was. He had chosen to lock himself away, hiding in his resentment and fear. Even when he'd finally found his way out, it had been on the promise of being

The Princess And The Orrery

loved and healed by Maria Sophia, expecting her to give him what he thought he deserved, to be his reward for all that he had suffered and lost.

There had to be a middle ground between the old and the new, facts and thoughts, belief and reality. A space where all elements could intersect and synthesise, becoming something better than the sum of their parts. It was harder, certainly. Riskier. Hells, if what he feared was true, the risk was greater than any he had ever faced.

Once, he would have forsworn it. Walked away and not looked back. But he had already lost one family...

"*Va,*" Seven swore. "*Es garvan famil uli, ik garvon famil ih.*"

He waved his hand over the lid of the strongbox, wincing at the pain and ignoring the quick, delicious tingle of magic. The box clicked, unlocked. He pulled the lid open.

Unlike the bed and the blanket, the contents of the box were perfectly preserved: books, a vial of amber sand, various bits of jewellery, and a couple of bags of coins. He put the jewellery on, enjoying the cool metal against his wrists and ankles, the slight sting of the earrings as he pushed them in. His fingers brushed the snake necklace, once more around his neck.

He was still not quite himself – he was covered in black blood, four of his fingers stung where the cool air brushed against skin that should have been hidden under nail, his hair tangled and, in places, alarmingly thin – but he was not, he felt, too far away from it, either.

He picked up the vial of sand and placed it in his pocket, leaving the money in the box. Next, he sorted through the small pile of books until he found the one he needed. It was smaller than the rest, the cover tatty and scuffed. It had been old when his grandmother had owned it. The last little piece of a home he'd never known.

Seven brought it to his face, opened the pages at random, and breathed it in.

There is a certain smell to paper, depending on its age. New paper carries the clean scent of the forest, of fresh air and waiting adventures. But older paper, paper that has seen it all, been there and done that, has a more jaded perfume. Old paper knows the dangers, and warns you in the only way it can:

F. D. Lee

Wait, it says. Listen to me, because I have been here before.

Seven closed the book and slipped it into his pocket, next to the vial of sand. He took one last look around his cave. He'd spent so many years hiding within its narrow horizons with only his own thoughts for company. Twisting in on himself, listening to the echoes of his mind.

He braced himself and disappeared, consigning the dank, empty cave to history.

66

Naima came to a halt by Amelia and Maria Sophia, and was shortly joined by two extraordinary looking people with alabaster skin that seemed almost ghostly against their black clothes. For one confused moment she thought they might be funeral directors, but Amelia seemed to know them.

"We have to destroy the orrery," Amelia shouted above the din of the panicking guests. "Melly, Hemmings, can you do it?"

It occurred to Naima, as Amelia shouted at the red-head, that this was the woman Amelia had attacked who had done something green and glowy to revive the genie. Once upon a time, she might have considered that odd.

Melly was staring up at the pulsating orb, the tentacle pressing against it. "No," she yelled. "I don't think so. Besides, if we do, won't that thing get out?"

The shell of the planet was visibly thinning wherever the thing tested it, the smoke inside melting into the air.

"If we don't, it'll get out anyway," Naima replied, also at a yell. "Look at the density of the orb, it's weakening by the second. Amelia, is there a way to shut it off? Stop it without breaking it?"

Amelia shook her head. "If it's like what happened before, it's not running off my engine. It's the *gu'lin vut*."

"The what?"

"The cog – it's a long story. It's something to do with Seven. It's connected to the orrery. I think… I think it must have brought that thing here."

"Yes," Melly shouted. "The magic must have brought it here. You all heard that awful drumming? Felt that sickness? We get it when we travel by Mirror, but never so strongly."

Naima opened her mouth to ask what the hell the red-head was talking about and then realised there was no point. Besides, she had an idea.

She pulled the vial of powder out of her pocket. "You get these people away. I can kill that thing."

Everyone turned to look at her.

"I was going to use this on Joseph. That thing is going to get through whatever we do. This is the best option."

"What is it?" Amelia shouted.

"It doesn't matter." Naima reached out and placed her free hand on Amelia's shoulder. "Just get out, take as many people with you as you can."

Maria Sophia pursed her lips, meeting Naima's eyes over her daughter's head. *She knows*, Naima realised. This was a thousand miles away from their original plan, which had involved Maria Sophia making a scene so that Naima could sneak up on Joseph and apply a small amount of the powder to his skin, dissolving him the way it had Celia.

Even that had been a risky proposition, a desperate plan reflecting a desperate situation. What Naima was suggesting now was far beyond desperation, but what choice did they have? They were at the end of the rope – a place where, traditionally, the options were to hang on or let go. Naima had been hanging on for months, dangling above the reality of her choices, refusing to fall.

Well, now she had a third option. She could hold the rope tight enough for the others to climb it, and then use it to beat the living hell out of whatever that thing was. If it meant that she had to untie it from its mooring to do so, well, so be it.

"Go," she yelled at Maria Sophia. "Get her safe."

Maria Sophia mouthed the words *thank you.*

Naima knelt in front of Amelia, pressing her forehead against the girl's so she wouldn't have to shout.

"I want you to listen very closely. None of this is your fault. You are clever and brave. There'll be people who try to talk you out of that; I was one of them, and I'm sorry. I was wrong. But if you let them win, you'll be wrong, too. You're a Sister, Amelia. You always have been. When this is all over, I expect you to keep exploring the philosophy of elementis… just, perhaps, not on your own, alright? No one should be on their own. Keep good people around you, and they'll help you avoid the bad ones. Understand?"

"I understand," Amelia said, her voice tight with emotion. "Naima?"

"Yes?"

The Princess And The Orrery

"You shouldn't blame yourself, either."

Naima smiled, some of the shame she felt easing. She stood, shouted at the others: "We need to get the guests out!"

Melly stepped forward. "We can help."

The one called Hemmings said something Naima didn't catch, but that looked like a question. He seemed to be in a worse state than any of them: black shadows under his eyes, skin clammy, unsteady on his feet. But he didn't seem to be refusing, just confused.

"Well, we can try," Melly shouted back.

Hemmings, his face a mask of exhaustion, nodded. Melly turned to Maria Sophia. "We can calm them down – can you get their attention?"

"Yes, but-"

Seven appeared next to Amelia. Other than staggering slightly, his arrival was entirely without ceremony. One moment he wasn't there, then he was.

His white tunic and trousers were covered in black stains, like he'd been splashing himself with oil. Like Hemmings, he looked decidedly unwell; unlike Hemmings, he seemed to be trying to downplay it, holding himself straight, brushing his hair from his bruised face, his lips turned up in a scornful half-smile. No one else appeared to notice the way his hands clung to the edge of his sleeves or the fact he was blinking rapidly, his legs held tight with the effort of standing.

Amelia flung herself at him, wrapping her arms around his waist. His empty blue eyes widened, and then an actual, genuine smile spread across his face. He ruffled Amelia's hair.

"I am pleased to see I was missed." He looked up at the orrery, the black orb pulsating above them. "Ah. I was right."

Naima opened her mouth to reply when everything went *really* to hell.

The black sphere burst. Free at last, the creature lifted its long, cylindrical head and tasted the air. Old, forgotten parts of its brain fired into life, a chain reaction of synapses long dormant resurging with the need that drives all things: to survive.

Pulling itself from the sticky, cloying afterbirth of its temporary womb, the creature crawled onto the orrery, enormous and driven, to satisfy its only desire.

Immense, ponderous, unfathoming and unfathomable, the creature's tentacles wrapped themselves around the device, halting the planets with a painful grinding of gears. It clung to the strange, uneven surface it had found itself on, shifting in heavy, rolling movements, beautiful and terrible in equal parts, until it was secure.

Denied for longer than its simple mind could comprehend, the creature was overwhelmed by the world it found itself in, the richness of it, the promise. If it had been capable of such complex thought, it would have praised whatever fortune had brought it to a world so overly ripe and ready to be plucked.

But all it knew was hunger, and all it could think on was the food that was waiting for it, now it was free.

Everything was chaos.

What little calm there had been disappeared the instant the monster broke free from the orrery. Its giant, coned head snaked through the air, its strange beaked mouth opening and closing, revealing sharp teeth and a jet-black tongue, its tentacles tangling around the planets, bending them out of shape.

This end of the garden was a bloodbath. There was only one exit from the balcony, a large arched doorway in the canyon wall, leading into the Palace. This was already wedged with bodies, and those nearest began climbing onto the shoulders of the people in front in a frantic effort to escape.

Other guests took their chances jumping from the balcony's edge, hoping perhaps to land on the cable cars ferrying up and down the rock face. Some did indeed make the jump, landing painfully on the carriage roofs. Many did not.

The Princess And The Orrery

Alfonso looked at the other cast members, seeing his panic and confusion mirrored in their faces. Christopher and Peter were staring, dumbstruck, over the wreckage of the party. The rest of the company were standing on the stage, in the places they'd held when the Baron's brother had made his speech and then disappeared in the arms of a blue man.

A lot had happened in the space of twenty minutes, and worse was coming. Hell, 'worse' was *here*. Whatever that thing was, it was now sprawled across the orrery, its thick tentacles strangling the device. Alfonso saw it whip out one of its long arms and grab at the mass of people in front of it, scooping up two men as if they were the cheap nuts the theatre sold. It lifted them to its open beak, lined with sharp, serrated teeth, and swallowed them whole.

Alfonso desperately searched the madness for Hemmings. He'd been standing right by the orrery with a group of women – Alfonso had only taken his eyes away for a moment to observe the horror that had released itself upon them, and when he looked back Hemmings wasn't there anymore.

Oh, God. What if the creature had got him already? What if somehow, when his attention had been elsewhere, Hemmings had been swept up in a long arm and devoured like he was nothing at all?

Alfonso swallowed, his throat suddenly so thick he could barely breathe, his stomach churning, his chest tight. He couldn't move, his feet were planted on the boards, his arms dead weights hanging from his shoulders. Around him, his fellow actors were blobs of frantic movement, some falling to their knees, others climbing the curtains, still others trying their luck in the mad exodus from the balcony.

But all he could do was stand, staring at the space where he'd last seen Hemmings, as the creature continued picking up guests and dropping them into its snapping maw. The part of himself that he kept on the surface – the part that watched, observing his feelings to use later, on the stage; the part that protected him – was gone. Alfonso disappeared. Michael disappeared. Jeremy, Mark, Rudolph, Bert, Cary... all the shells he'd constructed shattered and fell away.

It was just him, standing on the boards, looking at the future and realising he had no place in it, just as he had when he was fourteen, back on the farm.

And then his paralysis lifted, and he stepped forward. There was no point trying to run, there was nowhere else to go – and he refused to meet his end in the scenery. If he was going to die, he would die centre stage.

Alfonso spread his arms wide, opened his mouth to scream at the world-

-and was yanked back.

Hemmings had his forearm.

"What-? Where did you come from?"

Hemmings wrenched him back so hard he landed with a thump on the boards.

"Stay there and shut up," Hemmings instructed.

Alfonso couldn't produce any coherent words, anyway. His mouth opened and closed in shock as Hemmings and Melly took each other's hands and stepped forward, an earthy, shimmering green aura surrounding them, growing brighter with each step they took.

Alfonso's desperation eased, the churning in his stomach settled. A wave of something like tiredness washed over him… no, not tiredness; he was content. When had he last felt so at ease? He couldn't remember… a long time ago, or just recently?

He pulled himself onto his knees, staring at Hemmings and Melly as they lifted their arms, their hands still intertwined, and faced the seething mass of hysteria in front of the stage. The people nearest stopped pushing and shoving, turning instead to stare in wonder at the two of them.

Alfonso barely registered the blue man appearing out of nowhere with a dark-haired woman and a child, before vanishing again just as quickly. It was the little girl from the inn, the one Hemmings had been looking after. She held her hand out to him, and he found himself smiling as he took it.

The woman glanced at him, her eyes flicking between him and the girl – Amelia, that was her name. Then the woman nodded, apparently giving her approval, and marched to the front of the

The Princess And The Orrery

stage, where she began issuing orders in the clear, strong tones of someone who was used to having them obeyed.

"That's my mum," Amelia said proudly.

It was terribly strange. The monster was still working its way through the guests at the far end of the garden, picking them up and dropping them into its mouth. It was still horrendous. Alfonso could sense his fear and desperate remorse for those caught in its path, but his mind felt clear.

"What's happening?" Alfonso asked.

"We're saving you. As many as we can. Look."

She gestured towards the exit. The guests were helping each other up and moving in a steady crawl through the archway, into the Palace. It was nail-bitingly slow, but more people were getting through than they had been when they'd been pushing and shoving. Amelia's mother was organising the guests not already by the exit into lines, with the less able to move partnered with the more able. The rich, the so-called great and the good, and the slaves and performers, including members of his own company, were all united in maintaining this new hierarchy of needs.

"But what about the monster?" he asked, pulling his gaze back to the giant creature wrapped around the orrery, plucking guests from the grass.

"Oh, Naima will get that. And Seven's going to deal with the orrery. Everything's under control now. You should get inside the Palace."

"But shouldn't I stay here? Wait for Hemmings?"

Amelia shook her head. "He'll worry about you. You can talk to him later."

Alfonso thought for a moment. Things that had been complicated and frightening seemed, for some reason, suddenly very easy.

"Yes," he said as he made his way off the stage. "I'll talk to him later."

67

Naima caught Seven when he reappeared, steadying him. For a moment he tensed, and then she felt him relax.

"Thank you," he said, only slightly begrudgingly as he stepped away from her. Naima noticed again the dark blue bruises marring his skin, and sores, too, like fresh burns. It suddenly occurred to her she had no idea where Joseph was, nor what had happened inside the orrery to harm the genie so.

Seven, unaware of her observations, squinted up at the monster. "You have a plan, I assume?"

"I do," Naima said, refocusing. "You?"

"I do."

"Well, then. I suppose we'd better get on with it." She pressed her lips together, uncertain. Then she said, "Be careful. Amelia'll never forgive me if something worse – if something happens to you."

"Then I suspect you will have to prepare yourself for her ire, do you not agree?" Seven cocked his head, looking at her intently. "However, since it is very likely neither of us will survive what comes next, I would like to give you a gift. Attend. Every human I have encountered has desires which would shame a devil. The difference is not whether you want something selfish and wicked, but if you are prepared to break the world – or other people – to attain it. You, my Lady, are not. Your father would be proud."

He blew her a kiss, his hand coming up in a lazy salute, before vanishing again.

Naima stared at the empty space he left behind.

"Thank you," she said, wondering if he knew what his words meant to her and realising that of course he must.

Then, gripping the vial of powder, reassured by its weight, she ran to the front of the orrery, where the creature was pulling people from the crowd.

The Princess And The Orrery

※

Once again, Seven was inside the orrery. If nothing else, at least whatever happened next would ensure he'd never have to see the bloody thing again.

It was different, though, now it was no longer moving. It was dark, for one thing; the creature without blocking almost all the light. Whereas before it had been a jungle, alive and interconnected, it was now still as a cemetery, all Amelia's carefully designed components frozen in time, monuments to achievements now past, like the tombstones of long-forgotten relatives.

Which was all very well and pretty, but also not much help. Seven looked up, easily spotting the cog made from his necklace due to the unpleasant, crystalline mire it was resting within.

He stepped over Joseph's body and began climbing the ladder up the orrery, ignoring the burning of his exhausted muscles.

※

Getting into position was easy; the people caught at the end of the garden calmly let Naima through.

It had to be whatever Melly and Hemmings were doing. It was both a relief and deeply disturbing: her job would be much harder if the guests were still panicking, there was no doubt about that. But watching them step aside for her as they waited patiently for those in front to move forward while the creature devoured individuals at random was something she prayed she would learn how to forget.

If she had the chance to, anyway.

She wondered, abstractly, if her own current sense of calm was also a result of the strange magic being conducted by Melly and Hemmings. It felt different to the cloying blanket of compliance of Joseph's wish. Her actions were her own. She knew it because she also knew she could stop, turn, and run for the exit and never look back. But as much as she wanted to flee, she wanted to save everyone else more.

It wasn't that she was unafraid. She could feel her heart beating, the sweat on her palm as she gripped the vial, the tightness in her jaw. She was, in fact, more afraid than she'd ever been in her life, and yet she was still determined to do something about the situation she had helped to cause. Besides, the maths was simple. Not everyone would make it off the balcony alive, but some might. Some *would*, if she kept her courage.

Naima watched as the creature reached one of its great arms into the crowd. And then, at the last possible moment, she shoved aside the person the monster was aiming for and took their place.

The arm encircled her, suckers as large as her splayed hand pressing against her skin. She'd half-expected it to be wet and cold, but it wasn't. It was chilly but not unpleasant – smooth and dry, not unlike a snake. She could feel the creature's strength as it lifted her into the sky.

Early in her career, before she'd joined the Cultivators, Naima had been on tour with her father. Not a war tour; just visiting various other cities on some diplomatic envoy for the Six Points. They'd travelled all the way along the rounded southern coast of Ehinenden. Her father had been given a cottage on the beach, and Naima had spent her free time exploring the sandy, rocky coast. It was on one such exploration that she'd stumbled upon a strange rock: a coiling thing, with raised ridges that tapered at the centre and widening to a flat edge. A shell, almost, but not. It had been, without a doubt, mineral in nature.

Naima hadn't had the language, then, to describe what she'd found. She had, in fact, coined most of the terms now used routinely by the geologists in Castell y Sêr. But she'd known the moment she saw it that her world had changed. That her small, immediate life was over. She had become aware, standing on that beach with the stone in her hand, that the world was older and bigger than she'd ever guessed. That history stretched back further than her grandparents and the paintings of old soldiers on the walls of the barracks.

As she looked down at the opening mouth of the creature, its hard, snapping beak and reaching black tongue, she wondered if

The Princess And The Orrery

the world had once belonged to creatures like this. If their return was inevitable.

Well, bugger that for a game of soldiers, as her father used to say.

The creature released its grip, and she fell.

Seven reached the cog at the top of the orrery, breathing in wheezing gasps.

He had no idea what he was looking at, except that it was a mess akin to that which one might expect to find in a spittoon in a particularly unsavoury bar during a tobacco sellers' conference. Everything was covered in a thick film of clear, gunky sludge.

He prodded it, expecting it to be malleable and soft, but it was tacky and hard, like glue almost set. Pulling his grandmother's book from his pocket, he flicked through the pages.

The orrery shuddered violently as the creature outside moved. The book slipped from his fingers, falling as Joseph had done…

Seven lunged, catching it in his outstretched hand, holding onto the ladder by his fingertips. He pulled himself back, hooking his elbow around one of the rungs. His hair fell in his eyes, sweat dripping down his forehead, his lungs burning.

If anyone, ever, expected him to do something heroic again he would… well, he probably wouldn't be able to turn them into something small and easily stamped upon, but he'd certainly have a selection of choice words at the ready.

He went back to the book, racing through the pages. What if he'd picked up the wrong one? What if he'd misremembered? Did he have the strength to return to the cave, open the box to find the right book, and get back here before the creature killed everyone? Before it was strong enough to reach the city, if Naima's mad scheme failed, which it almost certainly would?

His search grew increasingly frantic as the orrery once again shuddered. A metal bar shot past him, inches from stabbing him in the shoulder, as one of the planets buckled under the creature's weight.

F. D. Lee

He was running out of time.

※

Naima fell, the creature's vast, black glistening tongue stretching out to pull her into the darkness.

She had one chance. If she released the powder too early, it would catch on the wind, scattering across the crowds below. Too late, and she would be in the thing's gullet, with no guarantee that she could open the vial. Of course, that might not matter. Sooner or later the powder would release itself, assuming that the creature's biology was similar to her own. But how many more people would die in the time it took for the vial to dissolve in that thing's stomach?

No, she had to get it right. She had to open the vial at the exact moment she felt herself on its tongue, its mouth closing around her.

※

He'd reached the end of the book and hadn't found what he was looking for.

Seven gave a wail of despair, the weight of his failure hitting him square in his chest.

The book was supposed to tell him how to stop the process of the *gu'lin vut*, to separate the cog from the machine and render the *es'hajit* useless, returning it to a simple device of human making. Now he had no idea what to do.

Another great rumble shook the orrery, bits of metal buckling around him while others fell, clattering, into the darkness. The only part of the wretched machine that seemed stable was what was inside the clear substance, with the cog at its centre. Seven readjusted his grip on the ladder, and, lacking any other idea, started going back through his book, forcing himself to pace his desperate search. It *had* to be in here. Narrative Convention was on his side, if nothing else.

The Princess And The Orrery

He was well aware exactly how weak such logic was, but when there was nothing else left to rely on, tradition was always there, waiting.

But this time, it seemed, even the dull predictability of Narrative Convention was against him. The book was useless. There was no way to remove the cog from the machine. And if it remained, it would only be a matter of time before someone tried to repeat Joseph's plan – Seven knew what people were like. Even if the creature ate every single person there and the outer planets all buckled and fell, the *es'hajit* would survive in this tangle of machinery and magic, this remnant of the genies' lost civilisation, and some idiot human would find it and think, *I wonder what this does?*

Seven let the book fall from his hand.

There was only one other thing he could think of. One last way to destroy the machine. Was he really considering such a thing? What would happen to him if he died – if he survived? When the witch called in her debt? What if, what if, what if...

There was no time. He had to make his choice now, or risk losing the chance to make it.

Seven, his elbow still looped around the rung of the ladder, unclasped his necklace. He stared into the snake's eyes. He'd worn his necklace his whole life, bar these last few months. It had grown with him, moulding itself to him. It was the last of its kind, just like him.

But it was also the only thing that made a such a machine possible, and thus it was a threat. Yet, without it, he would be vulnerable for the rest of his life, having to ration his power... or give it up completely. The thought made him sick, it was so immense, so incomprehensible.

Like all his kind, he had tried to balance the two extremes, allowing himself the heady thrill of magic while minimising the humiliating, unforgiving enslavement of the wishes.

And look where *that* had got him.

He plunged the necklace into the tacky, thick substance. He braced his legs against the ladder, his arms buried up to the elbow in the translucent gloop. The necklace strained, trying to reach the cog, but he gritted his teeth and held it back, forcing the cog to pull itself through the viscous matter to the necklace.

The orrery rocked and shuddered violently, and still the cog moved sluggishly towards the necklace. Seven heard himself muttering to it, willing it on, the necklace desperately trying to pull free from his grasp to meet its missing piece.

And then, just like that, the cog and the necklace were together.

Seven screwed his eyes shut and reached deep inside himself, layer by layer, until he found the source of his magic. In the eye of his imagination, it was a deep and vast lake in the base of his stomach, something he skimmed or occasionally, when he really had no choice, dipped a metaphorical hand into. Even when a wish had him, he did everything in his power to avoid submerging himself, fearing he would never find his way back to the surface.

Seven's grip on the necklace tightened, his blue skin turning white with the effort.

He jumped into the lake of magic within him.

68

Naima landed on the wet, hot muscle inside the creature's mouth, its saliva thick and slimy, sticking her clothes to her body, matting her hair.

She fumbled the lid of the vial open as its jaws closed, the tongue lifting her up to slide down its throat, and threw it towards the dark, swallowing muscles.

The tongue froze. Naima rolled over, scrabbling across the wet surface towards the serrated edges of the creature's beak, her hands and legs slipping underneath her. The creature began to shake, a thick foam bubbling up from its gullet. All around her there was the smell of burning, the strange popping sound of water boiling.

And then the scream began.

Naima reached forward, her fingertips pressing against the edge of the creature's beak, flashes of pain blossoming as its sharp teeth cut into the soft muscles in the flesh of her fingers. The monster started to convulse, its head slamming backwards and forwards. Naima saw more than felt the moment two of her fingers were bitten off at the knuckle, her blood like black ink in the half-light of the creature's mouth.

For a moment, she seemed to float in mid-air, her damaged hand above her with just her thumb, ring and little fingers silhouetted against the thin line of dusk visible through the monster's snapping jaws.

Her mind jolted back into focus at the same moment she hit the roof of its mouth before slamming back onto the centre of its tongue. The foam was rising up out of its throat in a column of expanding spume, thickening at a monumental pace. Naima watching in horror as the creature's flesh began to dissolve wherever the foam touched.

She pulled out her small scraping knife from her pocket. It was a thin, short blade, designed to pick out small clumps of mud or lodged stones from the old things she found buried in the earth. In a fight, she probably would have done better with a butter knife.

She swapped it to her other hand and then dug back in her pocket, this time pulling out a dusting brush. She gripped each tool and jammed them into the creature's tongue with all her strength.

The monster was still flailing, its mouth opening and closing, the roar of its distress deafening. The foam was just below her now, a few feet down its mouth. Naima pulled her right hand out, stretched as far as she could, and rammed it back into the soft surface, dragging herself up with it.

Hand over injured hand, the blood from her two raw knuckles tacky and hot against her skin, she scaled the creature's tongue, the poisonous foam rising behind her.

Seven was lost. Drowning in himself. There was no ending or beginning, no borders between the essence of himself and the heady insinuation of magic as it wrapped around him.

Wherever it touched, it left prickling pinpoint threads of pain and, beneath, the soft blossom of felicity, the sweetest, finest feathers of euphoria. Why had he been so frightened of exposing himself to this?

He let himself sink deeper, his mind pulling apart with each new contour the magic drew across his exposed senses, fraying, slipping free from his body.

There was something… a reason he had fallen so far into the power that lay at his centre, but he couldn't remember what it was…

Somewhere high above was a rumbling screech, dim and distorted. A scream…? But why? Who? There was nothing, no-one else but him. He was the world, stretched thin and all-encompassing, the beginning and the end of all things, the single note and the whole symphony.

Where his life had been a series of events played out in moments, suddenly it was a composition. Every beat and pause, every flurry and drop, were all drawn out in front of him to be viewed individually or simultaneously.

The Princess And The Orrery

Each note was unique and whole, each bar a melody, each progression leading into the next. There were moments of discord, the source of the pain that scraped across him whenever he channelled his magic, but there was also beauty, arrangements of sublime harmony.

Seven followed the music, watching his life play out.

His childhood, hidden in the desert with his parents, away from the jarring, jagged chords that were, he realised, the confused and contradictory desires of the humans, bleeding into the genies' melody, changing it, subverting it. But he, too, contained some of those same broken parameters, he saw that now. He was blended, a dual note that was part of his heritage and part of the world he'd been born into. He was an orchestration of many thousands of notes, each playing at jumping, inconsistent tempos; and yet, he was little more than a four-beat bar when he saw his own melody layered into the music that channelled the universes.

He looked forward, seeing his song tangled with another, the song of someone he knew... but something was wrong. Something was interfering with the music, trying to silence it. He could see so much, and yet there was a section of the score where the music was weaker, the notes faintly written, and his own amongst them, fading.

He wondered, neither alarmed nor particularly intrigued, whether that was his death. But as he watched, the silence grew, slowly erasing the symphony, spreading outward, backward, forward, upward, downward. And he was there, in amongst the deafening erasure, his melody struggling to be heard.

Seven pulled in closer, the hazy thrill of magic grazing and kissing his senses. He wanted to read the individual notes, to see what was silencing them. A knot in the flow of music. A rhythm that jarred and wouldn't blend.

He saw it and knew that the silence saw it, too.

Seven gasped, reeling back. The magic whispered to him, the music enticing him to remain. He looked upwards, through the weight of his deepest consciousness, to the dim, flickering light of his body, floating high above.

He swam up, towards himself, pulling his magic behind him.

F. D. Lee

Naima pulled herself forward, focused on the slit of light at the opening of the creature's snapping mouth. The smell of burning meat seeped into her pores, smoke stinging her eyes, the creature's screams so loud it felt like she was pushing against them.

Somewhere in the very back of her mind, a quiet, calm voice informed her she was going to die. That this wasn't just a particularly challenging climb, that she didn't have her ropes and harnesses. That she'd been stuck in an office for too long, that she was too old, that she should just give up and fall backwards into the rising foam.

Naima ignored it, telling herself instead that years of rock climbing, of searching for the lost secrets of the earth, of adventuring with her father, had taught her how to be strong. Had, against all logical expectation, prepared her to scale the tongue of a dying monster which she herself had murdered.

The muscles in her arms were white-hot iron, her legs slick with spit as she scrabbled to gain purchase. The creature was shaking now, spasming. Naima's body swung back and forth under her outstretched arms. More than once she lost her hold on her knife, blood from her missing fingers weakening her hold and leaving her hanging by a single hand above certain death.

She once again reached the tip of the creature's tongue, its hard beak frantically opening and closing as it wailed its demise. She pulled back with her small knife and plunged it as hard as she could into the fine cracks between the creature's pointed teeth, repeating the action with the handle of her brush.

This was the hard part. Holding tight to her tools, she walked her legs up, slipping and sliding, until she was in a vertical crouch, her left leg slightly higher than her right. She watched the creature's mouth, waiting for the moment it opened.

She hoped the soles of her boots were stronger than her fingers.

Waiting…

Her arms screaming…

Waiting…

Her thighs shaking, muscles exhausted...

The Princess And The Orrery

Waiting...
Now.

She leapt. Her feet landed on the knife and the brush, both of which gave under the sudden application of her weight. But it was enough. Ducking her head, she launched her body over the edge of its beak. Rolling her spine, ignoring the sharp flare of pain from its jagged teeth along her back and thighs, she tumbled over the precipice, and into the open world.

Seven screamed, channelling all the magic he had brought with him into his necklace, connected now with the cog. There was a moment of resistance, and then the necklace began to heat, passing from the depths of winter to the boiling heat of summer in seconds.

The clear substance began to bubble and dissolve, melting over his hands. Seven bared his teeth as he forced the magic into his necklace, supercharging it to the point of destruction. This was not the pain of raw magic; there was no hazy thrill of pleasure to accompany the agony. Only red-hot fire searing his palms, so that all he could do was try to breathe. He had thought the pain of the wish, without his necklace to protect him, had been unbearable.

He was wrong.

Fine cracks appeared across the snake, spreading like a network of rifts on the surface of a dying sun.

The necklace crumbled, leaving nothing but a heap of charred metal lumps in his hands. Seven turned his palm, and the fragments of his necklace fell into the darkness.

And then the orrery collapsed.

Naima sank into the soft grass, rolled, and ended up on her back about ten feet from the base of the orrery.

People rushed over to her, someone taking charge, mouthing words she couldn't hear at the others. Someone eased her up, ripping the back of her tunic open and pressing something against her skin. It took her a moment to realise they were stemming her blood. Another person started wrapping her right hand in a makeshift bandage.

She let them get on with it, her attention fixed on the orrery.

The creature was flailing madly, tentacles flying through the air. Its scream was no better outside it than it had been inside, a screeching keen that reverberated through her chest and stung her ears like hot needles.

Or perhaps not… the people around her were speaking, but all she could hear was the painful wail. A problem for later, Naima decided, her eyes fixed on the death throes of the creature. It was grasping at the orrery, buckling it. Even now, it was still reaching for people to swallow, running either on instinct or the desperate hope that it might, somehow, gain the strength to fight what was happening to it.

No amount of sustenance would save it, though. That much was clear. Great holes had split its body, deadly green foam bursting out and burning new cavities wherever it touched, fissures growing and joining. Parts of it had begun to melt, mixing with the foam, dripping down its slick body and further spreading the poison.

Tears poured down Naima's face as the creature struggled, its body heaving, its giant, orange eyes wide, panicked, pained.

And then its movements faltered, its eyes turning glassy. The creature slipped from the collapsing orrery, falling heavily on the ground. For a moment, it continued to breathe, its heavy body rising and falling, its arms turning in loops.

And then its body stilled, its last breath easing into the world, arms shuddering and falling, inert, across the grass. Next to it, the orrery was just so much bent metal and burned wood.

Naima fell backwards. Faces came and went, mouthing questions she couldn't hear. More bandages wrapped around her… but she looked beyond it all, at the sky.

The storm clouds were clearing, and the stars beginning to appear.

69

30 minutes earlier…

…Bea opened her mouth to scream at Carol when a bolt of lightning rent the air, bright white and blinding, landing somewhere in the middle of the city.

For a moment, they stared at each other, the shock on Carol's face mirroring Bea's own. But Bea reacted faster, shoving Carol aside and elbowing her way through the Ænathlin Again protesters when she heard someone shouting her name.

Bea looked for the source of the sound. All around her, the elves, imps, dwarfs and other such tribes that made up Carol's group were as confused as she was. Storms didn't happen in Ænathlin – the Rhyme War had seen to that. The majority of the Ænathlin Again fae had probably never left the Land, never seen lightning. It certainly seemed to be the case, judging by their terrified expressions.

"Bea, Bea!"

Joan was calling her! Bea's head swung, trying to spot the little house fairy. And then she looked up. Joan was on the roof of *The Quill and Ink*, waving at her. Swearing, Bea pushed her way back through the Ænathlin Again crowd. She'd just reached the door when Carol's hand clamped down on her arm, squeezing so hard Bea winced.

"This isn't over, cabbage mother," the imp hissed.

"Oh, whatever," Bea snapped, prying Carol's fingers from her arms and running into the pub. By the time she reached the attic, Joan had climbed back through the window and collapsed on the floor. Her face was ashen, tears streaming down her cheeks.

A hard lump formed in Bea's throat and fell to her stomach. Joan's face was exactly the same as her mother's had been the day she'd sat Bea and her brother, Mustard Seed, down to tell them that their father was missing.

"Joan, Joan, what is it? What's happened?"

"Oh, oh, Bea… Bea…"

"Joan, what happened?" Bea asked, trying to sound calm and in control.

Joan swallowed, her face a crumpled mess.

"It's the Grand, Bea. I went up on the roof to make sure nothing happened to you, I don't know, I didn't know what to do, and, and… Oh, gods… The lightning…"

Bea went still, the world narrowing to the space around her and Joan.

"What do you mean?" she asked, her mouth working on autopilot while her brain tried to comprehend what Joan was saying.

"The Grand, Bea. The Mirrors…."

"What?"

"I think… I think it exploded."

Epilogue

"I don't care how long it takes, I want a list of everyone working for the Palace, including the slaves in the manufactories," Naima instructed. "Either you can do it or I can find someone who can. Your choice."

The man grumbled, but nodded and scuttled away. Naima stifled a yawn, blinking in confusion at the rough bandage against her lips. She'd have to learn to write again – but then, she supposed, there were suddenly a lot of things she had to learn, and quickly.

She was finally making the changes she wanted. She'd been at it for hours, shaking off the doctors who insisted she needed to rest, even though her wounds – by their own admission – were healing magnificently. Almost unnaturally so, in fact. Naima had caught Melly's satisfied grin from across the room when the doctors had said that, and wondered just how good elven ears really were.

As for the men and women who'd attempted to stop her taking charge, well... a Palace full of people had seen her kill a monster. That kind of thing went a long way.

Of course, she had no real idea what she was doing, but she was discovering that running the Palace wasn't that different from managing the Cultivators. It was all just logistics, and she had years of experience in that.

Maria Sophia had helped, too. In fact, she'd proven invaluable, greasing wheels all over the place. It turned out Maria Sophia knew a huge number of neighbouring rulers, all of whom were more than happy to be wined and dined by her and her family – and introduced to the hero who had slain the monster of Cerne Bralksteld. A joke was already going around that 'the monster' Naima had defeated was the Baron, not the strange, terrifying octopus-creature. Publicly, Naima pretended to find it amusing, or at least not to mind it. Privately, she wondered if it wasn't more accurate to say that Seven had slain the real beast.

Seven, unlike Naima, hadn't fared so miraculously well.

They'd found him inside the orrery, trapped under fallen metal. He'd been carried to an empty bedroom and seen to by the same doctors that had cared for Naima. After they left, Melly had slipped into his room, exiting ten minutes later with a sheen of sweat to her skin, red eyes and a bleeding nose. The genie was sleeping, she'd said, but would recover.

Amelia had refused to leave his side until he finally woke up and she could see for herself that he was going to be alright. Now he was awake, Naima had last seen Amelia and Maria Sophia heading to the balcony, deep in conversation. She hoped they would be able to sort through their grief and estrangement. She was pretty sure they would. Cultivators didn't give up, after all.

Naima smiled and got back to work.

Amelia sat on the chilly grass in one of the few spots that wasn't covered in pieces of monster. She fished out another component from the orrery, wiped it down, and inspected it.

"This is a 67b… no, 67g," she said, placing it in one of the special cases she'd had brought from Starry Castle.

"Got it," Maria Sophia answered, writing the information down in the notebook Amelia had given her.

"Mum?"

"Yes?"

Amelia scratched her head. "Thank you. For helping me sort all this out."

"You're very welcome. It's interesting, actually. All these little pieces…"

"They're called parts, not pieces," Amelia said, unable to stop herself.

"Oh, yes, of course," Maria Sophia replied, a smile playing at her rose-red lips. "I'm sure there's a huge difference, right?"

Amelia rolled her eyes, making a mental note to explain everything properly when they had more time. Right now, there

The Princess And The Orrery

was something else she wanted to say. "I'm sorry about... about Jules. I didn't mean-"

Maria Sophia's hand landed on her knee.

"I know. I'm sorry, too."

They sat for a moment in silence. But it was a different sort of silence to the one that had permeated their castle back home.

That silence had been heavy and sad: the absence of Jules' ringing laughter; the smothering weight of Amelia's guilt; the long looks between her mum and dad; the whispered conversations of the staff that had stopped abruptly when they noticed her. *This* silence was friendly, easy. It was nothing more than a lull between words, a space in one moment that would drift, gently, into the next.

"So," Maria Sophia said, running her hand through her hair. "I was thinking we could stay here a while, together? I'd like to learn more about your Cultivating. Dad could come too – he can be spared for a few months, I think."

"Yes, that would be alright. As long as you don't try to get involved too much. I'm a Sister, now, you know. I have to be professional."

"Of course," Maria Sophia said, trying not to smile.

"Mum, I mean it – you've got to promise not to get in the way." Amelia reached into the pile and pulled out another part. She stared at it, not really seeing it. "Mum?"

"Yes?"

"Thank you for rescuing me."

Suddenly she was wrapped in a tight hug, her mother's words rushing against her in an urgent, breathy statement of intent.

"I will always, *always*, rescue you. Never doubt that for a moment."

Amelia squirmed, embarrassed beyond measure. And then, after a moment, she hugged her mother back.

"I know."

✻

Melly stood outside the genie's room, smoking.

Finally, he was awake and alone. It was time. She took a last pull, the end of the cigarette burning red, and then stubbed it out, knocked on the door and entered.

The genie was sitting up in bed, reading a book, a toy bear resting in the crook of his arm. Bandages covered his arms and chest, black stains seeping through the thick material.

It was not the image Melly had been expecting. She realised he must have looked worse, if such a thing were possible, during their frantic efforts to deal with the orrery and then later, when she'd snuck in to save his life. She must have been too tired, too focused – too afraid? – to notice.

"The witch returns," Seven said, his voice raw and thin. He placed his book down next to him, wincing slightly. "Amelia tells me I am now twice indebted to you?"

Melly nodded, closing the door behind her. "How are you feeling?"

"I dare say I feel much as I look. You are come about our bargain, I assume?"

Well, it seemed they weren't going to waste time with pleasantries. Melly took a seat. "You'll keep your word?"

"Some might argue that a promise given on the point on death is no promise at all."

"They might," Melly conceded. "What would you say?"

"I would say that I know who you are, *Melly*," Seven answered. "The Queen of the Fairies, as once was. I am aware of the bargains you make and what befalls those you deem a means to your ends. Our mutual friend the fairy is unaware of this truth?"

Melly lifted her chin. "I've changed since then."

"Ah, so Bea does not know, then. Tell me, knowing that I am aware of who you are, your history, do you still want me to uphold our bargain? Are you not afraid I might reveal you?"

It was no good. She took another thin, black cigarette from her case and lit it. She'd suspected when they first met that he recognised her – he'd made a series of snide little comments which, thankfully, had gone over Bea's head.

She wondered how he knew her, but then she'd been very… active… in Ehinenden during her reign. He'd certainly not been part of her court, but if he'd been anywhere near the Athenine

The Princess And The Orrery

forest, there was a good chance he'd stumbled onto one of her stories. Did it matter, anyway, how he knew?

"If you want to tell Bea who I was, I can't stop you," she said. "The only thing that matters is that you get the Mirrors working again."

"So you said. I confess to some level of confusion as to why you think I might be suited to such a task... that is, if you meant what you said?"

"I meant what I said. I saved your life in return for your promise to return to the Land and help Bea and her Plotter find a solution. Not in return for your death, powering the Mirrors."

Seven nodded. "Reassuring. And to my first question?"

"The genies were in the Land at the beginning, from what I understand. Nothing's clear, anymore. Even when I was a Narrator, the histories were vague... and I... well, I was distracted. Since then, the Teller erased it all. But I remember the tales of the genies during the war with Yarnis. You did something. Helped her destroy the pathways."

"Not I." Seven lifted himself up against the bolster, a wet-sounding cough escaping him. "I was born here, and certainly not during the times you speak of. The genies were scattered between this world and yours, amongst others. And now those who might have answered your question are dead, thanks in no small part to your dealings with the Teller."

Melly turned the cigarette in her fingers, staring at the smoke as it drifted up, disappearing.

"Yes," she said. "I won't lie. But I didn't understand at the time what he was doing. Not fully. And then I hid from it for hundreds of years. Ignored it." She turned her gaze to the genie. "Recent events have made me realise that isn't possible any longer. The GenAm is out of control. Not just at home, but here, too. The stories have to change, and that will never happen while the GenAm is still in place. While the Mirrors are under threat. So... Here I am."

"Here you are." Seven scratched vaguely at the bandage crossing his chest. She noticed he was missing a number of finger nails. "I will keep our bargain."

Melly exhaled, relief flooding her. "Thank you."

"You are welcome, though I confess I have my own reasons for agreeing to this madness." A faraway look fell over his features. "There is a question I wish to find the answer to, and to do so I must find the place where the music does not play. I know not why, but I think my purposes and yours will come to be the same." He shook his head, his countenance returning to what she thought of as his default: smug and self-satisfied. "It appears we are on the same side, my Lady. I certainly would not have predicted such a thing."

Melly smiled despite herself. "Narrative Convention."

"Ah, yes. Silly of me to forget." Seven closed his eyes, a long breath escaping him. When he opened them again, she had no way of knowing if he was looking at her or at something only he could see. "Tell me… do you ever tire of it?"

"Yes."

He turned to her, fine threads of hair catching on his pillow. "And still it continues, as do we."

"Yes." Melly brushed the ash from her skirt. "But perhaps we needn't continue alone anymore. I don't know if you care, but… well, I think you should know. John's alive. He's on his way here, with Ana. He still thinks of you as a friend."

The genie's eyebrows shot up his forehead, his mouth falling open. And then he smiled – a real, genuine smile that lit up his face, his peacock-blue eyes crinkling. He was always beautiful, but in that moment, bleeding and broken, he was radiant.

"Thank you, my Lady, for telling me."

Melly nodded and left him to his delight. Later, she'd have to work out a slightly more detailed plan than 'send the genie back and hope he does what he said he'd do', but for now she was satisfied that she'd finally, after all these years, done the right thing.

Hemmings wandered the Palace, unsure what he was supposed to do. Just a few hours had passed since the events on the balcony, and the only thing that seemed to have happened with any certainty was that night had fallen.

Not that you'd know day from night inside the Palace, he mused. He was quite intrigued by the idea of living inside the rocks; it would make a good thoughtsmithing project. He was reminded of the trolls back home, who often had to live in dank caves or other dark, forgotten places when they were on a Plot. They always had no end of complaints when they returned to the city. They said it made them meaner, somehow. Closed off. Distrustful. Angry.

Mind you, right now everyone seemed more confused than anything else. The Baron and his brother were dead, which meant that there was technically no ruler. The human woman, Naima, was keeping a lid on things for the moment, to the visible relief of the Palace staff, if not everyone else. Hemmings had learnt that a lot of people owed their fortune to the Baron's method of ruling and were resisting Naima's quick rise to authority.

Not that that was stopping her. She had already called in a young woman called Kamala to start planning new diplomatic relations with the neighbouring Kingdoms, and Maria Sophia had been busy writing letters of introduction while she'd waited for her daughter to leave the genie's room.

Hemmings suspected that Maria Sophia would be a formidable ally in Naima's corner. Melly had also sent a rider to Llanotterly, saying that Ana would want to see what was happening. He had no idea where Melly was now, but she'd been wearing a very strange smile when she'd said that. It had made Hemmings extremely grateful he wasn't one of the people who had raised concerns over Naima's leadership. He couldn't help thinking things were going to get even worse for the dissenters when Ana showed up.

He was also quietly optimistic that Melly might have changed her mind about sending the genie to his death, but he'd worked out a very rousing speech to persuade her otherwise, just in case. Now he was at a loose end.

He eventually found someone who could direct him to the banqueting hall, where rumour had it food was being served. In fact, when he reached the large, arched room, he was pleased to find not only huge, steaming bowls of soup but also hot bread, salted potatoes and spring salads. He helped himself to vast quantities of each, plonked down on the end of a long bench in the corner, and tucked in.

He was just debating a second bowl of soup when Alfonso dropped down opposite him.

"I've been looking everywhere for you. You'd think someone as pretty as you would stand out, but after today, I suppose everyone's definition of 'exceptional' has changed. Can we talk?"

Hemmings put his spoon down. "I'd rather not-"

"Alright, just listen then," Alfonso said, placing his hands flat in the space between them. "I didn't think you'd come back. That's why I changed the play. I had to do something with it, don't you see?"

"Do 'something' with what?"

"With how I felt. That's what I do, Sunshi- Hemmings. I feel things and then I box them away, all neatly labelled, so I can use them later. Nothing's ever wasted, not for me. It all goes into my performances."

"Well, I'm glad I could help," Hemmings said, unable to keep the bitterness out of his voice. "The play was very good. Everyone enjoyed it."

"For God's sake, you know that's not what I mean," Alfonso snapped, his fingers scratching the wood. "It hurt. Thinking you wouldn't come back hurt. I had to do something with it, or else it would have been pointless… wasted."

Hemmings' pressed his hand to his mouth. Alfonso stared at his hands. People bustled around them, getting food, talking, arguing. Life continued.

"Why did you think I wouldn't come back? I told you I would," Hemmings said at last.

Alfonso looked up. "Because you're a tourist."

"I don't understand."

"Look at you – I mean, well, not right now. But when you haven't been doing… whatever it was you did. Your clothes. Your hands. Your skin. You're a tourist, visiting poverty and hard work to see what it's like. You've got no idea about money or how things work. Bloody hell, you were sent to us by a King! People like you dip in for a few months and then, when you think you've seen a bit of the world, go back to your ivory towers with a nice little story to tell at parties. You don't ever 'come back'."

Hemmings dropped his head, shame burning his cheeks. Alfonso was right. Not in the exact details, but in the principle. He *was* a tourist. When he'd said he'd come back, he'd meant it. But... when everything was sorted out with Melly and the genie. When he'd had time to settle the idea with his mum and Chokey, who would both certainly have something to say on the matter. When he knew that Ænathlin was safe. But how long would all that take, really?

Human lives were short, passing in an instant. Hemmings was probably already forty or fifty years older than Alfonso. How long had he expected to spend sorting out his own life before... what? Retiring to the theatre and claiming his reward?

"I'm sorry," he said, his voice breaking.

Alfonso came to sit next to him. "I know."

"I meant it when I said it."

"I know. That's what made it worse."

Alfonso took his hand, brushing his thumb over his knuckles. Hemmings lifted his hand and dropped a kiss on Alfonso's, and then another and another. The actor chuckled, but it was stained with sadness.

"You are going to leave, aren't you?"

"Yes," Hemmings said. "But not because I want to. Not for parties or, or, or stories or anything like that. I have to help Melly save our home."

Alfonso sighed. "Well, y'know, I might have thought that was a load of crap, but after today I'm inclined to believe you two could do anything." A pause. "When will you go?"

"Soon, I think. We need to wait for the genie to recover and-"

Hemmings' hand flew to his mouth, but it was too late. Alfonso stared at him for a moment, and then burst out laughing.

"You needn't look so horrified – I think a fair few cats are out of the bag right now. I saw you and Melly appear out of nowhere with a blue man, and then you both glowing green – and that's not to mention the giant *fucking* monster that showed up and started eating people. Besides, those ears are a bit of a giveaway." Alfonso grinned. "You're a fairy, right?"

Hemmings groaned, realising too late that he'd lost his cap. He'd been swanning around the Palace with his long, elfin ears on display.

A second later and he completely forgot his anxiety. Alfonso's lips brushed against his, hesitant at first and then, when Hemmings kissed him back, with the kind of fervent passion that even the greatest of actors couldn't conjure from nothing.

Finally Alfonso pulled away, his breathing ragged. He stood up, the exact same challenge glittering in his eyes as it had that day on the road, and extended his hand to Hemmings.

"Soon is long enough. I reckon there's bound to be a few empty bedrooms in a place this size. So… are you going to sit there, looking all pretty and dejected, or are you going to give me a proper goodbye?"

Hemmings, blushing crimson, took his hand. It wasn't the happy ending he'd been taught heroes get, but it wasn't a tragedy, either.

And perhaps, sometimes, that was enough.

End of Book Three

The story will continue in the Pathways Tree, Book Four.

If you have a few minutes, please consider leaving an honest review for *The Princess and the Orrery* on Amazon. Your review will help new readers discover this book!

Sign up for my newsletter! Receive information about conventions, special offers, new titles, an invitation to join our Facebook group, as well as bonus content for *The Pathways Tree* series! You can unsubscribe at any time.

http://eepurl.com/dOUVtz

You can also follow me on Facebook (@fdleeauthor) or Twitter (@faithdlee), or email me at faith@fdlee.co.uk. It's always great to hear from you, and I always reply!

Thanks

I'd like to take a moment to thank the following people for helping me through the process of writing this absolutely ginormous book!

Big thanks must firstly go to Kit Mallory for all her amazing help and support. More than once, I felt like this book was going to get the better of me and Kit was there to set me straight (and remind me how awesome Melly, Hemmings, Seven, Bea and everyone else are!) I'd also like to give a huge shout out to my ARC team, critical friends, and BETA readers, who were thorough, encouraging and endlessly dedicated in their reading of this work (and for teaching me how to spell carriage!) Thanks also to Jo, Theo, Dan, Andrew, Paul, Pam, Linda, Kelly, Simon M. and Simon B., Gwen, Dan, Ivan, C.J., and Teddy for all your encouragement, advice and support.

As always, thanks are owed to Jon, who helped me work out the overall framework of the Pathways Tree series and without whom Bea never would have found her way out of the forest. Equally, I am forever and always indebted to Nina, Alex, Jo and Miranda, who have been and remain endlessly encouraging and supportive. I would also like to thank Liz Rippington and Jane Dixon-Smith for proof-reading and cover design duties, respectively.

A debt of thanks is also owed to Teddy, Gail, and all the Eastercon 2018 folk who came to my stall or grabbed me at the bar to very lovingly badger me about the delay between books two and three. I promise not to let any more studies get in the way!

I'd like as well to give a huge and incredibly heartfelt thanks to **everyone** who has shown such love and devotion to Bea and the gang. Words cannot express how much it means to me to know that I am not the only person who loves these crazy, brave, messed-up characters. Your comments, emails, messages and chats at cons always inspire and motivate me to keep going. Thank you.

And finally, thanks go to James, my husband, for keeping me alive.

Printed in Poland
by Amazon Fulfillment
Poland Sp. z o.o., Wrocław